Praise for *The Bu...*

"This crackling, lightning-bolt ener... ... even the lowest of characters recalls the work of Denis Johnson. [H]elped along by an energizing sense of humor and a virtuosic control of plot . . . Hart has created a Dickensian portrait of the barely settled Pacific Northwest."
—*New York Times Book Review*

"An ambitious and beautifully harsh chronicle of family, love, and deception. . . . A brilliant novel. Its huge scope and panoramic sympathies make it compelling and immersive . . . Hart's echoes of Cormac McCarthy—the brutality of landscape and character, the unrelenting hardship—are just a fraction of his original successes here in scope, character, and emotional magnitude."
—*Dallas Morning News*

"Mesmerizing . . . Hart has conjured a singular, searing world. When you step into this novel you submit to its dream . . . you believe in his large gift that leaves you stunned and breathless. A wonderful, unique portrait of a particular landscape I now see anew."
—Amanda Coplin, author of *The Orchardist*

"Brilliant . . . Hart paints a vivid picture of the brutality and venality of the old Northwest Territories."
—*Austin American-Statesman*

"Hart's sense of place is brilliant. [T]here are dazzling characterizations [and] a dense, keen, and illuminating narrative . . . of greed and ambition and of fathers and sons . . . Think the brutal realities of McCarthy's *Blood Meridian* set among the primeval forests of the Pacific Northwest frontier."

—*Kirkus Reviews* (starred review)

"A brilliant second novel . . . Hart's prose is dense and lyrically savage."   —*Publishers Weekly* (starred review)

"Not a writer of half-measures, Hart brilliantly re-creates the rugged life in the Pacific Northwest logging camps of the 1890s. A riveting, powerful tale."   —*Library Journal*

"Brian Hart's *The Bully of Order* does what only the best works of fiction can do: it brilliantly imagines those parts of life that history all too often fails to record. This is a thoroughly engrossing story told in mesmerizing prose. I highly recommend it."

—Kevin Powers, author of *The Yellow Birds*

"After a relatively quiet debut, Brian Hart has come back with a stunning second novel—a work [that] would qualify as a lifetime achievement for most writers. You do not have to read very far to see that Brian Hart has vaulted squarely into the first rank of American novelists."

—Philipp Meyer, author of *The Son*

"A very robust story about where I'm living now, Oregon. It's about the sheer madness and effort that went into logging in that area of the country in the 1800s. It's really an epic historical tale, and he's a fantastic writer."

—Smith Henderson, author of *Fourth of July Creek*

TROUBLE
NO MAN

ALSO BY BRIAN HART

The Bully of Order
Then Came the Evening

TROUBLE NO MAN

a novel

BRIAN HART

HARPER ● PERENNIAL

NEW YORK ● LONDON ● TORONTO ● SYDNEY ● NEW DELHI ● AUCKLAND

HARPER ● PERENNIAL

HarperCollins books may be purchased for educational, business, or sales promotional use. For information, please email the Special Markets Department at SPsales@harpercollins.com.

FIRST EDITION

Designed by Jamie Lynn Kerner

Library of Congress Cataloging-in-Publication Data has been applied for.

ISBN 978-0-06-269832-2 (pbk.)

19 20 21 22 23 LSC 10 9 8 7 6 5 4 3 2 1

*For my family
Tof
Kerri and Jürgen*

TROUBLE NO MAN

[-1]

THE DOG WORKS THE WIND, OUT AND BACK, BOTH SIDES OF THE road. When it stops ranging to mark a stump, the two men standing by take it as an all clear and hoist their heavy packs from the tailgate and sling their rifles. The red moon is an omen. They leave the truck partially hidden among the skid roads and slash piles at the edge of the clear-cut and follow the broken pavement uphill.

Three mile-markers come and go, and they leave the road and scramble through the rocks and past a wrecked school bus fifty yards down to a dry riverbed. In the shadow of the canyon they switch on their red LED headlamps. Deer tracks are stamped into the red mud but the ground is hard enough now to resist even a scuff and sounds almost hollow beneath their Vibrams. The dog keeps its head down and works its nose upstream.

They climb over and under the fallen trees and traverse a rock field. Weapons are passed hand to hand, packs removed, packs replaced. *No fucking way* is the initial response to the forty-foot-tall concrete ramp of the spillway, but flat-footed and careful, their boots hold. The dog has more trouble than they do and the younger man has to pull him along by the scruff of his neck. At the top, between the wall of the dam and the spillway, there's a shelf, eight feet wide, maybe sixty long, the edges lost in shadow.

The older man shrugs off his oversized camouflage backpack and sets it gently on the ground. He uses a black bandana to wipe the sweat from his face and the back of his neck. The other man's pack is smaller with much less hardware and weight, but with the strange acoustics of the concrete it's noisy and something rattles as he sets it down and earns a look from the older man.

"Yeah, I know," he says, and fishes out a small plastic bowl and squirts water into it from his CamelBak for the dog. Of the four reinforced steel floodgates, only one is open. The steel is twisted and one corner is dog-eared and the thick timbers that held it in place are splintered. While the dog drinks the two men squat down and peer beneath the damaged gate. The red moon blackens the deep cracks and depressions in the lakebed. The older man removes a monocular from his tactical vest and puts it to his eye.

"From here to the main house," he says. Ahab on the glass. "They'll be watching the road. And it looks like the fence and the gate have been repaired, so they'll feel safe. At this point I don't know what they'll have up and running, probably nothing. We used to have wireless cameras, a couple of drones flying grids, motion sensors all around the lake."

"So we'll shoot from here? How far is that?"

"We'll take position there." He lowers his scope and points to a pile of boulders in a slight depression fifty yards from shore. If there were water, that's where the fish would be. "I make it three, maybe three-fifty, to the house but they'll come closer."

"If they come out."

"They'll come out."

From inside his gun bag the older man removes four duct-taped brick-sized packages of Semtex and shifts things around in his vest until he can fit them into one of the larger pouches. He has two sidearms, drop leg and pancake, the former was his wife's. They watch the dog drink and their sweat begins to dry.

The younger man removes the bikini cover from his scope and checks the bolt, the safety. "Stay," he whispers to his dog. "You're going to stay." He could be deer hunting, putting the sneak on some muleys.

"Fudd gun with Fudd optics," the older man says, and removes one of the three rifles from his bag and slips it from its sock. "I can link to my phone," he says, tapping the stubby scope mounted on the rail. "I need you on my six."

"With the jargon."

"I'd feel better though, knowing." The first sign of fear lights his eyes.

"Fine."

The older man lifts his pack like a suitcase from the carousel and goes through the broken mouth of the spillway.

"Stay," the younger man repeats to the dog. "You stay." He sucks a mouthful of water from his CamelBak and lifts his pack by the loop and, careful of his rifle barrel, ducks low through the gate and easy, easy climbs down from the concrete ledge and onto the bed of the dry reservoir. Above him the moon is the tarnished head of a carriage bolt.

They nestle into the rocks. The older man pulls on a stocking hat, then takes the Bushmaster and switches on the scope. With his phone in his lap he syncs the two, passes the younger man the phone. He uses the rifle to scan the lakebed and the house and compound beyond, shakes his head and passes the weapon over in exchange for the phone.

"This is how you switch modes."

"OK."

"Show me."

"I got it."

"Doesn't look that way," the older man says. "Are you with me right now? I need you here, nowhere else."

"Death is my copilot and we're cruising for death."

"I'd rather you were crying again than talking that nonsense. You need to get your head right. We're doing this." He rises to his feet and adjusts his vest and his weapon, pats down his pockets. "You need to stop."

"I'm good."

The older man grunts his approval, nods his head. "I'll see you shortly."

He follows the dry channel from the boulders and stirs up a cloud of dust. From there he's on flat ground, one step after the other, then he's crawling up the crumbling bank to the shore. The ancient barbed wire is parted and he strolls upright and leisurely toward the main house, no available cover, a field of stumps. He's swallowed by the shadow of the ridge and the younger man puts the scope to his eye. At the chain-link security fence the Technicolor thermal blob in the scope cuts the wire and slips through. Unblinking, sweating, the younger man lowers the scope and waits for the crack of rifle fire because after that he'll be alone. He can't watch. He can't help but think of her.

It's the dog that's nudging him. He lifts his head and pets the dog and scans the lakebed with the scope. He searches the road and the darkened house and outbuildings and is temporarily blinded by the runway lights coming on, but there are still no lights in the house or on the road. No warm bodies. He switches modes on the scope so he can see the runway. Nothing moves. The dog lifts its nose to the wind.

The older man surprises him when he returns by way of the floodgate. "I doubled back and checked the road. We're good. Motion sensor tripped the lights on the runway, but everything else is down. Place is a shit show. No security. Beer cans, bonfire down to ashes. Drunk bastards." He extracts two cans of warm beer from his vest, passes one over. "Let's get settled in before you open that."

They spread out among the boulders and set their lanes and rests for their rifles. The older man has his big bag open and extra magazines stacked in groups by caliber. He puts his focus to the .50 but he has his M4 and a SOCOM 16 ready to go if they need to move. The other man only has his Remington 700 and an extra magazine, two tattered boxes of shells. They open their beers, cheers, and drink. The runway lights blink off.

"I have whiskey," the older man says in a whisper. "In the bag."

The younger man taps the flask in his breast pocket. "Walmart's finest." The dog curls up beside him and he rests his hand on the dog's neck and pulls on his fur.

They each drink what they have and don't share.

"Story of our lives," the younger man says. "Fuck you, get your own."

"I brought you a beer."

"I appreciate that."

"I was an engineer," the older man says.

"OK."

"You asked me once. I was never a soldier."

The younger man nods and takes a deep drink of his beer, stuffs the burp in the name of stealth and nearly vomits. "I was bitching about you one time," he says. "And she said to me, she said you were an autodidact. I was sure it was an insult."

"It's not."

"I know. I looked it up. She said me and you, the two of us, were birds of a feather." He finishes his beer and sets the can down gently on a flat rock. "I didn't like that."

"I built the infrastructure of war." The engineer points at the sky, a blinking light. "The last project I was on was a DOD satellite design team."

"That one?"

"No. I don't know. How would I know that?"

"Because you're a satellite engineer. Who else would know?"

The engineer finishes his beer and sets the can down. "My whole life has been preparing me for this moment. I've trained for this. I understand this world."

"You could be strapped in an electric chair saying the same thing."

The engineer lowers his head. He's an old man. "Maybe."

"The world's most dangerous nerd."

The engineer shelters the screen with his hand and turns on his phone, switches screens, shows it to the man beside him. "You want to or me?" It's a plain red button in a black screen.

"You do it."

The engineer presses the button. "Listen," he says. "Listen to me."

"I am. I'm listening."

"In forty-something seconds that place is going blammo and whoever comes out, we're gonna kill them. OK? I need you all in now. This is it."

"OK. Shit."

"I'm saying in forty-something—"

"Gotta be thirty by now."

"I'm saying good to know you and what are you doing?"

"Hey, man."

"I'm saying it's been a privilege. You're a good guy. A good family man. I judged you wrong when we first met. I thought you were someone you weren't. Maybe I thought I was someone else too."

"Jesus, Chuck. You're my hero. I mean it."

"Can you stop it with that? For once."

"I'm not ready, man."

"It doesn't matter. It's happening. It's happening. Hold on to that dog so it doesn't run. Here we go."

[0]

R < 25
CA 96118

T̲HE KEY, TURNED TWICE MORE, GAVE NO RESPONSE, NO CLICK or rattle, just a not-working mechanical nothing. One minute Roy was singing along with some ancient mixtape Toots and the Maytals—*I want you to know that I am the man who fights for the right, not for the wrong*—and the next, not even the murky lights of the idiot gauges would come on. The sudden quiet was unsettling. *Bam bam*. Roy glanced at Karen still sleeping in the passenger seat and touched the dash, a gesture, a war movie corpsman pulling his comrade's eyelids closed.

He'd exited I-5 fifty miles or so south of the Oregon-California border and hit the backroads hoping to see an ice waterfall his pal Pablo had mentioned once while they were sessioning the vert ramp in Corruptible Pete's quonset hut. Highway numbers scribbled on a scrap of beer box long since lost. Squinting at road signs through the storm, mouthing the words, places real and imagined: Lassen, Portola, the Weddell Sea, Graeagle, Scott Base. *This is what you get listening to somebody who does andrechts with no pads, not even a lid.* The arterial gulp of isolation, repeated, and then repeated.

So here they were: man and woman—Roy and Karen— destituters, plain-view hiders, no-place-is-homers, positionless, bearingless, kind of young, and truly restless. They'd tried to cross from one island of safety to the next and they'd gotten lost in the archipelago.

Karen opened her eyes and looked around, squinting. "What're you doing?" she said with a rasp, a light, not-quite-ex-smoker's hack. "What's the matter?"

"Carl just quit."

"What?"

"He just died. I don't know. Does your phone work? I got nothing."

She dug around in her bag until she found it. "Nothing. Where are we?"

"An hour since I turned off the freeway. If we go back. If we go forward, I don't know. We haven't passed anybody forever. I think we're fucked."

"Is fucked a place?"

"Watch yourself."

Roy was smiling as he climbed into the back of the van and wrestled his greasy, punk-patched jean jacket, his warmest coat, from the bottom of his duffel bag and pulled it on over his hoodie. He had no gloves and no hat, besides one of the mesh-back, trucker variety. His skateboard shit had a corner to itself: a five-stack of extra decks, three sets of shrink-wrapped wheels, extra trucks, a six-foot roll of grip tape, an old-timey orange tacklebox filled with kingpins, bushings, bearings, and mounting hardware. Skate mags, vids, stickers, and loose photographs in a Bacardi box. Another tacklebox grease-penned with red Xs that held bandages, tape, generic ibuprofen, Neosporin, vitamin C, and assorted herbal supplement bottles that had been refilled with Vicodin and Valium, Percocets and lorazepams.

The center of the van was heaped with unzipped sleeping bags, blankets and pillows, dirty clothes. There was a three-pack of condoms and a couple of empty wrappers by the wheel well. Not long ago, six months back, there'd been an abortion, Karen's second. Apparently the first had been when Karen was still in high school. She wouldn't talk about it, wouldn't tell Roy who the father was, said it didn't matter. When he pushed back, Karen assured him it wasn't anything creepy, she wasn't raped or anything like that.

"What's the big deal?" Roy had said, looking at the double lines on the pregnancy test. "Go take a couple of pills and boom, *finito*."

"That's not the way it is though," Karen said. "When you're an adult, there are implications."

"A butterfly fluttering its wings in China can make a tornado in Des Moines? Ripples in a pond? I say fuck all that interconnectedness bullshit."

"You don't know what you're talking about," Karen said. "All the time you act like you're some kind of hedonist, but you're just being a prick."

"I'm more of a nihilist than a hedonist."

"Nihilism is training wheels for assholes."

"OK, then I'm neither. I'm just, you know, whatever, doing what I can. Trying to make you not flip out."

"And the training wheels come off! You're a big boy now."

But they still went to the clinic and got an ultrasound and watched the required-by-law video and Karen took the pills. In the car, after they'd pulled out of the shameful back lot, there were tears. The poison or hormone, whatever it was, ran its course and Karen was in pain and there was bleeding and cramping, but Roy could tell it was the emotional side that was getting her down. Not even the grande-sized ibuprofen would help with that. He tried to be there and play nurse and rent her movies, pick up takeout, but as usual he fucked it up, rented movies he wanted to see, ordered food he liked. And after a few days of tenderness, he'd started thinking, *you need to move on, we need to move on,* and returned to his baseline of hard drinking and skating.

It was the human capacity of it all that bothered him, the Christian Science baggage carousel that spun around and offered hard numbers and data, or a living, breathing child. Having a baby didn't need to be a kill-or-be-killed situation. Maybe he'd do things differently now. Maybe they'd keep the kid. *Whenever you're ready,* he should've said, *I'm here. I put you in this place. I'll stay here until you're ready to go.* He'd get it right next time, or at least more right.

He gave Karen a kiss on the top of her head while she dug through her bag, then opened the door and hopped outside to pop the tiny worthless hood instead of battling with the knuckle-busting latches on the doghouse, because that was a whole other hole to go down. But he'd forgotten to pull the release for the hood, so, back in, driver's door open, reaching for the lever.

"Are we out of gas?" Somehow Karen had managed to put on lipstick in the three to five seconds that he was outside. He smelled the thick, animal-tested, tallow-vat smell before he noticed the waxy red sheen on her lips.

"We aren't out of gas." He upshot and wiggled a couple of stiff fingers, Brit bird, in the general area of her mouth. "I like that color. You look great."

"We've been on the road. I feel skeezy. Would you rather I look like shit?" She puckered her lips and gave him a few air smooches.

"No, I'm serious. It's a good color." He grinned and with effort thought he kept his malice from rising to a visible level. "Me and all the bigfoots and grizzly bears are impressed and super turned-on. Rock-hard yetis everywhere." Door shut, into the wind. He didn't know what he wanted from her. He wasn't mad, not at her, but the unwelcome, woman-hating voice of his stepfather, Steve, entered his mind anyway—

Range is cold.

"Like the off-ramp bums," Steve had said. They were at the Pala rez range, wasting ammo, talking groups and trigger pull, more or less ignoring their mutual distaste for each other. Steve ejected the empty magazine and opened the bolt and set his rifle on the bench. He held up a finger as in wait, then removed his ear protection and his amber shooting glasses. "Will not work for food if my tits can get it for free. Will bitch endlessly for no good reason. Will not stand by my man if I see any chance for chiseling. Will grind my man to dust. Anything helps."

Roy, hydroponically stoned, had trouble formulating a response, so he busied himself gathering the various brass from the bench and where it had fallen on the ground and dropped the casings in the small black sack they'd brought with them. Roy owned his stepdad at two hundred yards with the M77 but

Steve was unbeatable at twenty yards with his Springfield .40. Firearms were their only shared interest. Fathers and sons have had less, stepfathers and stepsons, much less.

Range is hot.

Steve held up a hand in the affirmative and made eye contact with their only neighbor: gray beard, 82nd Airborne baseball hat, tattooed hands, surgical long gun nestled into sandbags, synthetic stock with suppressor, topped with a Swarovski. Call me tack driver. American hero. He'd set his target at eight hundred yards, couldn't even see it without a scope or binocs. Roy watched his finger slide inside the guard and cover the trigger.

"Best cover your ears," hero said, without turning.

"I'm good," Roy said. "Go for it."

Now. The air pressure pulsed and dust kicked up in front of the shooting bench. The sound receded. Hero opened the bolt, palmed his brass and reloaded. Roy had cotton mouth. He'd like to shoot that rifle. There was lust. When he turned, Steve had his hands pressing his ear protection against his head, a gritted-teeth grin. The twerp. Roy held the bag of brass by the drawstring and let the blast from the next shot roll over him. He was sixteen and pretty sure he'd be dead before hearing loss was an issue. Three more shots and Airborne opened the bolt and moved around the table to his spotting scope.

Range is cold.

"You're talking about my mom," Roy said.

"I'm talking about women, and you better listen."

"Don't talk about my mom."

"Fine. Let's get outta here. I gotta be in Carlsbad by four thirty. I'll drop you at home."

Now look at Steve—rolling around on the plush carpet of his megachurch with his golden yarn ball of cat-toy enlightenment, thinking women are designed by the Lord Jesus to serve him. No, Stevie-dog, without women—without my mom—you wouldn't have accomplished dick all: no real estate license, no cushy church post, no home ownership. The truth, Steve? You can't (pan)handle the truth.

Always trouble finding the hood latch. Put your finger in the hole. Not that hole. He pushed the catch to the side and the hood opened. He'd need to unlatch the doghouse inside if he wanted to get to anything important. Metaphorically me all over the place. He hunched down so Karen couldn't see him. Self-awareness is a leaking tent, the more you touch it, the more it drips. He pulled on the wires he could reach, but they seemed fine, connected at least. He tapped the radiator cap, tugged on the belt. What did he actually know? Gasoline burned and made little explosions, oil lubricated, antifreeze cooled and kept parts from freezing, killed puppies.

Roy stepped back and looked around. The van was snow-crusted and listing toward the bank like maybe he'd wrecked instead of broken down. He imagined the black shadow of the state trooper that would slap the fluorescent green sticker on the glass marking it as abandoned. Last time the wrecking yard dinged him for three hundred bucks and he had to use a razor blade to get the sticker off, not that there weren't hundreds of stickers plastered all over the van already, but something about the cop sticker made him remove it. Official failure, was how it looked to Roy. Date, time, and location would be noted, unwanted and likely unaffordable services would be rendered. Brace yourself, help is on the way.

Hands shoved into his pockets, he blindly counted his

change with his fingers, organized it: quarters, nickels, dimes, flicked a solitary penny with the wind and it peened away with a space-shuttle slingshot bend into the bottomless snow on the other side of the bank. The mechanics of going home again were as much against Karen as the staged sentiment had always promised, but Roy had never wanted home. So Cal, born and raised, and he didn't care if he ever went back. He wanted adventure, wildlands and death rides, the authenticity of poverty minus the discomfort, a fruit-tramp lifestyle minus the work, minus the bugs.

Karen climbed out, pulling on her hat and gloves. "Can you fix it?"

"I don't even know what's wrong, so, no, I can't fix it. I don't have any tools anyway except for a skate key and a pocketknife. I don't have shit. Get back in there. Don't give me that look, I'm coming with you."

The heat was already gone inside but the protection from the wind was a welcome relief. Roy could see his breath. The windshield was quickly going from condensation to frost, skimmed in snow.

"There's no one we can call, huh? Even if we did have a signal." He was fishing for a specific response. He wanted to hear her say his name.

"A tow truck," Karen offered. "We could call a tow truck."

"Maybe if Mace had a phone," Roy said. "We could call Mace."

Karen glanced at Roy, then looked out the passenger window. "He doesn't. You know he doesn't."

"I just want to make sure we both understand that we're on our own now," he said, and slapped the back of his hand into his open palm as if he were in charge of NASA ground command. "This is it."

"Because we were with the angels or something before?" She leaned over and kissed his neck, yanked the hair on the back of his head.

He kissed her on the mouth, tasted her lipstick. Then he asked her if she remembered that guy they'd seen on the news. He'd been with his family, they were Koreans. They died when their car broke down.

"I don't remember that," she said.

"The whole family died. All of them." Actually, he thought maybe the family had lived and the guy had died when he'd wandered off into a blizzard looking for help. The Korean angle might have been wrong too.

Karen looked at him but didn't speak. She lifted her phone close to her face, and with a pointy finger, very carefully, turned it off. If he called her shrewd, he would mean she looked like a shrew. She nodded at the jingle of her phone shutting down. "No stick, no ant pile," she said. "Monkey starve."

He turned away, looked out the window. "I guess we should walk. We can't just sit here."

"Why not?"

"Do you want me to go get help and you can stay here?"

"And you leave me behind? Great idea."

"It's up to you. We can't get stuck out here in the dark. We'll freeze to death. Let's just go. Do you need anything out of the van?"

"What does that even mean? What we have in the van is what we need. That's why it's in the van." She waited for Roy to reply but he wasn't saying anything.

"I think we should wait for someone to come by," she said. "We have our sleeping bags and food. I don't remember this road and I grew up around here. I don't think we should just head out, you know. Stay with your vehicle is the advice I remember. Stay put. The snowplow has to come by at some point."

"I made a decision and now you're undermining it."

"What are you talking about? We can get it on. Nice and sweet, and later, after we screw, somebody will come by and find us and give us a ride. It'll be fun. Let's just stay. It's not like we're in a hurry." She tried to kiss him and he backed off. "Be nice to me," she said, with hurt in her eyes. "If I told you that you have a disgusting, smelly body, would you hold it against me?" she said.

"No."

"That's too bad because I'd rather have sex than pretend I'm Jack London with my one fucking match."

They'd already had sex that morning in a rest stop parking lot. Roy wasn't interested in another round. To Roy, all of this: the van, the road, the sex, everything, used to be better. He didn't know what this was, but it felt like someone was twisting the dimmer switch, bringing the darkness.

[1]

M > 35
CA 96118

T HE CHILD IS IN THE LIVING ROOM PLAYING WITH A DECK OF cards. Go Fish cross-pollinated with Crazy Eights. He can see her from the kitchen. She's safe. He's been left in charge. If he shows any fear or doubt or even fucks up a little, the child's mother will for good reason take this all away. He'll regress, the evolution of man in reverse. From the mud to the trees to the cities, space travel, back to the mud. Go fish.

The woman loves him, she's said it before, but she won't marry him now or say the words again. Not yet. She's a widow and the house will never be his house and the child is not his. If the little girl's father is dead, does that mean he can be her father now? Is that possible?

She has a makeup bag on the floor, emptying the contents and smearing whatever she finds on her arms and her face.

"I don't think your mom would like you doing that," he says.

She appraises him, judges his information, forms an opinion. "It's OK," she says.

"It's just that you're kind of making a mess and I don't know for sure but I think that stuff is expensive."

The little girl begins twisting the lids onto the small opaque glass containers and plugging the caps back onto the lipstick tubes and carefully placing them inside the green-and-gold satin makeup bag. He hadn't seen her go and get the bag or leave the living room at all. The child is fast and moves silently at times but is also capable of stone-heeled, window-rattling chaos if she's in the mood. "When's mama getting home? I want mama." And she's a mind reader.

"I think, I think she said an hour and it's only been about twenty minutes. Seems longer, huh? But she said an hour and that's not too long, right? Do you want to draw? She said we could draw. Remember, I'm pretty good at sharpening pencils." A reference to last week. He's establishing routine. He's going to be here. He's here to stay.

"No," the child says, not meanly but firm.

Drawings of rainbow-colored unicorn-type things are displayed on every wall, held there by strips of blue masking tape. The blue masking tape is something the child's mother has specifically talked to him about.

"Do you want to go outside instead?" he asks.

"Yes! Let's go see the bunnies!"

"OK, but you have to put on your coat and your boots."

"It's not cold."

"No, it's not too cold but your mom told me that if we go outside you have to wear your coat and your boots."

"I'm not sick anymore."

"No, you're all better now. Should I get your coat? Do you need help?"

"No."

He goes to the kitchen and comes back and tosses her a hand towel and with hand signals indicates that she should clean up and to his surprise she unscrews the cap on the cold cream and wipes some on the towel and scrubs her face. She uses a compact mirror from the makeup bag to double-check that she hasn't missed any spots. She is thorough and after she's finished her skin is red and puffy. She returns the towel to where it'd been on the counter next to the cutting board and puts away the cold cream and the mirror.

"Is it dark?" she says.

He points to the living room windows, at the obvious daylight, and immediately feels like an asshole. He is an asshole. He'd never fully realized what a prick he was until he'd started spending time with the child. Acceptable behavior has always been low on his list and this late in the day it's proving difficult to master.

"We still have another couple hours until the sun goes down," he says. "Plenty of time."

"Then I don't have to wear my coat."

"You do. Your mom told me you do," he says. "I don't care one way or another."

The girl retrieves her dead father's baseball hat from the hook by the front door. The hat says KC on the front and Go Royals in small cursive letters on the back. It has been adjusted all the way down but is still too big. She has long dark hair like her mother and she pulls it off her shoulders and does a half-ass job feeding it through the back of the baseball hat in a kind of ponytail. Her mom does the same but better.

"You're kind of half-assing that whole thing," he says before he can catch himself. "Let me help."

"What's half-assing?" There is no hurt in her face, no pain.

"It's nothing. Hey, do you want a hair tie or a barrette instead?"

"No." Now she's getting angry. She can smell his lies, his weakness and fear. Blood in the water. "What's half-assing?" She holds her hands out in a dramatic way that also favors her mother. "Tell me!"

"Looks good." He attempts a happy smile but feels like he might be sneering.

"It means it looks good?"

"Sure," he says. "You ready to get your boots on?"

"You're lying. And I'm not wearing my boots." She points to her bare feet. "My feet are half-assing, OK? So no boots."

"OK, let's go," he says, doing a weird flourish with his hand, a stranger unto himself. "We're half-assing our way right out the door."

She runs to the door and he opens it for her, Gentleman Jim, and they step onto the porch. He's snagged her boots when she wasn't looking though, and he holds them out for her and she unbelievably takes them. She pulls them on the wrong feet but he figures good enough even though the wrongness bothers him. He suspects she knows they're on the wrong feet and that bothers him too. But he follows her across the driveway and lets her open the temporary corral gate because they'd built it together, along with her mom, and she knows how to lift and pull at the same time to get the gate open, because he'd screwed it up a little and it took some finessing. She takes forever with the gate, not getting it open, and he has to fight the urge to take over. Let her do things. Let her be her own person.

The rabbits are separated into three different cages and when he switches on the single bulb in the barn they all turn broadside. They are white and the plan is to use them for food. The little girl seems to be fine with this. She opens the nearest hutch and reaches inside and pets the rabbit's ears. That's the only nice rabbit, right to left they get meaner. He isn't going to let the child open the last cage where the buck is kept because he's a monster, a Watership Downer with a ragged ear from rabbit fighting or a dog maybe. The man doubts if he can stop the child from opening the last cage without making her cry.

"When my papa shot Fargo did she bleed?" she says.

"I don't know. Who was Fargo?" The child has his full attention.

"Silly, it was our dog. We had Norton and Fargo was the one that Papa shot cuz she was dying. She's dead now."

He doesn't like it when she calls him silly, but again, that's his problem. "Where's Norton?"

"With Aunt Ape but he's old too and Uncle Ape says he might not make it through the winter."

"I'm sorry," he says. The response is inadequate. She waits for him to improve his position. "If he shot Fargo, Fargo would've bled."

"Like a lot?"

"I've never shot a dog. I've never shot anything but a paper target."

"She would've bled like a lot?"

"I don't know. It would be really hard to shoot your own dog. They're part of the family." Now he's gone too far. This is cliché is what this is. This is dishonest and here goes some more blood in the water. *I didn't know your dog. I can't speak to your grief.* He cocks his head and listens, hoping the girl's mother is pulling into the driveway, but she isn't. He considers lying to the child and telling her she is so he can get out of this.

"Papa cried at the table after we buried Fargo and said goodbye."

"Do you remember when that happened?" he says.

"Yes, but Mama told me the parts I forgot like with Papa." She shuts the first hutch and latches it. He's grateful that the rabbit didn't escape again. They're hell to catch. What was that line about nothing as foolish as a man chasing his hat? Haven't seen me charge into the blackberries after a bunny. He'd taken damage, new scars on top of the old ones.

The child opens the second hutch and reaches in. The rabbit cowers and turns. The girl reaches in further and when she touches the rabbit's fur it strikes the child quick as a snake with its forepaw. When the girl sees the blood on her hand she begins to cry.

He moves quickly to shut the hutch and latch it. The rabbit leans against its hutch wall in the corner, the ball-bearing-actuated drip waterer leaking against her back leg. Her nostrils move in a way that doesn't seem mammalian. You could drop that nose in the bottom of the ocean next to an anemone and it'd fit right in.

He doesn't know if he should pick the child up. She's really crying and looking up at him as if she needs him. So he plucks her from the ground and she wraps herself around him. He hugs her back and tells her it's OK. He catches her arm and wipes the little berries of blood from the scratch with his thumb.

They walk out of the barn like that and in the sunlight she stops crying. She lifts her head from the wet spot on his shoulder and pushes herself out of his arms without looking at him. After he sets her down she runs to the corral fence and climbs up until her arms are hooked over the top rail like a cowboy. He stands beside her, surprised that she's already forgotten about the scratch.

"Where're the goats?" he says. The art of distraction.

"Down there in the shade. Under the stinky tree." She lifts herself up higher.

"What's that?" He points to the field.

"Sandhill." She makes a decent chuckling crane call and the two big birds pivot like lawn sprinklers and look at her. "You try," she says.

He does and the birds run a few steps in the short grass and work their big wings and take flight. "I don't think they liked mine as much as yours."

"It didn't sound right."

"Ready to go inside?"

"Not yet."

They watch the birds fly over the county road and rise above the low hill on the other side, a rabbit-shaped hill, tucked in and brushy in the folds. For a moment he loses the birds in the sun but the girl points and follows them with her finger until he finds them. The birds circle around and land in the near field again. The girl stays on point like a bird dog and makes another crane call and it's as if she's had control of them the whole time, that she's guided them back to where she wants them, instead of the other way around.

[2]

M < 55
CA 96118

H E STEPS FROM HIS BICYCLE AND LEANS IT AGAINST THE SIDE of the funeral parlor. In the shade, with his back to the cinder-block wall, he lets the wobble drain from his legs. Smoke-gray sky, can't taste the ash any longer. His dismounts used to make her smile. Like a French mailman, she'd say. Bonsoir.

He can hear the dog rummaging around back, plastic on plastic like a tarp in a storm, rooting in the undertaker's trash pit, trying to get at whatever rodent or food scrap he's sniffed out. The man gives a donkey whistle and a forty-five-pound Malinois, coyote-lean and sharp-eyed with a black face and golden body, comes trotting from around the corner with a lidless plastic one-gallon container of—the man leans down to read the label—brown gravy in his jaws. Only an inch or so of congealed sludge remains.

"You're proud of yourself," the man says.

The dog lifts the jug higher and when the man tries to grab it he dodges out of reach and prances in the dust, high-stepping and tossing his head like a pony. As he comes around again he keeps his amber eyes on the man and presents his prize.

"I'm not playing," the man says. "Drop it. Pfui."

The dog does as it's told but gives the man a sideways look.

"You want to make me feel bad, is that it? OK. It's your stomach. Go ahead." He motions the dog closer.

The dog comes forward and gives the jug a swat and nuzzles it around and puts both of its front paws inside the wide mouth. While gripping the upper edge of the jug's opening with its teeth and giving down pressure with its feet, the dog aggressively twists its head side to side until the plastic rips open. With only a glance at the man, the dog thrusts its muzzle into the hole and settles into his meal.

When he's finished, the man calls the dog over and pulls him close against his legs and has a little bit of a wrestle and shove and then points at the ground beside his bike.

The dog lowers itself with its front paws close together and presents a recalcitrant profile. The man gives the dog a last jaw scratch and heads for the door.

Bells chime. The air is cooler inside. James Taylor on the radio. Heavy curtains cover the lobby windows but there's light coming from the wide doorway that leads to the chapel. The carpet is geometrically sun-bleached where the chairs, receptionist's desk, and wall tables in the waiting room have been removed. The inspirational artwork—pastel boats crossing rivers and stormy oceans, oily sunsets, watercolor fields complete with tractors and cows—have all been taken down. Against the wall, near the door, moving boxes are stacked to the ceiling and there's a handcart tipped into the corner.

The undertaker comes from the back wearing blue coveralls with his sleeves rolled up, drying his hands on a white towel with red stripes. When he sees who it is he nods and says hello. He tosses the towel onto the back of a chair and they shake hands.

"Glad you made it," the undertaker says, pressing down the wispy red hairs that remain on his head.

The man nods.

The undertaker finishes with his hair and motions toward the man's left hand. "How's the hand? Did you heal up all right?"

The man shoves his hand in his pocket and, as has become his habit, begins rubbing his thumb across the smooth scar where his finger used to be, presses down on the bone until it aches. "It's fine."

The undertaker takes a deep breath through his nose and after he lets it out their eyes meet once again. "Right when I thought I'd seen it all."

"We don't have to stand here talking," the man says.

"I told you I don't do deliveries," the undertaker says, a touch of playful anger in his voice. "I was beginning to think you didn't hear me or, worse, you didn't believe me."

"I remember," the man says. "I heard you. I got the note you left at the house."

The undertaker touches his hands together like a prayer, pink nails on clean freckled hands. "I wouldn't go without settling this."

"It's all right. I'm here now. Hell, Larry, I even put on a suit." The man wipes his hand over the breast of his black tailored merino jacket, touches the collar of his dress shirt. His face is sun-darkened and his greasy salt-and-pepper hair, only slightly shorter than his ragged three fingers of beard, points thickly in all directions as if someone has chopped up a pair of wool army surplus trousers with dull scissors and glued the remnants to his skull.

"It's better for a person's grief if they bind it off, close the loop," the undertaker says. "I believe that."

The man nods again. "Here I was thinking it was because I didn't pay you."

"Nobody has paid me in a long time."

"I'm ready if you are."

When the undertaker returns he has a small redwood box held out before him. The man accepts the box, feels the undertaker's eyes on the shiny scar of his missing finger. The wood has shrunk and the joints look bad. It weighs less than he would've liked.

The undertaker lifts the hand towel from the chair back and drapes it over his shoulder like a line-cook might do and goes to the window and hauls open the curtains. "I have a sister in Maine," he says.

"You're not going down with the ship then," the man says.

The undertaker turns and attempts his pitiable and well-worn, somebody-has-died-and-the-service-begins-at-one-sharp smile, but there's more to his face now, a new muscle group or a dead tangle of nerves, whatever it may be, the end result is a sincerity that—sitting through countless funerals—the man has always wanted to see. It's his true face, without religious pretension or the motivation of business, just the man. "This ship has sunk," the undertaker says. "And make no mistake, I went down with it. Same as you." He wipes his brow on the back of his arm. "I could give you a lift."

"Thanks, but I'm going the other way."

"It's about time." A smile spreads across his face. "Past time."

A CAR DRIVES BY OUTSIDE AND SOMEBODY YELLS. WITH THE MUSIC on the radio it's hard to tell what's said. The man and the undertaker both turn to look but can't see anything through the dust-caked glass. "Thanks again," the man says.

"Good luck to you," says the undertaker.

The door shuts behind him with a jingle and the sun bakes his suit against his body. The dog has disappeared. The tire tracks are fresh in the dust on the blacktop but they turn at the next block, heading toward the elementary school. The man whistles for the dog and waits but he doesn't come. He takes a deep breath. Another whistle, louder. No dog.

He shoves the box into his pannier, too roughly, and climbs onto his bike. He loses the dog's tracks immediately but can't bring himself to circle back. The dog is much better at finding him than he is at finding the dog. He goes slow with a light touch on the pedals.

At the FreshMart, sales placards continue to advertise the absurd: tasty and fresh, low prices, local and organic. A tipped-over water machine crosses the threshold of the double doors and empty jugs litter the parking lot. He whistles for the dog again, yells its name, still expecting it to trot up behind him and lick his hand, the back of his arm, as it always has. He wills the dog to appear and when that doesn't work he wishes as a child wishes on a star or a birthday cake. Powerball. Hope is a scratch ticket.

He rounds the corner and his skin chills in the shadow of

Preservation Hall—concrete-antebellum, scorched lintels, graffiti tagged, the last new building. From there it's all weedy foundations and trash-filled basements where the houses that were small enough to move were taken away on lowboy trailers years ago. Blackened chimneys tell a different story. Starts with insurance fraud and ends with pennies on the dollar, trash-bag carryalls, and kids' mattresses on the roof rack. He rolls a bullet-mangled stop sign and takes the last turn toward home. Riding by the abandoned lumber mill, he can smell the ghosts of the trees, their sweet resin.

The road is empty and the only tracks are his from earlier and going the wrong way. The farms are gone, wiped from existence. No hay sheds or barns remain, no animals, just dust. Alfalfa, formerly the dominant crop, is at this point an alien concept, replaced by star thistle and Scotch broom. Above the ag lands, tree stumps stud the hillsides and clear-cuts spread like pale mold in the black of the burns on the mountains. Pedal. Crank. Creak.

Two of the four windows in his tack room are broken and shards of glass sparkle yellow and white on the dusty floorboards. He leans toward the window and calls again for the dog. In response, a hot, smoke-tainted wind drifts in and stirs the dust, further dimming the sunlight. He takes the redwood box from his pannier and shoves it into his jacket pocket, does up the buttons.

He doesn't remember tying the noose but there it hangs. He's mildly impressed with his effort. Even with nine fingers. His ring finger and the tattooed ring that adorned it, burnt to ash in the box with his wife. Took it off with an inch-and-a-quarter chisel. Four books—two Haynes manuals and a couple of his wife's poetry collections, Jack Gilbert and Wendell

Berry—arranged log-cabin style on the back of his hand held the chisel upright while he brought the mallet down. It came off clean and hurt and bled about as much as he expected. Comparatively nothing.

He knocks the dusty noose around, a slo-mo speedbag workout. The milk stool at his feet was a gift from his eldest daughter to his wife. What happens when the idiot dog comes back? He's not coming back. He'll eat your feet, if you're hanging, whatever he can reach. You should kick off your shoes to make it easier for him. "Gravy-eating shithead."

The man waits, for what he doesn't know—a reason, a sign, an excuse, karmic reckoning—to put an end to this. Should he bind his hands? Is this an actual option again? Is this how it ends? Should he write a note? He doesn't want to change his mind. How would he even bind his own hands? Would a zip tie work? He has a zip tie somewhere. He thinks that no one will ever know, but what if they do? Why did he tie the noose in the first place? What if his girls find out that he didn't bring their mother to them like he promised because it was too difficult? *Insurmountable logistical problems. Sorry. I was too sad.* All the fatherly advice he's given them, examples he's set, good and bad, and none of it, not a word or misstep, would point to: If the going gets brutish, chop off your finger and hang yourself.

His suicidal calculations, chump math, are suddenly interrupted by the heavy thump of shotgun blasts.

Without thinking, he limps quickly from the barn to the driveway and rips open the passenger door of one of the two burnt-down-to-the-rims-and-shot-up pickups parked there and retrieves his rifle from behind the charred seat where he's stashed it.

Crouched at the corner of the barn, he checks that the rifle is still loaded. A dirty red pickup with a black fender has left the county road and broken through the fence, driving recklessly across the sunbaked field toward the house. The passenger is hanging out his window with a shotgun, shooting over the hood. The man follows the trajectory of the barrel and thirty yards ahead of the pickup catches the zipper of dust rising from the dog as it runs crookedly toward him, watches as he stumbles, falls, doesn't get up.

The man braces his arm against the barn, rests the rifle there and fires. Leads him by the length of the hood. The passenger is hit on the second shot and the driver jerks the wheel trying to pull him in and as he does the passenger tumbles out the window backward like a scuba diver. The driver brakes hard and the truck slides broadside and before it comes to a stop the driver is out and circling to the far side of the truck for cover. The driver yells but it sounds tiny like it comes from inside a box and it might as well. "It's only a fucking dog. You motherfucker. You shot him. You shot him." The driver leans in front of the truck's grille and fires seven shots with his pistol at the barn.

After a long minute of nothing but wind, a cloud passes overhead and the air cools in the shadow. Through the scope the man can see the dog isn't moving. When the driver leaves the safety of the truck and runs toward the passenger in the field, the man brings his barrel around to follow him. The driver pulls on the passenger's arm and begins dragging him back toward the truck but he must be beyond help because he lets go and picks up the shotgun instead and when he turns for cover, the man centers the reticle on the driver's chest and squeezes the trigger. He shoots him again when he's down and that's it for ammo so he thumbnails the bolt and spins it into the dead weeds and drops the rifle at his feet.

From the barn he crosses the southern corner of what was their garden. Ruined fence, smashed gate. What remains: Popsicle sticks with her handwriting on them, geraniums, his daughter's trowel because she never picked up her tools, the bottoms of Pabst cans for slugs, torn Visqueen and shattered PVC from the hoop house. Only the slightest hint of the work, the love, that went into this ground. The weeds won. The weeds always win.

The dog's hide is ragged and he has buckshot puckers in his hip, his fur matted with blood to the dewclaw. The man kneels beside him and holds the dog's head in his hands and talks to him, runs his thumb over the handsome ridge of bone above his eye.

As he lifts the dog to carry him to the trespasser's truck, the dog lifts his head and licks the man's face. The bleeding is a steady trickle from the buckshot wounds, not arterial. He can't feel any broken bones. The dog smells strangely like the inside of a car tire, like an inner tube. "Did they run you over, bud?" he says. He could shoot more. He wants to shoot more. "You'll be OK. I got you now."

He sets the dog down gently on the passenger floorboard and pushes the button and kills the motor. Behind the seat he finds a water jug and pours some into his cupped hand. He continues talking to the animal as it drinks. When the water is gone he searches the truck for some sign of militia affiliation but there's none to be found, not a sticker or a beer coozy or anything.

The passenger is sprawled on his stomach, arms out, palms up. The exit wound has shattered the right shoulder blade. Bone is visible through the hole in the shirt. A bloody piece of flannel

tied in a knot partially covers a ragged dog bite on his left forearm. The man rolls him over, industrial-grade acne and a plastic
gold grill, fake diamond bling. His shirt says: FAILED STATE—
CALIFORNIA CALIPHATE—89/97—NO SURRENDER. He was militia,
Jeffersonian. Could be worse.

The driver is older, bald, scars on his head and face. His
T-shirt is a crude map of California with a double-bitted axe
splitting the state longways. THE LINE BEEN DRAWN, it says. At the
approximate location of Redding, the shirt has a small oblong
hole in it the size of a disposable foam earplug. No other visible
wounds. Must've pulled the second shot. Stomach is beginning
to bloat or he had a hernia. Not lifting the shirt to see. Cured
what ailed you. Two fingers are missing on his right hand. The
man places his damaged hand over the dead man's. The passenger could've been his son, or maybe they were brothers or just
pals. The pistol is empty but the shotgun has two shells in it and
he saw more under the seat in the truck so he takes it with him,
leaves the pistol in the dirt.

He starts the truck and U-turns, parks as close as he can
to the bodies. It's like wrestling pigs getting them into the
truck bed. He says cocksucker and dumb fucking dickfors.
Idiots. Dead idiots. His arms and chest are slick with their
blood. He drives out of the field and down the driveway to
the barn. He isn't going into the house again. He hasn't been
in there more than a handful of times since she died, months
now, half a year. It'd taken him that long to get well, gather
the courage to pick up her ashes.

His daughters send messages to the TNK unit, they call it
tink, in the neighbor's barn a mile down the road, essentially a
souped-up HAM radio. It can be vector-adjusted to use Birke-

land currents and dynamic-array satellite guidance to encrypt correspondence. At least that's how the neighbor pitched it to him. A piece of expensive government hardware turned militia hardware once the neighbor walked off the job with it. But the neighbor and his wife, former Jeffersonians themselves, are dead now. Their cases upon cases of Mountain House meals and poly-tanks of drinking water remain, along with a filtration system and a wonky-at-best solar system, enough to run the tink but not much else. There used to be a few cows and a small garden and a laying flock of chickens, but once he was alone he'd butchered and made jerky out of the cows, then dutch-ovened the birds one after the other. He'd left the garden to die because green made him a target. Besides, he couldn't put his hands in the dirt without thinking of his wife. He didn't need more reasons for his various failures. He had all the reasons he could handle.

The tink is only a messaging system. He can't actually talk to his girls or hear their voices, and that's probably for the best. They're better off where they are. They made it. They said that the drive up wasn't so bad. People weren't violent, just worried and restless, tired.

You don't have to worry, he'd punched into the tink's miniature keypad that morning, after he'd put on his suit jacket and tied on shoes, I think we're ready.

> Yay! UR coming? How's mom?
> We'll be leaving soon.
> Is she all right?
> ——
> Dad?
> We'll be OK.

J wants to know if you fixed the truck.

Not sure yet. Don't worry.

Please hurry dad. It's only gonna get worse.

But he didn't know how it could get worse, then, as usually happened, his unasked questions had been answered.

HE TURNS THE TRUCK AROUND AND BACKS INTO THE BARN. THE bodies flop from the truck bed jointless and unruly onto a section of collapsed roof and broken lumber. Twisted and dead, he dislikes them even more. He hates them. He empties dozens of milk jugs of used motor oil, twenty years' worth, onto them and lights the whole mess on fire with a small butane torch he finds in a cobwebby corner behind the motor oil.

The only veterinarian he knows lives more than a hundred miles to the west, just outside Sacramento. She'll welcome them. She's the only friend they have left. But not believing for a second that the fuel in the red truck's tank will be enough to make it or that the auxiliary batteries will hold a charge, he loads his bicycle and panniers and an old buggy-style bike trailer they'd had since his youngest daughter was born into the back of the truck, tosses in an armload of loose tools, a tire pump, bike tubes, a pair of foldable spares. Thinking the dog can ride in the bike trailer if and when the truck runs out of gas. If he can even cram him in there. He finds an old turnout blanket in the tack room and slides it under the dog and then swaddles him tightly so he can't move. As an afterthought, he returns to the tack room for the last of the beef jerky and chucks it in the cab. Evil black smoke chases them out the barn doors.

Turning onto the two-lane highway at the end of the drive, he's surprised to feel relief, as if he's on the other side of a thing, made it through a long night or a fever. The speed feels good, the response of the motor, the power and control. The dog is panting with its tongue out, curled like a playground slide. He passes the neighbor's farm, the twelve-foot-high security gate is closed and padlocked, concertina wire tops the chain-link fence that surrounds the property. All the life the fence was built to protect is dead and gone but there's a small solar-powered Eton radio on the windowsill of the barn chattering away beside the tink giving federal food-drop locations and points of process and extraction. Occasionally he'd switch it to FM and listen to the militia rants, preacher babble, peaceful resistance groups giving sad explanations of their failures. Hopes and dreams turned taxidermy, hides and heads. The stereo in the truck had been cut from the dash with a Sawzall leaving a ragged black hole and a tangle of multicolored wires. There used to be music.

Through town, he scans the side streets out of habit and glimpses the undertaker lugging boxes up the ramp to his trailer. The motor stutters and he buries the accelerator keeping the rpms high, sensing now more than ever that momentum is his friend.

Another twenty miles and he makes a sound as the breath goes out of him. He touches his pockets, confirms that he's lost the box with her ashes. The truck slows as he lifts his foot from the gas pedal. The dog is panting on the floor, watching him with one glassy eye. The orange blanket is soaked with blood and the fuel gauge has already noticeably dropped, voltmeter at seven and falling. In his mind, he sees the redwood box being swallowed by flames. He settles his foot on the accelerator and drives on.

The on-ramp to I-80 near Truckee is clear and as he drives up the short hill and gains elevation he can see people gathered in front of the gas station below even though the pumps are gone. They aren't armed or looting, nothing left to steal, just standing and talking, and they turn and watch him go, one little boy wearing a backpack waves and he waves back. The Sierras are the mountains of the moon, burned black and without vegetation, and he can't see it, but he knows the lake is nothing now, an algal murk puddle, archaeology, remembers the bumper sticker: KEEP TAHOE BLUE. To conserve fuel he coasts out of the passes and doesn't touch the brakes as he swerves by, and sometimes crashes through, the smaller of the fallen trees. The broken pavement could break a tie rod but it doesn't. Gravity only wants him gone. The sky is unfinished with smoke and haze, waiting on Bob Ross to draw in the treetops and greenery. No depth left. How about some birds, Bob? Nice little birds. Happy birds. The unkind sun is chopped in half and Popsicle red at the horizon. Hardened mudslides and clumsy boulders cut the road but they've mostly been cleared leaving pale mud stains and bomb-pitted asphalt.

Darkness now. The truck only has one dim headlight. The closer he gets to Sacramento, the more he's dodging abandoned cars and trash, roadside stragglers, cyclists and cart pushers, instead of dried mud and wood. He loses time and burns fuel winding through the dark and bone-dry suburbs so he won't have to face the security checkpoints on the freeway, because he knows enough to know that if he can't prove the truck is his, they'll throw him in the cages and leave the dog to die.

He stops at the gate at the vet's house and lays on the horn.

When she finally appears, he gets out of the truck and comes forward so she can see who it is. He points into the cab.

"Somebody shot him," he says.

The smile leaves the vet's face and she pushes the buzzer to open the heavy iron gate and waves him in. She walks bent forward a bit with her elbows back and a limp, gifts from her final motorcycle wreck. She opens the passenger door and in the dome-light glow she checks the dog.

"Come on," the vet says. "Lift with me." She helps the man lift the dog until he's cradling it in his arms, then leads the way onto the headlight-lit porch and into the dark, cavernous cool of her house.

They pass through the entryway, a single lamp lit in the living room, an open book on the couch, and out a side door into a wide hallway with swinging steel doors. Dogs begin barking in the kennels and he and the dog both turn and look at the sound. The vet opens the electrical panel and flips a couple of breakers and the LEDs overhead snap to life and she leads the way to her office and the kennels.

He puts the dog down on the exam table like she tells him.

"Are you OK?" She gives him a hug, touches his face.

"I'm fine."

She opens an upper cabinet and pulls on surgical gloves. "You don't look it."

The vet's fingers work through the dog's fur, probing for injuries. He hadn't run out of fuel but the gauge was at zero for the last fifteen miles or so. He can't remember when he's last eaten. *I need to get rid of the truck.* He'd said that out loud. The vet tells him she can manage from here, and gestures him from the room. The dog watches him go.

Outside, he unloads his bike trailer and his bags from the back and stows them safely along the side of the vet's house, under the porch. He leaves the shotgun in the corner behind the front door. The gate shuts automatically behind him.

He drifts through the dark neighborhood and the intersection at the bottom of the hill without his lights, then follows the road to the west toward the highway. Dark roads, he lets the rumble strips guide him. A few minutes later the truck sputters and dies and he eases it onto the shoulder. He lifts his bicycle from the bed and pedals away.

That night the dog sleeps on a child's mattress on the porch while they nurse paper cups of Walmart bourbon and watch a stream of ants march across the banister and up the side of the house.

"Your hand," she says. "I keep looking at it."

He closes his fist and puts it in his lap.

"You don't have to hide it."

"I don't want to creep you out."

"Little late for that," she says.

The dog is dreaming with one eye open, making little yelps. Its hindquarter is shaved and iodine-stained, shiny staples bridge the incisions the vet made hunting for buckshot. The dream has a hold on the dog and he tries to run and it must hurt because he wakes up and gives a confused look at his hip. The man moves his chair over to pet him and talk him back to sleep.

"I'm the last of your Mohicans, aren't I?" the woman says later.

He looks at her and smiles.

A long minute passes. There are no jets in the black and hazed-over sky. "I might have something in the freezer for us."

When she returns she has a hoarfrosted pint of mint chocolate chip ice cream and two spoons.

"Put mine in the cup," he says, and slurps the corn liquor from the nugget of ice cream and squirms with the hot and the cold and the pain on his palate.

She holds out her gleaming spoon, sights down it like it's a weapon. "Not that you need another reason, but your dog getting shot is maybe number six thousand and twelve for you to give up on your little homestead and get out of here." She smiles as she watches the man slurp a hunk of ice cream out of his cup.

"I've been trying," the man says.

"So, you're going?"

"I left her there."

"What do you mean, you left her?" The vet shakes her head, takes a breath. "Honey, she's already gone."

"I left her ashes at the house. I have to go back."

"You haven't told the girls yet, have you?"

"No."

"I can usually get online a couple times a week. You could at least email them from here."

"I need to face them."

"Skype or whatever, that won't work. Email is about as good as it gets."

"I know. That's not facing them."

The man closes his eyes again and imagines the fire rolling over the redwood box. "It gets quiet here now." Eyes open, he sees she's giving him a strange look. "It used to be so loud."

"I don't want to ask the obvious," she says, "but how exactly do you plan on getting there? It's a long ways."

"I'll get there." Whenever he speaks, he feels the strings of confession. His soul is brittle. "I got my bike and a trailer for the dog."

She studies him with a long sideways look. "I can give you three reasons. It's too far. You're too old, and that dog is too big to lug behind a bike. Maybe you should leave him with me and get yourself a nice Chihuahua. There's a three-legged Jack Russell in the back that would be happy to go with you. Take the shotgun you left behind my door and the Jack Russell."

The man motions to the dog. "You said he'd be as good as new."

"He'll be fine. But it's gotta be what, twenty-five hundred miles?"

"You think I'm too old," he says.

"I already told you that. You are too old, you old dipshit. What about that truck you showed up in? Why didn't you just keep it and drive that?"

"It's not mine. I wouldn't make it out of the city before I got arrested. Too many checkpoints."

"You made it into the city."

"I was lucky."

"Whose truck was it? Why don't you tell me what happened?"

"Doesn't matter."

"You aren't going to tell me?"

"No."

"Fine, jerk. I don't want to know."

"You're right. You don't."

"OK. Take 49 up to the middle fork of the Yuba, then backroad it home. Nobody will bother you out there. It's all neighborhood by neighborhood here anyway, some are militia, but most of them aren't. People are planning on coming back from this."

"Are you?"

"I just take care of the strays." Her voice isn't devoid of hope.

He absently caresses the stump of his finger.

"Seriously, you could take my pickup."

"Not unless you're in it," he says.

The woman shakes her head and looks away. "The cops are all in barracks now," she says. "They're doing tours with the National Guard, working with the Border Patrol and whoever else. Around here, in the city, actual law enforcement is out of the picture except for the Code Enforcement, and the codies mostly don't do anything they don't have to." She eats another spoonful of ice cream, talks with her mouth full. "Welcome to Sacramento."

They finish their ice cream and their drinks and she takes his cup and puts it inside the empty carton and adds hers and stabs it all down with the licked-clean spoon.

"You're mine too, you know," she says. "You're the last man on earth."

"There's others," he says. "They're everywhere."

"Last man I'd eat ice cream with." She slugs him gently in the shoulder. "My nine-fingered friend."

He feels light and easy, happy. Didn't think that was an option.

"I'll tell you what I'll do," he'd said to his wife on that last day. "I'll take us on a last tour, a big trip."

"You don't have to. You just have to keep our girls safe."

"They're as safe as they can be right now."

"They're so much smarter than us. I know you think that we should've gone with them."

"We will. Don't worry. When you get well." He touched her hair and she leaned her head against his hand.

"Two old useless fuckers in Alaska," she said, "making our kids feed us oatmeal and wipe our asses." She looked up at him and smiled. She looked so tired.

"I can't do this, it's killing me."

"You wish." She smiled, all of her soul coming through.

"Even now you're flipping me shit."

"I'll always be flipping you shit."

"I love you."

"You don't need to say it."

"I need you to say it to me."

"I love you," she said. "You're my whole life. You're my heart."

[3]

M > 35
CA 96118

Y OU'LL BE TOO BUSY AND YOU WON'T WANT TO PLAY WITH ME
or do anything."

"That won't happen."

"You will. Mama will have a baby and you will. Myra's
mama had a baby and now Myra doesn't get to play. Myra gets
yelled at if she plays."

"I don't really know Myra or her mama. I only met her the
one time at the birthday party."

"My friend Myra."

"That's not. I know who she is. Don't cry. You don't have
to. I don't understand how you can have the maturity to be so
immature about this."

"You aren't my papa. You won't love me because you're not."

"Never. Goddamnit. I'm, hell—you're—we're each other's,

OK? Don't be a dick about this. Your mom isn't even pregnant. We just wanted to ask you and see what you thought."

"You don't be a—what did you say?"

"It's not going to be any different. Don't you want a brother or a sister?"

"I want a big sister."

"But you'd be the big sister. No matter what."

"Then I want a brother."

"Either way, we're a family. We each get the love we need allotted to us at any given moment. It's fluid, like water."

"What is allotted? Like a lot?"

"Kind of. It can be."

"Tell me."

"Love flows around, you know, sometimes one of us is in deeper than the others but we're never out of it."

"We can't get out of it?"

"No goddamn way."

"We conserve water."

"That we do."

"You won't forget to draw with me?"

"Never."

"Is it like a swimming pool or is it like a lake?"

"Yes, both of those." He taps his shovel against her little yellow toy shovel. "C'mon, these potatoes aren't going to dig themselves and when we're done we'll unleash the pigs." *Glean* is the word.

"They aren't on leashes, silly. They're in their pigpen or their piggy house."

"One pig's leash is another pig's pigpen. I'm a serious fella. And I mean it, you gotta quit calling me silly. Get moving. Let's spread these spuds out there on the ground so they dry in the sun. Your mama says that's the best way to clean them. They dry and you brush them off. No water required."

"I just said that. And you always say that. You and Mama. Silly."

"Oh, there it is again. We're trying to save water is all."

"Like when we brush our teeth? Or have a brother?"

"I probably kind of tangled things up with the love-and-water metaphor, didn't I?"

"I'm not tangled. What is a meta for? What does it do to people?" One by one she gathers up an armload of scabby Yukon Golds.

He sticks his shovel in and kneels down to work with her. "I need to be more careful with my—"

"What?"

"Words." He considers grabbing the wheelbarrow or a bucket or something to move the potatoes but doesn't see the efficiency in walking to the barn and finding a bucket and walking back. He uses his T-shirt like a basket and has the girl load him up.

"I want tattoos like you."

"Nope. No can do. They've run out of tattoos."

"What? Who did?"

"All the tattoos have been caught and captured and put onto people's bodies and there aren't any left."

"Are there mamas and papas?"

"Of the tattoos?"

"Yeah."

"No, they're all gone. Like the dodo bird. And before you ask, a dodo bird was a flightless bird that was hunted to extinction—you know what extinction is."

"Dinosaurs are extinct."

"Right. Tattoos, dodo birds, dinosaurs, opioid pain drugs, and strip clubs. Gone forever. This is the last row and we're done."

"I'm tired."

"You can go to the house if you want."

"No."

"OK."

"Can we let the pigs out now?"

"No, we still have to let these potatoes dry and then we have to bag them and move them to the cellar." Listing more than three things on a to-do list always pisses her off but he's continued to do it anyway, partly because he takes pleasure in pissing her off. "Your mom wants to move some of the electric fence over so they don't break down the garden fence again."

Her brow furrows and she crosses her arms over her chest, then just as quickly her face relaxes and she loosens her grip on herself. His lists don't mean anything will ever get done. She knows that as well as he does. "Are we still getting a puppy?"

"Talk to your mom."

"She said no."

"I'll talk to her again."

"If she gets a baby, I get a puppy."

"Sound logic."

"I do get a puppy."

"It doesn't matter if I say yes. It's up to your mom and she's still sad about your old dog."

"You told me."

"I know. I'm a repeater. Me and Fugazi. It's up to your mom."

The girl wraps her arms around a heap of potatoes and tries

to lift them all at once and drops all but a couple. She's smiling up at him. He brushes the dirt from his shirt and takes time to load her arms with potatoes and sends her on her way with a pat on the back. Haze from the fires in the distance makes it seem as if the sky is slowly lowering down on them and maybe it is.

[4]

M < 55
CA 94203

THE MAN SHADES HIS EYES WITH HIS HAND AND SEARCHES THE swollen river for the abandoned bridge pilings. The new bridge was supposed to replace the old I Street Bridge but the money evaporated before they even got to the deck. Tough old I Street had been owned by the railroad and they'd let it decline until they had to pay to have it torn down and hauled away. Black silt dunes rib the ground and form scalloped ramps onto the concrete. His front tire sinks to the hub and he's forced to dismount and push his rig. Among the broken walls of the power plant, hacksawed cables and pipes glint like jewelry on a corpse. Someone has tipped a crude ladder constructed of tie-wired rebar and driftwood against the lone standing cooling tower and the high-water mark is slashed with red spray paint, the words *Jefferson Was Here* scrawled above it.

He and the vet were going to ride bikes here together but

as they were leaving a Bosnian woman with her two young children showed up at the gate towing a trailer full of parasite-ridden sheep so he's alone, which he prefers.

Because the river brings her, again, to his mind, flowing water. She's drawing him in now. They'd come to this place, he and his wife. Left the kids with their aunt, twist-top wine, skinny dip in a filthy river, out to the broken bridge. They swam in their shoes because of the broken glass on shore. How long ago was that? All of his math involves his children, X and Y to locate himself. Her hair was tied up and when they got out he kissed her neck. She is the high-water mark. They'd made up a story for the kids about a broken water main to explain their soggy shoes. Had to cross a lake in the parking lot to get into the Walmart.

She isn't here. She's gone. The river talks to him and tells him this is a lie. *Dark side of the road. Don't think twice. It's all right.* He knows he won't see her again. But if someone else were to tell him that, he'd call them a liar. Because it feels like a lie, an untruth. The river knows. He will see her again. He has to. *No use to sit and wonder why, babe.* He's going in. He needs to feel the water, to be near her.

He unzips the rain flap on the trailer and the dog lifts its head and sniffs the air and together they watch the brown water swirl around the pilings on the inland-bound current. The dog seems content, even with the Elizabethan collar and the staples. The man squats down and gives him a soft pat, then takes off his jacket and shirt and folds them and puts them safely inside the trailer, blanketing the dog. He removes his shoes and his pants—he wears no underwear—and places them on top of his jacket. He smooths the layers of clothing and gives the dog a last ear scratch and jaw rub.

Standing naked, he has the hide and bulgy, quick muscling of a lizard, and is covered in several lifetimes of tattoos and scars. From any distance he appears stained and cursed, God-stranded and clearly forsaken outside the crumbling walls of human decorum. That said, he doesn't look out of place.

He crosses the ground gingerly, surfer sans board, and slides down the bank into the mud and froth and wades into the sloshing water until he leaves the bottom and mounts his crawl stroke. The brackish water smells of lawn fertilizer and burns his eyes and the small cuts and scratches on his hands.

Breathing hard, rubber arms, nearly equidistant from either shore, he climbs from the water onto the slippery remnants of the massive bridge piling and squats there on the broken concrete and rusted rebar. *I helped build this*, he'd said to her. *Explains the state of it.*

No one is on the water, no boats or barges. But on the opposing shore, among the flood garbage and the charred driftwood of almond orchards and Sierra forests, wadded against the rubble of burned and crumbling condominiums, he catches sight of six, make that eight, people huddled around a cook fire. No boats on shore, not even a skiff. Bald heads. Kelpers, the vet had called them, people who harvest kelp and algae. The man was surprised to learn of the inland kelp trade. The last time he saw this river it was just a brown trickle and the kelp trawlers, not to mention the algae blooms, seeded like oyster beds, novelties still, were operating well offshore.

He watches the drifting smoke, smells the toxic dust, tastes it like a broken filling in his mouth. "Talk to me," he says to the river. "Say something." He dives back into the blood-warm water and finds his stroke.

An outlaw trawler, hand gurdy mounted under a tarp-roof bait house, is motoring seaward, looking haggard with heaped gear and no hands on deck. The man stays low in the water until it passes. Breaking through the spray on the wave crests he looks for the kelpers on the far shore but can't find them. With the current and the wind, he loses three hundred yards to the drift and has to crawl over a jumble of slippery drowned cars and crawls the roof of a half-submerged Sprinter van to gain the bank.

Dripping in the dirt at his rig the dog sticks its head out of the trailer for a sniff and the man obliges him.

He stands naked and lets the wind dry his body. Little to none of his filth has been removed by the swim. He is thin and poorly used but it's obvious by the square of his shoulders and the way his weight settles pendulum-smooth onto the balls of his feet—if nothing else—he's durable. As he slips once again into the dry comfort of his no-longer-fancy black suit a smile haunts his face.

He pushes his bike and trailer up the gentle slope of a barren hillside. At the top he leans his bike against a stone bench and takes a moment to catch his breath. His skin is skimmed with a chalky residue and as the sun warms him it begins to itch. Behind him, a bum's road, a scar of single-track, worms from the broken trees back to the industrial four-laners and eventually the old freeway. To the northeast, on the opposite shore, what had been the vista from the bench, is the trashed capital, with its unfinished high-rises, abandoned tower cranes, and the dust that only gets deeper. The man is reminded of what craftsmen term the signature of the machine, where the cutting blade would mar the work. From space, there would be a discernible pattern, kerf marks. Up close it isn't collapse or even destruction, it's a natural process, like watching mold eat an orange in time-lapse.

The man mounts the bike and follows the single-track through the dead forest until he comes to a short sandbag wall, a defensive position. He hauls the bike and trailer over in two parts, careful with the dog, and reconnects them on the wide unmarked blacktop that loops through the warehouses on the other side.

The gate is down at the railroad crossing. He rolls to a stop and gets off the bike. In the distance, coming toward him track-side he sees five, maybe six of the kelpers stooped beneath their mossy hauls and dragging carts and wagons, pushing wheelbar-rows. The man maneuvers around the gate and climbs onto his bike. He looks over his shoulder, lifts his head at the kelpers, speaks to the dog. "Here comes the future." After a shaky start, they're smoothly under way, rolling. The kelpers shout some-thing but he isn't stopping. He's gone.

[5]

M >35
CA 96118

H E COULD'VE BOUGHT THE KIT INSTEAD AND HE WOULDN'T have had to figure out how the components went together. Plug and play, right out of the box. But he needed to know how everything went together because it was him that was going to be fixing it if it broke. When it broke. Now he needed to be an electrician. This morning he was a carpenter. Yesterday a plumber. This road is paved with self-reliance. If it were paved at all. He'd been skimming *Walden*, thought Thoreau a pussy, a whamby poseur of the highest order. Goats would've annihilated HDT. Never mind drought or children.

In any case, he'd saved a little money doing the solar himself, but really at this point it wasn't about the money. Insurance settlements had come in, his and hers, like twinned sinks in an oversized bathroom. Losses paid, hers for death, his for injury. His sink was in fact much smaller and truly pathetic beside her swimming pool of grief. But they didn't have to worry for a while, not about money at least.

He'd built the vented and insulated case for the battery bank and mounted the collectors on the roof and wired them in series. Then he'd strung the wire and connected the charge controller and inverter, added inline fuses. He'd followed the directions he found online, but the way the little girl was looking at him he was sure he'd messed something up and as soon as he connected the batteries, also wired in series, the whole system would burst into flames.

"Are you thinking?" the little girl asks him.

"How can you tell?"

"Because you look like this." She makes her monkey face and scratches her chin.

"I should just hook it up, huh? I have to commit at some point."

"Red to red and black to black," the little girl says. She hands him a crescent wrench.

He reaches inside the battery case and connects the leads. Nothing explodes or changes in the slightest. He switches on the charge controller first, then the inverter. The green light comes on. The dial needle jumps upward in the voltmeter. There's power coming into the system.

"That's that," he says.

"Why didn't you want to do it for so long?"

"I didn't know what would happen."

"What happened?"

"Nothing. It works." He's proud of himself.

"Mama says you'll burn the house down."

"No, she said I'd burn the house down if I tried to tie into the panel. I didn't tie into the panel. Not yet. This is just power for the barn and the goat shed and once I get the switch installed, backup for our well pump."

"How do you tie into a panel?"

"If I knew that, I would've done it. I feel like I did something wrong."

"Like bad?"

"No, just like a mistake. I feel like I messed something up or forgot something."

"The lights came on."

"Yeah, you're right. At least the lights came on so the batteries are charging. I'll try out the rest after they get a good charge in them."

There's dust on the road. When her mother gets out of her truck, the girl leaves him and runs to her and hugs her belly. She's a cuddler.

"They had another meeting," the woman says, smoothing the child's hair back from her face.

"Did you go this time?" the man says.

"Yeah, but I left early."

"What's going to happen?"

"Hard to say."

"The light came on, Mama."

"It works?" She points to the solar panels on the roof of the barn.

"So far."

"Big-city solar guy. You put the musk in Elon Musk. How about that? Is the house next?"

"Looks that way." He touches her belly, kisses her cheek, and steps beside her and grabs her homemade canvas bags filled with groceries.

"I have layer pellets in the back too," she says. "I got the last two bags. Florence says it might be a while before he gets more."

"OK," he says. "No problem. You go inside. Get out of the sun."

"What's for lunch?" the girl says.

"We still have trout from our camping trip," the man says.

"Eww."

"Trout and pickles?" the woman says.

"No," the girl says. "I want potatoes and ketchup."

"There isn't any ketchup," her mother says.

"I want ketchup, Mama."

"Then we'll have to make some more, won't we? We already canned the tomatoes. We're halfway there."

"Can't we buy some? Your ketchup is funky."

"Really?" She turns to the man. "Do you think my ketchup is funky?"

"No," the man says, grinning. "Yes. But I don't like ketchup from the store either."

The little girl watches the man climb the stairs with the grocery bags then runs up and opens the door for him. "I don't need ketchup, Mama," she says.

The woman stops the man on the way out the door to get the chicken feed out of the truck. "They were looking for volunteers to go with them when they take control of the courthouse."

"With guns."

She laughs. "They can't wipe their asses without a gun."

"What d'you want to do?"

"Have this baby. Be a family. Forget about them and everyone else."

"Forget about what? Who? What just happened?"

"I was hoping you'd say that."

[6]

R < 25
CA 96118

ROY STEPPED OUT OF THE VAN AND THE BLOWING SNOW SMACKED him in the face like a handful of gravel. He had his army-surplus duffel slung over his shoulder with some clothes, his skate pads and a helmet, a paperback or two, toothbrush, toothpaste, a one hitter, dugout, a bone-handled knife that he'd picked up at the Saturday Market, and, at the very bottom, a court summons from Multnomah County for criminal trespass and destruction of public property, all sausage-cased together by webbing and the skateboard strapped to the outside like a splint. Karen's kit was smaller and more elegant, a Swiss-made cycling bag. She had her shit together. Roy looked homeless.

"Do you want to shut the hood before we go?" she said.

"No, leave it. That way they'll know it's broken down."

"You don't think they'd figure it out?"

Roy locked the doors, shut the hood, and they left the van

behind. The drawstring was gone from his sweatshirt and the stretched-out hood wouldn't stay on his head unless he held it there and then his hands would freeze. The wind needled into his left ear and soon he had a crick in his neck from trying to protect it. Karen had her head down, hat pulled low with her hood over the top, trucking along, swinging her arms like a power walker.

"You can complain if you want," he said.

"Money in the bank."

"Are you warm enough?" Roy asked.

"Yeah, I'm toasty. Do you want my hat?"

"No, I'm OK."

She took it off and stuffed it into his hand. "Take it." Her bangs blew into her face, eyes watering from the wind. Her beauty was powerful, held real muscle. It twisted him up and weakened him. He put the hat on and wished they were back in the van so he could be sweet but the wind iced his will and the moment passed.

Karen smoothed her hair back and stuffed it into her hood and then cinched her hood tight around her face. He patted his pockets and remembered the cigarettes and the lighter in the glove box. "Wait here." He dropped his pack, ran the whole way back, struggled getting the door unlocked, found the smokes and lighter, and returned, lungs burning. He hoisted his pack and backed into the wind, lighting two cigarettes at once and passing one to Karen.

"Thanks," she said, and took a drag.

They walked on. Snow mounded on Roy's shoes and his toes went numb.

"Statistically," Karen said, "and I'm talking within a purely hypothetical model here, it seems like, after a certain number of these automotive bed-shittings—"

"Not to mention all the other day-in, day-out shit," Roy said, hand raised, ready to list them if necessary.

"After all that, it seems like someday we'd finally be transcended, thwupp, a place of wisdom and meaning."

"You're high," Roy said. "When did you get high?"

"I'm not high," Karen said. "I'm talking about depth, legitimacy, our karmic gears finally meshing." She held out her gloved hands to demonstrate the meshing of the gears.

"Karmic gears?"

"The odds are against the odds getting worse. You know what I mean?"

"I know what you mean." The cherry of his smoke, tormented by the wind, was being foreskinned inside the cigarette paper. His cold tattooed hand—karmic gears—his cold tattooed body—sometimes he didn't even recognize himself. He didn't know if this scar-tissue insecurity was a cultural thing or maybe even evolutionary but as of late he was sure of one thing: It got fucking boring. Roy's life and his boom-bap bass line of peacockery and failure got fucking boring. Talking about it. Wearing clothes. Getting work done, new ink. Haircuts. Eating. Living. Breathing in and out like forever.

Karen didn't have much ink, minor damage; a bird and a covered wagon, that was it. Once he'd overheard her at his mom's house say that she didn't see his tattoos anymore, couldn't name them if asked. He was invisible to her. He put on the show and she didn't even notice.

A hot-bodied grim reaper in a miniskirt and halter top holding a weed-eater graced his stomach, and on his chest and creeping up his neck he had DEK8D above an exquisitely rendered bald eagle. The wings went from one shoulder to the other, big as shit. Roy used to skate with some guys and they'd all gotten DEK8D tats. But Roy was the youngest and grommiest so his was the gnarliest. DEK8D Skateboards. Death Said Crew. You will know us by our trail of skull stencils, beer cans, weed smoke. A couple of skate mags had done stories about them. Roy still carried the clippings. With the press, they picked up sponsors, small companies, a skate shop or two, and made a video. For a while it looked like they'd all get paid, not just free clothes and shit, but it never happened. DEK8D and Death Said had doubled in size and then foundered and fell apart. Cocaine was a factor, so were liquor and women. To Roy, it seemed to be an organic process, and in his mind, true to skateboarding. Skate scenes, maybe music scenes too, were dependent on conditions and counter pressure. They sprouted and grew, died. You did some shit and it was great and maybe even beautiful and then it was over. You were in the dirt. What was next? Wait for the dirt, that's what.

And in the middle of DEK8D falling apart, because everything was so awesome already, Roy had gotten blackout drunk and center-punched his stepdad's Beemer into a palm tree. After the hospital and the police were done with him, he'd gotten a firm get-out-of-the-nest shove from Stepdad Steve and his mom and had officially quit high school with his senior year half finished and bailed on California altogether—left town on a 2:00 a.m. Greyhound with a backpack full of clothes and his skateboard. On the road, freeway rumble, bus murmur, he'd chewed a vike and chased it down with a shoplifted beer. He'd felt good leaving home, ready for whatever. *Just don't overthink it.*

From the Portland bus station downtown he'd called up a DEK8D guy, Pablo, who had moved to the Northwest a few years back. Pablo was having a party at his house while his mom was out of town. Roy had jotted the directions on the inside of his wrist with a black Bic and skated from the bus depot over the Broadway Bridge in a misting rain. He stopped in the middle of the bridge to scope the muddy river and the murky lights of the city. He wasn't in California anymore. This was something else entirely.

Over the next few weeks, skating with Pablo and his pals, Roy had fallen hard for Portland, skater heaven, his people, his town. He'd settled right in, and with his newly minted fake ID, he got a cash nightly job as a barback, and moved into a ramp house in Southeast with Pablo's cousin, Esky. He'd bought a mattress for twelve dollars at the pawnshop on the corner and skated it home and Esky had helped him haul it upstairs to his room. He could see Mount Tabor from his cracked single-pane window. The six-foot ramp in the backyard was sheltered by a metal roof so they could skate even when it was raining.

Bastille Day—he didn't know shit about that, something about storming a prison—and it was a party with a few bands and everybody was skating and swilling and later, when he met Karen Oronski, he knew that he was at the right place at the right time doing the right thing. He didn't feel lucky. He felt the lead-heavy hands of fate guiding him forward.

When he looked back, the van was gone, swallowed by storm and topography. Carl, same as Roy, had rolled off the line in 1980. He was an ex–California Parks Department vehicle. Roy and Karen had altered the stencil on the side to say Carl by scraping off the twenty extra letters and the legs from the K. It still had the orange gumdrop light on the roof and the ghosts of door badges, fleet numbers on the back. You cross the country in the van you can afford, not the van you would prefer.

"We're fine, you know," Karen said. "Now it's memorable, it might even be a little romantic."

Roy couldn't help but smile. "I didn't break the van," he said. "The van broke."

"I wasn't saying that you broke the van." She touched Roy's arm and he thought she might hold his hand and was glad when she did. "Babe," she said, "these things happen. They seem to happen to us all the time, but they happen to other people too."

"You paid out the ass for the brakes. And the fuckin' snow tires? We should've waited for summer."

"It's not the brakes or the tires that let us down," Karen said. "We weren't waiting. We're done waiting, remember?"

"We should've stuck to the main road, is what we should've done."

"It doesn't matter now." She smiled at him. "We've talked about this. We've always been waiting for the next show to go to or the next party or meal to eat or the next trip to take, but now we're really doing something. Even with Carl calling it quits, I feel like we're actually starting now."

"Starting what?"

"Our lives."

His stomach tightened at her dopey optimism. "What're you talking about? We weren't waiting. That's how people live. That's how everybody lives. If they're lucky. If they aren't, if they're truly fucked, they live in the moment. Child soldiers and refugees, they live in the moment. Them and people with cancer. Sick people. Victims. I'm not a victim. Not even as fucked as we are right now, I'm not."

"Be that as it may," she said, trying to calm him. "All I'm saying is now we have a purpose."

He moaned at the pain she was causing him.

"Don't act like it hurts you to hear me talk," she said.

"The purpose is that there is no purpose," Roy said. "The road is empty and the road is long." He held out his hand and presented the road in front of them.

She was silent for a dozen steps or more. "I feel old," she said finally. "You make me feel old."

Roy flicked his cigarette away with the wind. Karen knocked the cherry off of hers and put it in her pocket because she didn't litter. Her non-littering made him angry. She leaned into Roy's shoulder and fished his hand out of his warm pocket and held on to it.

"Carl isn't your fault," she said eventually. "This is fine. I'm glad we're here and we're together. This is our moment."

"Stop the cheese, please."

"I think you're afraid of me when I speak honestly."

"I'm afraid of drowning in a flood of purpose-driven new-age bullshit, not honesty."

She took a deep breath and shook her head, showing her disappointment as surely as if she'd said it out loud. "Listen to me, days like this are what give us form."

Make it stop, he thought. Her earnestness stared back at him as pathetic as a handmade birthday card. He couldn't handle Metaphysical Karen right now. To change the subject he said: "I don't know what else I could've done, you know, about Carl." Thinking: *wires, plugs, cap and rotor—the alternator that's as old as I am.* The alternator, that's what got them; there was his final carlike word. *Alternator.* He wasn't a complete whamby. He spoke man-talk.

"I'm glad we're together," Karen said. "I'm always glad we're together. Even when you're being an ass."

He took his arm back and shoved his frozen hand into his pocket. He could feel a fight or a moment of kindness coming on. The next few seconds would determine how it went, the clock was running.

"Know-how," Karen said, frankly. "We have no know-how."

"We're American made," Roy replied. "Red, white, and frozen blue."

She hip checked him and he veered off and almost went into the snowbank. "Look at you," she said, with a pitiful head shake. "Out here in the elements in your pretty pink hat and no gloves, your little skate shoes. All you need are some sweatpants that say JUICY on the ass."

"Watch yourself," he said, half-joking. "Cuba's under nuclear threat."

"No, I don't think so," she said. "More like, castration unnecessary, nominal testosterone."

"Celtics upset Nuggets today?"

"Adding a sports reference to insult?" she said.

"That's life on the gridiron."

"Or the back nine," she said, shaking her head. "OK, I counter with: Corporations understand national trade." A presidential pronouncement, complete with wooden hand gestures. Then she shoved him in the chest hard and ran. He chased her and when he caught her, he lifted her off of her feet and acted like he was going to throw her in the snowbank but he gave her a kiss instead. Right then, he made a pledge to himself—a new way of living—but he could feel it crumbling before he even put her down.

[7]

M > 35
CA 96118

THEY STAND IN THEIR UNDERWEAR AND WATCH THE LIGHTS from their bedroom window. In tactical terms, maybe a flying wedge or vee, or was that only for aircrafts? He's been trying to read up on the things they've been seeing, modern warfare and weaponry, paramilitary action. Mostly it was dudes with pre-ban ARs in trucks, or riding in side-by-side ATVs, dudes on foot with backpacks, running dudes. Running and gunning dudes. Still weird. Still abnormal. Almost a joke but they're serious.

He turns to her and her swollen belly looks hard and shiny as a melon. He puts his hand on it and she places her hand on his.

"*Red Dawn* but with peckerwoods," she says, lifts his hand and kisses it. She pulls on her pants and a sweatshirt. "Who am I kidding? *Red Dawn* was with peckerwoods. The Swaze."

"They'll keep going," he says. "They'll respect the property line at least."

"We don't know that," she says.

"No lights," he says. "Stay goth."

"I know. Total fucking darkness."

They've stopped going to town because of the roadblocks and the reporters, never mind the protesters. Porch lights were so last year, don't draw attention. Their nearest remaining neighbor has turned into a Jeffersonian militia honcho and these gun-happy orchestrations—night moves, she calls them—always make a stop at his place. But they've developed a plan for this and they're sticking to it.

He gets dressed and picks up the child from her bed and wraps her in her blanket. If she wakes, he'll say *burrito* because she likes to be wrapped up after her bath. It's their thing, swaddled, bundled in his arms, as he wipes the steam from the mirror. *Who is it?* Burrito. *Who's my burrito?* I am.

When he steps through the back door the woman is there waiting and she takes the child and the man picks up his backpack and slings his new rifle over his shoulder. He hefts the other pack for the woman and she slips under it. She passes the sleeping child back to him. They're already sweating. They lock the house.

No lights and no moon, but they know the way. Beyond the barn the land rolls into an old drainage. When the highway was built they diverted the drainage into a culvert to keep the water in the ditch beside the road. When there was water. Now it's a dry wash, an arroyo. One day when the man and the child were walking the gravel path of it they found a hole in the bank like a dog had dug there but exploring it further found a stone house, a root cellar, from the days of the settlers.

The child sleeps on the small bed the man built for her, while he and the woman huddle in the dark on pallets surrounded by winter squash and burlap sacks of potatoes, crates of apples, to wait for morning. He keeps his rifle on his lap and watches the door. He imagines shooting someone. The woman rests her head on his shoulder. He hopes she isn't thinking of killing but she probably is. When the shooting starts outside, he pulls the blanket up around the child's chin.

"They're just target shooting," he says. "This is all for show, training."

"How long do you think they'll keep that up?"

"Not long."

"I mean, how long will they just be shooting targets?"

"I don't know."

"I'm trying not to be scared."

"It'll be OK. I'll go and see what's happening in a little while."

"Can you feel that?" she says, guiding his hand to her stomach.

The baby moves like a knuckle beneath his palm, a sharp bump, maybe a heel or an elbow. They're quietly astonished, laughing to each other, and even though the shooting continues outside, it no longer registers, or not as much.

[8]

M<55
CA 94203

THE VET IS ON HER PORCH WITH HER BARE FEET RESTING ON A blue plastic beer cooler. She's wearing loose-fitting linen pants and a black sleeveless sweatshirt. She has the hood pulled forward so that it shades her face. Her arms are tan and sinewy as a marathoner's. As he approaches, she lifts her pants beyond her knees and picks up the bottle of lotion from the ground beside her. The scars on her legs look like something left by burrowing rodents. She squirts the greenish lotion onto her legs and rubs it in.

The man helps the dog out of the trailer and onto the porch.

"You're cleaner," the vet says, sliding her hood from her head. "Not clean but cleaner. Less dirty."

"Went swimming."

She wipes her hands on her pants and puts her feet on the splintery porch boards and slides her pants down. "Anybody bother you?"

"No. Saw some of those kelpers though. Other side of the river."

"You kept the dog out of the water?"

"He stayed in the trailer."

She picks up the bottle of lotion, offers it. "This stuff is amazing. Does wonders for aches and pains. Black market special. It may or may not contain opioids. Want some?"

"I already ate all of your ice cream and drank your whiskey."

"Suit yourself." She stands up and touches his arm. "I left something for you inside. And I don't want you to argue about it. I wouldn't offer if I didn't want to."

"I'm not taking your truck."

"I'm not offering it."

He opens the sagging screen door and enters the cool dark inside. A stack of bills thick as a paperback novel on the counter. He returns to the porch.

"I can't take that," he says.

"Go buy a car. Drive to your girls. I don't need that money. I'm strictly barter now. I have everything I need. I have friends that look out for me."

"I could pay you back."

"I'm not talking about it anymore." She slides a hair tie from her wrist and pulls her hair into a ponytail. "Are you staying for dinner?"

"If you want me to."

She walks by him shaking her head.

Three days later he maneuvers his bike and trailer through the unmanned blockade and heads south, enters the thick clouds of dust stirred up by the traffic on Folsom Boulevard, sidles into the stream of dust-mask walkers and cyclists at the margin of the stalled traffic. Many of the cars are wrapped in what looks to be landscaping cloth with holes cut out for the windshield. Taking the hint, choking on the dust, the man stops and ties a ripped T-shirt around his face and makes sure the fasteners are done up on the dog's trailer and he's sealed in tight. He shouldn't have brought the dog, but the dog wanted to come. So now he's doing what the dog wants.

He meanders through a burned-out business park and down a small dirt hill into the expansive, former-Walmart parking lot, now an open-air market, an ocean of green and blue tarps, tents, campers, junk cars, and pallet wood shanties, not joyless but desperate still. He is instantly a part of something here, as a wildebeest crossing a flooding river with the herd is part of something and also something else.

It is called the Buzzard, pronounced, for some unknown reason, in the French manner, same as *bizarre*. Before the floods it was the last surviving Walmart in Sacramento. They used to shop here. Not that long ago. After it closed, someone spray-painted a massive purple-headed turkey vulture on the western wall and it was renamed, retooled, reclaimed. The vet said that this was where business was done now, where he might find a legal, titled vehicle for sale.

Through the spud and beet vendors, solar and cycle power charging stations, and HAM operators that charge by the minute, he keeps moving. He stops and observes a rotisserie rack of what looks to be blackened meat thrumming with blue flies inside a gutted Airstream but the placard says it's only kelp. Nobody has tried to sell him anything, which is strange. Out of everyone, he's the only one in a suit.

A camo tent with a sign that reads: LUGGAGES, LINGERIES,

AND LEATHER. Smiley face. The proprietor is a teenager with an afro, naked to the waist with camo joggers and logging boots, tattoos of automatic pistols on his dusty chest. He sits leisurely among a jumbled stack of haggard roller bags.

"Where can I get a car?" the man inquires.

"Inside." The boy points at the cage doors at the front of the former superstore.

When he looks back the boy is standing in the lane watching him.

One of the three guards at the door comes out of his hockey-glass-and-hog-wire cage and circles the man's rig and gives him a hateful up and down.

"Doesn't look like you got much to offer, brother," the guard says. "But if I let you in, business is gonna be done. Hear me? You might not like what's on the bill if you don't come up with— let's call it currency—of some sort."

"Tell him to fuck off, Jeremy," one of the other guards calls from his cage. "Give it to the Lord."

The man reaches in his pocket and fans a few large bills.

"He's showing three or four hun, looks like he has more," Jeremy says.

"Well, fuckin' let 'im in then, but pat him down. And no bike and no trailer. He probably has a bomb."

Jeremy frisks him, feels his pockets, says he's OK, then opens the trailer flap and is startled by the dog.

"I'm not leaving my dog out here," the man says.

"You heard him," Jeremy says. "Just you." To his associates, "He has a dog. All fucked up. Lampshade." He holds his hands up to illustrate.

The man grabs his handlebars and turns to leave.

"Let him in," the one doing the talking in the guardhouse yells.

"Want me to search the trailer and the bike then?" Jeremy says.

"Don't bother." The talker peeks his head out so he doesn't have to yell—high and tight with product, mirrored shades, handlebar mustache. "Never in the history of suicide bombers has anyone been willing to blow up their dog too."

Jeremy opens the gate and motions him inside. "You aren't gonna blow us up, are you?" he says.

The man doesn't bother to answer.

The store is dark and cavernous and it takes a moment for his eyes to adjust and see that the aisles have been removed and the whole structure is being used as a parking garage, mostly for off-road and military-style vehicles. They walk to where the women's section used to be, and another guard calls him over and leads him down a wide hallway. The bike trailer squeaks noisily in the quiet. The heavily armed guard has a long beard and a ponytail and stands not much over five feet tall. They don't speak. Lights come on as they walk and turn off again as they pass.

At the end of the hallway is a double door painted red with three golden stars and an arrow set askance between them. The man looks over his shoulder at the dark hallway and considers turning back. If he'd known, but he had. Who else would it be? The almost-dwarf pounds on the door and a bell sounds and the lock retracts. The doors open and the man's escort holds them so he can get his bike and trailer inside but doesn't follow.

The room is shabby, back of house, but well lit and arranged like an office with a receptionist sitting at a fake wood desk, a set of closed steel doors behind her. Two armed guards dressed in black fatigues stand in the corners. One of them comes forward and takes the man's picture with his phone, then returns to his station. The receptionist is young and attractive, blond, wearing a yellow sundress that shows pale cleavage. She stands and smiles, hands on her desk, breasts shoved together. "You didn't come empty handed, did you?" She nods at his rig.

"I couldn't leave it outside."

"Of course. You can sit down." She points to a folding chair. "Would you like some water?"

"Yes, I would. Thanks."

She comes around the desk with a dirty plastic bottle and a well-used paper cup. She's wearing jeans under her dress and desert-brown army boots.

He holds the cup while she pours. Her hair is clean and shiny but her thick makeup makes her face look dead under wax. He drains the cup three times.

"Now, how about you show me what you showed them at the gate?"

He kicks out his leg so he can reach the bills in his pocket and shows them to her.

The woman takes them to her desk. She lifts a small metal case from a lower drawer and opens it and lays a bill inside. The lid snaps closed and she types in something on the keypad. Ten seconds later she opens the lid and smiles, holds up a bill. "This is counterfeit."

The man stands and takes the money and weighs it in his hand, holds it up to the light, finds the hologram and the watermark. "I don't believe you."

"It doesn't matter what you believe."

"I need a vehicle," the man says. "Just something that drives, has to have paperwork."

She lowers her head and gives him a look that he assumes she means to read as forlorn but it arrives deranged. "I wish I could help but you aren't giving me much to work with."

"I'm giving you cash to work with," he says. "And you're telling me it's counterfeit. I can't prove you wrong."

"I wouldn't lie," she says seriously.

"I don't know what you would do." The man motions to his bike. "Come look at this." The woman follows him and takes a step back when she sees the dog. The guards perk up and move in.

"What happened to him?" She squats down, lowers a knee, and gives the dog a scratch at the base of the lampshade.

"He's faking," the man says. Then he digs the rest of the cash from the pannier and holds it out for the woman. "Some of this must be real, right?"

She projects exasperation and takes the money and holds it up for her associates, gives it a shake.

The guards are close enough to touch him now. The woman gives the dog a last pat and stands up. "Take him to the lot." She returns to her desk, opens a drawer, and drops the bills inside. "It won't be pretty," she says to the man.

"I need paperwork too," the man says. "That's ten grand right there."

"Take it or leave it."

"You're trespassing at this point," one of the guards says. "You either come with me now or we're gonna have trouble."

"Counterfeiting can get you sent to the Dakotas," the woman says.

"I told you it's not fake and if it is I sure as hell didn't know it was."

Her manner changes again. She lowers her head and touches her sidearm. "We have options," she says. "You don't."

"At least give me a bill of sale. Something." He looks at his trailer. "I don't have anything else."

"What about the dog?"

"You aren't taking my dog."

"We're done then." She nods to the guard that hasn't been talking and he puts a hand on the man's shoulder. The man knows that this, if he chooses, could be where it ends.

The stone-age Prius is crumpled quarter panel, primer, and Bondo piebald with mismatched wheels, riding cockeyed on two donuts, and myopic with a spiderwebbed windshield. The batteries and charging unit have been removed so it's petrol only. It won't start at first and, if the gauge is to be believed, the tank is empty. The backseats are gone and the passenger seat has suffered fire damage and even after he puts down a blanket, the dog is hesitant to lie down. Even without seats, the man has difficulty cramming the bike and trailer into the back. The guard steps in to help him and when the hatchback finally closes, they are both fairly amazed. Next-level piece of shit.

Warning lights blink on the dash as the car sputters toward the exit. The windows won't roll down. The smell of burnt plastic is overwhelming. He should've kept the money. He should've done something else. He should've never come here. But he always wanted a Prius. The car dies and barely restarts before the battery is drained.

Outside, the man is stopped, idling at the guard gate. He waits for the puncture strip to be dragged out of the road and surveys the Buzzard. The kid with the afro is lost in the crowd. Jeremy the guard waves him through with a grin.

He's still waiting, revving the motor so it won't die, when he sees the two cops coming toward him, codies, pointing their pistols and yelling at him to switch the motor off. Get out. Get out.

The contents of the Prius are emptied into the parking lot. People stand and watch. The dog is returned to the trailer and the trailer is reconnected to the bike. He thinks they might let him off. He considers jumping on his bike and making a run for it. Twenty years too late for that. After exchanging a few words with the codies, Jeremy the guard gets into the driver seat of the sedan and reverses it back into the superstore.

The woman cody finishes searching the man's panniers and for some evil reason pours out the last of his water. "Do you have any ID?" she asks, as she applies a cable to his wrists.

"No," the man says.

"Are you in the system?" she says. "Don't lie either because if you are, we'll know soon enough."

"I'm not."

"Another Juan Masa," the male cody says. His accent is southern and he's tall and dark-skinned. He looks down at the man and holds his gaze, the whites of his eyes are shot through with broken blood vessels. "You got someone that we can call to pick up your dog? We can't allow it in the transport and if we call animal control, you'll never see it again."

He gives the vet's number and the cody sends a text. A moment later he holds up his phone and shows the man the vet's reply.

The male cody pushes the bike with the dog still in the trailer, while the woman leads the man by the cable tie through the Buzzard to their vehicle. People heckle them as a group but from a distance.

The man is loaded into the back of their transport and restrained with a retractable chain attached to his wrists like a dog leader. The woman cody takes his picture with her phone. The bike and trailer are leaned against the concrete base of a lamppost.

"Since you didn't lie to us—you aren't in the system," the woman says over her shoulder a minute later, "we'll wait until your dog's ride gets here, OK?"

The institutional white walls of the cargo bay and the bench are smeared with dried blood and what looks to be excrement.

An old woman wearing a sari comes to the driver's window but from the back the man can't make out what she's saying. The female cody eventually tells her to fuck off. After she's gone, the man leans forward to look for the dog and sees that he has his head hanging out of the trailer with his ridiculous lampshade.

The vet pulls into the lot in her little yellow pickup truck. The man has never seen her behind the wheel before and she looks uncomfortable. He doesn't bother trying to yell to her or signal. She wouldn't be able to see him through the smoked glass anyway. The female cody points at the bike and trailer and the vet waves and nods in the affirmative. She looks into the dark windows but she can't see him. The dog will be safe and that's enough.

They follow a four-laner south, out of the fractured city and through the suburbs. A few communities are making a stand—roadblocks and guard shacks, concertina wire—but most of it has been burned or bulldozed. Black canyons and burnt hillsides appear yellow under the dust-choked sun, black plumes of distant smoke, made more ominous and stark by the tinted glass.

"The Buzzard wasn't the place for you," the male cody says over his shoulder.

"I didn't know who I was dealing with," the man says. "Until it was too late."

"We've seen that fucking Prius sold a dozen times," the woman says.

"At least."

"They called you?" the man says.

"Last week's criminals are this week's paychecks." The driver opens a can of snoose and loads in a dip, offers it to his partner.

She pushes it away with a smile. "Your gut bacteria hate you," she says.

"They best get in line."

Dusty ag lands. There are no more houses, not standing at least. The odd mailbox tilts toward the road. What trees remain upright are stripped bare, thumbnail-raked stalks of rye grass. Large beige structures appear on the horizon as well as a grid of chain-link fence twenty feet high. It has the look of an industrial hog farm.

They turn off the highway and pass through an open gate and follow a potholed stretch of pavement into the parking lot and come to a stop. The codies open the doors and let him out. They stand in the parking lot and face the prison gates. The tops of the guard towers are visible above the roofline.

The woman cody cuts his flex cuffs with special pliers from her utility belt. "If you decide to walk out the way we came in," she says. "We probably won't say anything."

He shakes the cuffs from his wrists onto the ground.

"We're contracted to get you here," the cody says. "They're contracted to process you and keep you locked up. But right now, you're not under anybody's contract. Call it international waters or whatever. Call it the DMZ, or I'm not filling out the forms, or what's the fucking point. Take your pick."

The driver opens the door and stands up and speaks loudly over the roof of the transport. "Walk back to the road." He points. "Then you're gonna head east till you hit the tracks, turn left. Catch out when the train comes. Local slow roller so it ain't hard."

"All right."

"Fucking Buzzard, right?" the driver says.

"We don't want to see you again," the other cody says. "You get picked up for any reason at all and it's our asses."

The man nods and starts walking.

[9]

M > 35
CA 96118

HE TAKES THE CHILD DEER HUNTING EVEN THOUGH SHE ISN'T old enough for a weapon and he has to carry food and water for her and warm clothes. No good reason to drag her along. She'll be traumatized. But he and the child's mother have been arguing about everything and he had to get out of the house. Take her with you. Yeah yeah yeah. And build a shed roof on the side of the goat shed while you're at it since you stole half of my barn space. Chores, everything is a chore. If you want to eat, it requires twenty-seven different tasks. Never mind going out. As if there're any restaurants within fifty miles. As if any of that food isn't redneck trash or GMO poison, sugar and pesticides. As if he cares. As in he'd better or he can hit the road because she doesn't let that shit into her house, never mind into her child's belly. Never mind turning on a light switch without checking the state of the batteries first. The stupid future.

Poaching would be more accurate. The land isn't his and there's no longer a season on mule deer, or enforcement if there were. If he doesn't shoot it, some militia asshole will. He isn't worried about the militia assholes today though because they're celebrating their little Freedom Day in town.

"I'm tired," the child says, bundled up, robot stiff.

"Domo arigato, Mr. Roboto."

"What did you say?" She's going to bust his balls all day, this mean little girl, as if her mother were here in spirit.

Deep breath, no going back. "We haven't even walked anywhere yet. Look, there's the truck. We can still see it."

"I want to go home."

"Not until we walk up there." He points to the ridgeline. The ground is dusty and he hasn't seen any sign, tracks or browse. "If I were a deer," he says, "where would I go?"

"Home."

"OK. But where is the deer's home?"

"In town."

"No."

"We used to see them in town all the time."

"Because people feed them."

"Why don't we feed them?"

"Because feeding deer is low rent."

She knew what he meant by low rent. He'd explained it already. "But we feed the goats."

"Goats aren't deer. Look, we're almost there."

"Papa," she says. And he's more shocked that she's called him Papa than by the deer that's stepped from behind the ridge, and he misses his chance.

He scoops up the little girl and holds her under his arm like a bag of chicken feed and hustles up the hill to the ridge and sets her down. The buck he saw has disappeared into a thicket but there are two smaller ones and a doe working their way across the hillside below.

With his lungs burning, no breath, he sends his left hand through the sling and lies down on his belly, raises up on his elbows. The leather of the sling cuts into his arm above his triceps but he's locked and steady. He calls it one hundred forty yards. Easy shot. Then the doe spots them and they all stop browsing and look up at the ridge. He glances to his left and sees the child's shoes and she's behind him enough that she's safe. She's talking and he considers telling her to lie down and shush but the deer are looking at her and not taking notice of him at all. He isn't listening to what the child is saying. The deer don't know what to think of her, but she isn't a threat.

"Just keep talking," he says to her. "They like you."

He breathes in, lets it out halfway, and touches the trigger. The rifle jumps and kicks up dust and the child screams. He continues to ignore the child. He got a hit. He could hear it and he saw the buck jerk forward a little. Didn't he? He has doubts. Why is it still standing? He works the bolt and prepares for another shot. The smaller of the two bucks bounds off with the doe right behind him. The other one watches them go and staggers a few steps and drops.

The man turns to the child with a look of triumph and is met with tears. The day only gets longer.

"Don't cut him," she pleads. "Don't cut him open."

"Too late for that," he says. People always saying how things look wrong in death, leg twisted, neck bent; but not this deer, this deer, to him, looks just right. Lay down and died is all. Never mind the bullet hole.

He offers the child the CamelBak but she won't drink. He offers her dried apples but she won't eat. He's traumatized her. He can't figure why he thought this would work. She eats little fuzzy rabbits is why. She eats pigs that follow her like puppies everywhere she goes, right up to the moment when the mobile butcher guy, Brent, levels a snub-nosed .38 at their head. She eats chickens that have names. But the deer, for some unforeseen reason, is different.

"If you're this pissed," he says to her, "imagine what your mom is going to say." This cheers her up enough to at least move down the hill.

She begins crying again when she touches the deer's soft fur, but it isn't like before. She's hamming it up now, having painted herself into an emotional corner. His heart is still clubbing in his chest and he's fine ignoring her when she's like this. It feels like the right thing to do. The deer's tongue is out and an open eye surveys the haze, elegant snout with blood at the nostrils. They look at it, look at each other.

"Four point," he says.

"There's eight."

"They only count one side."

"Who?"

"I don't know. Deer hunters."

"Why?"

"Maybe they have trouble with numbers."

"Like they can't count?"

"I'm joking. You can't eat antlers."

"So they don't count?"

"I don't know. Probably not. Let's say thank you."

"Thank you." She runs a finger over the large tendon on the rear leg.

"Thanks, bud." And he means it. He's probably never meant it so much. "OK, we gotta get this moving. Here we go. Ready?"

She nods yes.

The skin. He makes the V with his fingers so he doesn't slice the paunch. He stops cutting and pokes around with his finger to make sure he's not too deep. A sharp knife, tested on heavy card stock, only used for hunting, only used for this. The hair is soft and rabbit-like on the belly and falls out easily, sheds worse than a dog.

He's up to his elbow now, hacking away at the inside of the deer's neck looking for the windpipe. Didn't bring a saw for the ribs, complicates things. His last deer was small enough he cut through the sternum with his knife. The windpipe feels like a radiator hose and warm. "Just give me a goddamn break," he says. The child is at his shoulder as he slices the remaining threads of diaphragm and pulls the gut pile clear. The lungs are jelly but he only nicked one of the front shoulders so meat loss is at a minimum. He's happy. This is an improvement. Last time he took out both shoulders.

"It smells." She's squatted down beside the bloating stomach, sniffing.

"Not bad," he says.

"No, animal smelly. Kind of smelly like the basement is smelly but without smelling like a basement."

He names the organs as he separates them. The child is interested in the heart. He explains to her how the blood flows in and out of the heart. She slides her thumb over the heavy ridge of muscle to the valve, then picks it up like an apple. Dark red blood pours from the valves and streams down her wrist.

"We have this much blood in us?" she asks.

"Yes."

"The baby in Mama's belly has a heart and blood but no fur or hooves."

"I hope not."

"That would be so funny if the baby had fur and hooves."

"That would be funny. Can you drink some water now? I can tell you're thirsty. Your lips are chapped. Are you hungry?"

"Yes."

He watches the child drink from the CamelBak and they split a goat-cheese-and-tomato sandwich on sourdough that he baked. They get deer blood on the bread but neither of them cares. Turkey vultures, three of them, are riding the updrafts, clocking the gut pile.

"Can I carry the heart?"

He has four bone-in quarters, organ meat, and tongue bagged on his back, strapped to his pack frame. He stripped the meat from the ribs and he's leaving them behind with the hooves and hide. The weight is bordering on unbearable and stupid. Once he makes the ridge, it's all downhill from there. He has the hide and the head stashed under a dead ponderosa. He can come back tomorrow. Dark clouds are crowding the valley and they don't have much daylight left. The kid is looking up at him, waiting for an answer. He thought he might be able to ignore his way out of answering her.

"You'll have to carry the liver and the kidneys, the tongue."

"OK."

He wants to dissuade her so he won't have to take off his pack. "It's going to be heavy."

"Not too heavy. I can carry it."

Like a power lifter he lowers himself down, then drops to his side, onto the pack, and wriggles out of shoulder straps. He unhitches the small canvas bag with the organs from the frame and ties it like a messenger bag over the child's shoulder. After he inserts himself once again into the shoulder harnesses and buckles the belt, he rolls to his hands and knees and like the slowest sprinter in the world coming out of the blocks gets back to his feet. The child goes first and he follows. Calculating their relative weight, length of stride, and muscle mass, he figures they're on more or less equal ground.

But at the top he's breathing hard and his legs are shaking, while the kid is doing her little hop-and-skip thing on the flat dirt of the ridge. He forgot to factor in youth. He considers leaving a quarter here and coming back. *If I'm going to leave one, I might as well leave two and make it easier. I can come back, grab the quarters, hide, and head. There's a plan.* He's about to shrug off his pack frame and split the loads when the little girl starts down the way they'd come, following their tracks through the dust and rocks toward the truck. He has no choice but to follow her. If he stops her, he might have a hard time getting her going again. She's inertia-driven and as he makes his way down with his pack, he is too. The blood is leaking onto her back from the organ bag and staining her coat and he's going to get it for that. Or maybe not. Maybe he did right today. The snow starts before they get to the truck and doesn't stop.

[10]

R < 25
CA 96118

ROY PRESSED HIS COLD HAND AGAINST HIS COLDER NOSE. MINUS the wind, walking wouldn't be bad. He almost whined to Karen but decided against it. Then a big gust hit, quartering away off his shoulder, and almost knocked him down. He considered letting it, giving the fuck up. Perhaps sensing this, Karen put her arm around his waist and they walked in stride.

He heard a sound like fabric tearing behind him. They turned together and watched as an apparition—twinned headlights framed in a boxy grill—appeared in the notch on the horizon. They moved to the side of the road and Roy pushed Karen out in front so whoever was driving would see that they were at least half-fem and therefore half-threatening, with his pink hat, seven-sixteenths threatening.

It was a white, bobtailed cargo truck and its tires broke loose when the driver braked too hard and it went sliding cockeyed, recklessly, right by them and came to stop blocking both lanes. They ran and then walked a little to catch it. The passenger door swung open as they came around. The driver was wearing Buddy Hollys and a Kings stocking hat and he waved them inside. "C'mon up," he said, and took off his right glove and offered his hand.

Karen stopped mid-step as if she were afraid. "I know you," she said. "From high school." She took his hand and smiled. "Karen Oronski."

"Shit. Howdy. Hi. How you been?" He pulled her up onto the seat.

"It's Aaron, right?"

"Yeah, Aaron Simmonds."

"Aaron Simmonds, this is my boyfriend, Roy Bingham."

The two men shook hands. Roy could tell that Karen didn't like being in the middle, being reached over. She leaned all the way back against the seat and tucked in her chin to be out of the way. Well, isn't this something, Roy thought, looking at her. Isn't this just peachy. Roy crammed their packs awkwardly at his feet.

"You wanna put those in the back?" Aaron asked.

"No," Roy said, "they're fine."

"I passed a van." He had a jagged scar that went from his right nostril, over his lips, to his chin. "Yours?"

"Yep," Roy said.

"What's wrong with it?" Aaron asked.

"No power," Roy said. "All the lights just quit. Alternator, maybe."

Aaron cleared his throat and put the truck in gear and, with a little jockeying to get straightened out, drove on. "I got tools.

You wanna go back and see if we can get it running? I can turn around up here a little ways."

"I think we'll just have it towed," Karen said. "Our insurance should cover it. We don't have service out here or we'd have called."

Aaron took off his glasses and wiped them clean with a blue chamois he snagged from the dashboard. "You aren't here for the funeral, are you?"

"No," Karen said. "Who died?"

"Simian Wattesly."

"Oh no," Karen said. "I was in the chess club with him. It was Simon, right? Everybody just called him Simian?"

"Yeah, he had those ears, milk jug ears, monkey ears."

"What happened?" Karen said. "Didn't he get elected mayor? My mom said something about that before—"

"Yeah," Aaron said, pausing for too long. "Then he fell headfirst into a pump station, landed upside down. There's water in the bottom, not much, but enough to drown in."

"Why was he in a pump station?" Karen said. "I don't even know what that is."

"It's like a big culvert on end that goes down into the ground," Aaron said. "It has a ladder in it and at the bottom there's a big pump and pipes going either way. The pump moves water from the treatment facility to people's houses." He glanced at Karen. "I'm guessing here that that's how it works. I've never been in one myself. It's kind of an educated, uneducated guess, I guess."

"OK," Karen said, seeming pleased with the explanation. Roy never explained anything to her anymore. Explanations were for young love, not for the veterans. *If you don't know everything I know by now, he thought, you never will.*

Aaron continued. "Simian was still working for the water company while he was mayor, drawing two paychecks, but I don't think the mayor really makes any money. It's a status thing mostly, as far as that goes. Some people pissed and moaned about a conflict of interest after the election, but who gives a fuck, right?" Aaron let go of the wheel for a moment, held his hands up.

Karen and Roy both intimated with their body language that they didn't give a fuck.

"He was all right," Karen said. "Kind of a Guy Smiley, but he was all right. I made him my bitch at chess."

Aaron smiled a closed-lip smile. "So you still have people here?"

"Not really," Karen said.

Roy almost said, yeah she does, her mom's place is still here and some kind of twice-removed half a stepdad named Mace is probably lurking in it, but he didn't want to get into the whos and whys and hows of Mace if by some chance Aaron didn't know who he was.

"Hey, I was sorry to hear about your mom," Aaron said. "It was in the paper."

"Thanks. We came back for the funeral but left right after."

"What about now? Another visit?"

"Pretty much," Roy said. "Road trip, journey."

"We might move here," Karen said, smiled at Roy. "See what's up. I'm tired of apartments and cities and traffic and yuppies. I want room to spread out for once. I want a garden. I want to grow some shit, know what I mean?"

"I do," Aaron said. "Feels good to get your hands in the dirt. My zucchini went crazy last summer. I couldn't give 'em away.

We made bread and pancakes and marinara but after a while you just get sick of it. I'd carve notes in them, like in the skin, and leave them in the back of people's pickups in town to mess with them."

Already bored, but thawing out, Roy imagined himself as a Cartesian deep-sea diver toy he'd seen at the amigo flea market as a kid. Push here it goes that way, push there the other. He wondered, *Is that what delivered me into this truck? Ease v. freeze?*

"What's in the back?" Karen asked Aaron. "Zucchini?"

"No, it's empty. I dropped off a bike for some guy in Redding earlier. I'm taking the scenic route home."

Karen's face was flushed and there were droplets of water in her hair where it had frozen while they were walking. She smiled at Roy again and he remembered he was wearing her pink hat and took it off and dropped it in her lap.

"A bike, huh?" Karen asked. "Are you like one of those chopper dudes on TV? Lost City Choppers or whatever?" She said choppers with an emphasis on the last syllable, chop-hers, and it made Roy smile.

"Mechanic slash builder, not a chopper guy, more café and canyon racer, street fighter. Not that I have anything against that chopper shit, some of it's cool. I like the ratty shit that folks do, you know, old *Easy Rider* magazine, David Mann shit, springers, suicides, big beard and a death wish, Frisco shit—that shit's pretty killer. Nobody can say it isn't, but I fuckin' hate the theme bikes folks are building, powder coat everything or worse, chrome everything. Flashy paint. Total clown shit, you know. I don't dig it." He removed his stocking hat and mussed his thinning hair, tussled his forelock. "Functionality is where it's at, low and fast, credible. Anyway, yeah, I have a shop in back of my house, right next to the garden, under a few feet of snow at the moment." He smiled at Karen. "April, my wife, she helps me with billing and taxes and stuff. We keep it simple, old Jap bikes mostly. I've sweated through every version of Honda's inline four motor, through the '70s and '80s at least, but I'm partial to twins, so I work on Triumphs and Beemers, too, but we don't see them as often."

The road ahead was beginning to drift over and Roy could feel a tap in the floorboards when Aaron punched through a big one.

Aaron turned to face Karen. "I was in the sheriff's department for a while, before this. I mean, I've always been messing with bikes, but before I opened the shop, I was a cop."

Karen and Roy both nodded, OK.

"You heard what happened? Maybe somebody told you when you came back before?"

"No, I haven't heard," Karen said. "Why'd you quit?"

Fired, Roy thought, *you probably got fired. Big fucking meat pie got canned. Sexual harasser. Blackmailer. Perp assaulter.*

"I didn't quit, not really," he said. "I crashed my squad car." He touched the scars on his face. "My partner got killed and a few other people were hurt. Hurt bad."

"I'm so sorry," Karen said.

"They said I might be able to transfer to another department, Truckee was an option. But I live here, you know? This is home."

"Well, I'm glad you stuck around or we'd still be walking," Karen said.

"I guess so," Aaron said, smiling. "Lucky you. Lucky me."

"I remember your letterman's jacket jingling when you walked down the hall," Karen said. "Like all your medals from wrestling and track or whatever that you pinned to it, clanking and rattling while you walked. That's weird you did that. It's a weird thing to do."

"It is, right?" Aaron patted his jacket as if the medals might still be there. "Some of my friends ran track but not me. I stuck to twisting arms and butting heads, wrestling and football."

"Your friends were assholes," Karen said. The words hung there and Roy sat forward in his seat and turned to see how Aaron was taking it.

"High school kids are all assholes," Aaron said.

"Yeah, but they were special," Karen said.

"Maybe," Aaron said. "Seems like they're all Realtors now. What kind of uselessness is that?"

"I don't know," Karen said. "What's three percent of a total douchebag?"

Aaron laughed heartily and transitioned it into a big feline yawn and reached to turn the heater down and Roy could see that he had gold crowns on all of his back teeth, top and bottom, on the right side.

"You moved before you graduated, right?" Aaron said.

"Yeah, I went to Portland," she said.

"But your mom never moved away though," Aaron said. "Did you live with your dad or something?"

"No," Karen said. "I went on my own. One of my sister's friends was going to school at Reed and working as a nanny. She found me a nanny job at the house next door to the one where she worked."

"She lived in the pool house," Roy said. "They gave her a car."

"They gave me a car to use," Karen said. "Portland was like the big, big city for me, you know. Coming from here. It was a good gig." Karen leaned away from Roy enough to get a hand up and on top of his head to muss his hair. "Then Roy and his friends drained and skated their pool and I got fired."

"C'mon," Roy said. "I didn't think you'd get canned. You weren't even there."

"I was at the coast," Karen said. "Me and the kids went to the aquarium while the parents took surf lessons."

"I don't get it," Aaron said. "Why'd you get fired if you weren't there?"

"The cops caught them. The family had met Roy before. He wasn't supposed to have a key. They didn't press charges, but—the kids used to call me when the new nanny made them mad."

"Why didn't you wait until you graduated before you left?" Aaron said. "You had to be close, right?"

A nervous smile crept over her face. "I got my equivalency in Portland."

"Family stuff?" Aaron said.

"No, not really," Karen said. "I'm surprised you don't remember."

"Remember what?"

"I had a bad reputation."

Aaron grinned, then cleared his throat, not sure if Karen was joking or not. "I never heard anyone say anything about you. I woulda punched 'em in the mouth." He showed Karen his hairy, purple-knuckled fist.

"I'm not positive, and I really don't care anymore," Karen said. "But I think they might've been your friends, the track stars."

"Are you serious?" Aaron said. He eased off the accelerator and the big truck slowed.

"You never did anything to me, or said anything." Karen pointed at the road so Aaron would keep driving, then touched Roy on the knee and gave him her it's-OK look. "We don't have to talk about it. It's all another lifetime now."

They continued in silence for a minute or more until Aaron smacked the wheel and startled Roy and Karen both. "Listen," he said. "I feel shitty about this. I'm sorry. I hung out with a bunch of dickheads when I was a kid and if they fucked with you somehow I should've done something."

"Ultra dickheads," Karen said. She wasn't going teary-eyed. She was stating a fact.

"Ultra dickheads," Aaron repeated. "Ultra douchebag fucking dickheads. Realtors."

"Amen, brother," Karen said.

They rounded a corner and in a cleft in a rock face Roy saw a column of ice rising into the storm and disappearing into the low clouds. He pointed and Karen nodded. Roy had been hoping to see people climbing the frozen waterfall, blue and red coats, yellow ropes, crampons and axes, fucking Yvon Chouinard, but there was no one there.

Roy's thoughts skittered through rotten sexual scenarios with high school Karen that would've resulted in her eventual abortion.

"How about you, Roy?" Aaron said. "What's your deal?"

"My deal?"

"I'm assuming you're not a Realtor and you're a bit inky for straight work." He traced his finger around his neck to demonstrate where Roy's tattoos were visible. "When I was on the job we used to call those—the neck tattoos—please-don't-hire-mes and the ones on your hands, we called those job blockers. Over the radio we'd say, white male, has full sleeves, job blockers, and a please-don't-hire-me on the left side, white T-shirt, black pants, red shoes, whatever."

Roy laughed a little. "I have some red Chucks back in the van, maybe I'm your perp."

"Nah, you're OK if you're with her." Aaron nudged Karen. "Even if you did get her fired."

"That was a long time ago," Roy said. Aaron smiled crookedly.

"He has, or had, some skateboarding sponsors," Karen said. "He's played in some bands." Karen rubbed her hand vigorously between his shoulder blades the way he liked.

"I'm a deadbeat," Roy said.

"You're not a deadbeat," Karen said. "You've chosen to live an exciting and nonlinear life. I love you for that. One reason of many."

Roy may've blushed. He felt better and his defensiveness drained away. She knew that he never planned on her getting fired for them skating the Ekariuses' pool. He'd only done it because she had an alibi. The cops had simply appeared, no warning. It was his run and when he slammed, he was slow picking himself up, remembered thinking: *Why is it so quiet?* No heckling. No oohs, no aahs. His friends were gone. By the time he hauled himself out of the shallow end, everyone was facedown on the deck beside the hot tub. A cop took his board. Another one pushed him down. *Do any of you assholes actually live here? His girlfriend does—*

"But—don't take this personally, babe—he might be getting a little long in the tooth for either of those," Karen said. "Shit or get off the pot, right?"

"Hardly," Roy said. "I'm just getting warmed up."

"So who'd you skate for?" Aaron asked. "Like Powell Peralta or someone? Tony Hawk."

"No, not Powell," Roy said. "Tiny companies, Abel and Pearl Snap wheels, Infinity Skate Shop."

"Huh, what bands?"

"You wouldn't have heard of them either. We didn't record, really. We mostly toured. I was in a band called Whale Eye that played Reno a couple of times."

"I must've missed it," Aaron said.

"It was just noise," Roy said.

"Parading as art," Karen said.

Aaron chuckled. "Why'd you call yourselves Whale Eye?"

"Because whale eyes look creepy, kind of like giant assholes." Roy shifted in his seat and smiled at Karen. His schtick, along with the rest of him, was out of its element. "Assholes that contain all the wisdom of the world."

"Like you," Karen said. "You wish." To Aaron: "They were like those bands that drop their instruments at the end of the show and let them feed back as they walk off stage, except they were still there, humping their amplifiers and screaming at each other without microphones."

"Like Sonic Youth?" Aaron said.

"Without the songs and lyrics," Karen said. "Or artistic sensibility. It was dysfunctional."

"We had songs," Roy said. "We had that one about eating horse meat in the Arctic. You said you liked that song."

"Bubblegum," Karen said, laughing. "Radio rock."

"Whale's eyes look like assholes?" Aaron said. "Wise assholes?"

"All they did was party," Karen said. "Who knows what he got into."

Out of the mountains, the shaggy, snow-covered hayfields opened up before them. They passed another broken-down car, hood up, a Subaru. The snowplow had bermed it in. There was a green sticker on the passenger window. Roy powered on his phone and had a signal so he found the insurance card in his wallet and called the insurance company and, like she was his best friend, the insurance agent or the operator or whoever said she'd send a wrecker within the hour. Karen told him to have the van dropped off at a place called Moody's Garage and Aaron backed her, said Moody was the best in town. Easy as that. After months of believing they'd been ripped off on their insurance, paid too much for services they would never need, Roy felt slick. Billboards appeared: Water—Jobs—Liberty—Small Government, Tractor Supply, RV Park.

"I'll take you where you're going," Aaron said. "Moody's or wherever."

"Do you mind dropping us at my old house?" Karen said. "It's kind of out of the way."

"Not a problem. Just tell me where to go."

The streets were gray and black with dirty snow, quaint brick buildings, a few barnwood, stage-stop-style fronts, two, maybe three stop lights. How did it go? If you blinked, you might miss it. If you lived here, you'd be bored by now. What nonsense, these little burgs. What was the point of these places? Old people were the only ones they saw on the streets and sidewalks and some of them waved to Aaron and he waved back. If this was ever going to be his home, it didn't feel that way. On the most basic scrotum and gut levels it felt unreal like maybe behind the buildings and under the streets there were alien operators controlling the whole show.

The house was yellow with a red metal roof and a sad, cobbled-together porch over the crooked front steps. A dented white pickup was idling in the driveway, its exhaust clouded the air.

"He's here," Karen said, too quietly for Aaron. "Mace is here."

Roy nodded. "And it looks like he's leaving."

This was the house that Karen had grown up in. Her older half sister, Whip, had died here. The truck in the driveway belonged to Mace, Whip's father. When they were here last, for Karen's mother's funeral, Roy and Mace had hung out some, run errands together. They'd picked up food from the deli counter at Leonard's. Their shoes were tinted green from mowing and weed-eating the grass. They'd set out chairs and cleaned out the firepit. Karen's mom had worked for the county at the Soil Conservation District and her coworkers were mostly geriatrics, but they were geriatrics that liked a few drinks at a wake. Mace had asked him about Karen and skateboarding and what their lives were like in Portland, but with his reviled, always guilty of something, convict manner Roy felt that with each word he spoke in reply he wasn't answering questions, he was entering into a conspiracy.

Mace's eyes were cold, almost reptilian, but sometimes they'd go dark and well over with desperate compassion. Karen called it the Disney effect, others called it bipolar disorder. Regardless, Roy still wanted Mace to like him, sick or not, crazy or not, and after he and Karen got home to Portland he'd started calling people homeboy, like Mace did, even though nobody called anybody homeboy anymore. Homey, maybe. Holmes, OK. Homeboy, that was some truly retro jail shit but when Mace said it, when he talked about his homeboys, when he called Roy homeboy, it was nothing to laugh about. He'd been with the Aryan Brotherhood in prison, had the swastika tattoo on his chest to prove it. Karen said it was about survival, not any kind of Nazi shit. Prison draws uncrossable lines. Colors stick together. If you don't like it, don't get locked up.

When Karen invited Aaron in for a drink, Roy glanced at her and shook his head. She smiled back at him.

"Better watch how you park," Roy said. "Don't want to block anybody in if they need to leave."

The smile withered on Karen's face as Aaron maneuvered the big truck around Mace's idling pickup. There were orange flags on red-painted bamboo poles stabbed into the snow to mark the edge of the driveway. Aaron killed the motor and got out, shut his door behind him. It was another long moment before Karen reached across Roy to open the door. "You can do it," she said.

"Can you?" he said.

"I'll be fine," Karen said.

"Good." He stepped down from the truck but when he

turned to grab his bag it was already in the air coming toward him and it knocked him backward into the snowbank.

"First step's a bitch," Karen said, as she offered him a hand to pull him up.

"Does that make you the first step?" Roy said.

"In more ways than you know." She yanked him to his feet and dusted the snow from his pants and guided him toward the porch with her hand on his back.

[11]

M < 45
CA 96118

THE KIDS ARE ASLEEP AND EXCEPT FOR THE LIGHT OF THE CAN-
dle on the bedside table the house is dark. There'd been
a splatter of rain earlier and the wet dirt smell of it had put everyone in a good mood. She's sitting at her dresser talking on
the phone when it suddenly squeals and crackles and the call is
dropped.

"They're messing with the cell phone towers again," the
woman says, holding out her phone. "C'mon."

He sits up and scoots over to her and puts his cheek to hers
so he can hear. This is their newest entertainment.

*Mom, I know. Mom, yes. Mom, I don't believe this. I can't un-
derstand how it happened. Me neither. Your brother's calling. Should
I answer it? Go ahead. Hey. We're all here. Hey, how's it going?
Shitty. I'm just sick when I think about it. Who are these people?
I'm physically ill.*

"Put it on speaker." He takes the phone from her and does it himself. "It won't wake them up. Don't worry."

They, I told you they were doing this, Mick. I'm going to throw up. Mom, it'll be fine. I don't really understand how people live there. What'd you mean? They've lived there forever and they just got crazier and crazier and with no water in the ground and the EPA sending water downstream for fish. They were fucked. Mick, please. Sorry. But they got organized and they got people elected. Wait, hold that thought. What they actually did is they got guns and trained an army and set up roadblocks and chased families off of what they were calling their territory. It's totally racist, not to mention fascist. Totally. But they were like farmers, don't farmers like need Mexican labor? Not when they don't have water and they have lots of guns. And now what? Can we go there? Can I visit? Why? Why what? Why would you? Because it's American soil. Technically. So I can visit. I wouldn't. No shit. You always want to put your nose in the middle of the biggest turd you can find. Mick, enough. Fine, just, Christ, let them have it. It's a dried-up shit hole. Hundreds and hundreds of square miles and they just stole it. If I were a Native American, I would be so mad. If you were a Native American, you'd be way more interesting. So glad you joined in, baby brother. That's really sweet. As if I wanted to feel shittier. Oh, cool it, you two. There's no way all of that is even close to being a shit hole, Mom, or worthless in any way. Mineral rights, you know. I don't know what else there'd be without water but what if they like strike gold. In California? I think they've found all the gold by now. Idiot. Fuck you. My God, you don't age, you just get more annoying. They should send in the actual army and blow them the fuck up. Hawk much? You want to scorch the earth just a skosh more? Just bomb it a wittle bit? Fuck you, Sam. There it is. Mick bleeds too.

I think they're all ex-soldiers anyhow, or that's what it looks like on the news. They're veterans of foreign wars. Oh my God. It's like reap what you sow, right. We train these people. Who's we? You couldn't train a ball to roll downhill. I'm so sick of you. We should visit. I'm not going near that place. You're a pussy. I am a pussy. I live in Los Angeles, Sam. I eat breakfast tacos and do yoga. I don't own a gun or want to. I actually think people that use guns for hunting should have to rent them, instead of keeping them like in their houses. Like renting skis instead of owning them. Why do we have to own everything? Wow, my son the Communist. How's that legal weed, Mick? Great. It's really great. Anyway. I heard there's going to be an amazing documentary on how the Preservation was formed, like the key players. It went all the way to the White House. Mom, wake up. He signed the executive order to establish the fucking place in the White House. Who doesn't know that?

"I don't even miss TV when this happens," the woman says.

"Men are more visual."

"Because they're limited mentally." She slugs him in the thigh.

"Fucker. Stop it. We're going to lose the signal. Stop."

"It changed. Is this different people? What is this? I miss them already. They're like my friends."

"Shut up."

"Wait, they're the same. I think."

Once all the militias joined together under the Jeffersonian flag, it was like only six months later and they launched their little campaign. Can you imagine? If they were anything except white men, they would be splattered on a wall somewhere. True. But instead they occupy a dozen national parks and wildlife areas and end up camped out at the Bonneville Dam. Boom boom boom. I can't imagine. From the Canadian border all along Highway 97, south to where Highway 89 intersects I-80. And it's not like Idaho and Nevada, Montana, Utah aren't itching to get in on this. You don't know that. Like you know more than me. Whatever, bong hit, Mick. Whatever, box wine, sis. At first Mimi and I thought it was something that maybe a SWAT team would take care of, then it was in the courts. Like they made a legal claim. Mimi isn't exactly a political mastermind, Mom. She voted. OK, Mom, sorry. She voted her conscience, unlike you. Poor Mick, no votey vote. Too hungover. All right. My vote wouldn't have made a bit of difference. It's all so corrupt. Grand understatement. The Preservation is like the Illuminati running a train on the Koch brothers' corpses in the clear-cut that was the Bohemian Grove. Oh my God. I don't know what that means, honey. You've lost me. Why would you say that to your mother? It's a joke. Lighten up. We can still take our country back. This isn't an actual secession, there's isn't going to be a fifty-first state. I know, Mom, you old hippie dreamer you. It just seems like at this point, you know, why? Do you think all of the people in those towns within the 89/97 corridor want to be under militia control? Yes, Mom, I do. I think they would've left if they didn't want to be there. They say they don't want government handouts or overreach. Mom, they don't know what they want. They say—

The broadcast ends in a series of loud clicks and goes silent. "My friends," the woman says.

"That was way better than listening to the Jeffs," he says.

"Wolf Mother to Massive Cyborg, this is Wolf Mother." She has a militia voice she employs daily, mostly toward her children.

"Imminent Peril to—"

"Like they could even spell that. Next time we hit a road-block, ask those turds. Hey, blue falcon, spell *imminent*."

"Maybe that was a propaganda campaign, subliminal warfare stuff," he says. "Do you feel more agreeable or less to the Jeffersonian cause now?"

"On a scale of one to ten? I'm a soft eleven." She drops into her bro voice. "Ultimate Fight Boss to Rip Chain. This is Ultimate Fight Boss, do you copy. I'm all sexy time and ready to party-party in my massive nakedness. How many clicks to my six?"

"You're a kook."

"Rip Chain, do you copy."

"Copy."

She gives him a kiss and slides her hand inside his underwear. "Raging Boner to—"

"Enough."

"I'll be the judge of that." She stands up to undress, waits until she's naked to blow out the candle.

[12]

M < 55
CA 94203

THE ARTIFACT OF A TRAIN CLATTERS TOWARD HIM OUT OF A murky cloud of dust. The engineer isn't paying attention, doesn't notice him or doesn't care to. The man waits until he spots an open boxcar. He watches over his shoulder and walks alongside the train and when it's close he hustles for twenty feet or so before he catches a rung and pulls himself up. Someone from inside snags him by the waist and gets him safely inside. A family, man and woman, four children, aged toddler to teenager. It's the father that pulled him in. He glances toward his kids and pats his chest. He's young, Latino, designer jeans and a threadbare dress shirt, a filthy dust mask on a string around his neck.

"*Protegeré a mis hijos,*" he says.

"I'm not gonna hurt anybody," the man says. He sits down and rests his hands on his knees.

The mother and her children are overdressed for the heat.

All of them have dust masks perched on their heads but they're newer and whiter than the father's, and still have the yellow rubber bands attached. They don't have any luggage, just a two-liter of water and a reusable grocery bag with oranges in it.

"*No los toque*," the father says.

"I'm more scared of them." The man makes a face at the children that shows how scared he is. The smallest smiles at him and pulls her shoulders toward her ears, leans into her mother. The other children stare at him like he owes them money. The woman reaches in the sack and pitches him an orange.

"*Gracias*," he says.

"You're welcome," she says.

The boxcar door is left open and as the train increases its speed the clattering and the wind get louder. The family pulls on their dust masks. Earth movers in the distance are scraping the wasteland in an effort to reclaim some arable ground. The air tastes grainy and leaves an LSD tang in the man's mouth.

Three of the four children are sleeping now, leaning against each other, rocking with the motion of the train. The eldest watches as the man peels and eats his orange, finally looks away as he wipes the juice in his beard onto his sleeve. He keeps the peels in his pocket so he can smell them later.

In a sun-blasted field of weeds a man stands up like a reconstituted scarecrow from his bed of dross and stares at the train. The man can't help but think of the settlers of this central valley and what riches they stumbled into. The man has a look at his shoes, his hands, his fellow travelers, then watches the man in the field as he lays back down in his weedy nest.

A few houses appear on the horizon, hundreds of burnt foundations like circuit board. People are walking beside the tracks. The man and the father stand and watch to see if someone needs help up, but no one chooses their car.

The train slows. They're among warehouses and abandoned factories, close to the freeway. A few minutes later the train grinds to a stop. The man can see the arc of a freeway overpass between the buildings.

"*Sal del tren,*" the father says.

"Checkpoint," the woman says. She and the rest of the family climb down with the father passing the two youngest to their mother and move quickly toward a factory that at one point had manufactured brake parts. The man follows them away from the unseen checkpoint and wanders across a parking lot and is surprised to see the vet waiting for him, outside her pickup, waving.

He gets in the truck and lets the dog lick his hand and tugs on its ears. The lampshade is gone. The vet is wearing the same set of scrubs as when he first arrived. She still wears her wedding ring but she's been a widow now longer than she was married. She reaches under her seat and drops a pair of dusty running shoes in his lap.

"Found these in the back of the garage."

"Thanks," he says. The man leans into the back and rubs his head against the dog's muzzle.

"He isn't chewing on his staples so I lost the lampshade," the vet says.

"How is he?"

"You weren't gone that long."

"But you took off the lampshade."

"He's a little stiff still, but he can take a punch. He's a tough cookie."

"He's a cookie. I'll give you that."

She puts the truck in gear and drives cautiously through the sweltering city. The dust thins as they get closer to the river.

"Squatters have all of this," she says, nodding at the high-rises, broken windows, scorched brick, and cracked marble. Clotheslines have been strung between some of the buildings. "It's like twenty square blocks, all the way to the river. The codies play like they're being humanitarians letting them stay but they can't move them. Nobody can. It's too many people. Where would they go?"

They drive in silence until they arrive at the floating bridge. The man puts on his new shoes, laces them up, a dead man's shoes.

At the roadblock the vet shows her papers and they pass through without issue. She takes her place in the queue behind a battered, propane-converted, rooftop-solar minivan brimming with children, their arms and legs too lolling out the windows.

"How'd you know to pick me up?" the man asks. "Those codies text you?"

"Yeah," she says. "They must've used my number to look up my name."

The man turns to see if she's messing with him and she's not.

"Unlike you," she says, "I'm a friend of the police. Always have been." She pulls forward onto the bridge and he can feel the ground shift. The wipers thump and screech the spray away. In front of them all the arms and legs have returned to the inside of the minivan. The man hangs his old shoes out the window and tosses them into the river. The cool air from the water settles into the cab as the wind swells mount. The dog begins to whine and the man reaches back and tries to calm him but he doesn't stop until they reach the other side.

On the vet's porch, the dog leaves his side and paces and sniffs around the bicycle and trailer parked beside the garage. The staples shimmer on the shaved pale skin of his hip.

"Do you need to take those out before we leave?"

"I thought you'd stay awhile, but if you're ready to go I guess you can do it. Snip in the middle and roll them out like a fish hook. No biggie."

"OK," the man says.

"I could take you out of the city."

"You've done enough."

"I wouldn't take I-80 if I were you."

"I'm not. I'm doing like you said, going out the back way through Sierra City."

"I have some food and antibiotics for the dog," the vet says. "It's not much."

"I wish I could repay you," the man says. "STT stole your money, said it was fake."

The vet laughs a little. "Maybe it was."

"I'm sorry about all this," he says.

"A man with debts who's sorry. What a novelty." She smiles a closed-lip smile and in some part of his brain he wants to kiss her. Perhaps sensing this, she steps away from him. "I'll miss you," she says. "I'll miss the dog more but I'll miss you, too."

He doesn't want to leave her here alone with the strays. "I'll tell the girls you send love," he says.

She nods and goes back inside. When she returns, she has a plastic bag dangling from either hand. The man is sitting on the ground rubbing the tender V under the dog's jaw.

"It's just bread, some salami, a couple of tomatoes, basil," the vet says. "Kibble and pills. Not much. Follow the instructions."

She points at the bag nearest the man. "I put some balsamic and olive oil in a pill bottle in there, so make sure it doesn't spill."

"Thanks." The man takes his time getting to his feet, like a dog would do, stretching on the way, and gives her a hug and a peck on the cheek. He can smell woodsmoke in her hair, along with a hint of lilac. Her work shirt smells of flea dip.

"Be safe out there," she says, patting his chest and pushing him away. "Take care of that dog. He's smarter than you, you can trust that. OK?"

"OK."

She holds the bike upright while he stows the food in a pannier. "I still remember the first time I met you."

"Be better to forget. Wasn't much to like back then. Even less than now." He buckles the pannier and meets her gaze.

"Things change." She smiles. "Some things, believe it or not, change for the better."

He mounts up and pushes off and thinks he hears her say something but when he turns she's watching him from the porch with her hand over her mouth.

[13]

R < 25
CA 96118

THE DOOR WAS UNLOCKED. KAREN WENT IN FIRST, ROY AND Aaron behind her. They dropped their bags in the mudroom and made their way through the cardboard box clutter into the kitchen. There was a rifle with a scope on the table along with a brass cleaning rod and a small orange bottle that said Hoppe's on it.

"Hello," Karen said. "Mace, we're here."

Roy could hear him thumping up the basement steps and the door flew open and pressed Aaron against the wall. Mace had shaved his head and his mustache was gone and he looked mutated without it. He was dressed in black jeans and a dingy white undershirt, no shoes. Mace picked Karen up and swung her around.

"What's this?" Mace said, when he spotted Aaron. He set Karen down and stepped back. "Officer Simmonds, ex-Officer Simmonds. What're you doing here?"

"He gave us a ride," Karen said. "Saved our bacon." She winked at Aaron.

"Hey, Mace," Aaron said. They shook hands. "Going for deer?"

"You bet." Mace picked up the rifle and slung it on his shoulder and gathered the rest of the gear from the table into a small duffel bag. "Let me get this out of the way so you can sit down." They watched him disappear back into the basement.

Karen opened the fridge but there was only protein drinks and gas station chicken, a few bottles of hot sauce.

"No beer," she said. "Sorry, Aaron."

"It's fine. No worries."

When Mace came back he turned to Roy. "Better come in for a hug, homeboy. My favorite little inkblot. How you been?"

Roy let Mace hug him and smiled at Karen. "Our van died," Roy said to Mace. "Lucky that Aaron came along or we'd still be hoofing it. Since you don't have a phone."

Mace held Roy at arm's reach and gave him a scary look. "That sure was nice of ex-Officer Simmonds." To Karen: "I don't have anything to drink, or eat for that matter. I was about to head out. You guys never said when exactly you'd be showing up." He glanced out the window. "Jesus, my truck's still running. I forgot. I'm probably about out of gas by now." He charged through the mudroom like he'd been shoved and banged outside in his bare feet and Roy watched from the window as he reached in and turned off his truck. When he came back they all looked at his feet.

"I've been trying to go barefoot more," he said to Karen. "Grounding, remember? You told me about it? It's supposed to be good for the orientation of your cells and shit." He grinned his snaggle-tooth smile. "Not that I want to be oriented in a cell anytime soon."

Aaron headed for the door.

"Thanks for the ride," Roy said.

"You're not leaving, are you?" Karen said.

"No," Aaron said. "I got some emergency whiskey in my truck. We can still have a drink. That OK with you, Mace?"

"Sure, man. Whatever you say," Mace said. Aaron went out looking a little hurt. "He got canned for drinking," Mace said.

"I thought he wrecked his car or something," Karen said.

"At eight a.m.," Mace said. "Still drunk from the night before. Killed his partner, his drinking buddy. They paid him to dry out. Taxes paid him. You'd think he woulda quit. Seven chances later. They only gave me three." He smiled again, eyes bright and joyful, other people's trouble.

"You've had more than three," Karen said. "And you know it."

Roy followed Karen into the living room. There was new furniture since her mom's funeral, like from a furniture store, not from Goodwill. "What's with all this?" Karen said.

"Nice, huh?" Mace said.

"Compared to the old stuff, yeah," Karen said.

"I sold all that crap to Benji Lanigan." Mace turned away from Karen, walked by Roy, and returned to the kitchen. They followed him. "Actually," Mace said. He had the fridge open and was shoving cans of Ensure into a paper sack. "I traded it. Benji took the furniture and I took that .308 you saw on the table." He rolled the top of the bag down and put it on the counter by the door.

Karen busied herself getting the ice and glasses, and when

Aaron came back with a bottle, she took it from him and poured. Aaron took his drink and wandered into the hall looking at the pictures of Karen's mom, Whip and her grandparents, Karen and Whip, Mace and Karen's mom, Linda, everyone together, a series of long-dead dogs, pretty much long-dead everyone.

"Ding ding," Karen said. "Enough with the museum tour."

"Sorry," Aaron said.

Mace set his drink down on the counter. He had a mean look on his face as he stepped by Aaron and went to the back of the house, toward his bedroom.

Aaron came and stood next to Roy on the torn linoleum, rattling and chewing the stale ice in his glass. "I don't think he likes me," Aaron said quietly. Roy shrugged his shoulders because he was most likely right. Karen had turned up the thermostat and the tablecloth fluttered in the warm draft of the furnace vent.

Karen sat down at the table. "He doesn't know what he likes," she said. "Have a seat."

"He lives here now?" Aaron asked, pulling out a chair and sitting down.

"Yeah, more or less," Karen said. "He bops around a lot, doing who knows what. Benji Lanigan? Do you know who that is?"

Aaron shook his head. "No idea."

Roy pulled out a chair but didn't want to sit at the table so he shoved it over to the counter and hopped up and rested his feet on it instead.

"Bopping around," Aaron said. "When he's not in county psych or getting stabbed in Susanville." Aaron kept his eyes on Karen as he took a long drink from his glass.

Karen didn't react to the news of the stabbing. "If you

were a cop," she said calmly, "then you probably know some things about Mace. He knows some things about you too." She glanced at Roy. "I'm not going to apologize for him."

Aaron held out his left arm as if he were testing the fit of his jacket. "There probably isn't a cop or an ER within fifty miles that doesn't know Mace," Aaron said.

"He got stabbed?" Roy asked.

"That's what I heard," Aaron said. "Gas station parking lot, several people involved. I don't think they ever caught anybody for it, though. Is he your stepdad? I never figured out how you two were related."

Karen was looking at the pale crescent in her thumbnail as she did when she was getting angry. "We're not related," she said. "He and my mom were high school sweethearts." She looked at Aaron for a long few moments. Sizing him up, Roy thought, deeming him worthy of precious information. "He came back, after my dad left. I was probably six or seven years old. My sister got sick."

"Half sister," Aaron said. The furnace kicked off and it was suddenly quiet in the house.

"Not how I'd put it," Karen countered, not lowering her voice at all. "Six of one, know what I mean?"

"Sorry," Aaron said in a whisper. "So that was his daughter? Whip was his daughter? What was her real name?"

"Sandy," Karen said. "Her name was Sandy."

Go ahead, Roy wanted to say, ask her another one. Ask her how Whip got her nickname. Ask her if it was cancer that killed her. Ask her what kind. Hope you have some sodium pentathol, head-gear, and a mouthpiece because it's gonna get rough.

"New furniture," Roy said, repaying Karen's earlier rescue.

"I guess we were wrong about Mace going feral." To Aaron, "We thought he'd be in here with lawn chairs and a barbecue, cooking meth or whatever."

Karen smiled at Roy. "Where did he go anyway?" she said. She called his name and he came into the kitchen dressed in a too-small peacoat, black Levi's, army-surplus desert boots, no hat.

"I gotta go take care of some shit," he said, picking up his drink and downing it. "I'll be back, not tonight, a couple days. I'll try and hurry. I feel like shit for zipping out the door like this."

"It's OK," Karen said. "We'll be here. Like Roy said, our car broke down. We couldn't leave if we wanted to."

"I can take you to pick up your van after Moody's done with it," Aaron said. "Give me a call." He reached into his pocket for his phone but couldn't find it. "It's in the truck. You want my number?"

"Sure," Roy said, taking out his phone. He acted like he was typing it in but he didn't.

"You leave me enough room to get by?" Mace asked Aaron.

"Yeah, I'm about to go anyway," Aaron said.

"I wasn't telling you to leave, buddy," Mace said. To Karen: "I'll see you two in a couple days." He snatched the paper sack from the counter and went out the door. Roy watched from the window as Mace not-so-carefully backed around Aaron's big truck and whipped around in a reverse slam as soon as the road widened a little. When he turned around he saw that Karen had been watching him watch Mace.

Aaron tilted his glass to Karen. "You probably never knew this," he said. "But my dad owned a dry-cleaning business and a coin-op laundry in Reno, the one on McCarran with the angel on the sign holding the pants. He inherited it from his dad."

"I remember that place," Karen said.

"He'd stay in Reno during the week. He had an apartment above the shop but he'd come home on weekends." Aaron looked down at his feet. "He died a couple years ago now. The store was turned into a Subway six or seven years before that, long time ago."

"Sorry to hear that," Karen said.

Aaron waved off the apology. "He put thirty years into that shop. For what? Cancer of the goddamn nose and throat? A shitty wake at Conkey's? It's depressing to even think about what that man put up with." He grinned. "I used to think he had another family down there and at his funeral I half expected to meet them."

"Anyone show up?"

"No, I knew everybody. No surprises." He refilled his glass, then Roy's and Karen's, raised his glass: "To homecomings." They drank. Aaron looked at Karen first, then Roy. "I was a good cop," he said. "You can ask anyone. I fucked up. I know I fucked up, but until then—it was everything." He nodded for a moment or two, then shook off his sentimentality and blinked his eyes clear. "Mace is pissed at me because I busted him once with an unregistered handgun. He did six months for it."

"That's a good reason not to like you," Karen said.

"Maybe," Aaron said. "But he's not supposed to have guns at all. He's a felon. Deer hunting? Season closed over a month ago. He can't get a hunting license any more than he can vote." His eyes were unfocused and Roy doubted if he'd been anything but a bully when he was a cop, if he'd ever been anything but a bully his whole life. Roy was born to hate cops. "I testified that the gun was unloaded in plain view," Aaron said, "or he'd still be locked up. He should thank me." The muscles in his neck thickened as he took another drink.

"And now you're a motorcycle man," Karen said. "Chopper man." Roy sneered involuntarily but Aaron didn't catch him.

"Yeah," Aaron said. "Some people don't make it where they want in this life." *Phony and prophetic*, Roy thought, *as if they were ever separated.*

"I don't know," Aaron went on. "I love motorcycles but it's not wearing a badge. Not even close." A long pause. "But you've done some shit, huh? You guys are still riding riot. Living life. Traveling."

"More like limping toward happy hour," Karen said.

"You've always been funny. I remember you in class cracking me up."

She winked at Roy. "Hear that? I've always been funny."

Roy smiled broadly with his proud love of her, but his guts were twisting.

Aaron wiped his mouth and looked at Karen then back at Roy, establishing a pattern that Roy considered to be a bit sexist but couldn't decide if it would be better or worse if he did the opposite.

"Did you ever go to college?" Aaron asked Karen. "I thought you'd be off to Columbia or Yale by now."

"No," Karen said. "I mean I went for a little while, a state school, not Columbia or Yale by a long shot, but then I met Roy and things changed."

"First the nanny job, now college?" Roy said.

She gave him a look that told him this was not the question to ask right now. Because she did blame him.

"You should go back," Aaron said. "You could do anything. Be a lawyer or a doctor."

"Maybe," Karen said, suddenly sheepish.

Roy thought, *Drink your drink and mind your own fucking business, pig boy. Ex–pig boy.* But it was true that Karen had given up big things for Roy—life goals, guiding lights snuffed out. He worked up a list of things he'd given up for her. It was a short list—strange and recreational cocaine use, not to mention the semi-professional, buying and selling, life-crushing cocaine use that used to pop up now and again.

"My two cents," Aaron said. "Go back. Get a degree. Change your life and in the long run, if you have kids, you'll change their lives too. The whole arc of the arrow changes if you get an education. I know that now. I learned it from my wife."

Sad Aaron, Roy thought. *Sad-my-life-didn't-work-out Aaron. These complaining, discontented motherfuckers get younger every year.*

Aaron offered his hand to Roy, said: "Anyway. Cool running into you guys."

Roy shook his hand and smiled back at him nodding, like: Yeah, bro, yeah. Now fuck off.

"I'll admit it," Karen said. "When I first saw you I thought, this guy? The football hero? The jock? Anybody but him."

"I'm old now. Glory days and shit. I hate how Springsteen songs now make sense." He crossed the kitchen in two steps, wrapped Karen in his big arms and squeezed.

Roy's hands had begun to sweat and his drink was empty. He couldn't think of a Springsteen song except that piece-of-shit pink Cadillac one.

Aaron picked up his glass and sucked it dry and then put it down, whack, on the counter. "Back to work."

"Thanks for the ride, man," Roy said.

"Yeah, no problem." Aaron smiled his big, tough, scarred smile and fixed Karen with another needlessly heavy stare. "You know what I think?"

"What's that?" she said.

"I think that maybe we're not so different, me and you. We both have our family tying us to this place, my dad, Mace and whoever else, it doesn't matter, and that means something." A big half-gold, goon smile. "Fuck you if you don't get it. That's what I think."

Karen smiled, but clearly didn't know what to say. Who would? She nodded yes but Roy couldn't read her eyes, then she leaned over and touched the big dork on the arm. She liked him. She really fucking liked him. She was happy to be near him. "It's not so bad to feel connected somewhere," she said.

Roy didn't know why she'd said it, but once she had, he sensed she'd needed to say it, or something close to it, for a long time and that it was true. She was in her house. She was home. All at once Roy wanted to get Aaron out the door and gone. He'd brought up Whip. Touchy stuff. And what did *tied to a place* have to do with anything? Does a masochist thank the rope? Probably.

"You aren't alone," Roy said to Karen.

"I know that," Karen said.

Aaron buttoned his coat, pulled up his collar. "I better get.

Tell Mace I said to chill the fuck out when you see him." He took Karen's hand for the second time. "Great to see you."

"Thanks for the ride," Karen said.

"I could give you some money for gas," Roy said.

"You could but I wouldn't take it. Call me when your rig's done and I'll give you a lift." Aaron went out the door and seconds later they heard the diesel clatter to life and he was gone.

Roy and Karen sat in the still warming kitchen, refrigerator buzzing, ice cubes melting in their empty drink glasses.

"What if I don't want to stay?" Roy said.

"Then, I don't know what," Karen said.

[14]

M > 45
CA 96118

THE LAYER HENS ARE SCRATCHING ALONG THE FENCE, ONE foot then the other, dry-dirt kickers, convicts searching for shivs, while the meatbirds are in their rolling jails in the pasture living in fear of nothing if not the goats jumping on the roof. Bonehead book about gardening with chickens set them back two weeks. Rows of bonehead books and magazines, stacks of them, never mind the websites, and what it came down to was fencing and weeding. All you need to know. Vigilance. His inner dirt farmer: *You get yerself some wire, some posts, a shovel, and you dig—if not for yer very life—then for yer sorry homespun dinner. Dig, boy, dig.*

Now, taking a break from the digging of cheatgrass from the garden paths, they stand side by side and work the dirt from their hands. She's seven today, his co-worker, his youngest, and that makes him, what? Old? A middle-aged father of two? There are moments when he feels nothing if not too old. Too old to be figuring out how to keep the daily operations rolling. Head above water. Too old to be complaining about all the work he has to do, and too old to actually manage it, even if he did just shut his mouth and get it done. Feels that way. Head underwater. Too old to keep up with a seven-year-old. Never mind the other one, the mean one, the teenager.

Three logging trucks, close together, stacked high with saw logs roar by on the county road. The Jeffs have repaired the biofuel plant in town and reopened the Sierra Pacific Mill. The smell of cut timber drifting in from the road is reassuring.

"Will new trees grow?" the girl asks her father. She has his eyes and is capable of disrupting the space-time continuum if she looks at him too long. At least that's how it feels.

"Forests evolve," the man says. "Remember when we talked about evolution? How time is the most important thing in the world?"

"We don't understand what it is," she says.

"People say they do," he says. "I don't." For some reason when she repeats what he's said back to him he likes it less than when her older sister does. She's a different person and he doesn't like inculcating them both with the same form of propaganda. It'd be like raising a monocrop, set them up for catastrophe, make them weak.

"Those trees aren't like our trees," the man says. "They don't need us to take care of them." After he says it, he realizes how untrue it is. He'll let it ride. The child is familiar with Northern Spy, York, Cripps Pink, and pie cherry. She's helped plant, harvest, graft, and stood watch with her family over the fires of the girdle kill.

"They just need time?" she says.

"And soil, water, and sunlight." He gives her a shove. "Chain-saws and skidders don't do them any favors though, do they?" He watches her eyes as she discovers the holes in what he's been saying. Do the trees need our help or don't they? *You know*, he wants to say, *if I told you exactly how the world is, you wouldn't ever sleep again, so quit looking at me like I'm a liar.*

Just then, the girl's mother comes out of the house, the older sister closes the door behind them. The screen door doesn't slam because he's installed a hydraulic closer/stopper thing. It'd taken him months if not years to get around to it but he'd done it. The teenager hates it. She wants to slam the door, was happier when she could. If it is possible to work yourself out of a job, this was not the place to do it. At night if he can't sleep he runs through the list of projects that need to be finished before it snows or doesn't snow, rains or doesn't rain. Rarely does he go to sleep satisfied. He keeps a notebook in the Shaker cabinet in the kitchen and he gets up and writes down his schemes and his lists multiply in the way rabbits do.

"They blasted the dams," the woman shouts from the driveway.

"What?" the man asks. "Who?"

"Some guys calling themselves Agua Critical," the teenager says, serious. "It was on the radio."

Stop acting so grown up, he almost says. *It's worse than when you act your age, which is saying something.*

"What dam, Mama?" the younger child asks.

"Three different ones, including Frenchman's. They put a dent in the one above Folsom but they say it's holding for now."

"What's the point of that?" he asks.

"I don't know. Piss off the Jeffs," she says.

"Other people live here," the older child says to her mother. "It's not just the Jeffs." She still remembers what it was like before the Preservation. The layer hens mob her feet wanting her to toss some scratch and she nudges them away with her foot only to eventually pick one up, the barred rock, reliable layer, a good bird, named Sevilla by the youngest.

"We live here," her little sister says.

He opens the garden gate and herds the girl through and shuts it behind him. The chickens don't expect anything from him. But death. To them, I am death. To all the animals, I am death. If they know it or not. Makes him think about his place in the world, the reach of comeuppance. Or karma, if you want to burn your palo santo about it. He pops hip joints with D2 steel and tans hides. He has goatskin rugs and rabbit-fur hats. To every season, turn. He catches his daughter under the armpits and chucks her onto his shoulders.

"We thrive, little one," he says, squeezing her little calf muscles. "We're not survivors, we're champs."

"I'm not a monkey," she says, popping her fist lightly off the top of his freshly shorn head.

It takes a moment to catch her angle. "Champs, as in champions. Not chimps, as in chimpanzees."

THAT EVENING THEY DECIDE TO WASTE SOME FUEL AND GO FOR A drive. The asphalt of the county road is cut with twin crumbling troughs in the southbound lane from the log trucks and tree bark litters the bar ditch. The Jeffs have doubled their security at the roadblocks, and after the first two they decide to turn around and go home. More and more they're in occupied territory. Strangers in camo with M4s directing traffic.

The only flood damage they see, outside of the mud and up-rooted trees in the fields, is the ruined bridge at Dotta Guidici, and that had been marginal for years. The man makes a note of the salvageable bridge timbers and plots a time when he can return and grab them, who he might call to help. Short list. Chains, cable and clevis, come-along, handyman jack, peavey, saw, unkillable Harbor Freight single-axle trailer. He builds a skyline in his mind.

"Surface water," the woman says.

"What, Mama?" the younger girl says, still looking out the window.

"The only water that matters is under our feet."

"Not the iceberg thing again," the older child says, tired of all things water. All things: her mother.

"You can't dam your way out of a drought," she says.

"It worked for a while," the man says, resisting the urge to make a pun. Dams make him want to pun.

"I'm tired of everything working for a while," the woman says. "I want it to work forever. I want these people to stretch their imaginations and try and see the long game."

"They can't see past their dehydrated chicken dinner," the man says. "You want them to build a coop and raise corn."

"The corn died," the youngest says. "Bugs killed it."

"Tough all over," the man says.

[15]

M < 55
CA 94203

TWINNED WALLS OF SCARRED BOULDERS PILED ONTO THE SIDE-walks funnel them toward the roadblock. He keeps the dog out of sight in the trailer. The codies on guard duty wear black tactical gear and blue dust masks. They have sidearms and ARs, ammo belts and high lace boots. A radio is blasting inside the Red-E-Shed guard shack, half-static, half-Slayer. "South of Heaven," classic rock. Sodium lights have been twisted onto hog panels with barbed wire. A three-phase diesel generator rumbles in the back of a hard-used City of Sacramento pickup. The man is almost certain they will be turned back but without pause the codies wave him through. They don't want him here any more than he wants to stay.

Cars lurch past and there isn't much of a shoulder. They go slowly and the oncoming headlights make the man's eyes weary and the night blurs. In the darkness beyond are the lights-out suburbs.

The stink of house fires has settled into the ground and is rancid in the air. FEMA zones, once protected, now bankrupt and abandoned. The feds bowed out and the utilities shut down and—with the exception of the militias, the too-dumb-to-go-anywhere crusters, and the truly helpless—the place is now empty.

His left knee clicks on each rotation of the pedals. First pain like first light. He says hello to the all-day pain. It will move through his body—knees, back, ass, wrists, neck—as the sun moves across the sky. No stopping now. No one to complain to. Let the body complain to the body. Let the mind find comfort in the distraction of the pain.

In the low hills above the city he stops and lets his sweat dry and within minutes the heavy quiet closes on him and chills his blood. He lets the dog out of the trailer so he can lift a leg but with his hip he squats. When he's done, he won't load up so the man puts his feet to the pedals, his hands in the drops. Knee click like a slow jazz finger snap accompanying the dog's four-step toenail percussion, looks back, hardly limping.

An hour later, out of the blackness, comes the otherworldly spectacle of scavengers removing a wind tower that they've dropped across the road like a lodgepole pine for firewood. Shattered hunks of white plastic and bent metal stump out of the dusty earth. The scrappers stagger in the blue-white flash of the cutting torch, eyes and teeth. The man and his dog go unnoticed as they leave the road. He pushes his rig through the dust in a wide arc to the other side of the hill where he throws his leg over his bike and rolls easy on the blacktop.

Red moon sliver, inland-bound on empty roads, dry riverbeds, and dustbowl fields. A line of cracked twigs that used to be an orchard. The wind blows hot, even at night. There are houses—he knows there are houses—but no lights. The dog wants to stop and nips at his ankle to tell him so.

He waters the dog in a sour cream container and has a few swigs himself. Using the edge of his overgrown thumbnail he punctures a dime-size blister on his palm. He lets it drain and as he slowly peels the skin off he thinks: Someday people will look back at this time and it will seem like it all happened over the course of a couple of months or years. They'll insist on an exact hinge point, a fault line, a political act. But there isn't a simple explanation, or even a person to blame. The answer is mistakes were made, better luck next time. He feeds the dog the skin from the blister and washes his hands in the dust and gets back on the bike.

When he comes to an unmarked junction he stops to check the map with his headlamp and he and the dog leave the highway for a ragged two-laner that climbs gradually into the hills.

They sleep in a concrete culvert that passes under the road. It is tall enough for the man to stand up in and the acoustics are familiar and, in a childlike way, welcoming. Others have slept here before them and there is a filthy foam pad but the man doesn't use it. The dog isn't so picky. Graffiti tells them to flee if the rains come or *you'll get shot like a cannon onto the rocks*. Smiley face. *I'm hobo loco because they didn't come*, someone has written. *Me 2. Me 3. I'll take mine on the rocks. I'm thirsty. Jeffersons are fags. Say that to their face. Pussy. My kingdom for some pussy. UR King Pussy. King Dripy Dick. King Butt Fuck*.

In the morning, after they leave the culvert, they only make it a mile or two before the way is severed by hardened mudslides. The man has to disconnect the bike from the trailer and make trips to pack his rig over the jumbled mess.

They pass through miles and miles of burnt forests. The sun bakes down on the dry slot of the Yuba. Choke on red dirt. Late in the afternoon, they take shelter in the cool stonewall vein of a rail tunnel.

He must've fallen asleep because when he wakes the sun has long since set and the dog is sitting outside in the meager moonlight like a stone lion.

Bleary eyed and saddle sore, the man gets back on the bike. They pass quietly through two ghost towns, one after the other, never see a light, and later, see roadside camps and flicker fires, and hear voices in the trees. He pushes the pedals down. The dog is in the trailer and the chain creaks under the strain.

Dawn finds them on ash-swirled blacktop. They're on what was Preservation land. Burnt and heavily logged forests on either side of the road but the deadfall has been cleared. The chainsawed eyes of the trees watch them as they pass.

At noon they come to a holdout compound with razor-wire fences and warning signs, security cams. Without a flag, there's no telling. The man parks his bike and walks toward the gate and the call box. Then he sees the three gold stars and the arrow. The blood is returning to his hands in a cactus handshake. He massages his finger stump and spits on the fence and calls the dog to his side and helps him back into the trailer. One of the staples is bleeding. He gives the dog a pill wrapped in salami and wipes the wound clean with an alcohol pad before applying the antibiotic ointment.

His legs go on without explanation, exhausted but emphatically still cranking the pedals, spinning the batter. He is in fact entangled with this thing he sits on and he is going to make it do what he wants. When he has the chance he is going to coast, sink a knee against the top tube and just take it easy, let it roll. With all the weight he's hauling the climbs feel punchy, even the low graders, and sometimes he has to get off and push. He feels lonely and helpless as he walks.

The sun has only just fallen when he coasts through a short S-turn, downhill section. At the bottom he's surprised to find green grass on the northern slope. He pushes the bike from the road into the tall grass and hides it behind some boulders. The dog unloads stiffly from the trailer, panting heartily, eyes narrowed from the heat. He needs sleep but they have water first, and he feeds the dog kibble while he has some salami and bread. There are birds here, unseen, but their chalky shit is on the boulders. The dog finishes its dinner, then settles in to licking its staples.

"You'd better quit that or I'll put the lampshade back on. If I had it. Bare-assed baboon," the man says. "It'll get better. Don't worry. Don't even sweat it, Frankenbutt." He digs in his tool kit and finds his cable cutters and his multitool and kneels down beside the dog. "Too early for this, isn't it?" He picks out the smallest wound, nearly healed, and snips the staple right in the center. The dog watches him but doesn't try to get up as he rolls the staple out of the skin. He drops the two pieces in his palm. "One down," he says. The dog licks where the staple had been and the man doesn't stop him.

He has his back to the road, petting the dog, looking for the birds, when the dog begins to growl. The man scans the trees while he rests his hand on the dog's head. Then he hears the trucks.

He can't see where they park but he listens to the doors close, one two three four. He hisses at the dog to be quiet and then busies himself cramming his sleeping bag into his pannier, but he's so tired that he's clumsy and can't seem to get his hands to work the way he wants.

Three armed men dressed in camouflage are walking toward the boulders. He can't tell if they've seen him yet.

When they see him, they stop.

"We've been looking for you," the one in front says. He has the militia insignia, the three gold stars with the arrow, on his shoulder. He covers the lower receiver on his weapon with one hand and points with the other. "Don't do anything sketchy, brother, or we'll punch your ticket."

"I'm leaving," the man says.

"Not yet." Another man, clean shaven and with a sharper outfit, digital camo, knee-high snakeboots, comes toward him as if to shake his hand, says, "Stay still." Then raises a sleek data-sat phone and takes the man's picture. They wait. A small flock of juncos pass low overhead and their wingbeats sound like horses running far away.

One of the militiamen steps forward and gives the dog a command to see if it obeys. "*Fuss,*" he says in German.

The dog leaves the man's side and plants its feet and barks excitedly at the militiaman. His hip is bleeding again. This isn't anger, this is the joy of the working dog.

"Fuckin' *sprechen,*" the militiaman says, smiling, hands up. "*Sei brav.*"

The man clears his throat and points at his side and the dog goes instantly calm and returns to the man and sits.

"That's what I'm talking about," the militiaman says, approaching. "May I?" he asks, and the man nods and the militiaman puts a hand out for the dog, pets it, roughs it by the neck.

"C'mon, can we keep him, Dad? Can we, please?" The other guys are smiling now, watching the dog.

The one with the phone shakes his head at the screen. "It's not loading, Sampson," he says to the dog lover. "Try and get this to work, would you?"

Sampson glances at his pals, slaps his gloved hands together, and takes the phone and begins swiping screens.

"Tell me whose land this is," the leader says to the man. "Where we're standing right now."

The man ignores him, finishes loading the bike. The men around him don't look familiar but he knows who they are.

"You aren't getting enough of a signal," Sampson says, passes the device back to the leader. "We need elevation. It'll work once we get outta this canyon."

"I'm not staying," the man says. "If that's what you're worried about."

"Do I look worried?" the leader says. "We're not the Jeffs. We're what the Jeffs were supposed to be, before they were corrupted."

"STT," the one called Sampson says with a hip-hop emphasis on the final T.

"Battle of Thermopylae," the leader says.

"You all look the same to me," the man says.

"We could put that dog to good use if you want to come with us. We can pay you, help you get where you're going."

"No, thanks," the man says. The dog loads into the trailer and he zips it shut. "I don't care who you are. I don't want to join. And I don't want you to follow me." He mounts his bike and maneuvers down the hill and is surprised when they don't try to stop him.

Near the road, three more men with rifles step from the shadows. Two trucks on the road behind them.

"*Sei brav*," the one called Sampson yells after them.

The man's heart is crashing against his chest and he is soaked in sweat. He pedals fast and never looks back. The sun goes red at the horizon and a mile later he can't see much beyond his front tire. *Sei brav*. Be good. Be nice. He looks over his shoulder but it's too dark to see the dog inside the trailer. "You don't be nice," he says. "Hear me? No *sei brav*."

[16]

R < 25
CA 96118

K AREN BROUGHT HER BAG IN FROM THE MUDROOM, SET IT down on the table, and looked at Roy.

"Don't get mad at me," Roy said, thinking: This will cheer her up considering Mace just split. "But Mace is just some guy. He isn't really your family. He isn't blood. At best, he's your half sister's dad who got stabbed in Susanville, a felon. To me, that doesn't add up to much."

She dumped the ice from their glasses into the sink and rinsed them and put them in the strainer. "I thought you liked him," she said, looking out the window. "I thought you had a bit of a man-crush on him."

"What're you talking about?" Offended, but desperate not to show it. "I don't have man-crushes on anyone."

She turned and faced him. The color was coming into her cheeks. She looked for a dish towel but there wasn't one so she dried her hands on her jeans. "Just seemed like you two were getting along. He likes you."

"All I know," Roy said, "is that we showed up and he left. What does that say?"

She pushed her hair back from her face with both hands and pulled a hair tie off her wrist and put it in a ponytail. "If you can't see why I'm here," she said, "and why it kills me that Mace comes and goes like that, like I'll always be here, like there's time later when I know there isn't. I don't know what to tell you. Really, right now, I don't think I have the energy to even try and explain."

"I'm tired too," Roy said. "You weren't the only one out there freezing on the road. You were sleeping. I was driving. I'd been driving all day."

"I know you're tired, but I need you to take a second and really absorb where we are and what it means to me to have you here. It means I trust you. More than anyone else in the world. I'm with you and I want you to be here with me."

He nodded in agreement but what she was saying was shot through with so much stupidity and childishness that he felt a bit disgusted. "I came here with you because I don't want us to split up," he said, "and just like you, I don't really have the energy to even try right now, but—"

"Stop," she said. "If you don't have the energy or the—" She hesitated, choosing her words. He hated when she took these pauses, like she was the deep thinker of the two of them. Been to college. If you're so smart, he wanted to say, you'd just spit it out without going over and over it. "Thoughtfulness," she said, "to be nice. Don't boombox my window. Don't say anything. It's fucking kindergarten."

"No, listen. I'm being thoughtful. But you're just climbing

into a coffin here. Everybody here, they're fucking gone, or they suck. Or both."

Her shoulders dropped and her nostrils flared and—was it relief he felt? He'd hurt her and he couldn't take it back. Could she ever understand that this was like gravity to him, the water droplet that had to fall?

"And what's up with you telling Aaron you had a bad reputation?" he said, following his lemmings of bullshit right off of the cliff. "What the fuck does that even mean?"

"I got pregnant. I told you." She paused. "Just like my mom did."

"OK. Maybe you should tell me what happened, like with Aaron's shitty friends, because hearing all that shit you were saying in his truck, I was like, what the fuck? Seriously, what the fuck?"

She was tired and her eyes, her smile, showed it. She used her hands to show the two sides of her statement. "Women are like, don't walk on me, and guys are like, but I want to, and then women are like, OK this one time, then guys are like, what's with all the boot prints, whore?"

"That doesn't answer my question."

"I blew the football team," Karen said. "All of them."

Roy leaned back and looked toward the darkened window, thinking: she's joking while simultaneously trying to remember how many men were on a football team, feeling his masculinity losing power—bad alternator—and in all kinds of trouble.

"I didn't blow the football team, asshole," Karen said. "Nobody walked on me. I wanted the attention. I knew what I was doing, mostly I did. They just, you know, all they saw were boot prints. They don't see you."

"You got pregnant, though," Roy said.

"Condoms break. Things happen, sometimes prematurely." She made a shooing motion toward his crotch. "We know all about that, don't we?"

Roy nodded, offended, but he was still wondering if the guys on the bench counted or was it just the starters, and did it include special teams too? He was getting turned on but he wasn't happy about it.

"I've told you all of this before," Karen said. "I had some shitty years. Whip died and my dad split. My mom was a wreck. But Mace showed up and straightened us out a little. He talked to Aaron's friends, the assholes. He might've even smacked them around, I don't know, and really it was worse after that than when they were acting like I was this huge slut. They wouldn't even look at me anymore. It was like I was poison."

"Why do you want to be here?" Roy said.

"I'm not afraid of my past. I'm not afraid of anybody. I used to be pissed at Mace for sticking up for me, doing what he did, but now I'm grateful. Not many people do that kind of thing for anyone anymore. If they even have the balls to face the problem at all, everybody wants to talk about it and go to therapy and shit, but not Mace. He put the fear of death into those assholes." As she spoke she looked frail and childlike and Roy wanted to hold her but didn't know how to initiate it or what it would mean if he did.

"But you still ran away," he said.

"It was just what I needed," Karen said, head up, a bit punch-drunk, teary eyed. "All of it. It makes me who I am. I'm OK with that."

And before she could take a breath and gather her thoughts,

or Roy could repent and they could really make up and move on, get this thing under control, he said: "Let's get Carl fixed and get out of here. Do something else, something we'd both be into. You know, have fucking fun. Maybe we could come back in the summertime. Then you could have your garden. Or you could sell this house and do whatever you wanted for a while. I don't want to see you go through this, reliving all this."

Her body stiffened and her eyes went wide, sadness was replaced by ferocity. "Were you listening to me? I'm not leaving. Where would we go anyway? That's a good question, isn't it? What would we be going back to? If we don't stay here, we don't have any place to go." Neither of them had said this out loud yet. This was a vacation with consequences. This wasn't a vacation.

"I don't have to do anything." Backpedaling, don't touch it— it's hot. "*We* don't have to. *We* could go see Neko and Yuri in Oakland and if we timed it right, we could catch some NorCal time, get some pre-harvest weed money. Or maybe Neko could find *us* some part-time something, drink-slinging work. You like the Bay Area."

"You don't listen."

"We could make it a big loop, circle around back to Portland. At least that way I could skate a bit, you know? See if I could shake a sponsor loose. There's plenty of folks we could kick around with."

"You're saying we but you mean me," Karen said.

"Don't start that shit. I'm always thinking us."

Karen shook her head, no.

"This snow is too fucking much," Roy said. "Icicles? What the fuck are icicles?"

"Besides frozen water?"

"I'm just saying, who knows? It might work out in SF, a new life is always out there, babe." He smiled at her, held out his good timin' hands. "There's always Mexico."

She was white-knuckling the back of one of the kitchen chairs. "I'm not doing that," she said. "I'm staying here. If you're going, I don't know what to say. I can't believe you would even bring it up. You haven't even given me a chance to unpack or do anything." Her eyes searched his. "What's wrong with you?"

"OK. Sorry. Forget I said anything."

She let go of the chair and hugged herself. "I'm still freezing," she said. "Aren't you freezing?"

Roy shook his head, no.

"Look, look at my forehead." She leaned toward Roy and he could see the tiny beads of sweat at her hairline. "I'm sweating and I still can't get warm." He reached for her but she stepped back with her hands up. "I'm going to take a bath," she said. Roy waited for an invitation. "Alone. You had your chance."

"Can I at least say that you aren't even trying to see it from my point of view?"

"Oh, but I do. I see you about to cave and I'm praying: not again. Please God, give him enough sack to do the right thing for once."

"Not again, what? What are you talking about?"

She clenched her fists and shook them in front of her like a pro wrestler declaring his indomitable power. "You *know* what," she practically growled the words. "You're like some idiot hippie that continually wants to tune in and drop out, fucking hokum acid trip dipshit attitude. Flee to Mexico?" She waved her arm and pointed a finger in a direction that Roy was pretty sure was north but he wasn't about to correct her. She went on: "Freedom, is that what you're getting at? You wanna be free? It's on and on with your freedom and your fucked-up ideas about liberty. Skate and fuck everybody else. Be a man, Roy. Stand the fuck up for once. Stand the fuck by me. For once have my back, like I always have yours."

"Take it easy. I just said Mexico because we'd talked about it before. Don't call me a fuckin' hippie, either."

She came over, straddling the chair his feet were on, and got right in his face like she might climb up and give him a kiss or do a striptease. "I can't call you a hippie? What can I call you, sweetie? Sir Roy the Bravehearted?" She smacked him on the forehead with her palm and the back of his head bounced off a cabinet.

"Call me fucking later if you're gonna be like that," he said, and he wanted deeply to hit her back. "Call me fucking gone."

"This is just like—"

"What? This is just like what?" He was yelling now, wide open, and in that way it was nice to be out of their apartment. He didn't have to worry about someone calling the cops out here.

"I told you, I don't even want to bring it up."

"Sure you do. You can't help yourself. Go ahead, say whatever you want to say. I don't give a fuck."

"How about you making us skip out on going to San Diego to your mom and Steve's for Thanksgiving? How about that? Because that was fucked."

"That was different."

"Yeah, how?"

"Because it was a fucking sad drunken summer that crashed into an epically shitty fall," Roy said. "I was jellied by the time it got cold."

"You don't get to do that."

"Do what?"

"Bring up my abortion to defend yourself."

"I'm not. Jesus. It wasn't easy for me but I know—I'm not comparing anything. Remember all the fun shit we did, though? I tried to make it normal again."

Karen gave him the look she saved for when she was explaining what Roy had done while he was blacked-out drunk. "You had some fun," she said. "But mostly I was alone, working, saving my money to fix Carl, like we agreed we would. Then you and your buds would come in the bar and drink for free and you wouldn't even stick around until I got off work." She held up her index finger. "Never tipped," she said.

"C'mon," Roy said, weirdly proud of not tipping.

"You let me walk home alone a lot. That's what I remember. Twenty-five rapey blocks, me and my pepper spray."

"We went to the coast," Roy said, feeling himself sinking into the quicksand. "I tried to teach you how to surf."

"You left me standing up to my tits in ice water to be pummeled by the waves while you duck-dived your way past the breakers and hung ten with your surfer brahs, your fucking Jack Johnsons."

Roy laughed a little. "They're more Perry Farrells than Jack Johnsons."

"I thought I was going to drown. Stuck in that stupid giant wetsuit with the hood. I couldn't even move."

"That's how you learn, though," Roy said, not joking; it was how he learned at least, minus the wetsuit and the ice-cream-headache cold water. Surfing in Oregon was different in that way than surfing in So Cal. "I should have stuck with you."

"Yeah, you should've."

He wanted to reach for her, to take her hand, but he still couldn't make himself do it. "What about when we went to Lincoln City—and to Bend—for those skate contests," he said. "That was a good time, right?"

"I didn't go to Bend with you. I had to work. And in Lincoln City, after the contest, you fucking ditched me and took off with the pro dudes on some Beach Boy vision quest."

"I did? No, you came with us. We were at the beach together all night."

"No, we weren't. You were an asshole to me in front of your friends and I went back to the motel and watched Sigourney Weaver kick alien ass, and you showed up at like four in the morning covered in mud and sand, soaking wet and cold, with pupils that looked like fucking black olives."

He gave her a quizzical look.

She continued, "I let you have the bed and I watched you toss and turn until you fell asleep. Then I went to the office and talked the lady at the desk into letting us check out late. I finally got you into the shower and got you a hamburger and a Coke and then I drove us back home. You didn't even remember that you won the fucking contest until I told you."

It was coming back to him now. He didn't have an argument. He had to stop arguing. "OK, listen, I don't even remember deciding not to go to my mom's. I don't. I remember apologizing to you about it, though."

Karen kicked the chair out from under Roy's feet and he pitched forward and slid off the counter and she got right back in his face and Roy almost told her that she was beautiful when she was angry, because she really was, and he felt awful about what he was doing to her right now. He tried to touch her cheek but she smacked his hand away.

"You made me call your mom, and Steve," she said, shaking her head. "That fucking colostomy bag of a man answered the phone and you—I can't believe you, telling me you want to leave right now. Fucked is what that is. Your mom even offered to buy our tickets so we could fly out, but because you made me lie we couldn't even accept charity, when charity was exactly what we needed. It's so fucked how much of a pussy you are when you pride yourself on being this strong-type guy, a tough mother-fucker that can take a hit." She did a little muscleman pose and mean-mugged him.

"Things aren't black and white. You always pretend they are but there's more to my deal with Steve and my mom than you give me credit for. It's complicated."

"It isn't black and white? So things are colorful. Like tie-dye. Like a freak flag."

"That's not what I'm saying."

She looked hard into his eyes and he looked back into hers and he could see the rims of her contacts. "I love you but you have absolutely no focus and that makes you hard to trust."

He was hurt now, what she was saying hurt him but he didn't show it. He didn't think so at least. "I've apologized to you for all of this," he said, "I don't know how many times, but it's not the same if I'm aware I'm doing it. It's called making a deci-sion and right now I think we need to make a decision."

"I'm done with you and your decisions. It's all bullshit any-way. You're just scared." She walked away. "Don't even think of following me," she yelled just before the bathroom door slammed shut.

"I won't."

He went and stood in the hallway and tried to organize his thoughts, looked at the Oronski family photos, the pale ovals and rectangles of the removed, like someone was behind him with a small mirror or a watch catching the light from the sun. Fighting in this house was the same as fighting in any other. Imagine that. The old ham-hander: No matter where you go, there you are. No matter where we go, there we fail. He couldn't see the long view, the history that built to the future. The pale spots where pictures used to be, memory stains.

When he heard the water in the tub, he went to the mud-room and hauled his bag into the bedroom and threw it on the bed. Karen's underwear was on the floor, black lace, not much to them, a remnant. He picked them up and gave them a sniff, not the white crusty part, but above it, her good smell, then dropped them on the bed and went to the living room and turned on the TV.

[17]

R < 35
OR 97203

Springtime mud show. The Pacific Northwest. The spe-cific more-wet. If it were sunny every day, what would he do then? Get a sunburn? Cancer? Tan and fit? Healthy living? Yogurt and yoga? Join the other death-fearing twats jogging at the waterfront or in Forest Park? *Fuck that*, he thought, more or less daily, hourly. *I'm the king of this bog.*

Somebody had brought a couple of tropical fish bath towels from the Fred Meyer to use as doormats and they were wadded up near the shallow end coping in the smaller of the three bowls. With spotlessly dry Vans, Roy stood on the deck of the big bowl drinking a tall boy and watching a storm front push closer and closer to the park. *When they roll in slow, they last longer.* Now he was a weatherman. Now he was the president of the meteo-rological society.

He wasn't alone. There was some tubby-bubby spock rocker

wearing bitch-ass slipon shoes, acting as if the shallow end of the medium bowl was his own personal miniramp, rolling back and forth: tail stall, fakie rock, tail stall, backside 50-50 for like three inches, fakie rock, tail stall.

Roy tossed his can and rolled in on him full tilt, locked into a frontside smith and took it all the way through the pocket. He pumped through the deep end to give the twerp time to be gone before he entered the shallow, and when he did he went hard into the opposing wall and threw his shoulder into a backside disaster so fierce and smooth and fast and loud it was like a beaver smacking his tail on the water, *whack!* Then down the wall with a backseat pump into a face-high frontside over the hip and, still holding his grab, he saw the twerp step off his board on the deck, another deep pump into a screaming, hard-carving, backside 50-50, focusing on the drop, choosing the exact coping tile where he would shove off, almost careful, absolutely measured and precise, getting every drop of speed out of his pump for the backside kickflip over the hip—this had been his whole afternoon, his whole day, his whole life— and he knew as soon as he cleared the coping he should kick his board away and run out but that little fucker with the slipons was still there with his retro shit, American Apparel faggotry, and fuck it, Roy thought or didn't think, luck favors the brave, Dennis Hopper all: Is that my leg? Is there any beer in that can?—and Roy was boosting over the hip and engaged the flip just so and, quick as that, he felt his board pressing oh so gently against the soles of his shoes as he launched toward the deep end wall—*I should grab, no grab, that's the point, be brave—be fucking brave*—but he'd drifted down the line farther than he'd planned and was almost into the pocket and his board was under him, down now, wheels barking, so he sucked up the transition as best he could and right when he was about to lose all hope and prepare for impact, he was snap-snap over the drain and going up the other wall, all arms a-waggle and hip jut, barely hanging on but stomped, stamped, and fucking delivered. All fucking day he'd been after this shit and now he had it. Then, a backside 5-0 stall—with a moment's pause for our fallen brothers—front truck *clink!* on the coping—and he pumped around the deep end and up the waterfall to the shallow end and there was slip-ons waiting for his turn so Roy charged in and went for a balls-deep rock 'n' roll, back wheels to coping, and tried to smash the fucker's toes but he jumped back and Roy missed. He was still smiling to himself for scaring the little fella when he went to bring the rock 'n' roll back in and lazily caught his front wheels on the coping and fell five feet straight to flat in the shallow like he hadn't done in years. A sack of pain-filled shit, he lay there on his back trying to get his breath. The sky was low and getting lower, great gray tumblers ripe with water, coming at him like a *Lawrence of Arabia* sandstorm, like death itself. Summertime rain.

His board was rolling around in the deep end. Slip-ons wouldn't dare drop in with Roy's carcass blocking his only available run. That fucker's cowardice—back and forth—not venturing into the strange angles of the rest of the bowl. Probably the story of that asshole's life. Follow the herd and don't get hurt, back and forth, repeat.

A raindrop splatted the size of a nickel next to Roy's left ear, then the sky opened and set up the drencher. Roy reconstructed himself to standing and stiffly retrieved his board and fairly crawled out of the shallow end to the deck.

"That was sick," Slip-ons said, picking up his sweatshirt. "Just beat the storm, too."

"It's a pool," Roy said, "skate it like one. Like you have a pair, with your bitch-ass shoes."

Roy left his dead soldiers where they'd fallen—fuck all the family-friendly assholes, gentrifiers and their fucking garden trowels and Home Depot staple-tagged barcode cedar fences—and finished his last beer rolling through the now-torrential Ore Uh Gun wetness to Sasha's car. He needed new bearings anyway, a new deck, a reward. There was pain, but he'd known victory. Worth it.

His elbow looked like it'd swallowed a grapefruit and his back was going to be fucked for a while. *That was sick.* That little turd didn't know sick any more than a guy looking through a telescope knew deep space. But that was the sickest thing he'd done in a while. True commitment, real bravery. He hadn't thought he had it in him. He felt brand-new and a sweet and wholesome feeling filled his heart. But then the little voice said: *Take it to the big bowl then, pussy. Take it to the deep. Work your speed in the full pipe and then try it.* Roy responded: *But I don't have insurance.* And if there was ever a way to know if you were old and washed all the way up, it was not skating the big bowl because you didn't have insurance. The elder statesman in Roy's head advised him that *we all have our own bitch-ass shoes, bunch a bitch-asses that we are. I am a man and men are a bunch of bitch-asses.*

His apartment was near the bridge, practically under it, and looked out on the trashy city park and the brown river. He had lived closer to downtown, but it cost too much now, if you didn't want to hassle with roommates, and what did you get anyway?

People—functioning, upwardly mobile, mostly white people, some Asians—citizens, just a bunch of outfits walking around, shopping, eating. When's the last time you got stitches? When's the last time you got hurt so bad you thought you'd shit yourself? *Bitch-asses. I was born to bleed, born to die, not shop.*

North Portland was still the real thing. Yesterday, waiting for the 75 bus, he saw somebody knocked out cold in front of Dad's bar. Little guy walked up to big guy, socked him in the face, and took his bike, middle of the day. These were grown men, not kids. The kids were even worse. Future condoville, sure, everyone knew it was coming, but for now it was a cheap place with something to see out the front window, fistfights, the greatest bridge, the churning river. Gimped as he was he had to use the wonky handrail to get up the stairs.

Sasha was home so he put his board in the closet and kicked off his shoes over the floor vent so they'd dry. He put her keys on the magnetic plate on the counter as he'd been instructed to do approximately twenty-seven thousand times. Light was coming from under the bathroom door and he could smell the essential oils. He was out of beer so he drank some of Sasha's wine from the bottle.

"Is that you?" she called from the bathroom.

"No, it's the rapist. I'm here to violate and dismember you. Not in that order."

"Can you bring me a glass of wine?"

He held the bottle up to the light and then opened the cupboard and splashed some into a glass. On the way to the bathroom he finished the bottle and left it on the coffee table.

She had her arms curled around her knees so he couldn't see

anything. Portland pixie, brown-eyed blonde, black highlights, curtains would match the drapes if there were drapes. He put the wine on the edge of the sink. "I'm going to need to violate you first, before you get that." He gave his zipper a tug.

"I don't think so, pal. Just give me the wine and leave. I'm not that into it right now, *it* being you and your gross wayward penis."

"It's not gross."

"Ick, is all I can say. Ick."

"Fine."

"Derby is in his crate, why don't you take him for a walk and stay gone until I go to work?" She smiled her Whole Foods checker's you're-a-thoughtful-and-morally-superior-customer smile and he wanted to slap her.

"It's fucking pouring outside," he said.

"Wear a coat. Take an umbrella. Derby loves the rain."

He placed her glass of wine well out of reach on the shelf above the toilet and left.

They'd found the dog running loose in the park when they'd first started dating. Sasha reported him to the shelter and kept him at her (soon to be their) apartment. No collar, skittish, unkempt, some sort of Scottish terrier, not the type of dog that usually goes abandoned. Nobody claimed him, so they kept him. Derby, the Derb, the Herb, skateboard chaser, mouse and rat killer, possum fighter, up to date on his shots and a nice little set of cojones and Roy liked to see them because nobody let their dog keep his nuts anymore. Roy fucking did. If it were left up to Roy, Derby would never lose his nuts. Even if he was a shoe-chewing asshole that had to be crated when he was inside or he would drive everyone to skin-picking, lip-twitching insanity. Nope, he'd go into the dirt whole. But he was still a puppy, or at least that's how Sasha called it, lots of good years to come for Derby. She wanted him clipped, thought his balls were weird. She talked about Derby but Roy heard her talking about their relationship, his future, his balls.

Roy's swellbow hardly fit in the sleeve of his raincoat and when Derby yanked on the leash to go down the stairs, Roy grunted in pain and switched to his good arm. He hooked the leash to the neighbor's doorknob and ducked back inside and quietly pilfered the last of Sasha's Vicodin left over from her wisdom teeth extraction. She thought she'd hidden them in the spice cabinet behind the cumin because Roy hated cumin but, *No, sweetheart, I found your pills and I ate your pills and to rub it in your face I'm going to dump the last of the cumin into the empty pill bottle and never say a word about it. See you in a month or however long it takes for you to feel the need to use cumin or painkillers again.*

In the park, directly in front of the sign declaring that all dogs must be leashed, he set Derby free and moseyed along behind him trying to muster the saliva to get the pills down his throat. No luck, so he donkey-whistled the dog back and released him, *Sorry, Derb,* and walked up the hill to the Safeway.

He left Derby tied to the bike rack with the junker Huffys and their plastic-bag seat covers and went inside and bought two cans of Steel Reserve and affirmed to the checker that he would prefer that she put them into their own individual paper bags, neat and tidy. Everybody needs a jacket, right?

Roy downed half of the first beer on the sidewalk in front

of the store and felt the pills finally slip loose. A perky white woman pushing a too-big toddler in a massive stroller gave him and his open beer a look as she approached the store.

"Live fast, die young," he said, and held up his brown bag can, cheers, for the toddler and the woman said, "It's never too late," and went inside.

Roy unhitched Derby with his free hand and let him run, followed him around the corner and across the back lot. He finished his beer and chucked the can and bag into the blackberry ramble alongside the parking lot and followed the dog down the sopping hill to the waterfront.

They posted up in the covered section of the amphitheater with a couple of other fellas drinking out of bags. Derby sniffed at one of them and earned a fuck off and a half-hearted kick.

"I'll stuff my shoe down your neck if you kick my dog," Roy said.

"Keep 'im away from me then," the man said, picking at a bloody patch on the back of his hand.

"Derb," Roy said. "Go shit." Derby trotted toward the waterfront, zigzagging and sniffing at goose turds, taking it easy. He did like the rain.

"I'm leaving, Thomas," the dog kicker said to the other guy, tugging the collar of his mossy yellow raincoat closed around his neck.

"See ya." Thomas was busy dismantling a pile of cigarette butts and rolling them into fresh cigarettes with a pack of orange Zig-Zags, and didn't look up as his friend trudged back into the rain. Roy watched him follow the asphalt path to the west side of the park and disappear into the trees, only to emerge moments later, bent beneath the weight of a massive camouflage backpack slung with garbage bags filled with cans and bottles, clinked and rattled away, reminding Roy of a bipedal dung beetle.

Derby returned and curled into Roy's side. Roy lifted his jacket and let the stinky little beast have a taste of his warmth. "You want a fresh one?" Roy said, holding out his pack of Drum.

"Sure." Thomas got stiffly to his feet and waddled over. He was probably in his forties, Native, braids, dressed in army surplus gear with a brand-new pair of high-dollar snowboarding boots on his feet. "Thanks," he said.

"No problem." Roy waited patiently for him to finish rolling his cigarette then took the pouch back and rolled his own. He finished his beer before he lit up.

"You need another?" Thomas said.

"Sure, you got one?"

Thomas dug around in his pack until he came up with a can of Hamms. Roy took it and thanked him. Twelve ounces of waterskiing bear piss hardly offered the necessary punctuation of a malt liquor tall boy and Roy had it drained in a few drinks. They smoked and watched the rain shatter the river. Cars thumped over the segmented decking of the towering green bridge.

"Shame about the salmon, huh?" Thomas said.

Roy hesitated. "What?"

"It was in the paper." Thomas twisted around and grabbed a fistful of loose news pages from the free paper that nobody read and held them up for Roy.

"I'm not reading that," Roy said. "You can keep it."

"Water got too hot. They all died going upriver. Cooked

'em." Thomas shook his head, took his time flattening the pages and folding them, then raised a cheek and slid them under his ass. "Those dams are gonna starve us out."

"Last I heard, the dams keep the lights on."

"I don't eat lightbulbs."

"It's not like they all died anyway," Roy said.

"You're jumping from 'what?' to being a marine biologist?"

"There's still salmon. They sell it in the store. On sale now."

"Not for long," Thomas said. "They were going to spawn and they died before they got there, that means they didn't reproduce. That means no baby fishes."

"Looks like it's lightbulbs for dinner," Roy said.

The rain came down like someone had paid extra.

"The good news," Roy said. "Looks like the drought's over."

"Whatever you say, Dr. Science," Thomas said.

Roy tossed his can in the corner with some others, pointed at Thomas's footwear. "Nice boots," he said.

Thomas lifted his foot and squinted at his boot. "They were handing them out, back of a van, down on Burnside, bunch a punk kids." He looked at Roy. Just like you, his eyes said. "Tossing 'em out like they were Christmas turkeys."

"Might be able to sell 'em," Roy said.

"To who?"

"I don't know. Try eBay."

"I got eBay. Let me just get my laptop."

"Yeah, sorry. They warm?"

"They're OK. Ugly as hell though, and nobody wants to pass you a bill if you're wearing more expensive kicks than them. Know what I mean?"

"Yeah." Roy stood up and hooked Derby back on his leash. "Thanks for the beer."

"No problem." Thomas was about to ask, so Roy handed him the Drum and let him roll another. "Them butts taste like shit, man," Thomas declared.

"That's why they call 'em butts," Roy said.

Sasha was gone, and there was no note, so they weren't splitting up, yet. Roy toweled off the dog with Sasha's still-wet favorite towel and man and dog parked on the couch with the thermostat pegged and watched Judge Judy and settled in to kill the hours until Roy had to go to work at seven. The pills were nice but he'd need more, same went for the beer. He felt lonesome and if it weren't for the muscle memory of slaughtering that backside hip earlier, he'd be fucking depressed, fucking down, low and low.

When he went to stand, a back spasm bent him in half and he had to hobble all please-ass-fuck-me to the kitchen so he could pull himself up with the counter and the fridge handle. Upright but still in pain, he rummaged in the freezer praying for secret vodka but had no luck. The postcards and photographs on the freezer door held his eye and made him wonder why he was still in this apartment with this woman and not somewhere else with some other.

Then, as he did with dismal regularity, he thought of Karen Oronski. He took a moment away from the reality of the dreary kitchen and his jacked back and went through the work of piecing her together. Her face was there, her longish nose and her heavy lower lip, and he could feel the weight of her body in his arms, the feel and smell of her hair as he buried his face in her neck. It was like a drug to think about her. He held her at arm's length and her smile came through her eyes too. He couldn't remember what her laugh sounded like. He tried on a few but none of them fit. This just happened. He could remember it yesterday. He felt a hollow spot open up in his chest. The moan coming out of his mouth broke the spell. There were other kinds of storms, outside of rain and snow, thunder and lightning, and Roy knew enough to duck and cover when one like this came on. He put the dog in its crate and grabbed his board and his bus pass and hobbled out the door.

[18]

R < 25
CA 96118

ROY WOKE ON THE COUCH TO HEADLIGHTS SPINNING THE SHAD-
ows of the window frames onto the walls as someone pulled
into the driveway. He sat up in the blue dark and turned off the
TV with the remote. Karen wasn't in the living room with him.
He went to the kitchen. A car door opened and Roy watched
as a man's shadow passed through the headlights. It had to be
Mace or one of Mace's friends. Without any real conviction Roy
decided he wouldn't open the door. He retreated to the living
room hoping maybe they hadn't seen him in the kitchen. The
knock was hard enough to rattle the glass.

"Who in the hell is that?" Karen asked from the bedroom.

"I don't know. Mace wouldn't knock, would he?"

"I'm hiding."

"You call *me* a coward."

She didn't have time to answer.

"Karen," Aaron Simmonds called between knocks. "Hey, Roy-O. Arroyo!" He rolled his r's somewhat expertly. "You awake?"

Roy straightened his sweatshirt and walked to the door licking the dry from his lips. The door opened before he got there.

"You're up," Aaron said, and reached in and flicked on the kitchen lights. "Good. Mind if we come in? We brought you tacos and beer."

"Hey thanks, Aaron. Wait, how many are there?"

"Just two, me and April, my wife. I'll go grab her and the grub and shut the car off." He turned as he was walking, spoke over his shoulder, "I don't know why I left her in the car. Where else would you be?"

Roy held the door when they came back. He shook April's hand but hardly looked at her. He wasn't quite sure what this was yet.

Aaron put down his paper bag of food and a six-pack of Dos Equis on the table. Roy took the beer he was handed and April found a plate and spread out and introduced the assorted chicken and beef and veggie tacos for everybody to share.

"We wanted to make sure you had food at least," Aaron said.

April was nodding along with her husband, smiling at Roy. "We felt bad," she said. "You come home and your car breaks down. It's awful."

"Yeah, it is sad," Roy said, but he wanted to say: *This isn't home. This will never be home.* Roy picked up a beef taco in a corn tortilla and soaked it in hot sauce from a plastic cup and wolfed it down in three bites.

"Where's Karen?" Aaron asked.

"She's in the bathroom," Roy said, opening a beer. "She'll be out in a minute. Thanks again for the food."

Aaron waved him off and April smiled and showed gapped front teeth, wide enough to stick a nickel in. Her hair was cut short and she wasn't tall and her short hair made her seem even shorter and more perky. She had a physical tightness about her he recognized of the high school athlete—bump, set, spike it, that's the way we like it—the dancer's heel pivot, half-duckfooted. He imagined them, Aaron and April, quite the pair, jocko couple.

"You caught me taking a nap," Roy said.

"Ask him," April said. She had a beer now too but she wasn't eating.

"Ask me what?" Roy couldn't read their expressions. He didn't know these people.

"We were in town having a few drinks." Aaron said, making the drinking motion with his thumb and pinky sticking out. "The Kings lost."

"Yeah, I watched the last few minutes."

"Fuck those fucking idiots. Crumb-chasing fucktards, drive me insane. Anyway, I told April about you and Karen, that I saw you, and me and Karen went to school together and that we had this great talk, and April wanted to meet you guys, so we stopped by."

"He didn't think to get some food," April said. "That was me."

"She's the brains," Aaron said. He had on a leather jacket and greasy black jeans, logger boots. Used to be a cop and from now on he would look undercover.

"You wanna come to Reno with us?" April said.

"I was asking him," Aaron said.

"Slower than your precious Kings getting to the point," April said. "It'll be fun." Her eyes were slightly crossed, big and brown. Maybe they weren't crossed, maybe they were just that big. She spun around and took in her surroundings. She grabbed Roy by the arm. "Can you see yourself here, like, living here?"

"I don't know. We just got here." He was close enough to smell the fruity smell of her shampoo. He grabbed a napkin and wiped the grease from his hand and the back of his wrist.

"Better figure it out, dummy." She seemed surprised at the coldness of her words but she was having fun anyway. No one was going to stop her from having fun. She gave him a pinch that hurt and let him go. "Where is she anyway? Aaron wouldn't shut up about her. He was starting to make me jealous."

Aaron shrugged his shoulders and held out his hands, oh you got me. April smiled and then smiled bigger.

"She'll be out in a sec," Roy said. "Are you coming back tonight or staying over?"

"We'll be back by morning," Aaron said seriously. "Dawn's crack, not a second later. Or sooner."

"All right. Let's go, then. I'll see if Karen wants to come."

"She has to," Aaron said, meaning, if she isn't going, neither are you.

"I'll tell her you said so."

Roy found Karen in the bathroom in her underwear, no bra, sitting on the counter next to the sink. She'd been clipping her toenails, the evidence in the basin.

"Did you hear them?"

"I sure did."

"You wanna go?"

"No, I do not. I'll come out and tell them as soon as I'm done here."

"But I have a plan."

"What plan?"

"It's a genius plan."

"Well, I love a man with a plan." She hopped down and traced her fingers over his penis through his pants.

"Grab your bag," Roy said.

"I got yours right here." She cupped his balls and squeezed gently.

He leaned down and kissed her deep brown nipples, Spike Lee style, right, then left, Mookie. "Your backpack. I'll carry my own balls tonight, thank you."

She let go of him. "Have you noticed that I'm not mad at you anymore? Do you want to know why?"

"Because I'm wealthy and good-looking."

"Because I love you." She kissed him on the mouth and Roy savored the wet, minty cool. "Wait," she said, "your plan includes coming back here, right?"

"Sure, but maybe not tonight." He hadn't lied to her for a while so he figured he'd earned one, or maybe he wasn't lying, maybe he didn't know what he was doing and that was the way he liked it. Let the furies decide. He left her in the bathroom to get ready and grabbed his kit from the bedroom.

"What's with the bag and the board? Going skating?" Aaron said.

"Maybe. I take it with me everywhere. Me and Karen might end up getting a room. It's kind of our vacation, you know. We need to have some fun."

"Poor babies," April said. "Broke down on the road." She

smiled at him and spoke in a whisper. "Tell me the truth, is she even here? Did she run away?"

"She's coming," Roy said. "She has to dry her hair."

Just then Karen strolled up with her bag on her shoulder: beautiful, capable, and all Roy's, perfectly contained. *You get one good one*, he thought. Then he hefted his bag and chucked it by the door, thought: *Maybe two.* A billion people on the planet, there were more perfect matches for him than he could ever handle, an endless supply. This went both ways, he was replaceable, everyone was. The big picture could justify anything. On an atomic level he was at peace.

Introductions and speculation about a destination, food and entertainment. Karen passed him another beer. Another sixer had appeared. She made herself a plate of tacos. Aaron and April were eating with her, had their own plates.

Roy went to the kitchen window, the one above the sink, and wiped away the steam and could see snowflakes drifting easily into the glass. *If you find yourself snowbound in the wilderness, it is important to be decisive. Don't go to sleep. You might not wake up.* From one of his dead father's wilderness survival books. *There is no such thing as cold and dead, only warm and dead. Dead muscles won't contract.*

Not that it helped you, Roy thought. *Fell off a rock face in Yosemite and died before I learned to walk.* He didn't know his dad's middle name or his birthday, only remembered meeting his grandmother once when she was on her last breath in the hospital. *You look just like him.* Like who? It didn't make much sense to him then and probably made less now. Childhood mirrors and faded photographs, all of which got lost when Steve took over.

When he turned around Karen was watching him and for a moment he feared she could read the intentions on his face, or at least recognize that his fight-or-flight instinct had engaged. "What are you scheming over there?" she said.

"Just glad to be out of the cold," he said. "Glad we made it."

"Do you want to stay?" she asked.

"Where'd they go?"

"April's in the bathroom and Aaron's warming up the car. Did you not hear any of what we said?"

"I was spacing out."

"Are you sure you want to go with them? We could stay. It's stormy out and I'm not mad at you."

"We should go with them. What else are we going to do?" This too brought a hurt look onto her face and Roy hated her for that, only for the briefest second, but his stomach recoiled and he hated her. She was making him do this, forcing him to pity her, and he wouldn't.

The drive to Reno from Loyalton took a long time with the storm and the slushed-up roads. Roy sat in the front and helped Aaron finish his pint of Beam, while Karen and April sat in the back and drank beer. Roy listened as they talked about Milan Kundera and boots, Fryes. April had lost a pair to foxes when she'd left her muddy boots on the porch. She had a biology degree from the University of Washington but she wanted to be a vet, planned on going back to school soon but didn't know when it would work out. She'd moved to town after she came to visit her brother, a FedEx driver that worked out of Truckee. She'd met Aaron at the hospital after her brother broke his collarbone mountain biking.

"Aaron was in the hallway, all copped out in his uniform,"

April said. "There'd been a wreck with like five cars and he was doing interviews, trying to figure out what had happened. I listened in."

"One of the drivers was having sex," Aaron said, "or attempting to. He and his girlfriend caused the whole thing."

"You're lying," Karen said.

"I'm not," Aaron said. "The girlfriend died. The driver can't walk."

"Holy shit," Roy said.

"He let me shoot his gun," April said.

"What?" Karen said, laughing.

"We hadn't even gone on a date yet," Aaron said. "I could've been fired." He passed Roy the bottle. "I was fired," he said quietly.

They were exiting the highway, spiraling down an off-ramp toward the lowly grid of surface streets. It wasn't snowing or even stormy at all and even with the city lights Roy could see stars. Biggest Little City. Aaron angled for the brightest lights, a moth, north star chaser.

"Not much to say about Reno," April said.

"Nope," Karen said.

"It's not bad," Aaron said. "There's some cool shit down here. Tons of skaters."

"Aaron said you were sponsored," April said to Roy, touching his shoulder.

"When I was a kid I was OK."

"Like Gary Coleman," Karen said.

"Just like Gary Coleman," Roy said. Thinking: Not that you ever did anything ever, when you were a kid or even now.

"I raced BMX," Aaron said.

Roy nodded but didn't give voice to his I-don't-give-a-shit thoughts.

"Yeah, it was fun," Aaron continued. "I went to races in Arizona and stuff. It's expensive, though. When I didn't seem to get much better, I plateaued is what my dad said, and the other kids, smaller, faster kids were winning all the time, I hung it up. Enter football. Hello, concussions."

The car was quiet. *There is no cold and dead when it comes to hypothermia because the heart can slow to three beats a minute. For the amateur it may be necessary to reheat the corpse to ascertain if the victim is dead.* I'm at three beats a minute, Roy thought, and if I hang around here I'm going to be warm and safely bickering with Karen but I'll be dead. Inside that house in the mountains with her, feeding the woodstove, feeding himself, fork and spoon, killing time watching basketball or hockey or whatever, TV baby, lost in the woods. He tried to imagine himself shoveling the driveway, stacking firewood, and he felt that old heat burning up the back of his neck, confinement. Or was it fear of work? He couldn't see the difference. One slip-up and he'd never escape. If Karen got pregnant again, she was keeping it. She'd warned him.

Aaron pulled into a parking garage downtown and, driving up the ramp, mentioned a bar up the street where they could start, take it from there. Roy had the feeling they'd end up in a titty bar if they stuck with Aaron and April long enough but he wasn't doing that. The tires squealed like a car chase in a cop show and Aaron leaned into it, playing the part. Roy was disgusted by his has-been-ness, used-to-be, ex-somebody. Close to home is what it was and Roy knew it. He was calling in an air strike on his own position. Used to have some sponsors. Used to play in some bands. What do you do now, like right now, what do you do?

They were three floors up and the searchlights of Reno traced a gambler's epitaph on the night sky. April gathered the empties from under the seats and arranged them in a half-circle around the minivan parked beside them. Roy shotgunned a beer and got it all down his shirt and wiped at it stupidly with his hands. Karen pinched his ass and called him trash. Aaron pissed against a low concrete wall, his head leaned back staring at the concrete girder overhead. The traffic noise from below thrummed through the concrete chambers with choral under-tones. Karen slipped under his arm.

"There's nothing wrong with us," she said.

Roy burped loudly and Karen waved away the stink with both hands. "We're gonna firebomb the fun into this town," he said. "We're gonna ass-fuck the fun into this town." He forced another burp and almost threw up. "Fuck this town."

"Don't let the whiskey drag you down," she said seriously. "We really can have fun tonight. Nothing's stopping us. Just take it easy."

"I'm easy, babe. I'm so easy I'm almost dead."

Inside, they got drinks. Aaron wouldn't let them pay. They took in the crowd, dizzied by the noise, rockabilly clatter, three-piece band, Horton Heat wannabes. They posted up in a dark corner with a shaky table. Nobody was dancing but there was the occasional rooster-strutting pork chopper, sock-hopping Suicide Girl. Same as it ever was, Roy thought. Some places won't let go. These folks are the sons and daughters, grandsons and grand-daughters even, of desert greasers, Highway 66 throwbacks, out-law bikers that have been picking at their collective melanoma and road rash since V-J Day. Roy liked them and the go-fuck-yerself-ness they off-gassed but at the root of it was just another wagon rut in the same old road. He was looking for the secret door, the way it hadn't been done yet, true freedom, true cool.

They had two more rounds, Karen got the second, April the third, and then wandered back outside, up the street, toward one of the big casinos. The night was cold and crisp with a diesel-exhaust-tinged wisp of cloud rag among the lights and buildings.

Aaron was saying something about blackjack and Roy said, "Yeah, man, let's go." The women followed a few steps behind and Roy almost said something, like that's the way it should be, but for once he held his tongue even though he'd have been joking. Of course he'd have been joking. Why did he think it, though? When was that pathway built? He didn't want to be the little man, the small man, that treated his woman badly. He'd always hated that, the duh-fucking-right obviousness of the male ego, almost more than the treatment. But the way that women can catch that tiny, undeserved anger like a mountain can gather a storm, well, that was biological too, wasn't it? The scene with him and Karen in the bathroom with the pregnancy test entered his mind, two pink parallel lines. Why didn't they design the test or at least the indicator so that the lines came together? Even a no-GED dropout like Roy knew that parallel lines never touch. Where's the kid supposed to fit into that equation?

Boots on the ground, the casino-ugly carpet, they watched part of the show, trapeze with nets, jugglers with fire. A security guard told them to keep it moving when they stopped on the catwalk for too long.

Karen says, "Something to see here, folks. Something to see. Move along."

"Funny," the guard said.

One of the trapeze guys was watching them get hassled from his little platform and for no reason Roy gave him a there-you-go-chief military salute. The guy smiled and sent one back and on his next turn hucked a double back flip like it was nothing, like he did it every day, and probably did. Where were the trapeze girls? What kind of show only had guys? Roy looked around to see who would field his question but the group had moved on. The guard was watching Roy, with a look of what the fuck, buddy. Get lost. He needed the door, the exit to where he was supposed to be, because it wasn't here.

Down the ramp and into the casino proper, Karen spotted a bar in the corner and they bellied up and Roy bought a round of two-dollar cocktails. On the sly he ordered an extra shot of well vodka for himself and was careful to take it without Karen noticing.

April went to the nickel slots while Aaron and eventually Roy and Karen sat down at the blackjack table. The dealer was a beauty and Karen caught Roy staring at the smooth cleft of black skin visible at the top of her casually unbuttoned uniform.

"You think she does that by accident?" Karen said in Roy's ear.

"What?"

"You're about to lose some money," Karen said.

"I don't know what you're talking about." Roy had two kings and he was staying.

"Sure you don't." Karen busted with a seven, and left the table, stood behind Roy to watch.

After three hands Roy was up twenty bucks. "Where's your accent from?" Roy said.

"Kenya," the dealer said. "Nairobi."

"Welcome," Aaron said.

The dealer nodded and smiled with her full beautiful lips together, then dealt the cards.

"As if it were up to you," Roy said. Karen clamped a hand on the back of his neck and he shrugged it off.

"What?" Aaron said.

"You don't get to welcome anyone. Ex-cop acting all United Nations."

Aaron turned to face Karen. "Somebody's a nasty drunk, eh, Karen?" he said, with a smile.

"Fuck you," Roy said. The dealer wouldn't look at him but she pitched him a jack of hearts and he thought she was flirting.

Aaron called for another card and busted, but he stayed to play. Roy took the comped drink when it came, well bourbon neat, drank it like a shot, and then scooped up his meager winnings and stood up from the table. He kissed Karen on the mouth even though she struggled against him and, without explanation, went to the cage and cashed in his chips.

He looked over his shoulder and Karen wasn't behind him so he went out the front door of the casino and onto the sidewalk.

The cold made him cough when he breathed through his nose. He'd forgotten to tip the dealer. He could go back in. The Karen in his mind caught up with him and grabbed his hands. She was smiling. She loved him. He loved her, too. All this love and it didn't make any difference.

"It can't go any other way," Roy said. But he was alone on the sidewalk. He hadn't felt so alone in a long time. He had to leave. He didn't care what she said. He walked by the garage attendant in his little booth reading the paper and up the ramp and found the car. Nobody was around and Roy didn't see any cameras. He didn't give a shit. He'd broken plenty of windows before.

Then Karen *was* there. She was actually right there. She'd found him and this changed everything, but only for a second, because he'd made a decision. It was already over.

"What're you doing?" Karen said.

"Wait and see."

She grabbed him to stop him but he pushed her back, not hard but he'd never shoved her before, never treated her rough. She gave him a shocked look and he threw his elbow against the car window as hard as he could and it still took three hard, bone-rattling smacks and his arm was throbbing to the shoulder when the glass finally shattered. He unlocked and opened the door, grabbed his bag with board attached, and shook the glass cubes from it. He wouldn't look at Karen. He wanted to plug his ears in case she spoke because suddenly this wasn't what he wanted at all. An arrow had been loosed and there was no getting it back. It was the time in the air, when there was only before and who knows what was after, and that was the worst, the in-between, after the release and before the strike.

He was standing in front of Karen, about to speak, about to explain when Aaron and April stepped from the stairwell. There was a long moment and Roy thought maybe he could talk his way out of this but he couldn't.

"Wait," April said, slow on the uptake. "Where are you going? Did you break our window?"

"Fucking Jesus," Roy said.

"Answer me," April said. "Aaron, make him answer me."

Karen had tears pooling in her eyes. "I'm sorry, Aaron," she said.

Aaron shook his head. "You could've just asked me for the keys, boss, told me you were going to get a room, which for the record is what I thought you were going to do. That's why we came up here, to see if you needed the keys. If you were getting sick. You could've said something." He held up his keys to show them, like here they are and they could've been yours.

When Aaron stepped toward him, Roy backed away. Aaron chucked the keys after him hard but missed and they went skittering across the concrete and smacked into the wall. Karen was standing there with her palms up. Aaron and April were looking at her, saying something to each other that he couldn't hear.

"Come on, if you want," Roy yelled. Karen shook her head no because she knew that he was going to leave her. He'd left her. But couldn't she see that it had only been for that moment and now the moment had passed, and passed again. There were no walls, only doors. He turned and kept walking, thinking any second he'd go back and apologize and buy Aaron and April however many rounds it would take to make it cool—he'd sob at Karen's feet—but he didn't. Later he would think someday I'll laugh about this but he never could. He would maintain that he was drunk but he wasn't that drunk. He knew what he was doing.

THE WHITE LADY CABDRIVER TOOK HIS BLACKJACK MONEY. ALCO-hol had him stunned and unsure, moronically attentive. The news at the bus station wasn't great, no bus to Oakland until nine in the morning. He sat on the bench in the bus station spinning the wheels on his skateboard. He read for a while, he had some Vonnegut in his bag and it made him feel better. KV was good with the big picture and not getting all screwed up by the small shit. He got it. He understood what it was about, he'd lived through the war after all, witnessed all kinds of horrible death and sorrow. After a brief nap and a few moments of dedicated thought, Roy realized how wrong he'd been.

Karen, to his surprise, answered her phone. Roy told her straight away that he'd been wrong, put it out there right off.

She was doing something else while listening to him, he could hear her moving around, and he wanted to know what it was but he didn't want to ask because she'd get defensive.

"I feel like you're too old to say this to, but maybe not." She quit moving around on the phone for a moment, then started in again. "Your actions have consequences. All the things you do, you're responsible for that."

"I'm going to Oakland. I want you to come with me."

She said no, she wasn't going, without even thinking about it for a second. "If you want to stay," she said, "I guess you can, but I'm embarrassed of you right now. I'm ashamed of what you did."

"Do you want me to say sorry? I'm sorry, OK? I made a mistake."

She was silent.

"Answer me, what do you want me to say?"

"I guess nothing."

"Where are you?"

"It doesn't matter. By myself. I'm alone. Aaron and April aren't here if that's what you're worried about."

"He's pissed."

"Of course he's pissed. They're both pissed. We're all pissed. We had to drive back from Reno in a snowstorm with a broken window. It was bullshit."

"I didn't need to do that, break his window."

"You didn't need to leave me standing there. You didn't need to treat me like that. I mean, if you're this ready to just leave me, then I guess there's nothing to do. Why'd you tell me to bring my stuff, when you were just going to ditch me?"

"I wasn't planning on any of it. You could've come with me."

"It's easy to say that now."

"It's not easy though. None of this is easy. You were pushing me to come here and do all this shit. I don't want to live in the fucking boonies, middle-of-nowhere shit."

"I thought you were with me. You know we could've had fun. Aaron and April aren't that bad. They're actually kind of great. I like them more than you. Right now I like them way more." She wasn't doing something else. She was trying not to cry.

And it was as if he'd crested a hill and it was easier now but then it was like there was a cliff on the downhill side and he was going over. "Get the fuck off me with your guilt," he said. "I can't stand it. You need to grow up."

"Get the fuck off *me*, Roy." She was screaming mad like he'd never heard her. "Get the fuck off of me." The line went dead.

Maybe this was for the best, but it didn't feel that way. It felt like he was making a horrible mistake and that it was happening very slowly and he could change it but he wouldn't. Romantics like Karen were nothing more than vultures, surrounded by death, pictures of the dead and abandoned houses. *History is for suckers. Not me. I'm going to live. I'm going to get on the bus and get out of here. I'm going to go. Be a man.*

[19]

R < 35
OR 97202

I T WAS HAPPY HOUR AND ROY WAS SICK OF THE SAD, BUMMER ON a barstool, Replacements-era regulars, so he hung in the back by the walk-in watching *Simpsons* reruns on the iffy, hit-me-again, no-remote TV, waiting for his shift to start. Day Shift Damian said he had coke but he wasn't going to share until he was off work in two hours.

With an empty six-pack of high-test microbrew at his feet, grimacing at a rotten courtroom TV show, the *Simpsons* long since over, Damian finally came back and waved him into the employee bathroom. A couple of lines and one stashed by the spare TP in reserve and he was behind the bar.

A gaggle of gas station beanies and black hoodies were trying to out-metal each other on the jukebox. There was a time for Mastodon, but barely post-happy hour on a Tuesday, as far as Roy could tell, wasn't it. He snatched a fistful of quarters out of the till and limped across the room to the jukebox and unplugged it, then, with some effort and more pain, plugged it back in.

"Not a word," Roy said, feeding quarters into the machine. "You guys are killing me. I'm not saying you're wrong. I'm not saying I'm better than you, but right now, I've got all the quarters. Don't give me that look. I'm gonna work with you. You'll like it." He loaded the complete *Ride the Lightning* album, followed by *Reign in Blood*, and then, preempting the demise of Damian's shitty cocaine, burned through the last of the quarters with Leonard Cohen and Velvet Underground. *South of Heaven* was playing when one of his regulars, an ex-carnie, Burning Man reject named Rooster, slipped him some Norcos and a half hour later his back finally went quiet. Almost whimsically, he thought he might get into the Jameson's. He was a bartending legend, a hero. He didn't just work here, he presided. It was always the same, night after night: ice-cold service and piss-warm beverages, decent jukebox and superior pinball in the back. Only a few played the machines anymore, though, rare was the pop of the replay.

Around midnight, some skate pro pals of Roy's showed up so he kicked everybody out and locked the doors and poured. An hour later they were all deeply embroiled in a drunken slappy grind competition in the bar parking lot. The judge was a shit-wig trog chick in a half-shirt Blazers jersey and a black mini-skirt, fishnets, and boots. Roy didn't like the look but he liked her body. She used a broken chalk square she'd taken from the pool table to mark where the competitors entered their grind on the curb, then, noting the distance and attaching initials to the hash, declared the winner. Which, as luck would have it, was Roy.

Joyous champion with a cold Pabst in his hand and another in his pocket, he found himself in a shoe-company-owned Sprinter van rocketing down I-84 to some other spot, a house party with a well-lit miniramp and no neighbors. He'd bested all the pros in the van in a battle of slappies and now he was among them, a wee hours contender. He thanked Independent Trucks. He thanked the northwest moss that passed for curb wax. He thanked the trog for the E and slid his palm over her fishnets and soon found the top of them and touched the smooth skin of her upper thigh, higher. He touched the silky smoothness of her underwear and she pushed him away. "I don't fuck around in vans," she said. "I have rules."

The rest of the boys, and two girls, were huddled up front around the captain's chairs arguing about which exit to take. Roy held the pill up for inspection, its unremarkable and nonthreatening dimensions, and popped it in his mouth.

Two days later he returned to Sasha's apartment to find his stuff under the landing stairs. The super had done a half-ass job of shoving it there after Sasha had tossed it all into the yard. There'd been phone calls. Derby was now his stepdog or more likely not his dog at all, and that hurt, more than Sasha's hatred hurt. He considered stealing the dog but didn't want to complicate things.

THE TROG CHICK'S NAME WAS LACEY AND SHE WAS WAITING AT THE curb in her Range Rover. Roy opened the back hatch and loaded what he wanted, which wasn't much, into the pristine cargo area. Then they were off.

The skate-shoe company was owned by the swoosh. Big

sneaker rolling with skateboarding was like big pharma selling medicinal weed, but with all of their backdoor advertising tricks and subcompanies they appeared to be from the streets. Roy didn't give a shit anymore. He didn't even know what selling out meant. Home brew or Budweiser, it was all the same to him. Homeless bartender v. pro skater. Just tell me where to sign.

Apart from a few of the really young guys on the team, Roy had skated with everybody else before. Jim "Nessy" Nestor—the Scottish gentleman—was their top pro and he and Roy went back ten years or more. They'd done a couple of van tours together when they were younger. He'd bumped into him a handful of times at Burnside too, and once in Sacramento, just after he and Karen split up. Nessy was big business now and Roy figured that it was probably a lot of his pull that got Roy signed.

But, according to Lacey, Roy had reached a marketable vintage, and over the last two days, to prove his worth, he'd thrown down some epic shit, cracked a tooth trying the kickflip over the hip in the big bowl and stomped it on the fifth try. Nobody could mess with that, not even Nessy. And it made the edit. So Roy would have a video part, and with that came a film stipend and a travel allowance, which was essentially a wad of cash handed to him by the team manager, Tony. He'd signed paperwork but it felt like just another session, another skate trip, with benefits. Like the hooker was paying him to fuck her.

Downtown, stopped at the light on Lovejoy, Roy felt a bit out of his mind. He'd quit his girl. He'd quit his job. He either had everything going for him right now or he was in deep shit. He glanced at Lacey and she was gnawing on her cheek and bobbing her head to what the fuck were they listening to? Robot crap, dubstep. Whatever. Her car, her system.

"Why didn't you do something with skating before?" Lacey asked. She was the West Coast advertising rep for the skate-shoe company that he now skated for, and come to think of it, her pull with the corporate people definitely hadn't hurt his chances either. The thing about succeeding was that you immediately ended up having to thank people.

"I've been skating," Roy said. "That's what I did with my skating."

"Commercially."

"Dreams are for kids."

"Presenting the lonesome, hard-ass, Roy Bingham." Lacey smiled and pointed at Roy. "I've heard your name for a while now. People talk. You are legend. Do you still have a board sponsor?"

"No," Roy said. "I was on the Bilge team until they imploded, but folks still send me stuff all the time. I don't pay for product, haven't since before I got pubes."

"You're like the guy that people say they want to be like," Lacey said, "but really they don't. I've spent enough time with you in the last few days to know. Nobody wants to be like you."

He placed his hands against his chest. "You can't buy this." He was joking but he wasn't. He'd signed paperwork. She *could* buy this. She had.

"The worst that could happen now," Lacey said, "with the team at least, is that you make some money and maybe sell a little bit of your soul. People do it every day."

"A sock with holes in it," Roy said.

"What?"

"My soul. It's a sock with holes in it."

Lacey smiled and touched his leg, slid her hand up to his

left-leaning bulge and squeezed. His cock was sore from all the fucking but in a good way.

"This place is posh," Roy said. "The Pearl, it's glitzy, right? Fucking downy, but nice. I remember when it was shit, warehouses and nothing else, a fucking dead zone. Couple of great loading-dock skate spots though. I'll miss that."

"It's OK," Lacey said. "It's shiny and new." She smiled at Roy. "But that's not necessarily a good thing, is it?"

Roy had gone with her yesterday when she'd signed the lease on her brand-new condo. The oven and fridge still had cardboard and Styrofoam packing material in them. The windows in the stairwell still had the manufacturer stickers stuck to the glass and the Otis guys were putting the trim on the elevators.

"Posh food, posh drinks, driving around in your posh ride," Roy said, thinking, *Now I say posh. What kind of a whamby am I turning into? Cheers. Bird. Suss.*

Like a mind-reader, Lacey explained to him the etymology of *posh*, how it came from England, old times, where the rich people on steamships, bound for India or wherever, preferred the port side of the ship on the way out and the starboard on the way back, port out, starboard home, but Roy couldn't be bothered. His silence seemed to upset her. She'd gone to Oberlin and had the pajama shirt to prove it.

"Do you know what *etymology* means?" Lacey asked.

He did or he had once but he didn't any longer. "Does it mean your hair stinks when it gets wet?"

She laughed and he warmed to her again, her earthy and robust sexiness, her big sad eyes that were only a degree or so from being just right, or just smart enough, just quick enough to strike him down. But she wasn't Karen. Never would be. Sometimes he wondered if it would be better to just go and find her and get it over with but he couldn't. Pride was a problem but more than that he was afraid she wouldn't be the person he remembered. She would've changed too. *Who're you again?* What if that happened? Like if she'd forgotten who he was. He actually shuddered while thinking this.

They both needed sleep and Lacey probably shouldn't have been driving. "It's the root of a word, right?" Roy said. "Like where it came from." He turned on her. "Like *Lacey* means you're delicate and pretty much see-through. Particularly pleasing while employed in sexual acts."

She smiled, but the hurt was in her eyes. "Have you ever had the feeling when somebody says something to you that it might be the meanest thing anybody has ever said to you?"

"Don't take everything so hard."

"It's happened to me twice with you. In less than a week." She sat up in her seat. "Think about that," she said with a forced smile. The clouds parted although the rain continued and the wet streets flashed as brightly as a fish.

He thought, maybe there's nothing wrong with her that a change of hairdo couldn't cure. Her smile was enchanting. He shouldn't be so cruel. This was a good thing they had going, but she had him feeling like a kept boy because he didn't have any place to stay and was in fact dependent on this woman for shelter and transportation. "Let's just go to your place and get some sleep, OK?"

"Are you gonna keep the asshole thing going," she said. "Or can you act like a human?"

"I'll be human from now on," Roy said. "At least for the rest of the day."

‹—◆—›

A MONTH LATER, ROY WAS SITTING IN THE MIDDLE-ROW SEAT OF THE Sprinter van, leaning against the window, picking at the spray-paint overspray on his hands, sweating beer. Westbound on I-70, headed toward some concrete skatepark in the pointless suburbs of Kansas or Missouri or somewhere. Lana del Rey was ironically on the radio but secretly they all loved her and would bitch if the music changed. Her song "Cola" had been repeated three times.

Derik, shirtless, sat beside him on the bench seat rolling a joint on a stolen red plastic McDonald's tray. Rasheed was in the back reading *Wired* with his headphones on. Yano from Fresno was up front messing with his phone. Brandon the boy hesher was asleep next to him, drool on his baby-face chin. Tony was driving, sipping a grande Red Bull, resting the can on his tubby gut. Roy and the B-Team. Nessy didn't mess with road tours much anymore, and for good reason. The van smelled like spilled beer, rotten fruit, balls, and hydroponic weed. Coast to coast in two weeks, more driving than skateboarding by a factor of ten. Five days in and Roy was ready to go home but he didn't know where that would be.

Derik licked the paper on his joint and pulled it smooth, held it up for inspection, offered it to Roy, *No, thanks,* lit it and hit it and left it smoldering in his mouth while he stowed his weed, along with a small pair of pink-handled crafting scissors and rolling papers, in a Crown Royal bag. He exhaled big and bounced a fist off his chest, a chest nourished by Wendy's, Budweiser, and marijuana, running lean on adolescent fumes.

"Roll your window down," Rasheed said to his cousin.

Derik did as he was asked and the gust of wind woke Brandon up.

"This shit used to look like all affirmative action," Derik said to Roy. "Real urban youth shit, right? City kids." He blew the ash onto the floor and hit it again. He'd made it clear that if he provided the weed, not to mention held it if they got pulled over, that he got double taps on the rotation.

Roy dead-eyed Derik, not in the mood. He wanted out of the van. He wanted real food. Mostly he wanted privacy. The freeway thudded beneath the tires, almost in time with the hangover pounding in his ears. Derik exhaled in Roy's face and passed the joint to Yano.

"See, we got amigos, Asians, a couple a hood niggas," Derik continued, shaking out one-two-three, thumb-index-middle on his right hand at the other skateboarders in the van. "We even got a Jew from Brazil." He took the joint back from Yano but waited to hit it. "And now we got Roy fucking Bingham. Team photo looks fucked up all over again. Like, who brought their dad to work? Grandpa and the Gang is what this shit should be called."

Roy made the talk talk talk motion with his hand, like a duck quacking.

"You got gray hair, nigga," Derik said. Yano started laughing and Brandon, too. Tony was focused on the road. Rasheed might as well have been in another vehicle altogether. Outside the window there were cows.

"I got some gray hairs," Roy said to Derik. "I don't have gray hair."

"Old-ass nigga," Derik said. "Look at you, all puffy and ill. It's almost tomorrow night and you're still hung the fuck over from last night. You white niggas don't age well. You look sick, zombie sick. Undead nigga." His smile cracked open and

showed his sparkling grill. "But you can skate. I'll give you that."
He offered a fist and Roy obliged. "Roy Bingham can throw the
fuck down, boy."

"Less talk," Roy said. "More rock."

"You straight, Roy," Derik said. "You straight." He hit the
joint again and this time when he offered, Roy took it.

The show went like this: Roll up to a local spot in the van
and the boys all pile out and mill and kick-wheel stopper pebbles
and kind of check what the fuck and see where the fuck you
could get speed for that shit or how to transfer from that to that
so you can get to there, smoke some cigarettes and roll joints,
have some beers and suddenly the crowd's deep and cheering
and Roy is six beers in going for lipslides on the over vert. King
of finding the sketchiest, die if you bail, Valhalla if you ride away
shit, and because of this he always got footage. Always. Something always went down when Roy was skating and it wasn't
as if it wasn't desperate because it was. He skated like each kick
would be his last, each stock ollie was—smack!—another nail
in his coffin. It'd taken him twenty-five years on a skateboard
to develop this kind of skate acuity, all mental, physically he
was pretty much fucked, but not so fucked that a couple vikes
and five beers wouldn't cure him. He might not look like much
but he knew every sweet fold and crease and bump and how to
get from here to there with speed and fucking style. All style,
all commitment. Not much flippy shit, even though he could
still more or less hit the lighter tech stuff, he didn't abuse it. Let
Derik and the lads handle the triple sets and the handrails. Roy
had to use his brain. His battered knees demanded it.

When he was young he thought slamming was the worst
pain he could feel. He hadn't worked jobs and been evicted

and learned bus schedules and lost the one he loved and gone to court-ordered AA and NA and gotten VD and acronymed himself into a deep septic hole of undiagnosed adult sadness. *Old man, take a look at my life.* What life, man-cub? Of what soft-serve state of existence do you speak?

Then it was one too many mornings with Derik yelling, "White power!" while Roy emptied his stomach into a hotel bathroom or parking lot shrubbery. He'd always been a pop-top charger, he had a reputation—wake 'n' bake, burn while you earn, beer for breakfast, six-pack for dessert—but he couldn't bounce back as easily anymore, and if he wanted this cash cow to keep crapping dollars and size-ten skate shoes, he had to make a showing. Which meant that he had to put a choke chain on the hard shit. Beer was fine, and (no edibles) weed, but that was it. If he got tired, as often happened after six hours of skating and swilling beers, instead of scoring some powders, he had to go to bed. Not even a Red Bull, find a pillow, get some rest. He was a grown-up after all and grown-ups, like small children, need routine, regular sleep and meal times.

In Denver, filming at a handrail on Sixteenth Street, Derik got in a scuffle with a security guard. *Catch a piggy. Fuck you. No, fuck you. Try and stop me.* They kept skating, skated circles around the security guard. The rent-a-cop reminded Roy of his stepdad. He cruised by and gave him a swat on the ass and an atta boy. The real cops showed up. Rasheed picked up his board and strolled down the street to a pizza place and had a slice and a ginger ale. Zack-O the filmer moved off and got footage from across the street. DPD wasted no time and in a few minutes Roy, Yano, Derik, and Brandon were cuffed and crammed into two separate cop cars and taken to someplace called Van-Cise Simonet. Tony was at Jiffy Lube having the transmission flushed in the van but two minutes after he got Rasheed's text, he was on the phone with a swoosh lawyer and working on bail.

Being processed was a process. Derik got bragging rights with his assault charge. Roy was runner-up with resisting. Everyone got destruction of public property. Derik was of the opinion that waking up in jail was better than going to sleep there. Nobody slept. Derik got in a fight with some mullet-headed tweeker and ended up knocking him silly with a haymaker. Roy shoved one of the tweeker's buddies but didn't have to swing. Yano and Brandon jumped in too and it was understood that if they'd been in there alone things could've gone differently. Brotherhood. They were let out a few hours after dinner. Instant potatoes, white bread, and kidney beans.

Roy picked up a staph infection in jail, festered in his road-rashed shoulder, put him in the hospital for a few days. Broad-spectrum antibiotic, vancomycin, as if it were designed for skateboarders. Steven Seagal marathon on TV. Plenty of rest.

After the lawyers started pressing, everything was thrown out except for the destruction-of-public-property tickets. It was good news. They had more footage. More mayhem. And Tony had some *Night of the Living Dead*/flesh-eating bacteria/Roy Bingham Lives T-shirts printed up and they tossed them to the crowds at demos. Some of them ended up on eBay for two hundred a pop.

[20]

M > 45
CA 96118

As a family they load into the truck. Dust in the road. Dust on the hillsides blurring the ridges, bleeding into the washed-out sky. A dozen sheep are in the field, paddocked in last year's pasture. The layer hens are pecking around the base of the hop vines. The pigpen is empty, gate open, feeder tipped over, they're feral now. Somewhere there are goats but their range is boundless. The man hunts them now as he does the pigs, spot and stalk. He has coyote and fox pelts nailed to the goat shed, as much warning as decoration.

They don't bother with car seats for the kids. There's been a general reduction in speed as well as traffic. As in none. Pulling onto the county road, they don't fasten their seat belts, fuses have been removed to stop the beeping. On rare occasions it feels easy-going and countrified but more powerful than that is the need to get out of the vehicle quickly.

"I bought groceries there for over twenty years," the woman says.

"Never mind the gouging," the man says. He's driving. His pistol is shoved into the slot above the stereo on the dashboard. The license plates for the truck are in the tray between the front seats along with the screws and a screwdriver if they needed to put them on. If, for some reason, they have to cross the border.

"Are we going to buy anything?" the older child says.

"I don't know, honey," the woman says. "Cheryl said they were giving whatever was left away."

"Where's Cheryl going to go?" the younger child asks. "Marnie and Oliver are supposed to come to my birthday." She's had a hard time making friends. Marnie and Oliver are younger and look up to her.

"They aren't leaving right away," the woman says. "I'll ask and make sure they're still coming to your birthday."

"But she won't work at the store?"

"There won't be a store after today."

"They'll move away?"

"Probably."

The little girl is near tears. "Are we going to move?"

"No," the woman says. "We're staying. We're not going anywhere."

The man glances at her and she looks out the window.

Signage advises them not to leave the pavement, to slow down and prepare to stop. The militiamen at the roadblock wave at them to slow down but they're allowed through without stopping. The numbers written on their windshield with shoe polish proclaim their status as permanent residents. Updated codes appear in their mailbox every Tuesday, thanks to the neighbor.

A twisted and burned SUV is in the ditch where it'd attempted to drive around the roadblock and hit the land mines. Even the youngest child has stopped noticing it or asking what happened, why they don't take it away. *What happened to the people?*

In silence, they pass the parking lot where the woman's drive-thru coffee trailer used to be. The broken skirting and the tire chocks remain. The trailer had been stolen months ago, another one just like it on the other side of town disappeared the following week. A police report was filed in Truckee but they wouldn't find it and they wouldn't come here and look. Somewhere some militia guys were sipping espresso.

The contents of the store have been moved to the parking lot and strewn onto rolled-out sheets of clear Visqueen. A few people push shopping carts but mostly it's just pick up a spatula or a package of disposable shish kebab skewers or a hotpad. Junk show. The man already wants to go home.

Then he spots the boy whose parents were killed in the SUV at the roadblock. Jerzy, is his name. Last they'd seen him was at the funeral, wearing the same getup as when he showed his steer at the county fair. War orphan. His dad had been the lead man on a road crew. His mom was a teller at First National Bank. Country people. Nobody knows for sure why they skirted the road block. Doesn't matter. The results are the same. Jerzy's with his guardian now, the well-driller, Sullivan. Both of them are filthy and their pants are crusted in dried mud. Been working. Smell the diesel from here. What child labor law? Everybody needs a well, now more than ever. Soon enough, we will too. Must be on their lunch break, stopped to see the hubbub. Sullivan leans down and says something to Jerzy and they turn to leave. The man watches them cross the street and climb into Sullivan's pickup.

His eldest daughter smacks him in the leg. "Hey, there's Jerzy!" She runs to the sidewalk and waves to the truck as it drives away. Jerzy turns around in his seat to wave out the back window. They had the same teacher last year. Might not even be a school come fall.

"K-I-S-S," is all the younger girl gets out before her sister smacks her in the shoulder.

"Enough," the man says.

The woman sees her friend, Cheryl, short hair and a sundress, near the chained doors at the entrance and goes to join her. The man stays with the children and watches the scavengers.

"Can we go see if there's anything we want?" the older child asks.

"No," the man says. "There's nothing here for us."

"Why did we come here, then?" the older child asks.

"So your mom could talk with Cheryl. It's all just junk."

They watch an old man attempt the tablecloth trick with the plastic, fail, and drag it to his sedan and wad it into his trunk and drive away.

"Guess he found something," the man says.

"You haven't even looked," the younger child says. "You don't know what you could be missing." Things he's said to her, redirected back at him.

"Fine, you guys go see if you can find anything that we need."

The children leave him and fall in with a few other kids that are smashing bubble wrap and making forts out of cardboard boxes.

The woman leaves Cheryl and returns to the truck.

"Is she OK?" the man asks.

"No."

"Where's she going?"

"She says she's going to stay as long as she can. She has the keys to the store and she wants to move in there after everyone leaves."

"No water means no sewer. She can't take her kids in there."

"Should I ask her to come to our place?"

"We talked about this."

"I know."

"I like Cheryl. I want to help."

"I know."

"Her husband."

"Her ex-husband."

"He's Jefferson and if they find out she's at our place—I don't know what would happen, but it wouldn't be good."

"We could let them stay for a week or so," the woman says. "Nobody would know."

The man watches as the younger child puts a box on her head and runs full tilt into her older sister and falls on her ass. He expects her to be crying when she lifts the box from her head but she's laughing. Cheryl's kids are there too, the boy is a few years younger than the girl.

"A week," he says.

"I told her two."

"I figured a month," he says. "Are they riding back with us?"

"We'll pick them up at Pioneer Park."

"I'll get the girls."

"Don't tell them yet," she says. "And don't tell Oliver and Marnie either."

"I won't."

The man crosses the parking lot. Cheryl catches his eye and nods to him. He smiles back at her and picks up a box and whacks the younger girl on the butt with it. "Time to go," he says.

"We just got here," the child says. Her face is flushed and he can tell she's only a bump away from crying. Her sister enjoys being the bumper.

"Say goodbye to your friends."

The girls say goodbye as adults would, as an actual last goodbye, and it's hard for the man to watch. He'd like the world to be different.

Cheryl and her children step out from behind the settler's cabin in the park. They have backpacks on and grocery bags clutched in their fists. The man gets out and loads their stuff into the bed, takes note of the coffee beans in one of the plastic bags.

"You're going to have to lie down under the girl's feet, OK?" the woman says. Cheryl nods and her kids leap into the open rear door and squirm beneath the older girl's feet while their mother crams herself in behind them. The woman drapes a blanket over them.

"We only have one roadblock," the man says. "Ten minutes and you'll be able to sit up."

"Hang in there," the woman says.

"We're fine," Cheryl says.

They slow for the roadblock. Cheryl's youngest, Oliver, won't stop talking.

"He needs to quiet down," the man says.

"Oliver, be quiet," the younger child says. He listens to her.

The militiamen move into the road and one of them holds up his hand to stop them. The woman gives the militiamen a beauty queen wave and a phony smile.

"Shit," she says, still smiling.

"What's happening?" Cheryl says.

"We're fine," the man says. "Be quiet and we'll be out the other side in a minute." He comes to a stop and rolls down his window.

"Why don't you get that goddamn thing out of here?" the man says, points to the scorched SUV.

The nearest militiaman smiles and approaches with his finger outside the trigger guard. "Serves as a reminder, doesn't it? What could happen." He leans in to look in the cab, sees nothing, keeps walking, looks in the back. The man watches in the side mirror as he reaches in the truckbed and comes out with something. He smacks the bed rail twice and the other militiaman steps aside and waves them through.

"We're good," the man says, accelerating.

"What'd he take?" the woman says.

"Can we get out?" Marnie says. "My legs hurt."

"Come on out, sweetheart," the woman says. "Come up here with me where there's room."

The girl crawls from beneath the blanket and the woman helps her over the seat into the front seat of the truck. Cheryl lifts Oliver onto her lap and wiggles in between the two girls.

"That wasn't bad." Cheryl says.

"I'm pretty sure he stole your coffee," the man says.

"Son of a bitch," Cheryl says.

"Mom," Marnie says.

"I don't even care."

CHERYL AND HER KIDS STAY FOR THREE WEEKS, AND WHEN HER ex-husband pulls into the driveway in a four-wheel-drive van spray-painted camouflage they aren't surprised. He isn't visibly armed, didn't come looking for a fight. His children are happy to see him. He doesn't make threats or rage as Cheryl swore he would. He repents. He's scared. He wants his family with him. Cheryl surprises everyone when she decides that she and her kids will go with him. The ex-husband says they're being reset-tled in Chico. He wishes them luck. They never see Cheryl or her children again.

[21]

R < 35
XX 001

THEY FLEW OUT OF LA FOR A THREE-WEEK TOUR IN EUROPE. Nessy met them in London, dragged them to a football match, various pubs, and he and Roy and Yano started talking about renting a house, maybe Rasheed and Derik too. They put Tony on it. *Find us a house by the beach so we can check out all the beaches.* Tony sent them emails with potential listings but they wanted to see them in person before they made a decision.

On their last day in London, Roy and Rasheed were taking it easy watching Nessy and the boys skate a broken ledge that dropped off into a banked cobblestone wall and runout. It had rained earlier and the cobblestones looked as if they were sweating. Derik slid out and took a heavy slam but got right back up and waited for Brandon to try his frontside disaster for the twentieth time. No luck but Derik switched gears and went for a nosepick instead and stomped it. Everyone watching smacked their boards against the ground like they were broadswords against shields. Nessy kicked toward the bank leisurely and instead of trying anything he just carved up it and popped a little ollie and rolled away.

"Me and Nessy," Rasheed said to Roy, "we come from an older civilization than you."

"You're saying California is civilized?" Roy said.

"New York," Rasheed said. "Places that have history. There's never been a war fought in California, not in modern times. Only skirmishes. Mexico."

Nessy came around again, this time kicking full tilt into the banked wall, and ollied three feet up to the ledge and locked into a backside 5-0 and reverted on the drop and went through the cobbles switch. A chorus of skateboards hammering on cobblestones.

Birds passed through the gaps in the buildings. Roy and Rasheed had their boards under their feet, back and forth, *click click, click click*. Nessy was off his board, talking to some girls by his Land Rover, pointing at the lights on the roof rack and popping his hands open, pow, making the girls smile.

"We got Old World depth," Rasheed said. "Irresistible to females." He smiled, did a seated ollie higher than most people could do standing up.

"You love California," Roy said.

"It's OK. It ain't home." Rasheed looked over his shoulder at the sound of honking horns. "This feels more like home than anyplace in California."

"It's all the same to me," Roy said, jet-lagged, hungover, numb. "There used to be style and, you know, individuality, but now there's just marketing. Cities are cities are cities."

"Marketing is only a symptom." Rasheed stood and gave Roy a swat on the shoulder and picked up his board and took a run at the bank and back-tailed it like he was rolling to the Sevey to grab an ice cream bar, smooth as could be.

Roy had been the same person the whole time, probably used to skate better than he did now, but with the recent advertising push, his image had morphed and slid into a narrow but lucrative slot. He was fine with it. The shoes were hot and the ads were everywhere. His full-pager, face and bare chest covered in his own blood superimposed over him step by step throwing a freeway ollie to nose blunt on an overpass rail, then, like a suicide, grabbing frontside and going over the edge and landing on the banked wall, six or eight feet below, somehow rolling away down the super steep and filthy concrete (a sleeping bum and his pack in the background) carrying way too much speed to enter the flat of the two-laner below, but still hanging on and somehow at the last second making the impossible death ollie over the curb and clearing the sidewalk while he was at it and he was rolling, arms up—Conquistador! Then the Prius hit him and sent him ragdolling out of the frame. So long, canine tooth. Hello, new scars and memory loss, blood and more blood.

Nobody knew that it had taken him four tries to make it, four hard slams, before he was lucky enough to roll out and get hit by a car. There was a lesson in there, Roy could feel it. He was a salmon swimming against the dam.

The team manager, Tony, sent him a text saying he could expect a mid-six-figure settlement from the Prius. The shoe-company lawyers were all over it. The woman behind the wheel hadn't been speeding but she'd rolled right through the light. They were in LA so they'd actually pulled a permit to film that day so she was fucked. She'd lose her license for sure and she might go to jail. The best ad of the decade, hands down, man shit, war eagle, death ride, champion blood orgy. Roy swore he'd buy a Prius with the settlement money, fucking love those cars, so soft and quiet.

IN SPITE OF RASHEED'S COMPLAINING, THE TEAM EVENTUALLY rented a big house in Ventura near the beach. It had six bedrooms and a pool and they kept water in it because it was square with no tranny and partying and swimming and bobbing around on an air mattress was sweet. Roy realized, with money, not everything was skateboarding. Very few things were in fact skateboarding. Skateboarding had always been free, one of the things he did because he didn't have any money, but he didn't have to just do things that were free anymore. Now he could do whatever he wanted, as long as he killed it every time he skated. There was pressure to succeed and he began to miss the days when he skated broke and unknown, free to kill it or crumble and the only one that had anything to say about it was him.

Depressed, feeling washed up and done, going through a bit of the mid-lifery, Roy bought a motorcycle from the Triumph dealer in Carlsbad, paid cash, one of the reissue Bonnevilles. Over the next couple of weeks he trolled around YouTube and eBay and put drop bars on it and changed the exhaust, added rearsets, nixed the stock cluster, and replaced it with thumbnail-size tach and oil-pressure gauges. No speedo. It wasn't long and he was on the bike more than he was on his skateboard. They said—and it was true—that you didn't know fear, you hadn't lived, until you'd white-lined on I-5.

Rasheed bought a built XS 750 from a bike builder in the Hollywood Hills, all black and bored out with a Dyna and rearsets, fast and throaty, and the two of them took a couple of trips up and down the coast, bedrolls strapped to skateboards, strapped to the back of their seats. Derik couldn't get a license and had to stay home unless he wanted to ride all Ace and Gary with his cousin. Nessy didn't even like to drive a car and opted out of the moto adventures, said it wasn't his thing. Yano won some potato-chip-sponsored contest in Atlanta and bought a first-generation cherried-out CB 750 with the prize money even though his only bike experience was piddling his girlfriend's Vespa to the beach and back.

It was March 8 and Rasheed missed a corner on 101, twenty miles from home, washed right through it and went off the edge. He had dinner reservations with his girlfriend that night. Roy wasn't there but Yano was and he never touched his bike again, left it on the side of the road with his helmet in the dirt and when it was trucked back to the house it just sat there in the garage. Nessy was in Japan and got stuck there during Fukushima and couldn't get out of the country in time for the funeral.

In the Tribeca Sheraton Roy watched disaster footage of Japan as he put on his suit and combed his hair. He rode to the cemetery with everyone else in a rented Escalade. Tony was driving. They didn't listen to music.

Rasheed's mom hugged him, and looking at her made Roy cry too. He and Derik hit it hard at the wake and cried like children and both said it should've been them and meant it.

Roy woke up on the floor of his hotel room. He had brand new skate shoes on but they weren't his. Last he remembered he'd been wearing the dress shoes he'd bought with the suit.

He crawled to his feet and went to the window, surveyed the city. Bottle rocket water towers. All those rooftops, blue-tarped AC units and dead garden plots, gathered at the feet of the skyscrapers. He checked his pockets. His wallet was there but it was empty. Two linty Hydrocodone and a roach wrapped in tinfoil. His suit jacket was wadded up by the door and his phone was in it. He replied to Tony's texts and downed the pills with a Heineken from the minifridge. He drew the blinds and texted Derik and got in the shower. Two more beers when he got out and he was passable. He could eat. Derik was staying at his mom's. Roy didn't know how to get there. Tony was at the door.

Derik didn't fly back with them, nobody could find him, wouldn't answer his phone, and everyone was worried, but he called Roy a week later from some secret celebrity rehab center the swoosh sent him to and said he was OK, getting through it. The shoe company rolled out a special signature model in memoriam. Roy couldn't decide if that was insulting or not. He quit painting DEATH-SAID and DEK8D-SKATES all over everything and rattled out RASHEED LIVES instead.

[22]

M < 55
CA 96118

A FLAT TIRE, CHANGED IN THE ROADSIDE DUST. NO SIGN OF THE militiamen or anyone else since he'd left the highway for the backroads. He thought they'd follow him. He'd waited to be sure. He's in the high country now, cirques and dry lakes, tarns. Mudslides scar the lower hillsides and the mountains above are lunar gray and forest fire black. He wouldn't be surprised if meteors rained down. Hopeless squared. Far away, against the dull sky, turkey vultures spin like burnt paper above a fire.

Scrubbing the grease from his hands with a wad of dead grass, he spots three mangy mule deer moving through the drainage below. The dog starts after them but the man calls him back. He can see their ribs and the knobby bend of their spines, hip bones. The buck carries his small rack with a bowed neck and gets tangled in a mess of dead alders and falls down briefly until he fights his way free. The doe look footsore as they leave the buck behind.

The man shares the last of the salami with the dog. When they finish he snips two more of the staples on the dog's hip and eases them out with his multitool.

"Snitches get stitches," the man says. "Or staples."

The dog sniffs at his injuries and gives them a quick cleaning with his tongue.

They enter city limits, head down, suffering a crosswind, the red sun. Transmission lines and transformers have been removed from the power poles that are still standing. The manhole covers have been stolen and the asphalt is buckled and torn from the steel tracks of crawlers, excavators. The undertaker is gone and he left the front door open but the blinds are closed. He doesn't stop pedaling. The dog lopes alongside. The biomass generator at the mill has been completely dismantled and taken away. Crows and magpies hop and squawk in the city park and he nearly wrecks trying to see what's dead.

The neighbor's security gate, along with a section of the steel fence and posts and concertina wire, has been heaped across the road. Black shapes in the field so he slows but still doesn't see any vehicles or people. Nothing happens quickly on the bike, plenty of time to work through what could be waiting for him at the barricade. He doesn't have an option for going around. He's only a mile from home. Judging by the pinched bricks of asphalt, it was the same tracked machine that had been used in town. They've tagged a few of the posts and the road itself with the word *traitor*, misspelled once, triater.

They've come and gone. Fifty yards down the long dirt driveway a burnt-down-to-the-steel-wheels pickup leans into a bomb crater. Farther, pieces of what appears to be a blasted-apart ATV litters the field, axle and roll cage, steering column, coiled black suspension spring sticking out of the dirt like a spirochete. If there are bodies he can't see them. The man had planned to send a message to the girls with the TNK but they will have taken that along with whatever else they could find. The dog tests the wind and head down goes tentatively toward the neighbor's but the man calls him back.

"We're going home," he says to the dog. "We're not going there."

The dog stops, turns to look back the way they've come, then flinches and dips down with all four legs. A ripping sound tears by the man's ear and the dust jumps in the ditch. A power pole gives up a tangle of creosote splinters. Three shots in quick succession and one of them punches through the trailer fabric with a swack. The dog is already running and the man pedals fast with his head low, directly into the borrow pit and dumps the bike. On his knees, he whistles for the dog. From the ditch they move together into the field and fall into the slit trench, a whole series of which surround the neighbor's house, serpentine as the stream channels in a marsh.

The shooting has stopped. They're in the dirt now, low and safe. The man that dug these trenches said: *Options are what you make of them. Force multipliers are essential.*

He crawls forward, careful of booby traps, searching for markers. The dog keeps behind him.

A shadow darkens his path and he turns with his hands up and waits to be struck or shot but it's a bird, several birds—vultures—slinging here and there across the sun. He can feel his heart beating in the chromium cobalt of his partial denture. At the fence, he lifts the steel grate and slides under and pulls the dog after him.

With his head just high enough to see, he searches for the shooter but doesn't see anyone, knows in advance that he won't, senses the reticle slide onto his face. Nothing to do but run for it.

Out of the trench, they cross the dusty pasture to the neighbor's barn and the man opens the heavy steel door and lets the dog go in first. The door slams loudly behind him. *Turncoat* scrawled in the rust, painted on the wall. The TNK is gone, empty shelves, not a single battery or power cord. The concrete cool of the barn settles his nerves but they aren't staying. The dog raises its head and sniffs the air.

Out the side door, they hide behind the lumber crib and wait. The sun is lost in the haze, pale as a bleach spill, somewhere between noon and dusk. An hour passes and no one comes down the road. The man half-hitches the dog to the crib post.

"I don't want to tie you up but you don't listen."

The man hurries around the corner of the house and stops beside a dusty brick-lined flowerbed with a rusted ornamental harrow as the centerpiece. Sight lines to the road are blocked by the house. No one is about.

The three larger stones and the antique harrow are shoved aside. He brushes away a layer of dirt and digs his fingers beneath the heavy oaken cover and with effort flips it over to reveal the steel hatch hidden beneath. He crawls on top of the wooden lid to give his knees a rest from the hard ground and pebbles. He knocks gently on the hatch for no reason, to hear the sound. Curtains flapping in the broken windows of the house. Nothing else moves. Then the dog is barking and he turns to see and there's a gun in his back.

A man's voice tells him to stand up. He does as he's told. The dog's barking has turned into a howl.

"Don't turn around," the voice says.

"All right. Take it easy. I'm not armed."

"Let's go, make sure your dog stays tied up." He marches the man to the lumber crib and watches as he ties a proper knot, then walks him over to one of the two large propane tanks in the yard and makes him sit down.

"If you think for a minute I was trying to hit you with those shots, you're fooling yourself." He's wearing a two-piece ghillie suit and the composite stock of his Kimber has STT and the three stars and the arrow insignia carved in it. He's twenty-five or thirty years old, black cropped hair and a sparse beard.

"You live up the road," the militiaman says. "I've been to your house, the burnt barn." He glances over his shoulder to the road. "It's like the Bermuda Triangle down here. People come in and don't come back."

"I came back."

"Yeah, where's your family?"

"Gone."

"You buried them," the militiaman offers, pleased with himself.

The man doesn't reply.

"And you went to the lake." He slings his rifle over his shoulder and squats in front of the man. He has a silver wedding band and dirty fingernails. "There were families, women and kids, sleeping in the main house. Did you know that?"

"You want me to say I'm sorry?"

"We're here together," the militiaman says, smiles. "That's all the sorry I need."

The man lowers his head, thinks: *Don't run, you'll just die tired. I'm already tired.*

"You'd think it would've been something as simple as proximity," the militiaman says. "How we found this place. But it wasn't. It was that HK your buddy was carrying. Registered to his wife, but from before they were married. It took us months to track down a marriage certificate. Then she wasn't on the note for the property so we had to dig through more paperwork until we found an address. I'm talking paper files. All the digital files, financial anyway, they all been hacked and blacked, zero-sum game when it comes to tax collection, 'bout time." He blinks and wipes the sweat from his forehead with the back of his hand. "Sweating like a priest in a preschool over here." He leans his rifle against his leg and—"Stay put"—quickly removes the top of his ghillie suit. He ties the arms of the suit around his waist. He's wearing a Dave Matthews Band T-shirt underneath.

"But we got people for that," he says. "People all they do is track fuckers down." He hefts his rifle and with his left hand reaches inside his ghillie suit bottom and produces a data-sat phone and keys in a message. "We'll be having company for dinner. They want to meet you. See what in the hell your buddy has stashed in his hidey hole."

The militiaman trades the phone for a can of Kirkland snoose from his pocket and loads his lip. He spits, offers the can. The man takes it and puts a pinch in his lower lip. Together they look at the bunker hatch across the yard.

"You mind if I stand up?" the man asks. "My legs are gonna cramp if I just sit here."

The militiaman nods yes and takes a step back and watches him stand. "It's like the old army shit, right?" he says. "They'd carry fucking everything, cannons and shit. Bring it along. Have Salvatore and O'Dell and Washington lug it up the hill." The militiaman spits again, taps the snoose can on his rifle butt and puts it back in his pocket. "You know what kind of cannon we use? What kind of food we eat? Whose beer we drink? Fucking yours. We don't carry shit. We commandeer."

The tobacco is twisting his stomach. The man spits, then hooks it with his finger and flips it on the ground. The militiaman turns and studies him.

"What're you going to do with my dog?"

The militiaman shakes his head and takes a moment to carefully wipe a bit of dust from the forestock of his rifle, smiles to himself. "All right. Move your ass. Let's see what we got going in that bunker."

Standing above the hatch, the militiaman takes him by the arm. "You'd tell me if we're about to go boom, wouldn't you?"

The man nods but when the militiaman lifts the handle and they both hear the click, the man drops to his stomach and sprawls on the heavy wooden hatch cover and hangs on.

A shock hits him in the chest and he's lifted a few inches off the ground. With the sound of a cast-iron skillet being dropped on a concrete floor the steel door of the bomb shelter jumps from its hinges and smashes into the militiaman's upper arm and spins him around. The dust swallows them.

The man's fingers are bleeding and it feels like someone is standing on his chest. But he gets to his knees and reaches out and pulls the rifle by the sling from under the militiaman. Through the warning tone ringing in his ears, the dog is barking. The man wants to tell him it's OK, that he's coming, but he doesn't have enough air in his lungs to speak.

He stands on unsteady legs and levels the rifle at the bloody, unconscious militiaman and pulls the trigger but the safety is on or it's jammed and he's fumbling with the action when the militiaman suddenly sits up and screams in pain. His arm is hanging, disjointed, broken from the socket, and arterial blood is pumping steadily from under his shirt. The man finds the safety, fires a reckless shot into the militiaman's chest and he falls to his side and goes quiet.

The dust is clearing. He sits down and cradles the rifle in his lap. He touches his face with the back of his arm and it comes away bloody. He has to move. There are other explosives set to go after the hatch. He knows this because the neighbor told him. He has to move. The dog is running toward him now with the chewed-through rope flagging from his collar. The man holds on to the rope and lets the dog pull him to his feet and to the far side of the barn, and when the charges rigged to the drained propane tanks finally go off, the whole structure sways but doesn't fall.

The neighbor's house is ripped in half and the roof is on fire. Without warning his legs go out. The dog is beside him, leaning on him, shivering, it licks the blood seeping from the man's ear into his beard. With trembling fingers he picks out the largest of the splinters and rocks embedded in his shins and hands but the smaller ones will require some cutting. He leans on the rifle to get to his feet and with the dog at his side walks through the field back to the bike and, with an overwhelming sense of *what the fuck*, continues north toward home.

At his driveway he stops and waves the dog ahead to make sure no one is waiting for them. He unloads four shells from the rifle and wipes them clean and reloads them. The barrel has a ding in it, possibly from the hatch door, but he sights down it and it's straight. The hot wind worries some loose roofing on the house, a nervous, chattering sound, and within the crumpling newspaper racket of the wind there continues the almost angelic ringing sound of permanent hearing loss.

The black smoke from the neighbor's makes a low column that feeds the general haze. The dog circles the house one last time then sits down in the driveway and waits.

The man lays his bike down and with the rifle on his shoulder limps to the ash pit of the barn. When the dog barks the man walks to him and finds the unopened box in the driveway near the truck where he'd dropped it. He slings the rifle on his back and kneels down and picks up the box and holds it to his head. The dog comes close and sniffs at the box and the man drapes his arm over the animal and gives him a kiss.

He stows the box inside one of his panniers, fastens the buckles, gives the whole thing a shake to make sure that it's secure. They each have a drink of water and the man takes a moment to gather his courage.

The dog goes into the house first and nudges his bowl around the kitchen as if he still eats there every day. Broken glass and crumbled drywall, splintered furniture and broken tile. Militia boot prints, a few spots of dried blood if you knew where to look. The photographs that remain have been smashed and stomped on. The man leans against the sink and connects the dots on the hole-punched appliances, stirs the thick dust on the countertop with his finger. He doesn't try the faucet because he knows it won't come on.

He stops in the doorway of their bedroom. The clothes he changed out of are on the bed. He strips and puts them back on. He leaves his suit folded neatly over the bloodstain on the mattress. When he leaves he shuts the front door behind him. The dog walks out toward the gate and the man mounts his bike and follows.

It's well after dark when the militia convoy comes storming through, lights ablaze. They don't slow, and after they pass, the man and the dog climb out of the ditch and move on.

[23]

R<35
CA 93001

HE SKATED ALL DAY FRIDAY WITH HIS OLD PAL PABLO AND some other Portland folks that were in town and that night ended up hooking up with a massage therapist/skate groupie he met at his regular sushi place. On Saturday, after awkwardly supping a wheatgrass-and-blueberry smoothie with the massage therapist—she didn't want his number—Roy rode the Bonny to San Diego to see his mom and stepdad.

The house hadn't changed much, Steve kept a tidy kingdom, fresh paint, luxurious lawn, Japanese maples. They'd weathered economic gloom and boom and were sitting pretty in a paid-for house that they could sell for—Steve ventured in the first few minutes Roy was there, as if on cue—a million, maybe a million five by next year.

They ate roasted chicken and potatoes with a three-bean salad in the oversized dining room at the teak table with the woven placemats and pottery serving dishes that his mom had made when he was little. He didn't know if she still did pottery or what she did with her time. She'd cut her hair short and let the gray take over. Her skin was tan and her nails were painted burgundy. Steve was wearing a baby-blue button-up shirt with Dockers, his uniform. Grecianed hair, a couple of inches of side-burns to let his flock know that he was, in the name of Jesus, still cool and rebellious.

Roy's half sister was supposed to be there too but she was on call. *Yes, she's a doctor*, Roy thought. *You don't have to remind me every time I come here.* When he told them the details of his sponsor-ships and approximately what he was being paid his mom said she was proud of him, but Steve didn't get it and it wasn't long before he started in with his Roy-v.-half-sister-Lisa knife-throwing rou-tine where Steve was the magician, Lisa was his silent and beauti-ful assistant, and Roy was the idiot standing in front of the target.

"Lisa will finish her residency next month," Steve said. "She'll have her pick of where she wants to go. Top of her class. She had a lot to deal with too," Steve lamented, "what with the diabetes and being dyslexic."

"She's a smart one," Roy said.

"Maybe it's the hurdles we face that define us," Steve said.

"Or if we want to jump over them at all," Roy said. "I choose—what'd you call it? Going around?"

"Circumnavigation," his mom said.

"Right," Roy said. "Thanks, Ma."

Steve touched his hands together. "I wonder sometimes what you think about when you're alone with your thoughts."

"Money, cash, hoes," Roy said. Steve smiled lovingly at his wife.

"You're taunting him," his mother said, studying the art deco, frosted-glass-and silver-armed chandelier over the table.

"But every day I pray over him," Steve said. "Every day I pray and I ask God what will happen if he ever has children of his own. How will he act then?"

"Just like you, chief," Roy said. "King of my castle."

Steve's faux bonhomie went suddenly dark. "You're a lowlife is what it is. Look at you. You're a dirtbag."

"Only my friends get to call me that," Roy said, happy with how things were going.

"He's saying that you aren't his friend," his mom said to her husband.

"Steve isn't anybody's friend," Roy said. "Maybe Jesus will be his friend." His mom shrugged, rolled her eyes, and pulled out another eyebrow hair.

"He makes excuses," Steve said, holding a palm up to his wife, "but by my lights his life is a total waste."

"OK," Roy said. "Let's sum up the life of Steve." He leaned in and spoke quietly, something that had always stopped Steve from interrupting. "You went from being a nickel-bag weed dealer to passing the real estate exam—on the third try—to court-ordered rehab to weaseling your way into being the co-pastor/co-weasel of what, low and behold, became a money-hungry megachurch. Is that about right?"

"You have no idea what I've been through," Steve said.

"And the last bit," Roy said, "what I like to think of as the paving of the charitable path, paid off this house and branded your Botox ass with that smug little shit eater that you evangelist assholes like so much. As if real estate prices and ocean breezes were the equals of salvation and brotherly love. As if bullshit was in fact steak and eggs." He pointed at his plate. "Or chicken and potatoes, as the case may be."

Roy's mom got up from the table, raised her hands in silent exclamation, and went into the kitchen.

"Fine, I won't try and help," Steve said. "I won't lift a finger. It's your soul."

"Amen," Roy said, and downed his beer. With a smile, he gathered his mom's plate on top of his own and took them into the kitchen. He grabbed a drumstick from the casserole dish on the stove and found his mom on the back porch having a cigarette. He chucked his chicken bone over the fence into the neighbor's yard, wiped his hands on Steve's overwatered lawn, and gave his mom a hug. When she asked goodheartedly about grandkids, Roy bummed a drag off her smoke and gave her a hell-no look. Steve had shut himself in the den to work on tomorrow's sermon/watch porn and didn't show himself again. Roy apologized to his mom, gave her a hug goodbye, and rode out.

THE NEXT WEEKEND HE WAS INVITED TO A SKATE-FILM PREMIERE in LA. He recognized only a few of the heads in it, the rest were next-generation groms, raised in perfect concrete skateparks, some of which he'd helped build. Assholes used to take time out of their days to pull their cars over and kick the shit out of skateboarders. You used to have to know how to fight or at least take a punch. Now the kids not only had permission, they were encouraged. Sure, OK, the kids ripped, no debate there, but they were hatchery fish with weakened DNA, corrupted by their lack of corruption. They weren't wild. What kind of American boy grows into a man without running from the cops or getting attacked by a homeless person? How could they learn about the perils of freedom without consequences? *How did I get so old and when was the last time I went skating just to skate, no filmer?* The credits rolled and he slunk out the side door.

He met up with Yano and Derik afterward in the hotel bar where Tony had booked their rooms. Yano fished an envelope out of his jacket and handed it to Roy.

"What's this?" Roy said.

"Title to my bike," Yano said. "It's still in the garage, right?"

"Yeah. I haven't touched it," Roy said. "I mean I've started it a few times but I haven't taken it out."

"It's yours."

"Man, you should keep it."

"I don't want it."

"I'll take care of it. I love that bike."

"Don't wreck it," Yano said. "And know that I don't give a shit about the bike."

"I won't wreck, man." He knocked on his own head and Derik laughed, gave a sideways grin.

"You're a fuckin' dork, Bingham," he said.

"I know," Roy said. "But I'm old so it's endearing."

"Proud a that shit now," Derik said.

"There's no fighting it," Roy said.

Derik had been out of rehab for two weeks, but it obviously didn't take because he was lapping Roy and Yano on beers. No hard liquor though, which was a step in the right direction. He said he'd been editing old footage to make a biopic about Rasheed. They talked about going skating but didn't make any solid plans.

After they left, Roy got his room key and went to his room and sat on the bed for a while, looked out the window at the traffic below. He flipped the key onto the bed and rode home.

Waiting in his mailbox was a letter from Karen Oronski. His mom had forwarded it to him. He examined the handwriting on the envelope. He picked at the seal. He smelled the flap where she'd licked it—unless it was one of those peel-and-stick jobs—but he didn't open it. The blood was pumping in his ears. Karen existed in a dimension separate from the one he had been occupying since he left her. In some part of his forever-juvenile brain he felt that if he opened the letter his whole world would suck into a black hole and he would disappear. He slid the envelope into the inner pocket of his leather jacket and zipped it in.

Tony called the next day and asked if he wanted to skate some shitty New Mexican death pool for an ad shoot, and Roy said sure, why not, because he wanted the distraction. He changed the oil and filter in Yano's CB, lubed the chain, changed the plugs, and replaced the pod filters. After he put some air in the tires, with grease-blacked hands, he strapped his board to the seat.

The two Red Bulls he got for breakfast made him twitchy. Traffic was muck. He fought his way out. He rode it like he stole it. He rode it like he didn't give a shit about dying and it made him feel like he would never die.

He sweated out the hottest part of the afternoon in Barstow, parked at a plastic table under an umbrella beside a taco truck in a dirt lot, and chased his four carne asadas with a couple of gas station tall boys. Train noise crushed car noise, replaced by jet noise, quieter then. What a shit hole. What. A. Shit. Hole.

Down the road, back on the bike, he checked out some taran- tulas and a roadkill rattler, watched the sunset paint the bluffs. He ventured that he could do this, motor the west, for the rest of his days. He envisioned a trailer park. He would die out here, riddled with melanoma, a failed liver, and a blue heeler with a red bandana for a collar—his only friend, a dog that bites. He missed Rasheed. He didn't want to die. The desert wanted him to die. But Karen's—still unopened—letter was like a golden ticket in his pocket, a get-out-of-jail-free card. Die alone in the desert, or open the letter.

The motel clerk passed him a greasy six-inch square of ply- wood. He thought for a moment that it was a new form of room key, like there was some digital fob thing encased in the wood that could release the lock. He thought, *This shit is going too far.* But the clerk must've read the confusion on his face and told him to put the wood under his kickstand so it didn't melt into the blacktop and fall over. Then she gave him a couple of shop rags so he wouldn't use the towels from the room.

"C'mon, I'm not that much of a trashball," he said, but he probably was.

The deadbolt wouldn't lock properly and they'd lied about the HBO but he didn't care. He bought a six-pack at the gas station next door and drank it while listening to baseball on TV and not opening Karen's letter, which as it turned out took him most of the night.

Tony texted him directions and Roy plugged in his head- phones so he could listen to Google Maps tell him where to go. He followed instructions, if not the speed limit, and felt like a secret agent.

The sponsors provided coolers of beer and strippers/models for the photo shoot. He skated with the boys and groped the models and bled and did burnouts on the deck with his motorcycle. It was a party and the girls were pretending to be into him or they were into him but his thoughts were now with Karen.

So without telling Tony or anyone else that he was leaving, he hopped on the CB and rode into the sunset with a stupid grin on his face, his head working double duty with a monologue about why and why not to read Karen's letter. He could swerve eight feet to the left and get a face full of Peterbilt, or eight feet to the right and launch the mesa, pick his exit, go big, two hundred feet to a rock pile, a one-way no-chance Evel Knievel.

He was going fast now, passed two semis blind on an uphill, hit triple digits at the crest and the wind caught him broadside and tipped him just enough and he had a moment of wobble that made his blood go cold. Tank slapper, they called them. High side. Who died? he imagined the cop asking him when he got pulled over, standing over his twisted corpse.

He dropped a gear and swooped into a long corner, taunting the red in the tach. He was low enough to drag peg and the suspension had been rebuilt but it was still as old as he was and the bike porpoised at the apex but he was used to that too. He felt that nothing could surprise him but he also knew the danger in that kind of thinking.

He saw the snake for about as long as it took him to think: I see the snake, and then he ran over it, tunk tunk, like a garden hose. He couldn't see it in his mirror. He wasn't stopping. *Look where you want to go, not where you don't want to go.* Motorcycle wisdom. *Don't look at the snake.* He felt that Rasheed was with him and then he wasn't. He clicked into fifth and rolled the bike wide open, felt the music of the inline four find its harmonies. He did his best thinking on a motorcycle. He also did his best non-thinking.

At dusk he topped the tank and wandered across the lot to some blistered desert roadhouse on the banks of the Gila River and before he'd even had time to get properly buzzed he'd gotten stomped and had his motorcycle stolen.

"Apparently, there are real bikers," the cop said to him in the ER as he was being stitched up. "And then there are guys like you. Bad timing. Wrong town, wrong bar, wrong bike. Wrong outfit. Do they call it an outfit?"

Roy didn't bother with a response.

The cop was young and capital-N Native, ex-military judging by the USMC tattoo on his forearm. "We have some suspects, but you'll have to ID them. I mean, there's footage from the gas station across the street but you can't really see any faces but yours. Can't even see them make off with your bike."

"I just want my bike, man," Roy said. "I don't want to press charges."

The cop nodded, like, good idea. "We won't find your bike. It's gone. Did you have anything with the bike, like saddlebags or anything?"

"No. I was traveling light. Just the bike." He wasn't about to say that he had a dopp kit under his seat with the toolkit and a skateboard on the back.

"Do you have insurance?"

"Liability." He didn't have insurance.

"Well, there you go."

The doctor finished tying the knot on his stitches and snipped it. "You're all done."

After that, the letter from Karen was the only thing he had. They'd taken his wallet and his phone. Another tooth gone, broken nose, fourteen stitches. He had a picket-fence thing going now, he'd have to see a dentist and get some falsies. Old age falls on you like snow from a roof.

Tony wired him money and FedEx–ed him a phone and a charger. He stayed in the Desert Chalet motel, shaken, hurting, wary to move. Someone was supposed to drop off a rental car for him but they were fucking around. New Mexico was fucking around. New Mexico couldn't be serious. He sent the desk clerk, a skater kid who recognized Roy, for food and beer. At one point he went outside and drank ice-cold Tecates by the pool but he couldn't go swimming because of the stitches, not to mention the wonky pain in his ribs made it so he couldn't breathe deeply. His tongue was raw from squirming around in the hole where his tooth had been. He was ashamed. Ashamed that he couldn't defend himself, ashamed that he was prey when all this time he'd thought of himself as, if not a predator, definitely not somebody to fuck with. Wrong and wrong again.

Tony texted that the video from the gas station had gone viral. Roy opened the attachment and watched himself backing away from four men with his hands raised, helmet in his right, and as the first guy came at him he swung at the last second and brained the guy with his helmet and the guy fell down but the other three were on him in an instant and he swung a few times but mostly missed and his helmet was taken away and tossed and they just beat the shit out of him until he was wadded up in the dirt. He watched them take his wallet and shove him underneath a semitrailer, before helping their buddy to his feet and walking out of the frame.

"Sick intro footage, couldn't be better," Tony said happily, when Roy finally answered his phone. "I'm sending you a new version of the video. Check out the side of the truck. Seriously, man, Roy Bingham v. the fucking world. *Epic* is too small a word. You're my champ. The people's champ."

"I gotta go." Roy hung up and watched the new version of the video. The logo on the side of the truck had been altered digitally from whatever it had been—*Mayflower* or whatever—to the shoe-company logo. After the fifth time through he started to get used to it and take a bit of pride in the one solid shot he'd gotten off. At least he'd fought back.

"They stole my bike," Roy texted Tony. "Yano gave me that bike."

"We'll buy you a new one. Two."

"Is there video of me waking up?"

Five minutes later, "C attached. UR like honey badger! Will edit down time to add Lazarus to the end. He lives! Cheers."

The complete clip was seven and a half minutes long. The fight section from beginning to end took all of twenty-two seconds. Lights swept over the tractor trailer, no logo on the side, a plain white truck. Another semi pulled through and blocked the shot for a minute or less and kept going. Nothing moved but shadows. Roy tried to remember what he'd read about being knocked out cold, severe concussions, long-term damage, depression and anger, substance abuse problems. At four minutes, forty-three seconds Roy's leg moved and he rolled to his stomach and crawled out from under the trailer. It took him a few tries to get to his feet and a minute or so to get steady enough to walk.

His face was black from the blood coming from his scalp and his cheek, his mouth, and his hair was loose from its tie and all over the place. His eyes were that crazy night-vision green, and with his fists hanging at his sides he looked insane. He was scanning the parking lot for his bike, but to the lay viewer it probably seemed like he was looking for another fight. He spat a mouthful of blood into the dirt, then bent down and picked something from the wet spot. A tooth. And that was where Tony or whoever cut it, him standing there peering at the tooth in his bloody hand.

Afterward he'd gone back inside the bar and the bartender had called him an ambulance. She poured him a beer and gave him a bar towel to clean up with and a shot glass to put his tooth in.

"Who the fuck were those guys?" he'd asked her. He'd remembered their motorcycle jackets. "What the fuck is a Bandido?"

"I didn't see anybody," the bartender had said. She was in her fifties maybe sixties. Didn't look like she'd made the best decisions in her life but she was apparently wise enough not to make another bad one.

"I didn't say a word to them," Roy said, whining a little. "I didn't say a word to anybody."

She took the bloody towel in her hand, not worried about the blood, and passed him a fresh one. "Maybe they were offended by your silence."

"How far is it to walk to the hospital?"

"Too far for you. Ambulance won't take but a minute. My ex-son-in-law will be driving it. He's an idiot. I bet he'll let you play with the lights."

He drank the beer even though some part of him knew that he shouldn't be drinking after he'd been knocked out.

The ambulance driver came in and said, "Hi, Ma," to the bartender and Roy dumped the tooth from the shot glass into his hand and shoved it in his pocket and followed him out to his rig.

He opened the bay doors and had Roy sit down on the bumper while he rooted around in the back. He returned and opened a thick compress and pushed it roughly to Roy's head wound and told him to hold it there, then he took his blood pressure and shined a penlight in his eyes. "You pass," he said, and led Roy to the passenger door and opened it for him and motioned him inside.

"You can sit in the front of the bus with me tonight so's you don't dirty up the back." The EMT had to help him into his seat.

"Thanks," Roy said.

HE'D FORGOTTEN ABOUT HANDWRITING. ONLY HIS GRANDMOTHER had sent him handwritten letters and they'd been more or less indecipherable, not worth Roy's effort. He'd shake out the pages looking for the check, then chuck it. He was surprised at the joy it brought him to see where Karen's wrist or the edge of her hand had smudged the ink, or where she'd crossed out a misspelling, then mauled it with further changes and iterations until nobody outside of a forensic lab could say she didn't spell it right somewhere in there. They'd been apart for most of a decade but her voice rose clearly from the page, maybe more than it would have through a phone, and he couldn't even begin to understand why.

He'd half-expected to read that he had a child and that she, it would have to be a she, was in grade school now, but that wasn't the case. Karen was where he'd left her, in her old house. She said Mace had come while she was in Reno and left his truck and five thousand dollars in an envelope with his keys and a signed title. He'd taken his guns and most of his stuff from the basement, kind of trashed the place, left in a hurry. The mystery of Mace, still crazy. Maybe he'd joined a monastery. She'd used the money that Mace had left, along with the money from the sale of his truck—she'd driven it for a while first—to open a drive-thru coffee stand like the one she'd worked in on Stark. She had two employees now and was thinking about opening another location just for weekend traffic. Through Aaron and April she'd met people, made new friends. At first she'd thought Roy would come back.

She'd been married but her husband, Aaron Simmonds's brother-in-law, April's brother, had died in an accident. He had been a truck driver for FedEx and his truck had gone off the road and he'd been killed. Not instantly, he was in the hospital for two weeks before she and April pulled the plug. They had a kid, Wiley.

Her sadness spilled into his self-pity and made him feel so small that for a moment he was overwhelmed with emotion. He could still hear Toots and the Maytals—*I want you to know that I am the man who fights for the right, not for the wrong. Helping the weak against the strong*—playing in the van when the van had died.

He opened another beer and let the suds work into the holes where his teeth used to be. Mouth breathing, he caressed his worthless broken nose.

He'd gotten in the habit of looking for Karen in every woman he saw. Onto every woman he got together with, he'd not so subtly superimpose the recollected parts of her. Results were mixed and then they were bad—just bad, not good. You couldn't change a person, a woman, you couldn't will them into something they weren't. But wasn't that what people did, attempt to reshape others, along with everything else, to their will? Or died trying. Roy had often wasted months searching for the depth, the mystery, in whatever woman he was dating, looking for their heart, and then, not liking what he found, not finding Karen, he usually split quietly or, if he was bored, he'd set the charge and stand back, wait for the boom. Whatever worked. There wasn't anything *about* most people. Most people were filler. Karen wasn't. This part of him, this emotional drag, was unique in that he couldn't destroy it, couldn't unhitch it. No matter how he tried.

[24]

R<25
NV 89501, CA 96118

AFTER HE'D LEFT THE PARKING GARAGE IN RENO AND TAKEN the cab to the bus station—after Karen had hung up on him—he called his pal Yuri in Oakland and found out from Yuri's girlfriend, Sue, that their other friend Neko was out of town and wouldn't be back until next week. They had an extra room, though, and they would let Roy and Karen borrow their car if he wanted.

"I'm by myself," Roy said.

"Why?" Sue said.

"It just happened."

He could practically hear Sue shaking her head and glaring at him. "I can't believe you." She passed the phone to Yuri.

"You got my guitar?" Yuri said.

"No, man. Fuck. I forgot about that. I don't have it."

"Where is it?"

"You know where it is. It's in the same place as it was before."

"Unless someone bought it."

"Unless someone bought it."

"You told me you'd get it back."

"C'mon, man."

"Asshole. Pawned my guitar. Not just a guitar, a Gibson L6S. You're an asshole."

"Listen," Roy said, "I can hear you going Yeltsin on me so I know you're pissed and I'm sorry. I'm really, really sorry."

"You fuck," Yuri yelled, sounding very much like someone impersonating a crazy Russian. "You fucking turdhammer, you selfish lowdown sack of dead cats."

"Take it easy. I've had enough already without getting it from you."

"You've had enough?" Yuri's voice doubled in volume. *Here we go*, Roy thought. "You're like Kurtz going upriver, working for the government scum and wagging your ass around the campfire and high-fiving the fucking golden-hearted quote un-quote savages."

"What does that even mean?" Roy said.

"It means you're a double-dealing son of a bitch. It means, who the fuck are you, man? Are you my friend or are you just some shitbag?"

"OK, I'm a shitbag and I'm your friend. I'm sorry."

"Yeah, OK." Yuri cooled off quickly, always had. "You know, we both read the same books but apparently I'm the only one that can retain information."

"Or a girlfriend," Roy said.

"You don't even know," Yuri said. "You don't even know how fucked you are. You might as well have a brain tumor. Cancer of the ass. You without Karen is like what's the point?"

Roy told him basically what had happened: the van, Aaron, Reno. Yuri softened his tone.

"Sue's pregnant," he said.

"Oh shit," Roy said. "What're you gonna do?"

"What'd you think? We want kids, man. We planned it."

"Cool. That's cool. I didn't know that, you know, you guys were doing that already. I thought you'd wait or whatever."

"OK, so we kind of planned it. We figure if not now, when."

"Yeah."

"Anyway, she isn't showing yet. I haven't told a soul but Neko. Sue told her sister, but that's it, so if blabbing happens, I'll know it was you."

"I won't say a word."

"Things are gonna change soon," Yuri said, "but when you get here we can find something to do. There's a new indoor park outside Sacramento, we could meet there, or since you already bought your ticket you could ride the dog all the way in and we could make dinner at home and maybe go watch some crappy band or something."

"OK." Roy didn't care. He didn't have any place else to go.

Yuri was working full-time as a plumber's apprentice and going to night school three nights a week. All of it sounded like a nightmare to Roy, but he wasn't about to say it. Yuri and Neko were part of the old Death Said/DEK8D crew, Roy's best friends, and they had the tattoos, not to mention the scars, to prove it. If they were doing something, he'd back them.

Roy turned off his phone and checked the bus schedule one last time. With his jean jacket for a pillow he tried to sleep. Too paranoid. He looped the shoulder strap of his pack around his ankle so no one would walk off with it. The Reno teen spawn lurking at the south entry had clocked him, noted his position. They'd be over if he stayed awake. They wouldn't be able to help themselves. *Sup*, they'd say to each other. *Sup*, with their arms out like they might curtsy, gangster stepping and picking their zits, hauling saggy pants up with their undersized pale hands. An overweight cop in a tan polyester getup and a cowboy hat was watching the door crowders. Something would happen. *Sup, juggalo. Sup, dawg.* Roy wanted to watch it happen but he wanted sleep more. He wanted the fat cop to open fire. If everybody in the bus station died, he wouldn't care. The world wouldn't care.

The speakers were blown on the PA and every time there was an announcement Roy's head throbbed.

A man in a blue tracksuit was standing over him, listing slightly from the weight of a bulky leather satchel. When their eyes met, Mace set down the bag and gave Roy a strange look.

"You're not here to meet me, are you?" Mace was confused or angry, his facial expressions switched back and forth like a weak signal on the radio station being overtaken by a stronger one. "Where's Karen?"

"What are you doing here?" Roy was on his feet, the usual amalgamation of old hip and knee injuries needling under his weight.

"Where's she? Where's Karen?"

"She's gone. She—we split, man. I'm here by myself."

"If you hurt her, I'm gonna crack your fuckin' skull." He smiled and his lip was split and oozing pink blood and it made Roy's stomach ache.

"So, separately, solo, where are you going now?" Mace said.

"Karen writes me and says you two are staying with me through Christmas and now you're gone?"

"I'm leaving. She's staying. I give no shits about Christmas. Not one." Roy felt like he should be absolved of explaining things to Mace. "You bailed as soon as we walked through the door," Roy said.

"I had plans that couldn't wait. You," he smacked Roy in the chest with the back of his hand, "you're coming back with me." His eyes went dark and evil and Roy settled onto his heels and waited but nothing happened.

"I need to go," Roy said. Just stick to the plan, he told himself.

Mace ran a hand through his stubbly gray hair and again looked around the bus station. "You drove out here. Where's that shitty van?"

"We told you, it broke down."

"You drove all the way out here in your shitty van so you could turn around and ride the dog home?" Mace phrased it like a question but it wasn't. The bones, tendons, and muscle of what he was saying was that Roy was not leaving. It wasn't going to happen.

"I didn't plan this, man," Roy said. "I'm not going home. I don't have a home to go back to." All he had to do was get on the bus and everything would be fine.

"I had some things to take care of," Mace said. "My truck is parked here." He pointed toward the exit. The ICP kooks had departed. The path was clear. "You know how it goes, Caltrans cams, parole. Listen, I busted my ass so I could get back up here to you guys. Did in one day what should've taken three." Mace gave Roy his most solemn nod.

"I don't know what you get up to, man," Roy said. "I don't care."

"You wanna know," Mace said. "Look at you." He placed his hand on Roy's shoulder, a too-touchy convict. "Fighters, you know, boxers, the great ones, they don't win by punching, they win by thinking, by making adjustments on the fly."

"I'm not fighting anybody."

"Everybody's fighting somebody, homeboy," Mace said. "Even you, which means you gotta be elastic. You've gotta be adaptable. It's where the real strength comes from."

Roy wanted to sit down and take his shoes off because wearing the same socks and shoes while he slept and sweated and walked around always gave him itchy feet. He wanted to scratch his arches until his footskin began to shed and lodge under his fingernails. He wanted to pull his toes until they popped. He wanted to live in motel rooms forever after or at least for a week or so. He wanted to walk away from Mace and not look back, but none of these things happened. Instead he put on his jacket and shoved his hands in his pockets. He wasn't sure if he was angry or not, he felt that he should be, but in some ways he felt relieved. If he went with Mace, he was off the hook. He already missed Karen and if he missed her this much now, imagine how much worse it was going to get.

He turned and hoisted his bag and walked toward the parking lot and a few moments later felt Mace's hand on the back of his neck and it sent a shock through his body.

Roy twisted loose of Mace's hand. "You know, she was dying to see you. She hauled my ass out here and we fought about it. We fought until I was at the bus station." It felt good to bicker and make Mace feel bad and he wanted to hang on to it because behind it, his guilt about Karen was swelling. He'd left her. He'd walked off and left her with no one, like he said he would never do. The years and failures had eaten away at what he was able to accept but this was too much. She deserved better. She deserved a hell of a lot more than a parking garage in Reno.

"It hasn't been easy between us," Mace was saying. "You out of everybody should understand. She has these standards that I can't always live up to." He held his hand up in the air. "High fucking standards."

"No, she just has standards. You and me are the fucked-up ones, not her." Roy looked at Mace. "I thought I was going to Oakland."

"No, you're not. You're coming with me. We're gonna fix this."

Poverty-class holiday travelers walked by with determination, not leisurely but late, hauling their garbage-bag luggage and herding their children. Mace pointed to where he was parked and Roy followed.

At Moody's garage Roy was informed that the van had died due to a faulty relay. The overweight mechanic said it took him five minutes to find and repair the problem and the part cost twelve bucks. Roy gave him his last twenty. When he backed it out of the garage, he waved Mace off, like go home. I got it.

The smell of the van, the silence imposed by Karen's absence, the sensory blankness of her not being with him, of nobody being there at all, upset Roy to the point that he couldn't listen to music. Music felt like a betrayal. He drove with the window down, sipped from some old coffee he found in the cupholder and was saddened when it tasted like lipstick.

He looked in the rearview and Mace was swerving along

behind him. At the house Mace parked him in and Roy wasn't buying that he'd done it by accident. He waved to Mace when he walked by but stayed in the van. If Karen was inside, she could wait, or let her come to him. He wasn't ready to grovel. He climbed in the back and took off his shoes and socks and squirmed into a sleeping bag and eventually went to sleep.

When he woke the sun was low and it was freezing in the van. The windows were fogged and it was quiet. He watched his breath plume. He was shivering. He fished around beside the wheel well until he found a beer and slugged it down in three slushy headache drinks, then pulled on fresh socks and tied on his shoes and opened the slider and pissed in the virgin yard of snow.

Karen was not there. Nothing had changed since they'd left. He went back outside and hauled all of Karen's things inside and put them in her room, arranged them the way she would've. He put some of his stuff there too, but not all of it, nothing important. He needed to make a statement that he was willing but not that he was incapable of leaving.

He didn't see Mace anywhere so he made a box of mac and cheese but with no milk or butter he ended up pitching it in the trash. When the furnace turned off he heard a new noise. He followed it to the basement and found Mace lifting weights under a bare bulb.

"Did you find her yet?"

"No." Roy went to the workbench and looked over the gun parts and lubricants and tools. He pulled the handle on a small gun safe but it was locked.

"Nothing in there for you." Mace slipped the collars onto the weight bar and then watched as Roy expertly assembled the Springfield .40 on the bench.

"My stepdad has the same pistol," Roy said.

"Did he teach you to shoot it?"

"You can learn a lot from an idiot." He worked the slide a few times and took it down again.

"I'm listening," Mace said.

"Ex-cop Aaron said you're not even supposed to have one gun, let alone a whole safe full of them," Roy said.

"If nobody had what they weren't supposed to have, nobody would have anything."

"Really? Well, Confucius say he who goes to bed with itchy butt wakes with pink eye. Sun Fuckin Tzu."

Mace counted under his breath through his push presses and when he'd finished dropped to his back on the mat and knocked out twenty-five speedy sit-ups. Back on his feet he used a chain to dangle a twenty-pound plate from his weight belt and with knees bent so his feet wouldn't touch the floor went through a pull-up and dip routine on the bars he'd set up.

"What the fuck are you doing all this for?" Roy asked.

"I'm getting older. I need to keep up my muscle mass. I have to." He unhooked the plate from his belt and pitched the hook and chain into the corner and put the plate back on the rack. He loaded the bar resting on the cage with more weight than Roy thought was wise and ducked under it, shrugged it onto his back. He took a few careful steps forward and steadied his eyes on Roy's. "A man has to be capable." The veins stood out on his neck and on his forehead as he dropped, nearly touched his ass to the floor, and lifted the weight back up. His Rocky II sweat suit was soaked with sweat. *Get up cuz Mickey loves ya! Yer a bum, Rock.* Mace did the last five reps quickly, measured his steps backward into the cage, and set the bar down.

He came out of the cage and sat down on the mat to stretch, grabbed his toes, dipped his head. "We have to do something, homeboy. We all do. We can't wait for things to come to us. You'll see." He fixed Roy with a heavy stare. "You're waiting for her to show up here, is that it?"

"You're here. Her stuff is here. This is her house."

Mace got to his feet and cracked his neck left and then right, as if he were about to get in the ring. "I believe there are types of men," he said, pointing at Roy. "You're a germinal type, like a sprout that hasn't been hardened off yet. I'm trying to save you that pain. I'm telling you it's better if she lets you down than if you let her down. It's better for you. You can build on it if it's her fault but not if it's yours. You'll be living in quicksand if you leave her, sinking all the time."

"Don't worry about it," he said. "She'll come back here. We can talk then. We'll figure something out."

Mace caught him by the hood of his sweatshirt and slammed him against the wall face-first. "I'm not asking anymore, home-boy." Roy didn't struggle, he was terrified, too scared to fight back. Then Mace let him go, unwadded his hood for him, and gave him a pat on the back. "My wallet is on my dresser. Take a hundred. Go and find her. You'd better make an occasion of it. Reparations. Don't come back here without her."

Roy had to move Mace's truck to get Carl out of the drive-way. The snow had started again. He tried Karen's phone, dreading that she might actually answer, but now it was dead, voice mail automatic. She was somewhere. The laws of physics required that she had to be somewhere. But, and this is what had him looking at the horizon, *she might be just where she needs to be, and now I'm in the van. I'm on the road with a hundred bucks in my pocket.* The fish has spit out the hook, but Mace was right. He had a responsibility. He owed her.

He went to the tiny public library and used their ancient computer to find Aaron's business address on the yellow pages site. The street was a block off the highway, sad houses with mismatched fencing and junk cars buried in snowbanks. He parked the van behind April's broken-windowed car, a garbage bag taped over the hole. The box van was in the back of the house, parked beside a detached garage with a welded stick-figure motorcycle and rider mounted on the gable. The problem with searching was that you might find what you were looking for.

He called her phone again but it was still off. He left the van running and went and knocked on the door. He waited. He watched Carl spew exhaust and he looked healthy, jackrabbit strong, ready to travel. Great set of tires. No one answered and Roy was relieved. He walked back to Carl and climbed in and drove away. He'd never thought he could lose her like this, actually lose her because he couldn't find her, or worse, that he'd quit looking altogether.

[25]

R<35
AZ 85333

FIRST THING IN THE MORNING HIS PHONE LIT UP WITH A TEXT from Tony telling him that the video of his beating had made the national news. Getting out of bed took time and the pain was significant. He was afraid of going to the bathroom. His face was stiff and swollen and his stitches were oozing. He dialed the front desk and asked Jimmy to bring him some decent coffee, food.

He spent the day watching TV and sleeping. He dreamed of Karen and took it as an omen.

In the evening, there was a knock on the door and Roy stood up and opened it, figuring it was Jimmy, but it was two of the guys that had rolled him instead. Roy went to slam the door in their faces but they pushed their way in.

"Ain't here to thump on you," the shorter one said.

"I didn't tell the cops anything," Roy said, feeling like he was playing a part in a movie.

The tall one was in the minifridge and he pulled three beers and put them on the table. "Sit," he said.

Roy sat down with his back to the wall. The tall man tossed Roy's wallet and his phone on the table and then sat across from him. The short man stayed standing. They both wore flannel shirts and Dickies and the shorter one was wearing Rasheed's signature shoe. They were older than he thought they were when he met them, but they weren't much older than him.

"Where's my bike?" Roy said, checking his wallet and finding his cash and cards intact.

"Out front." The tall man held out his beer and Roy lifted his own, like cheers. "My name's Smith and that's Jones."

"Like the song," Roy said. "'Smith and Jones Forever.'"

"I don't know that one," said the big guy.

"Silver Jews."

"What?" said the smaller man.

"That's who sings it," Roy said. "The song. My bike's really out there?"

"We regret any inconvenience," said Jones, a crooked smile.

"You guys stomped me and kicked me under a truck," Roy said.

"You gave our buddy an orbital fracture when you hit him with your helmet," said Smith.

Roy couldn't help it, he smiled. "I told the cops I wasn't pressing charges but they don't seem to care since that video is all over the place. I'm guessing you've seen it by now."

"Yeah," said Jones.

"That's the thing," said Smith. "We didn't know who you were."

"I'm not the governor's nephew or something," Roy said. "I don't matter one way or another."

"I used to skate," Jones said. "I probably wouldn't a rolled you if I'd known who you were."

"My board was on my bike," Roy said.

"You caught us at the end of a three-day bender," said Jones. "Nothing was making much sense for me at that point. Jap bike, punk ass. All I saw."

"Me too," said Smith. "Anyway, your bike's out there. I kept your board though, figured you could get another. They just give 'em to you."

"Sure."

"No hard feelings." Smith stood and held out his hand and Roy stood and shook it, then shook Jones's.

When he was alone in the room, he caught himself smiling in the mirror and did a double take on his busted face and quit smiling and sat back down. *I used to skate too*, he thought. *How many times do you hear that?* How many times had some crazy bastard in a gas station parking lot or in a bar told him that he used to skate with so-and-so at some pool somewhere and maybe he'd been there and sometimes he had.

The key was in the CB and it fired right up. He didn't see any scratches. They'd burned through a half tank of fuel but they'd welded their logo, a silver-dollar-sized badge, onto his frame. He left it idling and returned to the room and grabbed his wallet and both phones, his trusted helmet. When he looked back, the door of the hotel room was wide open and the lights were on.

HE RODE SLOWLY THROUGH LOYALTON BUT DIDN'T STOP. HIS BODY ached. He was scared to get off the bike. He was pretty sure he had bugs stuck in his stitches. A few people waved and he waved back. There was a new grocery store and the downtown blocks had been refinished and there were two competing real estate offices side by side, an art gallery, a T-shirt shop, a deli. *Welcome to Jefferson*, a billboard said. *Coming soon. The 51st State.* He didn't know what the hell that meant and he didn't remember the place being so hoedown touristy but then again he didn't trust his memory as much as he used to. Rolled the last stop sign and with a twist of the throttle the CB pulled smoothly, front tire off the ground a couple of inches, as if it were hungry.

The barn was painted bright red. He could see it from the road and at first he thought he must have the wrong place because there wasn't a barn and then the house was different too and he was sure he was lost. He stopped at the side of the road and killed the motor.

The barn's foundation was so new that around it there was just backfill and nothing had started to grow yet. Roy had only seen barns falling down. He didn't know they were still building new ones. The house was maybe remodeled or new, but the driveway was the same, the trees, the dogleg bend. Open fields, the nearest neighbor was maybe a mile back. He'd never noticed how truly country this place was. Hayfields for as far as he could see. He listened to a sandhill crane pair croak through a call-and-response routine and finally spotted them on the rise across the road moving through the hayfield. He fired up the bike and turned down the lane standing on the pegs.

Parked, with his helmet off, he could smell the rankness of the goats. He stood next to his bike and took it in. The house was a bungalow with a wraparound porch, light blue paint and white trim, a swing set, and a large, lush garden with raised beds and a fence like a penitentiary keeping the goats out. He watched as they came up from the field, a dozen or more white goats, walking leisurely along the fence line, jerking their heads and testing the air.

When he looked again, Karen was on the porch. Her dark hair was long and held back from her face in a braid, but otherwise she looked much the same, maybe a little thicker in the hips but she'd always had curves. She had on a faded black *Disintegration* shirt with a blurry Robert Smith on it, black jeans tucked into rubber boots. She wasn't alone, there was a child with her, a little girl, with dark hair to match, in a blue-and-green striped sundress.

Roy set his helmet on his seat and walked to the bottom of the stairs. The child was watching him, half-hidden behind her mother's legs. Karen looked more annoyed than surprised. He was waiting for her to say something. She put her hand on the child's shoulder and guided her down the stairs.

"You aren't Wiley, are you?" he said.

The child nodded and ducked a little further behind her mother.

"I'm Roy." He was squatted down now, level with the little girl, and watched as her eyes found the stitches on his face.

"What happened?" Wiley asked.

"I fell down," Roy said. "I fall down a lot."

"Why?"

"I don't know. Somehow I just can't avoid it."

"Are you Mama's friend?"

"That's right," Roy said. "I'm a friend of your mom's."

"This is a big surprise," Karen said.

"You look great," Roy said.

"Don't start with a lie." She gave him a hug but she kept her distance and stepped away quickly. "I never thought I'd see the day when my hair was the same length as yours," she said.

"I was going for Iggy."

"You're no Iggy."

"Yeah, probably not," Roy said. "Wiley, do you like motorcycles?"

"She does not like motorcycles."

"I do, Mama. I do like motorcycles."

"You do? Well, you better come over here and have a look at mine. Maybe you could sit on the seat for me and make sure everything's OK. You could do that for me, couldn't you?" He held out his hand and the little girl took it. "I need a mechanic."

"She'll need her boots," Karen said. "Wait here."

"She doesn't need boots," Roy said. "What kind of hippie commune is this requiring shoes?"

"It's the exhaust pipe on your bike I'm worried about."

"Right." Roy stopped on the stairs. "We need to wait for your mama to bring your shoes."

"I want my boots."

"She wants her boots," Roy yelled. "A biker needs her boots." The little girl was scowling at Roy, mad-dogging him. "How old are you?"

"I'm three."

"How old am I?"

"You're six."

"I'm six. Feels like I'm six. I've been really excited to meet you. I've missed seeing your mom. She's about my favorite person in the world."

"That sounds like lie number two to me," Karen said, passing over a tiny pair of cowboy boots.

"Wait, hold it. You lied to me," Roy said. "You said you had a little boy. You said in your letter that Wiley was a boy."

"No, I didn't."

"Mama, I'm not a boy," Wiley said.

"I know, sweetheart."

"You did. Look." He retrieved the letter from his inside pocket and handed it to her. She opened it. He watched Wiley put her boots on the wrong feet while she was reading.

"Put those on the right feet," Karen said.

"I am." Wiley took her boots off and switched them. "I am, Mama."

"See?" Roy asked.

"You misread it."

Roy took the letter back and reread it. He'd made a mistake. The little girl was halfway to the bike by the time Roy put the letter away and caught up with her. He lifted her onto the bike but she was too small to reach the grips without lying down on the tank.

"Does everything seem OK?" Roy said. "It was riding kind of weird on the way up."

"It's OK. Mama, it's stinky. I'm done."

Karen picked up her daughter and Roy followed them inside. The living room was furnished simply with bookshelves like a library and wood floors, no TV but a nice stereo, LPs, toys and paper and colored pencils scattered everywhere. The sun shone in the south-facing windows and there was a cat sleeping in the warm spot on the floor. "That's Wiley's cat, Sample, that isn't supposed to be in the house."

"He's sleeping, Mama."

"When he wakes up, put him out," Karen said. To Roy: "There were these people—your people, dirty skater people— passing through town that were selling kittens but they'd taken the sign from someplace else that said free samples and had crossed out the words and written five bucks and kittens. We freed this one."

The little girl curled up beside her cat and gently touched the hair on the tips of its ears.

Karen led him into the kitchen, butcher-block counters and cabinets with no doors, a green-and-black checkerboard floor like a diner, a chrome-edged table in a breakfast nook, hanging pots, magnet bar knife rack, a commercial oven with six burners and a griddle.

"I guess I can give you a beer," she said, as she opened the fridge. "Even though you might get drunk and do some stupid shit."

Coming from the solitude of the bike to any social situation could be jarring but he was completely unprepared for how easily Karen could knock him off balance. He wanted to apologize but he probably just looked scared.

"Too soon?" Karen smiled without malice and passed him an unopened beer. "You better be tougher than that showing up at my house unannounced."

"I should've told you I was coming."

Karen shrugged.

They each opened their beers and clanked them and had a drink.

"This isn't the same house," he said. "I looked at it for a while from the road before I turned in because it didn't look right. It was like a box, none of the covered deck or dormers or anything. Was there even a barn here?"

"I sold the old house, just the house, like, the structure, and they came and took it away on a truck. Apparently it's on some billionaire's mega-ranch now, north of here, by Frenchman Lake. I always picture it being used as hunting quarters for chubby dudes, fat rich guys farting the night away, spooning."

"And you built this?" Roy said. "Why didn't you say anything about that in the letter?"

"I guess I didn't see that it mattered. In the grand scheme, you know." She looked toward the living room at her daughter.

"It's really nice," he said. "A fresh start." He didn't intend to sound bitter because he wasn't, at least not with Karen and her life, but there was sand between his words.

"How about you?" she asked, passing right by his petulance.

"Nothing fresh about my starts," he said. "Same old shit. Living, skating, contemplating the view from nowhere."

"At least you have a motorcycle now." She pretended to flip her hair. "Sexy locks."

"Yeah, and here I am getting mileage out of what? Being older and crustier than everyone else?"

"It's still just skateboarding," Karen said. "Try not to over-think it."

He took a step toward her and she held up a finger and

cocked her head, no no, and stopped him. "One of Aaron Simmonds's buddies built this house," she said. "Remember Aaron? The other motorcycle guy? The OG motorcycle guy?" She gave Roy a sideways look and Roy stupidly shook his head but he remembered—and was sure she knew he did.

"I broke his window in Reno," Roy said.

There was a sadness in her eyes but it went away quickly and the brightness returned. "He'll be thrilled to know you're back in town," Karen said, smiling, scrunching her nose cutely. "What really happened to your face? Did you do that skating?"

"No, I got my ass kicked and my motorcycle stolen." He smiled to show her his missing teeth. "I got it back. Some bikers rolled me. There's a video, it's all over the Internet."

Karen opened a laptop on the counter and quickly found the footage. She covered her mouth and shut the laptop.

"Why did they do that?" she asked. "What'd you do to them?"

"Nothing. The cop said, wrong place, wrong time. Actually, he said wrong place, wrong outfit."

Karen gave him a sad smile.

Roy laughed, couldn't help it. "They brought the bike back after the video got out," he said. "Told me they'd been on a bender and didn't know who I was or they wouldn't have rolled me."

"Precious," Karen said. "Outlaws with hearts of gold. Dirtbags loving dirtbags. Did y'all have like a 'mama tried' moment?"

"They said they used to skate."

"I'm the only hell she ever raised." Country accent, cock-eyed grin. "Yer famous, right? Can we be nice to you for no reason?"

"I get it."

"To me, all of you are a bunch of poseurs, bad actors. Where have all the good men gone?"

"I wouldn't know."

She nodded. "As if you or anyone else can even tell the difference anymore. Shit is sad."

"OK," he said, but she was right. Smith and Jones probably sold meth and were involved in human trafficking. That's what real bikers did, right? He didn't know. He didn't want to know. A good man would.

"Can't handle the heat," Karen said, "stop making me burn you."

"All right. Listen." Roy took a breath and bobbed around a bit to pump himself up. Emotional calisthenics. "The whole thing, getting my ass beat, it's kind of why I'm here. I was in a motel room with nothing but your letter and I realized, this has been still happening, this thing with me and you, for a long time."

She smiled and it was suddenly obvious that he'd made a mistake, that he'd misread her letter completely—more than just thinking that Wiley was a boy—that she'd just been saying hello and that now, standing in her kitchen, he sounded a lot like a crazy person, a stalker.

"I haven't seen you for ten years," Karen said.

Roy shook his head. He could explain, he could try. "One of my friends—Rasheed—he was on the team with me. He wrecked his motorcycle. He died."

"Sorry. But I still don't see what that has to do with me, or us."

"That's only part of it, though. There's this other part." He leveled his eyes at her. "I started thinking I could be dead or I might as well be, like, what does it matter. Like death was a state of consciousness or something, like getting high or something. And when I read your letter, I thought, I'm, you know, doing a half-ass job of being alive if you aren't in my life. I need a reason." Roy wouldn't feel more exposed if he removed all four axle nuts and dropped into a thirteen-foot bowl.

"I'm sorry about your friend and that you got beat up, but I was drunk when I wrote that letter."

"Drunk when you mailed it?"

"No, I was sober by then but I was so mad at myself that I sent it anyway." Another earth-tilting Karen smile. "Postage is pain leaving the body."

He touched his stitches to see if they were bleeding but they weren't. "When we were together it was the happiest time of my life," he said. "I fucked it all up."

Karen put her hands on her cheeks and shook her head. "What have you done with Roy?" she said. "Where is he?"

When he smiled his face hurt, stitches stretched skin, bruising sloshed fluid, scabs tore loose. Now he was bleeding. He could see Wiley in the living room, carefully drawing on an oversized piece of paper. He let out a long breath. "My point is," he said. "I don't know what my point is. Maybe when I bailed, let's say I got half, like we got divorced."

"I should've got a lawyer because you didn't deserve half," she said, the hurt filling her eyes. "You deserved much less."

"I didn't deserve shit," Roy said. "I deserved a kick in the head. I still do. I'm sorry. I'm so sorry for what I did to you. But I've always known that the half I got, it wasn't the half that mattered. And sitting in that motel room reading your letter, rereading your letter, I realized that since we split I'd kind of pretended like you were always there, like you were still with me."

"I wasn't. You were fooling yourself."

"I know that."

"And you think you can just roll up on me like this? Because you're going through a rough patch? You don't know what a rough patch is, bucko."

"It's not like that."

"Oh, shut up and keep your puppy eyes in their sockets." She looked toward her daughter in the living room.

Roy lifted his beer and took a drink, nodded OK, took a step back. "Didn't you tell me once that you wanted a kitchen like this, legit, commercial grade. A cook's kitchen. You always had the cooking shows on."

"Did I?"

"I think so."

"Maybe you're thinking of someone else."

"I'm not," Roy said. "It was you."

There was a hummingbird at the feeder outside the kitchen window and they watched it come and go and come back.

"Did you think I'd let you stay here?"

"I can go."

She gave him a look that he would describe as depthless, without end. "You can sleep in the barn tonight but that's about as far as I'm willing to trust a stranger."

"I'm not a stranger."

"You're the definition of a stranger."

"To myself."

"Gross." She shook out her hands, drying the paint on

her nails, making him smile. "No self-pity or pseudo self-examination in the kitchen, whatever the hell that was."

"OK."

"You can have dinner with us. There aren't any options in town so don't ask to take us out to eat or something. We eat here." She turned at the quickening sound of Wiley's approaching footsteps.

"Sweetheart," Karen said to Wiley, "can you help me make a bed for our friend Roy in the barn?"

"I want to sleep in the barn, Mama," Wiley said.

"Not tonight," Karen said. "Roy needs to spend some time alone. He has a head problem."

"Like the man at the bowling alley?" Wiley asked.

"That's right," Karen said.

"What happened to your brain?" Wiley said to Roy. "The man at the bowling alley hurt his brain and now he's mean."

"I'm not sure," Roy said. "But it's not as bad as that. I'm not mean."

Karen smiled at her daughter but spoke sharply to Roy. "If you're thinking this is a two-way street," she said, "you're wrong. You're walking on, like—" She used her hands to give him the approximate dimensions. "Like a dirt trail with feces, human and animal, and oil spills instead of mud puddles and you're the only one on it. You're all alone on your turd road."

"When you put it like that," Roy said, "it doesn't sound so bad."

"Turd road?" Wiley said, laughing. "You don't want to be on a turd road, silly."

They had hamburgers and kale salad for dinner and afterward watched an animated movie on Karen's laptop about a little girl named Rosalita and her big red rooster and the adventures they had on their avocado farm. Roy gave Karen a shocked look when Wiley leaned against his shoulder and held on to his arm. The movie ended and Wiley went to bed and Karen sent Roy to the barn with a glass of water but no contact of any kind.

He stayed up, sitting on the army cot Karen had set up for him, and listened to the stinking goats moving around and breathing. He stayed up thinking about Karen's life and Rasheed's ending. He felt incapable of being honest with himself unless it was self-hatred. He needed more out of himself. He needed to evolve.

Later, he went outside to piss and purely by accident caught a glimpse of Karen undressing in her bedroom window. He didn't look away or try to hide. She couldn't see him. He didn't think she could. Her light turned off and he watched the stars, the rising moon. Irrigation pumps droned in the night. He felt like he'd never sleep again. He felt the earth under his feet and it was moving.

[26]

M < 55
CA 96130

THE DOG WAKES HIM AND HE ROLLS TO HIS STOMACH.

"Who's there?" he asks, steady as he can manage but his voice still breaks groggy and thick. No answer and his blood drops cold. "Listen, I say the word and my dog'll chew your face off." He has the militiaman's rifle at his shoulder, scanning for movement. The scope is worthless. If it's militia, they'll kill him. They could be hunting him. Of course they are.

Silence. Then footsteps. "I don't mean to bother you," a man's voice, East Coast accent. "Smelled your fire from the road."

"You alone?" He can't make out anything except the slightest shuffling of feet.

"I am. I'm not anybody that's gonna hurt you."

The stranger steps from the shadows of the trees into the moonlight and the dog lowers his head and shifts its weight to its back legs. The man keeps the rifle leveled at center mass. The visitor is black and lean, dressed in all khaki with an army-issue boonie hat pushed far back on his head. His eyes sparkle in the firelight and his smile isn't trying to sell anything.

"Will it bite?" he asks.

"Not if I don't tell him to. God help you if he does."

"When's the last time God helped anyone?"

The man lowers the rifle. "If you hurt me, the dog gets you. If you hurt the dog . . ."

"I'm not hurting anyone."

"Grab some wood and we'll build up the fire so we can see each other. Take it from there."

"You don't look so good," the visitor says. "Are you hurt?"

The man touches his face. "I'm fine." His whole body is stiff and aching from the explosion, yesterday morning he could hardly move, and the ringing hasn't faded in his ears.

The visitor smiles. "I might have something for you." He turns and disappears into the darkness and the man and the dog move into the shadows and wait for his return.

From the darkness, a tube of Neosporin and a bottle of ibuprofen pitched onto his sleeping bag. The visitor returns with arms loaded and dumps a mess of twigs and limbs onto the coals. He stands and stretches his back, removes his hat, bald on top, bushy at the sides, and runs a hand over his scalp before dropping to a knee and blowing the embers to life. There's a pint of vodka or gin sticking out from his back pocket.

The man squirts a worm of ointment onto his finger and works it into the meat of the bigger scabs on his face and arms, where he'd had to dig the splinters out. "Which way you headed?" he asks, pops four ibuprofen.

The stranger ceases his huffing and puffing and blinks the smoke from his eyes. "North, you?"

"North." The man chases the pills down with a drink of ashy water. He can see the glint of the stranger's bike frame in the firelight.

"Are the J's still holding Lassen?" the stranger says. "The national park?"

"The feds had it, but last I heard they gave it up."

"It's right around the corner, right? Like a few miles." The man nods. The fire leaps up all at once and the visitor gets to his feet and offers his hand. "I'm Sol."

"The dog is Pecos," the man says, taking his hand. "I don't care what you call me."

Sol clutches his hat to his chest and smiles. "The world's going to shit and I meet a man with no name." He holds out his hand for the dog and it comes forward to sniff and Sol gives him a scratch. "I thought it was the horse that was supposed to have no name."

"I don't have a horse."

"Of course not." Sol passes over his bottle of vodka and leaves the firelight to get his rig. The man doesn't drink. He leans over stiffly and puts the bottle on Sol's side of the fire, sets the Neosporin and ibuprofen beside it.

When he comes back: "I'm from Philadelphia originally but I'm on my way up from Texas now," he says. "I was working down there for the last six years or so."

The man nods, OK. He keeps the rifle in reach.

Sol swigs from his bottle, speaks. "I came through the mountains, drove through New Mexico and Utah, so's to miss the nonsense on the interstates, but I got robbed at a campground

near the Utah border, took my car, everything I had." Sol unscrews the cap on the ibuprofen and tosses a few in his mouth
and chases them down with liquor. "After that I stumbled onto
an old Mormon place, a compound I guess they call it, lots of
canned food and water I could draw with a handpump."

"Nobody was there?"

"No, and hadn't been for a while. The livestock, cows mostly
and maybe some sheep, goats, I couldn't really tell what was
what, were dead in the fields."

"You could've stayed."

"I could've," the visitor says. "I spent a month waiting for
someone to come back but they never did. Nothing but wind.
Nothing to read but the *Book of Mormon*. That is a tremendous
book. I don't know if you know this, but according to them, my
black ass is cursed."

"I wouldn't take it personally," the man said.

"I won't." Sol put his hat back on. "But I had to get out of
there. I was absolutely losing my mind. So I loaded up their
little tractor with all the fuel I could carry, every can, jar, water
bottle I could find. I still smell diesel." He takes a moment to
sniff his hands. "Almost made it to Provo. You know, there're
people there doing just fine. They won't even let the J's and the
other militias pass city limits."

"So they're a militia too."

"True. That's right. But they all had names. Every one of
them. I didn't meet any nameless people there."

The man looks at the dog and back at Sol. Sol points at the
militiaman's rifle, the STT emblem carved in the stock.

"I'm not militia," the man says. "I took this off of one of
them."

"Explains the cuts and bruises," Sol says. "Anyway, I got my bike and more supplies from the Mormons in Provo. Very fair, honest people, doing fine, more than surviving. Maybe I should've stayed. They were all like growing food, pumping water, birds singing, children playing, happy happy." Sol smiles again and the man takes a sip this time when it's offered and hands the bottle back. "Texas is a cinder if you get tired of going north," Sol says. "Don't go there. Utah is town by town. Nevada, fuck off. Fuck Nevada."

The man smiles. "Reno will burn you down."

"Didn't make it out that way."

"Good thing," the man says. "I lived south of here, not far, a little town. The dog got hurt and I had to go to the vet in Sacramento, and when I came back the town was gutted. They used heavy equipment, stripped everything. It's not the Jeffersonians anymore."

"I know," Sol says, nodding at the rifle. "It's them now. They're worse than the first ones."

"I have water," the man says. "If you're thirsty."

"Thanks," Sol says. "I filled up at the rest stop, same as you. I saw your tracks in the dust." He points at the man's rig. "What kind of bike is that?"

"The kind with two wheels."

Sol shakes his head. "Anybody ever tell you you come off as a bit of an asshole?"

"Lots of people."

Pecos is curled beside the fire fast asleep, suddenly he lifts his head and growls. There is the sound of rustling leaves but there are no leaves and when they look up they can see the blur of an ancient four-rotor drone as it speeds by in the darkness.

The man gets slowly to his feet with the rifle. The dog is sniffing at the air and the man can hear the whir of the drone in the distance, once again coming closer. "You should get away from the fire," the man says, as he and the dog walk into the darkness toward the bike.

From his coat pocket, Sol produces a small pistol and pops a couple of shots like a cowboy and by some miracle hits the drone and it crashes high in a tree and hangs up in the dry branches. Sol whoops and he's laughing like a maniac as the man pedals away. It isn't long until Sol catches up to him and they dismount together and leave the road.

They stash their bikes under some deadfall and the man wanders into the dark with the dog looking for a place to hide. He slides beneath a downed tree and pulls Pecos against his side.

Sol comes stumbling after them lugging what looks to be a piece of carpet but is in fact a half dozen lead aprons stitched together with monofilament line. Sol slips under the tree beside the dog and they huddle beneath the lead aprons like children under a blanket and wait.

"I was an X-ray tech in Dallas," Sol says. "After all the news about militias using thermal imaging to find refugees, I had an idea where it might be going. I *borrowed* the aprons from different hospitals I worked at, thinking maybe I could get them to people that could use them but, before I could, the power went out. When I got robbed at the campground, these were the only things they didn't take. Heavy as hell but worth the trouble."

They sit still and listen to the silence, the panting dog, then Sol continues. "There was a fire in my apartment building, fires everywhere downtown. They burned down—" Sol takes a deep breath and the dog licks him in the face and he laughs and the man can feel him shudder. "They cut gas lines and waited for the repairmen to come and fix it, then they shot them. If anybody tried to get out, they shot them. They lit it on fire. My boyfriend, most of my friends, they were waiting for me to get home from work. It was our anniversary."

They hear the trucks approaching, headlights sweep. The lead blanket is pulled lower over their bodies. Brakes squeak, doors open. Voices, the sound of breaking limbs, laughing.

"Come out, come out, wherever you are," someone yells. The night is dead quiet, windless.

"Here, pup. Here, boy." A dog whistle.

"*Fuss*," another voice. "*Fuss*." The man knows who it is now, the same ones as before. *Sei brav.* They're following him. They know he's here. He's sure they will find him, then doors close and motors start, one two, and the gravel sprays. Silence.

Sol pushes the blanket off of their heads and gives the dog a pat, gets to his feet and dries his eyes on his sleeve. "I think they're gone," he says.

"We'll see soon enough." The man searches the horizon for brake lights, listens.

"Are they looking for you?" Sol says.

The man looks down at the rifle. "They might be."

"Ponyboy one, fascists zero."

"I'm up by more than one."

"So they are looking for you?" He doesn't answer. "Someday, it's gonna be them versus the Mormons," Sol says. "I bet you anything. Like Shiites and Sunnis."

The man rolls up the lead aprons neatly like he's rolling a sleeping bag and passes them to Sol. He returns to the scattered fire and kicks the embers from the ground and gathers his wadded sleeping bag and repacks it in his pannier. The man and the dog watch the sputtering coals until Sol comes to join them. Without a word, they get on their bikes and pedal away.

"Wyatt Earp would've been a warlord," the man says.

"Who?"

"Never mind. Shit happens fast, is all. The west is dead."

[27]

R<35
CA 96118

WILEY WAS ON HER COASTER BIKE IN THE DRIVEWAY. ROY could tell that Karen was trying to decide if he was lying or not. They spent quite a lot of time like this, accounting for Roy.

"After I left here, I got a job in Sacramento," he said. "I lived in Carl for a while. I was skating a lot at night. Pretty much as soon as I got back to Portland I ran out of money and I was back to sleeping in parking lots and at Burnside with the heathens until Justice and Leon invited me to park in their backyard next to the ramp. Remember their place off Forty-second?"

Wiley wrecked her bike in the dirt and Roy and Karen watched as she crawled out from under it and pushed her too-big helmet out of her eyes.

"Yeah," Karen said. "Justice was dating that girl from Israel."

"Elise," Roy said. "He married her. He converted first, got cut, then he married her. They said their vows on the ramp." Karen raised an eyebrow, impressed, but didn't say anything.

"I must've got used to sleeping in Carl," Roy said, "because pretty soon I got a job with Owen and Sed at DreamLine building skateparks and Carl was home sweet home. We went all over. One summer, I helped build two spots in Washington and the next I worked on a monster in Idaho. Two years gone. I learned a lot and I thought I was pretty smart about concrete and cutting forms and flat work but Owen canned me anyway. He got sick of me telling him what he should do."

Wiley laid down her bike in the driveway and started toward the porch. Karen told her to put her bike away in the shed if she didn't want it to get run over. The little girl did as she was told and when she topped the stairs Roy gave her a fist bump and took her helmet like she was a jet pilot. "Can I have some water?" she asked.

"Last I checked the glasses were in the cupboard and the water came out of the faucet," Karen said. Wiley raised an eyebrow, just like her mother, and opened the screen door and went inside. A dust cloud moved over the road and onto the field.

"We're going to dry up and blow away," Roy said.

"This is global discomfort," Karen said, "not global destruction."

"Tell that to Florida," Roy said. "Tell that to eighty-five percent of the world's population living on the coasts."

"You'll get statisticular cancer if you keep that up. Eighty-five percent? Where'd you get that?"

"Made it up."

"You and Barry, you guys—you men—you want the end. It excites you, gives you apocalypse boners. Better watch what you wish for."

"What do you mean, Barry? Barry, your neighbor Barry?"

"Yeah, Barry Miller. He moved in, I don't know, three or four years ago. He's another prepper douche, doing that whole militia thing, Jeffersonian breakfast meetings. They have powwows at his house and shoot guns, dress up in commando outfits, accessorize."

"When in Rome," Roy said.

She narrowed her eyes at Roy, sizing him up. "I'm still not sure if our brand of domestication suits you but you don't strike me as the militia type."

"That's why I'm still in the barn. Because you can't figure me out?"

"Are you complaining?"

"No, I love the barn. I do."

"If you want to complain, you can go sleep in Barry's barn."

"I'm not. I won't."

"This has all happened before, right?" Karen said. "Drought, fire, strife, dead forests, the threat of world war. Actually, this has happened forever. It's never stopped. Moves continent to continent. It'll be our turn soon but not yet."

They stood for a moment and watched a few of the goats take turns leaping on top of the propane tank, falling all over one another, butting heads.

"It's going to be hard to eat those things." Roy opened the door for Karen.

"We generally cook them first."

"That'll help."

"I'm still surprised that you ate rabbit," Karen said. "Tougher than I thought."

"Wiley did it first or I would've bailed," Roy said. "You're the one that killed them and skinned them."

"Goats should be no problem for a rabbit eater." Roy followed her inside and stopped the screen door with his heel so it wouldn't slam. Wiley had pushed her stepstool in front of the sink and she had the faucet on and was letting the water pour through her fingers.

"Don't waste water, sweetheart," Karen said.

"I'm not, Mama." She was in a kind of trance and didn't make any move to do as Karen had asked. Roy reached over her and turned the water off and she gave him an angry and terrified look and started screaming *no no no*.

Karen gave him a thanks-a-lot look and picked her up, squirming and crying, trying to punch her mom, and took her down the hall to her bedroom. "You played right through your nap, didn't you?" Karen said. "You're so tired."

"I played outside, not in my nap! I didn't play through my nap! No!"

Roy stayed in the kitchen and listened to Wiley's angry screams for five minutes, logged his time on the clock on the stove. It made his jaw ache, then, just as he was about to go outside, to surrender, her screams went to quiet sobs and pleading, "Mama, mama, mama." A minute later it was quiet. Karen came back into the kitchen.

"Sorry about that," Roy said.

"It's fine. Next time give her some warning. You just surprised her. She was tired."

"If you let me stay, since I'm not planning on going any-where—" She looked at Roy and her face was so much like Wi-ley's at the moment when he'd turned off the faucet—after the water had stopped but before she'd registered any anger—that he couldn't help but smile.

"That's a big if."

"OK, like I said, if you let me, miracles happen, who am I going to be to her?"

She placed her hand on his heart. "The cart at this point is in a different solar system than the horse but I'll humor you. I'd expect more from you than your stepdad ever delivered. You get me? No casual dismissals, no lying, no bullshit."

"Steve? I can beat that. I'm better than him eight days a week."

"I know." Karen stepped away from Roy and grabbed a dishtowel and wiped up some of the water that had splashed onto the counter. "So let's run this whole fantastical hypothetical out. If you stay, what are you going to do about skating?"

"I told you, I can skate anywhere."

"But you have an image. What will you do about your im-age?"

"Fuck it, image ain't shit."

Karen reached out tentatively and took his hand. "First of all, I don't want to hear how you got by, OK? I guess we should be clear on that. You know that I was married and that was pretty much it for me. I don't want to hear about where you've been."

"I won't say a word."

"Not that you wouldn't have mentioned it by now, but do you have kids?"

"Not that I know of."

"Are you trying to be funny?"

"No, that's what people say, what guys say. Not that I know of. It's supposed to be funny."

"Fatherless children, I didn't think you of all people would think that was very funny."

"OK, I don't have any kids."

"That you know of."

"Sorry I said it."

She lifted up his shirt to see the tattoo of her name. "I can't believe you crossed me out."

"I regret that. I'm sorry."

"You crossed me out along with the rest." She stuck a finger in his ribs. "What the fuck is a Darlene? Christy? Monica? This is evidence of some serious, serial assholery."

"I've changed."

"You're such a liar, even your skin is lying."

"What about that? That's not lying."

"Crossed out my name."

"I'll get it fixed."

"You're still sleeping in the barn."

"Me and the goats are hatching some big plans. Wait and see. Total goat domination. Militias don't stand a chance against me and the goats."

She finally kissed him, really kissed him. He finally held her.

THREE MONTHS LATER HE JOCKEYED HIS TRIUMPH OUT OF THE back of his new/used pickup and rolled it into the barn. That afternoon he stood outside waiting for a lumber delivery. Karen and Wiley were barely visible out in the field, Wiley, riding high in Karen's backpack, waved at him and he waved back. He was going to build a skate bowl in the barn. If he was staying, he'd need somewhere to skate. He was staying.

His first visitors to the bowl were Aaron and April Simmonds. Through the open barn doors Roy watched them park their bikes—cool canyon racer Hondas, same vintage and cut as the CB that Yano had given him—in the shade of the apple tree near the house.

When they ventured into the barn and said hello, Roy did the same. Then, "If you're gonna kick my ass for breaking your window, I don't blame you, but can you wait until I finish this?" He'd spent yesterday building forms and all of the morning pouring the concrete coping for the bowl in sections and was in the middle of the final piece.

"No hurry," Aaron said, and wandered off to take his time inspecting Roy's motorcycles while April cooed over the baby goats making all the noise in the stall nearest the new ramp.

Roy finished and loaded the wheelbarrow with his trowels and floats and buckets and went outside to the frost-free faucet to clean up. The sun was high and it felt good as it warmed his shoulders. Aaron and April came outside and after Roy dried his hands on his shirt, he offered his hand to Aaron and Aaron took it.

"I'm not gonna kick anybody's ass," Aaron said. He'd gone all the way bald and shaved his head now. He had a beer belly and some tattoos on his arms.

"I might," April said, and slipped off her motorcycle jacket without turning around to face him. Athletic build, cut, with tough girl shoulders straining against her black T-shirt.

"I'm sorry about what I did, about your window," Roy said.

"Don't worry about it," Aaron said. "It's not like you're the first one to do some stupid shit in Reno."

April swatted his hand away when he offered it and gave him a hug. "You have some big fucking shoes to fill here," she said in a whisper.

Roy nodded but didn't say anything. April looked as if she might cry. Aaron slung an arm around her shoulder. "Nice bikes."

"Thanks," Roy said. "You too. I was about to make lunch. You guys want a sandwich?"

"Sure," April said. "Where are the girls?"

"They're at the Coffee Stop," Roy said. "Karen's putting in a double-bowl sink. I offered to help but she said she'd do it."

"She built the first one more or less on her own," Aaron said. "We helped her with the roof and my buddy did the electrical but she did all the plumbing and put in the counters and everything."

"I guess that makes me redundant," Roy said.

"Only if you were as useful as she is," April said.

"Ouch," Aaron said.

"OK. OK. I got turkey and I got ham," Roy said. "I'll prove my worth with sandwiches. Let's eat."

Karen and Wiley came home later and found the three of them on the porch drinking beer. Aaron and April stayed for dinner too but left before it got dark. April worried about deer on the road.

Karen put Wiley to bed, then she and Roy stayed up in the kitchen drinking the last of the wine.

"That's the first time April has been back out here since the wake," Karen said. "But I'm at their house all the time. They watch Wiley for me."

"She seems OK," Roy said. "She told me I had big shoes to fill."

"April," Karen said, shaking her head. "Did you think Aaron was gonna give you a smack?"

"I did." Roy drained his glass and set it down. "I gave him my CB," he said.

"You what?"

"I gave him one of my motorcycles before you got home. Signed the title and everything."

"Why'd you do that?"

"It was the one that Yano gave to me, the one that got stolen. Yano was riding that bike with Rasheed when he died. The bike was there. And Aaron, in a roundabout way, was the one that got me thinking about bikes in the first place. I owe him."

"You're a whimsical little thing." She gave him a big wet kiss and held on tight to the hair on the back of his head.

They locked the door to the bedroom so Wiley couldn't surprise them and did their best to be quiet.

LATE IN THE FALL AS A DRY, DUSTY SNOW BLANKETED THE FIELDS, the swoosh team was filming in Roy's bowl, the Goat Bowl, as it came to be known. He'd put a Porta-Potty out back and a woodstove in the barn and if he kept it fed it stayed warm enough to skate and not worry too much about the pain of a cold slam. On the last night of filming Roy got too drunk and ended up sleeping in the barn.

Early the next day Wiley arrived with a paper sack full of

breakfast burritos wrapped in tinfoil and a large thermos of coffee. Roy stoked the fire in the stove and when the boys got up he let Wiley hand out burritos. There weren't any coffee cups besides the thermos lid so they cut the bottoms off of beer cans with pocketknives and used those. Wiley found her board and Roy helped her put on her helmet. Everybody climbed on the deck to eat and watch the kid skate. She dropped in and got cheered when she made it a halfway up the deep-end wall. On her next drop she went faster and took a tumble, called it quits. She teared up but without her mom there to console her, she just took off her helmet and climbed out of the bowl and sat down next to Roy and watched the skateboarders eat and roll cigarettes and finish off the coffee, then she and Roy walked to the house together.

"Mama says you're in trouble," Wiley said, as they stood at the mudroom door.

"What should I do?"

"Be nice. You have to be nice and say you're sorry when you're in trouble."

"OK."

"Where's Turtle?" she asked.

"He wasn't in the barn. I don't know where he is." He'd gotten the dog for her off of Craigslist in Truckee. Golden retriever, dumb but sweet. "When'd you see him last?"

"He didn't sleep in my room. Mama said he was with you."

"I don't think so. We'll find him. He's around here somewhere."

Wiley pulled open the door and Roy followed her inside. Karen was in the kitchen with NPR on the radio. "There's more coffee," she said, without looking up from the book she was reading.

"Thanks for the food," Roy said. "The boys told me to tell you."

"I spit in them. All of them."

"That's OK. Sorry about last night."

"I'm not mad."

"I'm still sorry. Six beers too many. It's an old story."

"Get your old story in the shower. I can smell you from here." She looked up then.

"I just hadn't seen anybody, skated with anybody for a while, guess I got carried away."

"Stink. Shower. Clean clothes."

"Thanks."

"Roy."

"What?"

"I really did spit in them."

"You say that like it's a bad thing."

By the time he'd gotten dressed and had some more coffee, the boys had the van warming up in the driveway. Karen and Wiley were upstairs. He could hear them talking. He heard Karen say *Turtle*. He put on his insulated coveralls over his clothes and pulled on his snow boots and his parka and went outside to the machine shed and started Karen's Kubota tractor with the snow-blower attachment and let it warm up. On the way to the barn he turned off the van. He could hear them skating inside and he opened the door just wide enough to yell at Tony that he was going to blow the driveway before they left so they didn't pack it down by driving on it.

"Don't forget to cup its balls," Nessy called from the deck of the bowl.

Roy was laughing, still a bit drunk, on the way to the tractor.

He'd forgotten his gloves so he steered with his hands inside his coat sleeves. Blue sky, white snow, the cool rumble of the little diesel. The churned powder from the blower caught in the wind and drifted back on him in rainbows, coating him in a layer of snow like an Arctic explorer. When he went by the house again, Wiley was watching him from the living room window and he could see Karen in the kitchen. He waved stiffly and Wiley waved back.

The neighbor, Barry Miller, drove by in his big Dodge truck and ignored Roy when he waved good morning. Barry never waved. Roy retracted his coat sleeve and gave the finger to the cloud of snow dust retreating to the south.

"Have a nice day, asshole," Roy said, and as he whipped the tractor around to make the final pass, he saw the dog's leg, the golden color in the ditch. The dog was dead and frozen solid. He didn't know if he should tell Wiley. He had to tell Karen.

He lifted the dog from the snow, frozen blood on its head, and set it down on the floor of the tractor. He ran the blower on the way back because dead dog or not he still had to clear the road.

When he climbed down from the tractor, Karen must've seen the dog. She came outside and Wiley was right behind her.

"He got hit by a car, sweetie," he said to Wiley. "He's gone. I'm sorry." The boys were coming out of the barn now, laughing, stopped laughing when they saw the dog.

Wiley came forward slowly and touched the dog's fur. "He's bleeding," she said. Tears were forming. Roy looked away, shook his head at Nessy and the boys, nodded to the van. "Go ahead and go, man. We got a tragedy here. Good to see you."

Karen lifted Wiley up and hugged her. "No, Mama. I don't want to leave. Where does Turtle go now?"

"We'll have to bury him," Karen said.

"The ground's frozen solid," Roy said.

Nessy pulled his hood on to protect his ears from the wind, touched Wiley on the head, looked to Roy and to the dead dog. "You might not know it by looking, but we are the best diggers in all of America. There are none better. True fact." His accent was reassuring. He gave Wiley a smile and a nod. "We'll take care of him for you, darlin'. You don't have to worry about a thing."

MIDDAY AND THE SUN WAS HIGH. WARM ENOUGH TO STAND IN A T-shirt from all the pick swinging and spud-bar wielding and shovel chipping. A ragged bunch of tattooed skateboarders smoking cigarettes, sipping beer. All the hangovers had been sweated out.

Roy wrapped Turtle in another blanket and with Karen's help lowered him into the hole where his stinky plaid dog bed was already waiting. Wiley used her small shovel to help cover him up.

The van drove away and Karen and Wiley and Roy stood in the driveway and waved goodbye.

"I like your friends," Karen said.

"Yeah," Roy said. "You OK, sweetheart?"

"I miss Turtle. I miss him," Wiley said.

He'd successfully fought back the tears all morning but he cried when Wiley reached up and he lifted her to his shoulder.

[28]

M < 55
OR 9XXXX

Dawn and they can see the dead gray rock of Mount Shasta. Ash is in the air and the road is skinned with it. The high alpine snow is gone, the glacier buried under ash or melted away. Graffiti on the rocks at the edge of the road tells them that the ranger station and highway junction ahead are in militia hands. After consulting their maps they leave the highway and take the back way over the old Military Pass Road. The sun is low as they push their bikes through the burnt forest. They make camp on the northern flank and discover snow sealed to ice under layer upon layer of ash. They use sticks and rocks to scrape away the grit and mud. Each of their small camp cookpots is continually topped up and left fireside. Water jugs and bladders are refilled. They split one of Sol's Mountain House meals for dinner, chicken parm, before passing out early.

In the morning Sol wanders away from the fire with his .22 Browning pistol, muttering something about a squirrel. The dog naps while the man tends the fire. The skies are gray with low clouds that move toward them easily. The air smells charged, as if it could rain. As the sky darkens he wonders if it might snow.

There's a pop in the air that almost sounds as if it were made by the fire but two more follow and he recognizes gunshots. Pecos hops up and sniffs the wind. The man grabs his rifle and follows Sol's tracks hesitantly into the dead trees. The way is uphill and it isn't long before he's breathing hard and beginning to sweat. He smells sulfur first, sees the steam. It's a hot spring and in the morning chill the steam is thick and he can't see anything until a breeze pushes a lane open. Then he spots Sol, squatted down with his knife out, gutting an animal, a deer. It has small forked horns. The dog gooses Sol and makes him jump.

"Oh Lord," he says, on his feet and laughing. "Look at this. Can you believe this?"

"This is somebody else's place," the man says.

"Not anymore."

The pools have been constructed with stone and mortar and there's a mossy pipe stubbed out of the rocks where the hot water comes out. "We should go," the man says. The pools, two small ones and a larger one, are marked by cairns, heights of which are relative to the water temperature. No militia graffiti, no defensive positions, none of the usual trash, shell casings, cigarette butts. No fresh footprints either.

Sol waves his knife at the man. "I'm staying. You do what you want."

"Fine. I'm going for our rigs, then," the man says. "I gotta put our fire out too so no one sees it."

The dog stays with Sol waiting for more scraps and the man feels a little insulted.

On the way up the hill with Sol's rig, he hears more gunshots, five, six in a row. The dog barks and keeps barking, and it gets louder, comes bounding down from the forest and runs by without more than a glance. Then Sol comes charging out of the steam, churning up dust, going as fast as he can.

"Bear," he says. He has his pistol in his hand and he keeps coming, runs right by. Over his shoulder: "Leave the bike. We'll come back."

The man follows Sol downhill, hobbling as quickly as he can.

"Did you shoot it?" the man asks. "Is it wounded?"

"I shot at it but I don't know if I hit it." Sol slows so the man can catch up. "That dog of yours is a huge coward."

"Smart is all."

Sol starts coughing and laughing at the same time. Hanging from his pocket is a hacked tenderloin. "Bitch won't get it all," he says.

They rebuild their fire in the ash pit at their first camp and pan-fry the tenderloin with a little bit of snow and ice tossed in to keep it from sticking, but it sticks anyway.

"I say we go up there and see what's left," the man says.

"You can."

"How many shells do you have?"

"There's a box of 'em. Fifty or so left. You can't kill a bear with that peashooter."

"You can kill anything with that if you hit it in the right place."

"Not if it kills you first, and if I hit it, it's going to be pissed. I vote for using your big bad militia rifle."

"It's too loud. You can hear it for miles."

"Then I vote for getting my rig and heading down the road, grateful for what we got."

"I thought you wanted to stay at the pools. Spa day for Sol."

"Not if I'm a get eaten in the process."

The man picks up the pistol and ejects the magazine. Sol stands up and digs a few loose shells from his pocket and passes them over.

"Where's the rest of your ammo?"

"Shells are in the bag on my handlebars, under my bandana." Sol stoops and picks up his tin plate from the ground and finishes the last bite of his dinner. Talking while he chews, "If you aren't too horribly maimed, could you bring my bike back with you so I don't have to haul my ass up that hill again?"

"Keep my dog here."

"Like he'd go with you."

The man takes the rifle too, just in case. The sun is high as he belly crawls from the trees into the cove. He rests the butt of the pistol on his hand resting on the rock. The rifle is loaded and ready beside him. He sees the deer first, its horns. Then he sees the bear sitting on its ass with its back facing him, a massive black lump. He checks the safety and takes a breath and shoots the animal three times in quick succession in the base of the skull. It stands suddenly and spins around and paws at its injuries, teeth snapping as if it's biting at yellow jackets. Then it sees him and lowers its head to charge but its front legs give and it pitches forward and begins lurching toward him with only its hind legs churning, head in the dirt. The sound is more of a moan than a roar. The animal's dark eyes search among the trees beyond the pools and it tries to turn but its front legs are limp and it can only manage to roll to its side. The bear's cries get louder and more desperate.

The man takes aim and shoots it six more times and when it stops struggling and goes quiet he reloads the magazine with shaking fingers and stalks over to it and sees its lungs working still and puts the pistol barrel to the side of its head and pulls the trigger until the clip is empty. He backs off and waits while it twitches out its final sparks of warm-blooded electricity. His hands won't stop shaking and his heart is pounding blood in heavy gushes that resonate in his ears.

It's a sow and she is seemingly rooted to the ground. He touches her side and feels her ribs, lifts her leg, and is repulsed by the crusted dugs. Later, when they cut her open there is milk. Her stomach is full of mud. Pecos finds a young cub floating in the smallest of the soaking pools. It has an entrance and exit hole on either side of its small body, red froth along one side of its jaw. Sol holds it in his lap, touches the bloodless entrance wound.

"I went camping with my brother-in-law and some of his friends outside of Bozeman," Sol says. "I was the pity invite, but I didn't care. I'd never been to the mountains before. I made my sister make them take me with them. We hiked into this lake and went fishing." He set the bear cub's body on the ground, covered it with his bandana. "I'd never seen anything like it. Have you ever caught a trout?"

"Yes, Sol," the man says. "I've caught a trout."

Sol raises an eyebrow. "Then you know what I'm talking about. It's amazing. They had to, like my brother-in-law and his buddies, they had to take my pole away or I would've just stayed there."

The man thinks of a time when he and his family went fishing on the Feather River. He'd hooked his own hand, caught no fish.

Sol continues, "We hiked back to camp, and after we fried up our trout, we were drinking in this campground, big campground with campers everywhere. The moon came out." Sol stops and motions to the sky, the moon. "Like tonight, it was bright, and there were kids with their families, you know, playing and toasting marshmallows, but later, like eight mojitos later, I was about to go to bed and we saw this van come into the campground, slow moving, no windows, like sketchy, and this lady is calling for her daughter—Samantha! Samantha!—over and over. And I remember seeing this lady earlier, because she was pretty and I caught my brother-in-law checking her out and I gave him my I-will-cut-your-outdoorsy-white-balls-off-if-you-so-much-as-think-of-cheating-on-my-lovely-and-so-much-better-than-you-sister look, and this woman at the campground was with her whole family and the daughter was probably five years old and had no business whatsoever wandering around at that time of night. Like what the fuck, you know? And we're all, every one of us, fairly blasted on mojitos and beer and I say to Bob, my brother-in-law: 'Bob, that van is just wrong,' or something, and Bob runs over to it, heroic stud that he is, and makes the van stop. We all go over and we're trying to see inside but the driver and the passenger, these hobo-looking white motherfuckers—no offense—dirty as hell with fucking pine needles in their hair and torn clothes, like they've been rolling around in the dirt. No hygiene at all." Sol raises a hand. "Seriously, no offense."

"Fuck you," the man says.

Sol laughs. "Capturing little girls, is what I think. I think they look guilty and they're leaning forward and trying to cover the windows with their bodies, like blocking us so we can't see in the back. And they're saying what's the trouble and we ain't seen no fucking kid and we'd appreciate it if you got out of the way and Bob says, 'They got something in the back.' So I try the slider but it's locked and the driver hits the gas and about runs over one of Bob's friends, seriously almost kills him.

"At this point the adrenaline is way up and we're seeing ourselves as heroes and the whole campground is quiet except for this van tearing out of there. We pile into Bob's truck with Bob driving and me sitting shotgun with the other three dudes in the back. What a posse, right? Tally ho! Bob hands me a pistol from under his seat and we're flying through the woods and I'm looking at this hunk of metal in my hand thinking I'll kill those dirty cracker motherfuckers—no offense—if we catch 'em. I'll shoot them dead."

"Did you catch them?"

"Bob chased them so relentlessly down those little dirt roads that he made them crash and one of them was thrown from the van and he was fucked up, like dying, and the van was rolled onto its side and the one still inside was bleeding too, had a big open cut on his head. You could see his skull."

"What about the kid in the back?"

"We're standing there, like, OK, we caught them. Now what? I wouldn't say I was suddenly sober, but I was suddenly not so sure of what exactly I was doing there. Mind you, I'm still holding the pistol, standing in Bob's headlights, and I like pass it to Bob, like sorry but I can't go to prison or kill someone. Eight mojitos or not. Honestly, at that point I think I kind of forgot why we'd been chasing them in the first place. The carnage we'd caused was just overwhelming. Then we hear this crying sound from inside the van, just the saddest sound, and I reach in the window and unlock the door and Bob pulls the slider open and there's a bear cub in there in like a pet carrier thing for cats. The door must've popped open during the crash and the bear cub climbs up and runs right by us into the woods. We just let it go. Just let it run."

"What about the guys bleeding on the road?"

Sol nods. "Bob and I finally got our shit together and extricated the one from the tree and got him onto level ground. We gave him blankets from inside the van. The other guys helped and we did the same with the head injury. They weren't as bad as we thought at first."

"They weren't dying," the man says.

"I don't know. I hope not. They were talking by the time we left. They were pissed. So, we went back to the campground and packed our camp, threw everything in the back of the truck in a heap and called an ambulance from the pay phone at the campground. I was on a plane home the next day." Sol cocks his head and holds out his hands. "We saved that little bear."

"You're like PETA, except for the attempted murder part."

"Vehicular manslaughter, I checked."

"I bet you did," the man says. "Where's your sister now? Where's Bob?"

"The last I heard from them they were in Homer. Bob was working as a foreman on a desalination plant. I have three nephews and a niece. I'm sure they're fine." Nervousness creeps into Sol's voice.

The moon is blocked by storm clouds and haze. They still haven't finished butchering the sow. At first they attribute the sound to the sleeping dog having a dream but as it gets louder they get to their feet. It's coming from the trees. Sol stands and follows the sound. The man holds on to Pecos. Both men are bloody to the elbow.

"What is it?" the man asks. "Take your pistol."

"It's another cub," Sol says. "Keep the dog back. I don't need a gun."

"I got the dog."

Ten paces and Sol is lost in the darkness.

The man can hear Sol talking, low and steady. "What're you going to do?" the man asks. "You can't just grab him. It'll shred you if you pick it up."

"Shut up for a second," Sol says.

A long minute passes and the only sound is Sol's calming voice. Then the cub is screaming like a pig would do and in a moment Sol returns to the firelight with the small angry animal wrapped tightly in his jacket.

"It's like catching a bat," Sol says, happy as could be. "You just wrap them up. Now hold him while I make a cage or a pen or something. Don't look at me like that. I'm keeping him. Bear rescue number two for me."

"You're crazy."

"Here." And without warning Sol passes him the terrified animal and it takes everything the man has to keep it from squirming free of the jacket or get bitten.

"Hurry up with whatever you're going to do," the man says, "or I'm letting this little bastard go."

"Just hang on." Sol has his knife out and he's cutting saplings and laying them on the ground. The fire is dying and they're both exhausted. The man wants to sleep.

"He'll chew right through that shit," the man says. "This is ridiculous."

"You'll see."

"Not if you don't hurry up I won't." The man tells Pecos to stay but the dog is livid. "Use rocks. He can't chew through rocks."

"Shut up and let me work."

The man wrestles with the bear, it's as strong as a piglet too, twenty-five or thirty pounds, can't be weaned yet. He readjusts the jacket, careful of its teeth and one free paw, until it's cinched in and swaddled tight, then he pins it between two large rocks and sits on it with one hand holding its head down. The tragic sounds coming from the bear make the hair on his neck stand up. He wants to let it go, but what happens to it then? He knows what happens. Maybe they can keep it alive. The dog finally listens and lies down and with interest watches the cub as it tries to twist its head far enough to bite the man on the ass.

"I'm telling you, that tree-limb shit isn't going to work," the man says.

"Noted," Sol says. But he stops cutting the saplings and grudgingly takes the man's advice and begins stacking rocks to make a three-foot-by-three-foot box then ties the saplings together with paracord to use as a lid. It takes him half an hour and the fire is only coals, clouds have moved off, stars are out, Orion, a red sliver of moon.

At Sol's invitation, the man drops the bear into the rough enclosure expecting it to climb right out but it squirms free of the jacket and just watches as Sol pins down the grid of saplings with more rocks.

"See?" Sol says proudly. "Safe and sound."

The bear circles the enclosure, puts his paws on the wall.

"Here he comes," the man says.

"You can go now," Sol says. "Take your little dog and leave us alone."

"Fine with me."

The bear cries on and off throughout the night and Sol stays with him, talking and trying to get him to eat some of the venison.

At dawn he finds Sol curled in his sleeping bag beside the stone cage, and when he looks in, the bear is sleeping with its back to the wall nearest Sol, as if it can feel his heat.

[29]

R > 35
CA 96118

Roy heard the midwife's truck pull into the drive, saw the lights on the wall. Snowing hard and windless last he checked. The front door opened and shut, Sissy said something to Wiley to make her laugh.

Karen and Roy were sitting up on the edge of the bed when Sissy and Wiley came in. Lying down put too much pressure on Karen's bladder. They'd been all over the house searching for a comfortable place to be.

"Are you ready, Mama?" Sissy took her coat off but kept her stocking hat on, gave Karen a peck on the cheek. "You look amazing. We've been preparing for today. We are so ready for this. You're going to be brilliant. I can see it. Can you see it, Papa?" Sissy had medaled twice in Beijing, gold in the downhill, silvered in the slalom, then broke her femur while up by two seconds in the super-g. She lived in Truckee but the midwife collective she was part of worked as far north as Susanville. When she stood next to him, Roy had no question that she could take him in a fight.

"She looks ready to burst," Roy said.

"She looks stunning. The last thing she looks like is that she's going to burst." The midwife shot Wiley a check-out-this-guy look.

"She does look beautiful." He smiled at Karen but she shook her head. No need to lie. Call it what it is: ready to burst. Wiley climbed on the bed and rested her head in her mother's lap.

Sissy worked through her list, blood pressure and pulse, clocked the contractions, nodded at the progress that'd been made since Roy had made the call, then settled in to whisper encouragement and brush Karen's hair from her face while she ignored Roy. He was used to this. Sissy was expert at making him feel vestigial. Watching the two of them—not to mention Wiley—there was an overwhelming sense of time winding down, an era coming to an end.

When they relocated to the living room, Karen had Roy put the kettle on for tea.

Sissy took a moment to further unpack and organize her midwife gear. Roy wondered if she knew how much better actual medical devices—Doppler, heart monitor, thermometer, even the forceps and scissors, compresses—made him feel.

"Someone new is going to be living in your house soon," Sissy said to Wiley.

"I know."

"I'm excited, are you?"

"Yes."

"She's mellower than either of us," Roy said.

"Are you a little scared?" Sissy said.

"A little."

"It's going to be fine. You can help me."

"I already helped Roy fill the tub and test the water and put the towels out."

"I see that," Sissy said. "You've done a great job."

"Come here, honey," Karen said to Wiley. Soon they'd settled into a game of Crazy Eights on the floor in front of the stereo, Desmond Dekker going on about the Israelites and Bonnie and Clyde. Roy had spread Visqueen on the floor beneath the tub to protect from splashing. He'd done the same on the mattress on their bed. Two brand-new trash cans were in the kitchen, one for linens and the other for other stuff. Made him feel like a contract killer.

Roy opened a beer but Sissy snatched it away and put it facedown in the sink.

"I miss happy hour?" Roy said.

"You did good with the tub and the towels. Hang in there."

"I really wanted that beer." He shook out the beer can and put it in the recycling.

"Harden the fuck up, cowboy," Sissy said quietly. "You only get one chance with this."

"That's what's got me worried."

"You can do it." She slapped him on the back. "Be a man. You know, for her."

Sissy made everyone tea. Roy's had a splash of bourbon in it.

Karen was sitting up in the birthing tub, breathing consciously, clutching her kneecaps so tightly there would be bruising that stayed for a week. They'd rented the tub and Roy thought that was weird but what wasn't? It came with a liner. How many kids had been born in that thing? Karen's breasts were swollen and the veins were risen on her chest and on her belly. Dark nipples. So the baby can see them with its undeveloped baby eyes, is what Sissy said. He could feel the heat coming off Karen. Her face was flushed. Underneath Roy's obvious fear, there was arousal.

"You're not breathing," Karen said. "Breathe with me."

He looked into her eyes and watched her breasts and followed her breathing. The water in the tub looked pink like maybe it was tinted by blood.

"We're not going to the hospital, then? This is it," Roy said.

"Are you nuts? No, we're doing this here. You couldn't get me into the car right now if you tried."

"Are you bleeding?"

She looked at the water. "Maybe. It's OK. We're going to be fine." Roy thought he should put some music on. Desmond Dekker had ended. Wiley and Sissy were in Wiley's room. He could hear them talking but not what they were saying.

"Hey," Karen said, touching his hand.

"I'm losing it," he said. "I feel like I'm gonna pass out or jerk off. I can't tell which. Maybe neither. Or both."

"You're OK." She took hold of his hand and squeezed. A contraction racked her and she crushed his fingers and he started to take his hand back but stopped himself in time.

Wiley's footsteps went banging through the kitchen and then Sissy said something they couldn't understand. "This is an emotional time," Karen said to Roy. "It puts you through a lot, feelings that maybe you haven't felt in a long time, or ever. It's fine. We're gonna be fine."

"What should I do?" Roy said. "I need you to tell me. I need a mission."

She let go of his hand and moaned through another contraction. "Go get some air. Look at the moon and the stars, then come back to me."

He gave her a weak smile. "It's still snowing. I can't see the stars."

"Tell Wiley to come here. I want to talk to her."

Roy sent Wiley to her mother. Sissy came from Wiley's bedroom with a skate mag in her hand.

"I'm going outside for a minute," Roy said.

Sissy removed her stocking hat to reveal her shaved-in breast cancer solidarity head and gave it a rub, then took a seat at the kitchen island with her cup of herbal tea and began flipping through the skate magazine. "If I see taillights, I'll chase you down." She held up the magazine, Roy's Prius ad had won a best advertisement of the decade contest. The old is new again. "Do you guys train for this stuff?"

"No."

"No conditioning work or anything, strength training?"

"Just skating. I quit smoking for a while, more or less."

One stunt person to another, a fraternal nod. "That's goddamn crazy."

He pointed at the door. "I'm not leaving. I'm just going outside."

"Don't be scared," Sissy said, without looking up from the magazine. "It'll happen when it's ready to happen. We don't rush and we don't panic."

Roy nodded and grabbed his coat and stepped outside. He gulped in the cold air and shook his head, trying to rattle his brain into focus. The snow continued. He'd already gone through six pairs of gloves shoveling snow this winter.

The goat shed was ripe with goat stink but he hardly noticed anymore. He checked the charge controller on the PV system that he'd rigged to power the barn too and it was enough to keep the lights on and the water from freezing in the goat pens but he'd have to climb the ladder again tomorrow morning to clean off the panels. Winter was hell on his batteries, he was on his second set already. Triage was how it felt most days: Fix fence, shovel, dig, repair, get by and don't stop or the whole operation grinds to a halt. As with everything, he and Karen would have to figure something else out long-term.

He pitched Despot the billy some hay and wrenched on his horns. Despot was disgusting, pure stinking destructive horny goat. Roy admired him, respected him even, but he was annoying in his need to destroy everything: fences, gates, feeders, whatever he could find. He'd gotten out last week and dented the shit out of the quarter panel on Roy's pickup. Just because. The nannies were sweeter and they got grain and nose rubs. Roy had a talent for milking. He'd built their stanchion with help from YouTube. He was OK with the killing and the butchering now, had to be, the guy they used to hire to do it had left town. Necessity normalizes. But Karen was the one with the skills. He made a mess of anything he cut into and the joke was cube steak. Cut it all into cube steak.

The chicks were being housed in a storage room off the back of the goat shed. He closed the door behind him and the smell of woodchips and ammonia hit him first. The heat-lamp-huddled birds had a calming effect on him. He'd built the brooder out of some old double-pane windows he'd saved from the county landfill. A box of glass held together with screws and a piece of scrap wood laid across the top for the heat lamp to clamp on to.

The little white and yellow birds had kicked litter into their food so he took the feeder out and cleaned it and refilled it with the fresh stuff that reminded him of Grape Nuts. He'd filled a five-gallon bucket with water earlier and he topped up the chickens' water jar from that and screwed on the plastic base and when he replaced it he made sure they all took a drink but one didn't get up from his corner. The other birds wouldn't get near the loner.

Roy picked it up and saw that it was breathing but it was slow and it didn't try to squirm from his hand. He knew he should kill it but shut the thought out because it seemed like bad luck to kill anything on the day his child was being born. He dipped its beak in the water and thought maybe it had swallowed a little but there was no way to tell. He gently lowered it onto the warmest spot under the heat lamp and mounded up the chips on it and made it a little bed. The other birds chirped and ran and climbed onto the miniroosts he'd built with #2 pencils and toy blocks he'd pilfered from Wiley's old toybox. They trampled the sick bird uncaringly. They gulped down water and scattered their feed, little prehistoric monsters.

On his way back to the house, head down against the storm, he heard Karen screaming. He ran as fast as he could through the snow and broke the upper hinge on the screen door as he ripped it open.

Karen was still in the tub, on all fours, facing the low flames in the woodstove. Water had been sloshed all over the floor and Wiley was on her knees beside her mother, pants wet, shirt wet, arms glistening. Sissy was at Karen's ear, talking to her. Roy scooted in beside Wiley and put his hand on her back.

"Where the hell were you?" Karen said.

"You told me to go," he said. "I was—I'm right here." Snow was melting on his face and his hands were tingling as they warmed up.

"Let yourself be," Sissy said to Karen. "Push and let it happen."

"Fuck Jesus," Karen said. "Oh fucking Jesus fuck."

Roy dropped to his knees and pulled Wiley tight to him and she looked up at him with unblinking fear. They were scared together. "Can you sit on the couch, sweetheart?" Roy said. Wiley wordlessly did as Roy asked. "We might need a little room is all. Are you OK?" She nodded yes.

Sissy moved to the other side of the tub and put the heart monitor against Karen's belly, static, a disconnected guitar amp, then the *plop plop plop* of a heartbeat. Karen's hand shot out of the tub and latched onto Roy's jacket, his dirty chicken shit goat shed stinking jacket, and he broke her grip like a grappler and ripped off his coat and threw it across the room. He came around the tub to face her and held her hands. She looked into his face and she scared him. How close was this to death? Suddenly her body seemed to coil into itself and he could practically hear her bones cracking and she stayed that way for too long, long enough for him to panic, but she released and Sissy was smiling a little but her eyes and her hands and her actions were dead serious and steady as stone. She'd put away all electronics, anything with a wire. She had towels and blankets ready. A little net like you'd use in an aquarium.

"Here we go," Sissy said. "Get in there, Papa."

Roy looked at Sissy, unsure if he was taking his clothes off or just climbing in.

"You're going to catch the baby." Sissy demonstrated what she wanted Roy to do. "I'll help you if you need it."

Karen moaned loudly and reached between her legs with one hand and Roy put his hands under and felt her pubic hair then something else and it was smooth and round. It was in his hand and he had the shoulders and the head and he might drop it, palming the head like a grapefruit, beyond slippery, he couldn't see what he was holding at all, then Sissy was there and lifted the child out of the water. Roy had never seen anyone perform a task so expertly. Roy was astounded. The child made its first sounds. Sissy gave Roy a look, saw right into his panicked soul. He just barely had the sense to help Karen as she rolled onto her back and sat up in the tub. Sissy wrapped the little girl in a blanket and passed her to Karen and she held her to her chest. The blanket drifted in the water. Sissy went to work with her little fishing net, tapped whatever she was pulling out into a small trash can she'd brought from the bathroom. Roy brushed Karen's hair back and touched the baby's head. Her mouth was working and the cry was so small and tender Roy's strength went from his legs and he felt like he might pass out.

"I gotta wash my hands" was all he could manage. He went to the kitchen sink and did a thorough scrub, dried his hands with one of the clean towels on the table. He watched as Wiley left the couch and went to her mother, stood behind her. Karen reached back and pulled her close.

They waited until the blood stopped pulsing in the cord and then Roy cut it. There was more waiting and crying. Karen was saving the afterbirth. Roy brought her robe and helped her from the tub and moved her to the couch. They sat as a family and looked at the child, rubbed the vernix and tested it between their thumbs and fingers.

Sissy eventually asked Karen permission and took the baby to what she'd established as her clinical area on the kitchen counter. She had a digital scale that assembled in two parts and she weighed the baby and used a tailor's tape to measure her length. She listened to her heart with a stethoscope and examined her ears and eyes. Wiley and Roy helped Karen to the bathroom and helped her rinse off in the shower.

Sissy had given the baby a beanie with the birthing-center name and logo embroidered on it. She took pictures with her phone and Wiley brought Karen's camera and took some pictures with that too. Roy used kindling and some red fir he'd been saving to stoke the fire.

After she put away her scale and packed her bag, Sissy connected a length of white garden hose to the tub and ran it out the front door and off the porch.

Wiley stepped carefully over the hose and knelt down in front of her mom. "It's a girl, Mama."

"She is a girl," Karen said. "How are you, sweetie?"

"I'm fine, Mama."

Roy leaned over Wiley and looked into his daughter's face. He saw her and she was all there. He couldn't speak. He wasn't breathing. What was this? What new planet was this? *What world did you come from? How did this happen? How is this coming as a shock?* Karen reached out for his arm. She looked as if she'd just stepped out of a sauna.

Just then Sissy came from the bathroom, toweling off her hands, looking more Volkswagen mechanic than midwife.

"That's that," she said. "I knew this was going to be an easy one. I told you," she said to Karen. "You did great." She smiled at Roy. "Ah, don't hide it, it's always the toughies that cry. Best day of your life. Congratulations, Papa."

He nodded thanks but if he spoke he didn't know what he would say. He wasn't crying. The baby, his daughter, was stretching her face like she'd just pulled it on and her eyes were rolling around shockingly loose in their sockets. How many babies were just born around the world? How many people had died? *Will this child live through a war? What happens if there's a war? There is always a war.* His wires were crossed. What about the sick chicken? Forget about that. He was responsible, directly, for a human life. That would never change. He'd fuck it up, of that he was sure.

"How about when it's empty you and me haul this tub onto the porch?" Sissy said to Roy. He nodded OK. To Karen, "I saved the afterbirth for you, Mama. We'll dehydrate it and put it into gelcaps like we talked about."

"Thanks," Karen said.

"Sure," Sissy said.

"You want a drink?" Roy asked Sissy.

"I wouldn't say no."

Roy poured two tall bourbons, cheers.

"I have a sister," Wiley said proudly. She jumped to her feet and did a little dance, booty shake.

"You have to watch over her, though. OK?" Karen said.

"OK, Mama."

The baby had already latched onto her breast. She was moving right along. Wiley was fiddling with the baby's fingers. Roy had his drink, was odd man out.

"Seems like there should be some type of trial period," Roy said. Karen gave him an uncomprehending look. "I mean, she's ours now. Like forever."

Sissy glanced at Karen and knocked back her drink. "I guess you can take the skateboarder out of So Cal but you can't take So Cal out of the skateboarder."

"It's a lot of responsibility is all," Roy said. "You at least have to go through a background check to get a gun. People, anyone, can have a baby. It's crazy."

"Why are you talking about guns right now?" Karen said.

"Are you getting another gun?" Wiley said.

"No, I'm not," Roy said. "Not anytime soon. It's just weird that any person can just have a baby. That's all I'm saying." He was trying to make light but his concerns were serious. Wiley nodded because she agreed. He downed his drink and tipped his glass at Sissy. "C'mon, Spacek. Let's get a move on."

"Don't call me that."

"For the So Cal business. Fair's fair."

"You're lucky your check cleared," she said to Roy, as they hoisted the tub. To Karen. "You really did do great, Mama. You too, Wiley. Come see me in a couple days and we'll see how everybody's doing. We have some paperwork too, but it can wait."

They named her Sarah after Karen's grandma. She slept in their bed that first night and they couldn't get her out of it for years to come. For Roy it was like checking a 9-volt with his tongue. A weak battery, or even a dead one, would give you a little kick but get a fresh one and there's no question. He could taste that electrical kick, see it in Karen's face, and it gave him the feeling that his life before Sarah was a game played with other people's money.

After two weeks of sleep deprivation by way of late-hour diaper changes and general farmstead collapse by way of neglect and winter weather, not to mention the innumerable and overwhelming father-daughter mind-melds that warped and re-warped his soul, the feeling that this was somehow scripted or preordained and that their lives mattered overtook his doubts, smothering his logical mind, which repeated to him endlessly that no one counts, that mankind is a germ. Looking at his family, his old frameworks went soft and rotten, teetered and swayed. If these people didn't matter, then nothing did, and if nothing mattered, they still would.

[30]

M < 55
OR 9XXXX

Hᴇ'ꜱ ᴡᴏʀᴋɪɴɢ ꜱʜɪʀᴛʟᴇꜱꜱ ᴏɴ ᴛʜᴇ ʀᴏᴄᴋꜱ, ꜱᴄʀᴀᴘɪɴɢ ᴛʜᴇ ʙᴇᴀʀ hide with a flattened steel can. Bloody dots cover his back like a pox. He found the first tick embedded in his leg when he'd undressed to soak in the hot springs. The more he looked, the more he found. Sol had tweezers. They took turns. The deer and the bear were covered in them too. Their discussion about Lyme disease hits a wall with the U.S.-government-created conspiracy theory. Call it cooties. Call it a bum deal. Bug bite. Call it: If you don't die, nobody cares. And then nobody cares. The mud scooped from the hot springs helps with the itch.

Meat is draped blackly on crisscrossed paracord and on a length of barbed wire the man found up the hill and stretched tree to tree like a clothesline. The drifting smoke of four separate fires mostly keeps the blowflies from landing. The bear cub is still in Sol's stone cage, quiet now, its muzzle bloody from the venison Sol has been feeding it.

Something wakes the dog, a sound or a smell, and now he's up and moving out of the smoke, watchful, sniffing the wind. When he barks the man stands up from the bear hide and sees them coming up the hill. He grabs the militiaman's rifle and puts it to his shoulder.

The one in front has a modded AR, the other two have hunting rifles, wooden stocks and scopes. They stop as a group when they see the gun pointed at them. They're dressed in civilian clothes, T-shirts, Carhartts, baseball hats.

"We heard you shooting yesterday," the one in front says. He is middle-aged, bone thin and haunted-looking with angry red scars on his hands and creeping up his arms. "We figured we'd come and talk to you, tell you what's what." He takes off his baseball hat and wipes his brow. His hair is gray and rusted-looking and overgrown. His head has the look of a ruptured cottonwood seed.

"Are you militia?" the man says.

"No," the leader says, putting his hat back on. "I'm a Californian. I'm an American. I grew up in these woods. My father and grandfather logged these hills. I raised a family here." He glances at the two young men behind him. "My sons."

"I'm lowering my weapon," the man says. The bear cub is crying again. The sound from the stone cage is one of desperate pain or of farmwork, an unhappy hackle raiser.

"What do you have in there?" the older man says, taking a step forward.

"Bear cub," the man says.

His sons shake their heads in disbelief, scowl at the idiocy.

Then they turn as a group and watch as Sol comes walking down the hill, daintily, foot to foot in his European underwear, his laundry folded over his arm. He stops when he sees the men in camp.

"They're not militia," the man says.

Sol takes a few steps and sets his clothes down on a rock, holds his hands up. "If you want to eat, we have plenty," he says, offers a smile. "I'm going to put some clothes on now so don't shoot me."

"We'd have killed you already if we wanted to," the taller of the two sons says.

"That may be true," the gray-haired man says to his son, "but we're here because if we heard your shots, then STT did too. You should get going. Take what meat you can carry but don't stay here."

"And don't come back," the tall son says. The smaller brother nods in agreement.

"OK," Sol says. He looks at the man, nods OK.

"We'll pack up," the man says.

"They'll be coming from the ranger station or near it. You don't have much time."

"Thanks," the man says.

"That rifle you have tells me two things," the leader says. "Either you were with them or you killed one and took his weapon."

"I was never with them," the man says.

"Bullshit," says the tall son. He points his rifle at the dog. "That's a cop dog or a military dog. I make you for Jefferson or STT, fuckin' Western States sure as anything."

"Don't point that at him. I said we're leaving." The father

waves his hand at his son and he lowers his weapon. The man sets the rifle down at his feet and shows them his hands. Sol pulls his shirt over his head.

"I'm letting that damn bear go," the tall son says, and he's about to say something else when a shot rings out and a spot like a large drip of paint or a cherry pit appears on his forehead, pink mist like a halo. Five maybe six more shots snap by and the old man and his sons jerk and twist and quickly crumple as if a spell has been cast. The shooting stops and Sol raises his hands and drops to his knees. The man catches the dog and holds on to it and waits for what's coming, doesn't bother picking up the rifle.

The militiamen come through the smoke, moving fast, barrels up, and kick the weapons away from the dead men, wordlessly set a perimeter. They're dressed in their standard mismatched—Real Tree, desert, digital, jungle, Mossy Oak— camouflage uniforms. The dog lover, Sampson was his name, smiles at the man and slings his weapon. The man waits for him to say something but he isn't talking. The leader arrives, weapon slung, offers his hand. The man refuses to take the bait, stands on his own, brushes off his pants.

"I thought we lost you," the leader says. He turns and motions for Sol to lower his hands and get up. "Signal went out for days then it came back."

"What signal?"

"Your dog. We put a trace on him. First time we saw you." He points at the dog, its neck, makes crawly fingers.

The man glances at the dog. He remembers the militiaman petting him, slapping his hands together when he was finished. *Sei brav.* Flies are lighting in the blood now and on the bear meat.

The one doing the talking drops his pack and lays his rifle on top. "My name's Printz and that's Sampson—he hasn't shut up about your dog by the way—and that's Danish and Lott, Hick, and Latham." He smiles at the dog as he takes off his coat. He's wearing a second pistol in a shoulder holster, a utility belt with a knife and ammunition. He leaves his pack and his coat on the ground and slings his rifle back on his shoulder. "Bad dudes." He passes a hand over the bodies. "They don't look like much, but as a family they've been raising hell around here for the better part of a decade. This is a big day and we only have you to thank for it." He nods vigorously at the man, like you better believe it. "You're our Judas goat. Do you know what that means? You did all the work. They came to you." Then he notices the rifle at the man's feet. He picks it up, turns it over and traces his fingers over the stock, the carving. The other militiamen are closing in now, trying to get a better look. Printz passes the rifle to Sampson, who ejects the magazine and clears the chamber.

"It was Dave Matthews's," the man says.

One of the militiamen, Lott, laughs. "That answers that," he says.

"Shut the fuck up," Sampson says to him.

"He was a fan," Lott says. "I'm not talking shit."

"Both of you be quiet," Printz says, nodding to the man. "We've met already, but who're you now?" he says to Sol.

Sol is standing with his hands open at his waist. He glances at the man and smiles before he speaks. "Solomon Morris Sheridan the Third," he says.

"Uppity little bitch," Sampson says.

"No, that's my sister's name," Sol says.

"Fuck you," Sampson says.

"What's with the rash?" the one called Latham asks. "Are you contagious?"

"Ticks," the man says.

Latham squirms and scratches his shoulder. "Fuck that," he says.

The bear cub cries and gets everyone's attention. Printz peers in to see, then waves his comrades over. Danish, beefy arms and a blond flat top, spits chew spit at the bear and walks away. "Fucking stupid," he says.

Printz watches him go. "Don't just wander off," Printz says after him. "We still have work to do here. I want this cleaned up before nightfall."

"Yeah, yeah," Danish says. "Let it be written."

There's a slot in the rock down the hill, a big broken smile, and the militiamen roll the bodies one after the other into it and then kick in duff and smaller stones to cover them up.

As the sun slips behind the mountain, the temperature drops and the steam thickens. The militiamen take turns in the pools, with one standing guard at all times. They have ticks too but not as bad. They have their own tweezers and headlamps. They make a contest out of it. Sampson wins with thirteen. Printz is the last to use the pools, tick-free and he gloats. Once he gets dressed and pulls on his boots, he picks up his pack and his weapons and walks over to the man, squats in front of him.

"Water sure is nice, isn't it?" Printz says. The man glances at the pool but doesn't answer. Printz has wide-set, calculating eyes and thin blond eyebrows. "This is a delicate matter, so I want to talk to you one on one." When he speaks intimately, there is the click of false teeth. The man gets a sense of what's coming.

"Was he dead when you found him?"

"No."

"Was anyone else there?"

"No." The man doesn't know what message Dave Matthews sent to his comrades, if he and the dog were mentioned.

"Are you going to make me ask?"

"He shot first."

Printz nods, tugs the hair on the stretched bear hide and the barbed wire screams a little. He brushes the bear fur with his hand. "I'm willing to forgive you for what you've done, but I'm going to need something in return."

"You can have the rifle."

"I'm not talking about that anymore." Printz leans in, talks too closely. "Our sweep, our mission, is to reestablish Preservation control. That means neutralizing or expelling the remaining Jeffs as well as independent and federal forces that we come across."

"I already told you, I'm not interested and you can't have my dog."

"Hear me out. When we hit the Columbia River, we're taking a boat from there, back down south. We'll be working a different angle on the coast, delivering aid instead of doing security patrols, hearts and minds. We got families too. This is the good fight. We're helping people. Helping the country." The man shakes his head no. "Damn, brother, you aren't hearing me. I'm talking about you coming with us. You and your dog. Sampson tells me the dog is only as good as the handler so you're in." He touches the man's arm. "I think you owe us that much."

"I don't owe you shit."

Printz raises his eyebrows, sniffs the air, smiles. "How far are you headed? What's your endpoint? If I had to guess, I'd say

Alaska. Everybody out here says that's where they're going. Pilgrims. You know how many of them actually make it?" Printz again studies the man's face. "Canada is the problem. You have to make it to Juneau if you want to go north. The goddamn Canadians hold everything to the south of there. We lost the inland passage. Can you believe that? The United States is losing territory on both borders. This is how it starts."

"Are you done?"

Printz smiles a tight-lipped smile, continues. "The dog is coming with us, and if you piss and moan about it anymore, I'll put a bullet in Solomon-fancy-pants-the-third's nigger head." He gives the man an aw-shucks wave and a whack on the shoulder. "Uppity bitch, right?"

The man doesn't argue. He and the dog watch Printz walk away, cross the rocks to where the others are digging into the ragged hunks of venison roasting on a spit over the fire.

"Aren't you the hot ticket," the man says to the dog.

The sad, plaintive cry of the bear cub echoes from the stone enclosure.

"Shut that fucker up," Danish says, "or I'll shut it up for you."

"There used to be two," Sol says.

"So?" Danish says.

"So, it could be worse," Sol says with a smile.

"What're you going to do with that thing?" Printz asks Sol, digging a long tan finger into a can of Copenhagen and sliding the dregs into his lip. "Let it grow up and eat you?"

"I could train him to dance, we could join the circus," Sol says.

"You're more than halfway to being a freak already," one of the other militiamen says, Lott is his name. He's taken his hat off and he has blue and green tattoos on his shaved head. He smiles a half-silver grin and nods to Sol and then to the man. "So are you guys a couple?"

"Traveling companions," Sol says. "How about you? Is one of these gentleman your special fella?"

"I'm married," Lott says.

Sol waits.

"To a woman," Lott says with urgency.

Sol smiles, sure you are. "You know, I read somewhere," he says. "*The Brothers Karamazov* maybe, of a man fighting a bear, but they'd pulled his teeth and his claws. That's not a fair fight, is it?" Sol says. "I like my fights fair. How about you?"

"I like to fuckin' win," Sampson says.

"Copy that, brother," Danish says.

Sampson approaches the dog, kneels down and checks out the scars on his hip. "I didn't get a chance to ask before but it's from a shotgun, right?"

"Yeah."

"Motherfuckers," Sampson says. "Who trained him?"

"Who says he's trained?"

Sampson smiles, shakes his head. "Trust me. I know. Been around dogs my whole life."

"Eats his own weight every week."

"So do I," he says, laughs. "Czech?"

"Some."

"German?"

"No."

"He takes hand signals. I've seen you use them."

"He's a pain in the ass."

The one called Latham, the medic, has his pack open and

he's cleared a place on a large flat rock so he can clean his weapons. He's sitting cross-legged with his hood up on his gray sweatshirt. "You should let the bear go," he says. "It's a fuckin' bear, right?" In a few practiced motions, almost as if he were playing, or showing them a magic trick, he takes his pistol apart. "How many bears are left?"

"He'll die if I don't raise him, though." Sol holds up his hands. "He's too young to be on his own."

"He'll die anyway," Printz says, without looking away from the fire. "He's already dead. Kick those rocks in and walk away."

The blood is still dark on the ground. The fires have all been left to die and the smoke is punching up the air. The man goes back to stretching and trimming the hide, no one is talking anymore. Later, Sol gives the man a pat on the back and wordlessly returns to his tent and zips the door after him.

Lodged in a tangle of hair on the back of the dog's neck the man finds the tracking devices, they look like blackened fingernail clippings but when he tries to bend them they snap and he can see they're made of plastic. He uses his knife to cut them free. When he's finished he hauls the dog into the coolest pool and dunks him and searches again but can't find anything.

In the morning, the man packs his rig, loads it with not-quite-dry bear jerky and bones for Pecos. He's leaving what's left of the venison for Sol and the bear cub. Lott and Danish walk down to the road and return separately, an hour later, roaring up the hill like off-road racers in a matched pair of late-model Hi-Jet troop carriers, carbon-fiber frames, three feet of travel, spool-up power like an RC car. Sol helps the man get his bike and trailer into the cargo cage and gives him a hug goodbye.

"Take care of yourself," Sol says. "Maybe I'll see you up the road."

"I hope so." The man secretly passes him a piece of paper with the coordinates of where he'll be in Alaska. They part ways with a final handshake and it isn't until miles later, riding in the back of the STT rig with the dog, his bike and trailer, that the man digs for a fresh water bottle and discovers that Sol has given him three of the six lead aprons.

[31]

R < 25
CA 96118, CA 95605

ROY KICKED OFF HIS SHOES AND SOCKS AND WORKED THE PEDALS barefoot as he motored along in Carl, listening to High on Fire. The snow in the passes was turning to rain. The heater, along with the stereo, was cranked. He had his one hitter out and things were feeling a little better, weed blurring the hard edges of Karen's absence. The ski-area traffic absorbed him into the herd.

There was a new indoor skatepark in Woodland, a suburb of Sacramento. Yuri had mentioned it on the phone, then Roy remembered that he'd read about it in some magazine. It was the only place he could think to go. He asked directions from a woman in a Raiders jacket with a tiny tattooed star on her cheek like a beauty mark. She thought he was talking about a roller rink until he reached back and held up his board. He changed clothes in the parking lot and ran through the rain with his board and helmet and went inside.

The kid working the gate was a stranger but once inside Roy recognized a few of the guys on the eight-foot ramp, two pros killing it and an old guy who wasn't, an editor at a skate magazine in SF. Roy had met the editor years ago, when he was working on an article about him and the DEK8D guys. He'd skated with the two pros, Jim (Nessy) Nestor and Justin (FBI—fucking big Indian) Gilles, as recently as last summer in Portland.

Roy said his hellos, gave a couple of bro hugs and a handshake, waited his turn, then dropped in. His legs were tight from driving so he worked the ramp for speed, loosening up, laid down a few long grinds, but on his fourth wall he boosted a hefty back stair, and from then on he charged, went for whatever showed up in his mind as he pumped for speed down the opposing wall. He was out of shape though, and he reeled it in before his legs gave way and he bailed.

"Off the bench," Nessy said, as if he were impersonating Sean Connery. "From the corridor, if you will, Mr. Bingham delivers."

Roy took off his helmet and scratched his head and watched the editor run through his limited bag of tricks, stiff and not very fast, kind of spazzy. He was better on the page.

"You still live in Portland?" FBI asked.

"I'm in between." Roy clicked his helmet back on. "Don't know where the fuck I'm going."

A photographer that everybody knew, George Pacecek, was coming up the stairs to the deck. George set down his camera bag and gave Roy a high five. "What the fuck, Roy? What's the occasion? I haven't seen you farther south than Klamath Falls for ten years."

"Not that long," Roy said, and had to step back because FBI was boosting and making the whole ramp shake.

George opened his bag and worked on getting set up to take some photos. The editor went over and talked to the photographer, pointed at the lights and at some kids skating the street course.

With the camera equipment it was a little crowded on deck so Roy crossed over to the other side of the ramp and waited for his turns. Later in the session, after Roy had made the nosepick off the handrail at the back of the deck and hauled his body once again, smoothly with a frontside grab, into the transition, Nessy came over to his side to shoot the shit.

"George got that whole sequence," Nessy said, swigging a beer with a rubberized, transferable Coca Cola label on it. "Roy Bingham murders."

"Born to kill," Roy said.

"What're you doin' tonight? Wanna get some beers with me and FBI?"

"Sure."

In the morning, Roy was in the back of the van in a bar parking lot, hungover, cash reserves down to ones, stripper rich, with maybe a quarter tank of gas. He found his phone and it said "service unavailable." Karen paid the bills and she wasn't going to keep his phone on. He knew it would happen, but not today. Nessy and FBI were expecting Roy to call so they could caravan to SF, but with no phone and no phone numbers, he couldn't. So here he was, in fact, penniless and living in a van in Sacramento. At least it was raining.

Not knowing where else to go, he went back to the Woodland park, but he wasn't going to spend the money to get in until he saw someone he knew that might be able to get him in for free. He smoked the last of his weed and napped in the back of the van. Late in the afternoon a pickup pulled into the parking lot across the street. A black guy got out wearing a hoodie, shorts, and two knee braces, and grabbed his board and a duffel bag and headed for the door.

Roy got out of the van. "Liston," Roy said.

When he saw Roy he stopped, held his bag up to get some shelter from the rain. "Bingham?" Roy nodded. "What the fuck you doin' here?"

"Waiting to skate."

"Well, come the fuck on, man."

Roy went back to the van and grabbed his shit and followed Liston inside. The kid at the door knew Liston and remembered Roy from the day before. He waved them in for free.

Liston lived in West Sacramento in a run-down tract home on a double lot with a big corrugated steel shop. He offered Roy a spot to park his van beside the shop until he got situated. He was married with two kids but his family was in Florida for the holidays. Liston couldn't get time off work to go with them. He had a miniramp in the back corner of his shop and they went there to skate some more after they left the park.

"You're a mechanic now?" Roy asked, working the lever on a drill press.

"Machinist," Liston said.

"What do you machine?"

"Whatever they tell me."

Liston had a beer fridge in his shop and an old oil furnace that kept it toasty. After the first night in the van, Roy moved into the shop and slept on the ramp.

"How'd you get into this?" Roy said, passing a hand over the workbench.

"I got locked up for a while."

"I heard."

"When I got out, my PO got me a job at an auto body place and the owner thought I was less retarded than his other employees—which is hardly a vote of confidence—but he helped me get into some classes. I did the community college thing for a year but my daughter was born so I quit and got a job."

"Is it good money?"

"It's fine. My wife works too." Liston put down his beer and tried a kickflip to noseblunt for the twentieth time and failed again. He hit the flat bottom hard and was slow getting up. "Weren't you married?" Liston asked.

"No, me and Karen never got married." Roy dropped in and nailed Liston's trick on his first try.

"Fuck you, Bingham. I'm turning the heat off tonight."

"Come on, man."

"Fuckin' lockin' up my beer too."

Roy couldn't bring himself to ask Liston for a loan so he asked if he wanted to buy some skate decks and wheels he had floating around in the van.

"No, man. I don't need that shit. And my family comes back day after tomorrow so you need to get sorted."

"Do you know anybody that wants to buy a van?" Roy said. "I'm kind of stuck right now."

Liston shook his head. "I know a guy that might be able to give you some work."

"As a machinist?"

"Fuck no, Bingham. Laborer. Shovel and broom. *Pala y escoba. Nada mas.*"

"Laborer?"

"As in, to labor. *Jornalero.* The bottom, brother."

Roy squirmed a little. "I don't know, man."

"Are you kidding me?"

"What?" Roy said. "I'm not saying no, am I? I just want, like, more information."

Liston went to his workbench and wrote something down on a greasy piece of steel with a chalk pencil, came back and handed it to Roy. "If you call him, you can say I gave you his name. But don't call him if you're just gonna dog out on him and bail without warning."

"I'm not looking for a career," Roy said.

"You can skate, but you're a fucking moron." Liston dropped into the ramp and kept talking. "You're gonna be homeless. That's gonna be your career." Liston raised his voice an octave. "I'm not looking for a career," he said. "I'm just gonna fucking mooch off my buddy Liston until I win the lotto."

"All right," Roy said. "That's enough a that." He dropped in on Liston and snaked him and made him fall, kept skating and locked in at least five tricks in a row that Liston would never be able to do in his whole life, before he finally wadded up and slid to a stop in the flat bottom.

"Call him," Liston said. "But only if you're gonna work. Hear me?"

"I hear you," Roy said. "I fuckin' hear you."

The man's name was Clem and he lived in a mossy sailboat at the marina with two Scottish terriers named Swerdlow and Mankowitz. He never asked how Roy knew Liston or why he was living in a van. He invited him on board and had him fill out an employment form in the surprisingly tidy galley. While he was doing that, Clem went to the marina office and photo-copied his license. When he returned he gave Roy his license and a piece of paper with G-9 written on it.

"You can park there if you want."

"OK, thanks."

"You can use the bathrooms but if you're going to shower try and do it after they lock the gate at ten."

"OK."

The next day at dawn Clem drove Roy to the new bridge that was being built upriver from the failing I-Street bridge. The dogs went with them, tugging on their yo-yo leashes, and stop-ping constantly to piss and sniff at turds and trash. The river was diverted by a series of dams around the construction project. Barges were anchored in the water end-to-end in a continuous chain that created a temporary work platform. Clem explained that once the ambient temperature had fallen enough to slow most of the runoff the engineers had shut the upstream dams and weirs and built the temporary dams in sections so the crews could work on the bridge without being underwater. Only one of the bridge columns had been poured so far but Clem said there were three more that would go in before they could start on the deck.

"I'm in the office until they have the columns done," Clem said.

Roy got a bit of a thrill imagining himself working high above the river with Clem, but Clem got him a job in the yard instead, driving a telehandler in the mud, fetching materials that were ordered over the two-way radio. He never left the shore.

His foreman, Enrique, was from Chihuahua and he could speak English—Roy had heard him—but he wouldn't speak it to Roy or any of the other peckerwood laborers working in the yard.

Clem went to Thailand for two weeks in March and let Roy stay on his sailboat to watch the dogs. On a moonless night he borrowed Clem's Zodiac and motored out to the new bridge. He tied up to the piling nearest the power plant and scaled down the back side of one of the temporary dams into the dark pit below.

He stood out there in the middle of the river and listened to the water and thought about Karen Oronski. He thought about his life but in an unchangeably distracted way that took him nowhere. He was lousy with decisions. He was only good when he was moving. He was only good with Karen and when he was moving.

When he returned to the marina he put the dogs and their food, their dishes and beds in the van, then went back to the boat and disconnected the batteries and locked the doors and hatches. He took the dogs to Liston's and left them in the shop, figuring Liston would find them first thing. They had food and water. They'd be fine. Roy was northbound, a little bit of money in his pocket, free.

[32]

R < 45
CA 96118, CA 94015

THE BABY HAD JUST GONE TO SLEEP AND THE SUN WOULD BE UP
in an hour.

"I need to get out of here," Roy said.

"Why?" Karen said. "Why don't Wiley and I get to get out
of here? Why do you?"

"Give me a few days. I need out. I need sleep."

"Don't talk to me about sleep. You get more sleep than anyone."

"I'll bring presents."

"I don't care about presents." Karen touched her painfully
swollen breasts through her sour-milk T-shirt. "Take these and
feed the baby and let me go. How about that? Take my tits and
set me free. I don't want them anymore and you probably won't
either once the milk is gone and they sag and I look old and
ugly."

"Never."

"You better still love me when my tits go wrong."

"I'll try."

"Don't make fun of me."

"I'm not."

"You are."

"Not so loud, you'll wake everyone up and then we won't even be able to argue in peace."

Karen hung her head and shuffled over to Roy.

"You think I don't need a vacation?" Karen said into his chest.

"I know you do. But let me go first since really you can't go anyway until Sarah is weaned."

"This is the biology of misogyny."

"I know. It isn't fair." He was a farmer now and like any farmer he had a gift for complaining without actually saying anything. He could complain by just looking at you.

"You've been riding around on your new toy quite a bit," Karen said. "I know you're not always working. I see you popping wheelies, ripping around like Steve McQueen, pretending to check the irrigation lines."

His new bike was an ancient '84 XR 500 that in the last century had been built out as a desert racer with an oversized tank and extra lights up front. Roy had bought it for five dollars at an estate sale and limped it home. With the carb and tank cleaned out, a new fuel line and an oil change, the bike was ready to go, pure thumper.

"I'm a desperado, out riding fences."

Karen smiled. The weight she'd gained during her pregnancy was long gone and she was back into her old clothes. Roy wanted to get her new clothes. Her arms were thin, too thin, Roy thought. Everybody was too thin.

"You can go," Karen said, as Roy pulled her to him and kissed her. "I'm up next, though. Me and Wiley are going to do something fun without you and your spawn."

"OK."

"I don't know what yet, but something."

"There's always Mexico."

"Shut your stupid mouth," she said. "Get out of here. Go."

He packed light and, outside of sending Yuri a text to let him know that he was coming, made no plans. It felt good to be back on the Bonneville after the XR but it had been a while so he took it easy. He rode the back way out so he wouldn't have to go through town and see what else had happened since they'd boarded up the unfinished Jeffersonian Preservation Hall, or go by Barry Miller's, where it seemed like every other week their neighbor was putting up a new security fence. He had the corny red, white, and gold Jeffersonian flag flying atop his ridiculous supermax-style gate, so you'd know where his allegiance stood or crouched or cowered, whatever his allegiance did.

The Binghams' other neighbors, hay farmers mostly, along with their friends from town, Aaron and April, they'd all left. There'd been no goodbye parties, no forwarding addresses. The trucks and lowboy trailers arrived and lifted the houses from their foundations with I-beams and hydraulic jacks and hauled them to Frenchman Lake or one of the other billionaire or militia compounds that had sprouted up near Susanville or Redding. The house movers went about their jobs like insects, dung beetles, slow and steady, somewhat clumsy but ultimately effective. Roy didn't blame people for selling out, for leaving. Often he wanted to join them. But last week Roy had tracked down Sullivan, the well-driller, and paid him a deposit. Another well, another door opens. Just because everyone thinks one thing doesn't make it true. If Karen wasn't ready to quit, neither was he.

The bike was running rough so he hit high revs in an attempt to burn it clean. He envisioned the combustion chambers, gummy spark plugs. Dust coated his visor and he wiped it clean with the back of his arm, old leathers, dingy gray and cracked.

The Yuba and the Feather, both dry and loaded with dead-fall, were followed by the mud puddle reservoirs, after-party sad, trampled and dusty, denoting dead towns. It would take more than a good winter to fix this. Another summer like the last and Roy figured it was done. They'd have to leave like everyone else. Unless Sullivan found some new pocket of groundwater. A philosophy of wait-and-see that might in the long run kill them.

Winding through the mountains, clicking through the gears, falling into turns, then he hit a straight stretch and looked around and was suddenly filled with fear because at home he hadn't been able to admit to himself what exactly was out here, the pure desolation. He'd been so busy working, being a father, keeping the lights on and water pumping, that he'd convinced himself that maybe this whole rickety apparatus would actually hold strong, because it always had before. But from elevation with a long view, he could see that it wouldn't.

And it didn't get any better once he hit the highway. The bike tightened up though, and the jets cleared and it quit popping. He settled in at eighty-five and let it roll. Die-off was apparent on both sides of the road. The border of the Preservation was inconsequential, one side was as trashed as the other. The little towns and off-ramp fuel stops looked like they'd been bombed. Police tape and chain-link barriers and graffiti were the constants. And the tagging wasn't the usual sort. It was the kind of thing you saw when the National Guard was called in, status reports written on the walls and rooftops four feet tall, so they'd be visible from the air.

Roy listened to the news on the radio. He knew about the earthquakes, the floods and fires, the running battles with the militias, the attack on Twentynine Palms. His mom and Steve had sold their place in San Diego years ago and moved to a retirement community in Maine, so they were fine. The epicenter was way north of there anyway. Everybody was always blah-blah-blah saying SF was on the chopping block but it had missed them completely.

He sped by a water tower that had been tipped over and cut in half, maybe to catch the rain that didn't fall. *You could skate that*, he thought.

He'd read that more than fifteen million had already left California. The Midwest was bone dry and fracked out and everybody talked like the East Coast might as well be on the other side of the Gobi. Militias over there, too. Rust Belt Regulars fighting for their own little bit of Preservation. Coast regions of Oregon and Washington and now Alaska were overrun with refugees, but since the political fracture of the Preservation had been compounded by the physical fracture of the earthquake, they didn't have the infrastructure left to maintain a growing population. Everybody was either federally battled or federally maintained, but how long could that last? Fighting wars on two fronts overseas, not to mention all the new militias and the Jeffersonians at home. It wasn't that something had to give; it was that it was gone and it wasn't coming back. Maybe Alaska was the place to be. Maybe it always had been. Canada wasn't taking anybody else. They'd built their own wall. Do unto others.

The Bay Bridge was blocked with protesters. Banners were strung from rail to rail but Roy couldn't read them as far back as he was in the line, a quarter mile at least. He angled out of the traffic jam and drove across the median, over a sidewalk and into a boarded electronics store parking lot and called Yuri. His friend gave him new directions that took him far south but Yuri said it would still be faster.

Yuri and Sue lived in an affordable housing project that had been carved out of a block of row houses in Daly City. Roy parked among some other motorcycles and scooters at the edge of the courtyard. A small apple orchard surrounded the massive garden in the center of the complex. There were orange trees too, and avocados. Hop vines ran up the walls.

The door opened before he could knock and Sue greeted him with a big smile. She was a small Chinese woman and she gave him a powerful, lung-cinching hug. Yuri, his old friend, skate trash with a Russian mafia father, clapped him on the back and shoved him inside and put a beer in his hand.

The living room had two chairs and a couch with a low table in front of it, bookcases against the wall. Efficiency kitchen, but it had a nice view of the courtyard. Roy couldn't imagine living in an apartment. Where would he piss? Indoors? *I don't think so.*

"Where are your boys?" Roy said.

"Probably going through your shit," Yuri said. "Stripping your bike and selling the parts to buy bathtub vodka."

"They're still at school," Sue said. "Which is where I should be. I told them I'd come back in for a few hours tonight but I'll be home by the time dinner gets started." She was younger than her husband but she looked tired, worn down.

"I'm doing dinner then?" Yuri said.

"So smart," Sue said, and gave her husband a kiss.

When Roy picked up a twenty-year-old issue of *Thrasher* from the bookshelf, Yuri told him that his boys, they had three of them—six, nine, and eleven—all skated. They had two more beers while they looked through magazines, held up photos for each other to see.

"I remember that place," Yuri said.

"What about him?" Roy said, holding up the magazine for Yuri to see. It was a photo of his old teammate Rasheed, doing a massive backside 180 kickflip over a dirt-and-boulder parking-lot-to-parking-lot gap.

"Looks fake," Yuri said.

"I saw him do it," Roy said. "I was there."

"No shit?"

"No shit."

"Whatever happened to him?"

"He died riding his motorcycle."

Yuri gave him a sideways look. "I didn't know. With you?"

"No. I wasn't there."

"How about the rest of the guys? Nessy and Yano?"

"Last I saw them was when they came through to skate at my place, years ago. We had fun. Got footage. Shit, they had to help me bury Wiley's dog, middle a winter. I almost forgot about that. I know that Yano started that XIT shit with Bradford and it took off huge for a while. Nessy is swoosh royalty. Golden ticket. I haven't heard anything bad so I'm thinking they're OK."

"That's one way," Yuri said.

"It's too easy to say everything's fucked, you know? Or all my friends are gone. Or we're all doomed."

"I wasn't saying that," Yuri said, grinning. "I was just surprised by your fucking optimism."

When Yuri's boys came in from school they stacked their boards behind the door and took off their tattered shoes, came into the living room shoving and gave Roy the stink eye. They all had long hair and torn clothing and looked to be about five minutes from being feral, mini-Genghis Khans returning from ruling the steppe, Mad Maxicans. Roy liked them instantly, the future. When they saw his helmet and asked about his bike, he took them outside and gave them all rides on the back and even let Oscar, the oldest, try to ride it by himself but he dumped it and chewed up his knee and Yuri said that was enough. He'd just gotten the cast off his arm two weeks ago. Before that it had been stitches. Before that it had been food poisoning. Before that a broken leg. Before that appendicitis. Before that he had been born premature. The future needed health care.

Sue taught biology at the community school that was integrated into the apartment complex. Yuri was on staff as a plumber. There wasn't room for Roy in the apartment but there was an outside sleeping area for guests and, after a dinner of roasted beets, farmed crawdads, and brown rice, Roy picked a hammock and sacked out to the sounds of sirens and helicopters and woke before dawn to the burbling of the drip irrigation in the garden.

Yuri kicked his hammock a few minutes later. Roy got dressed and followed him out of the apartment complex. They walked down the hill to a coffee truck and then wandered through the streets until they were looking out to the ocean where the kelp boats were busy taking their hauls.

"They're like the snails people buy to keep their aquariums clean." Yuri tipped his coffee at Roy. "Human condition is what that is. The bed we made."

Roy leaned back on a bench and took in the air. "Do you eat it, the kelp and shit?"

"Yeah, all the time."

"Not bad?"

Yuri smiled and scratched his head, his face settling into a grimace, gray stubble and laugh lines. Old friend. "It's patriotic. That's what they say. Just like a victory garden." He took a slug of his coffee. "You know that the oil companies hold all of the undersea cables now."

"I heard. Ransomed access."

"Your Wi-Fi is gonna get slow."

"Any slower and it'll be dead." Roy had the lid off of his coffee, smelling the steam. "Where did the big wave hit?"

"North of here, Jedidiah. Smacked into the redwoods."

"Did you feel the quake?"

"Yeah, you?"

"No."

"So listen, there's an apartment opening up. I think we can get you in. Sue has some pull. So do I."

"What would we do with our animals?"

"You might be able to bring some of them. The chickens."

"There's a guy drilling wells up by us, has a kid working for him that's the same age as Wiley, smart as hell, like a little engineer. They've had some success, where no one else has. I paid 'em a deposit. We're on the list. We hit water, we'll be set."

"If," Yuri said.

"When. Not if." Roy couldn't remember the last time he'd had coffee that wasn't brewed in their kitchen, let alone arrived in a to-go cup. Sometimes they didn't have coffee at all, for weeks. "Maybe you should move up there with us."

"No school. No hospital. No work. Lousy with militia fuck-bags." Yuri stood and walked to the edge of the sidewalk. Gulls turned at the edge of the cliffs. "You saw my kids. They need medical help, like every other day."

"There's plenty of work at my place," Roy said. "Just none that pays. None that gets you an apartment."

"Don't give me that company-man shit. Where's Wiley going to school? And when Sarah gets older, what then?"

"There's an online thing. It's not bad."

"Until BP and Shell don't get their payola and the Internet goes down for good. Then your dumbass becomes what, Professor Dumbass? Professor Dial-up?"

"Fuck, I don't know. Do something. Like you were saying, we all have to do something."

"I was just asking. Sue and I talked last night and—I was just asking."

"I appreciate it but we aren't going anywhere. I don't trust cities anymore. I don't trust people in general."

"That's too bad. I took the day off so we could hang."

"I trust you, man, and Sue. But I don't know anybody else around here. And at this point, I don't think I even want to."

"What do you want to do today, then? Dig a bunker? Stockpile ammo? Lithograph some fucking pamphlets?"

"No. I need to get some clothes for Karen and the girls."

"Little Roy on the prairie. Get me some candy in town, Pa."

"Fuck off. Sue can tell me where to go, can't she?"

"I'll go with you. What the fuck else are we gonna do? Skate? Get drunk?"

"After we go shopping, sure."

Roy only stayed two nights. It was the last time he'd see Yuri and Sue, their boys, the last time he'd see SF. If he'd known, maybe he would've stayed a bit longer. They had gone skating, though, borrowed Oscar's board, which was how Roy liked to remember Yuri—standing on the deck at the deep end at some graffiti wasteland hotel pool, a beer in his hand, calling Roy a pussy.

"Get it," he'd said. "Get in there and get some, you broke-down, goat-farming, militia-ass motherfucker."

Going up the coast, Roy had to cut inland where the road had been lost. Yuri had told him as much, and Roy had seen it on the news already, but riding toward it he couldn't quite compre-hend the scale. Whole stretches of the coast had been evacuated, mile after mile of real estate swallowed by the tide. He twisted the throttle and ran fast east, sang Youth Brigade, *and we'll sink with California when it falls into the sea.*

[33]

M < 55
OR 9XXXX

Hᴇ ᴅᴏᴇsɴ'ᴛ ʙᴏᴛʜᴇʀ sᴛᴏᴡɪɴɢ ʜɪs sʟᴇᴇᴘɪɴɢ ʙᴀɢ, ᴊᴜsᴛ ᴅʀᴀᴘᴇs it over the trailer and moves quietly out of camp. He's sick. The diarrhea started as soon as they left the hot springs, now with the muscle aches in his neck and lower back, hips. He wonders how Sol is faring. The militiamen are still sleeping. They have colorful tents like they're at base camp or in a scout group. The dog stays close as the man coasts by the two vehicles parked in the trees. The sun has yet to light the treetops, never mind the quick-charge solar cells on the militia rigs. The wind is cold and the man's hands ache on the grips. He rounds a corner and is surprised to see Printz standing in the middle of the road.

"Morning," Printz says. "I figured you'd be along." He slings his rifle over his shoulder and hangs his thumbs in his chest pack.

"We'll wait for you down the road, how's that?"

"I don't think so. There's some people we're gonna meet today and I want the dog there in case someone else knows we're coming." Printz takes out the small black folder where he keeps his maps. "I'll tell you a secret. If the Jeffs take control again, they'll just hand over everything to whoever asks, the feds or the chinks. They don't care which. Their organization is compromised." He flips through the pages, searching for the one he wants. "And I'll tell you right now, if they catch you, they won't ask you to work with them, be part of the team, because I'll make sure they find out you were with us and they'll kill you, brother. No question." Printz keeps flipping through the maps.

"Who pays for this shit?"

"You'd be surprised."

Once Printz settles on a map, he slides his finger over the stacked-up topo lines, smiles. "It's gonna be a tough one today. Look at this. We drive up here and then we have to hoof it to the top. Rough country." He traces a circle with his finger.

The man releases his grip on the handlebars and lets his hands fall to his sides. The bike rests against his leg. "What if I say no?"

"Now, c'mon. We all like you. We're friends, right?"

"I don't have a choice but to be your friend, do I?"

"No, you don't." Printz laughs and jostles the man by the shoulder. "You'll be a good soldier someday. I know it." The man is surprised by Printz's strength, by his own weakness, his age. His skin hurts like he has the flu.

Printz stows his map folder and swings his weapon forward and rests his right hand on the butt. "When I was a kid, my parents grew tomatoes. They had greenhouses, like fifty of them. This was no back-porch operation, they had lots of people, illegals mostly, wetbacks, to be honest, working for them, trucks and trailers, greenhouses, warehouses bigger than airplane hangars. I'm telling you, they grew tomatoes. I'd ride in the trucks to the processing plant sometimes. It was in another town, maybe two hours from where we lived." The man waits silently for Printz to go on. He needs to go and squat in the bushes again.

Printz switches the safety on his weapon from on to off while he studies the man's face. "Tomatoes are delicate," he says. "They don't travel well, there'd always be spoilage, even on that short little drive we made to Glendale, but it all went into the vats, all of it, whatever was in the trucks went into the cans. And you know what? Nobody could taste the difference. You get me?" He leans closer, lowers his voice. "You're acting like what's happening out here is murder but it's not. It's a campaign. It stops being murder when it's war."

"So why don't you kick my ass or kill me and take my dog?"

Printz gives the man a warm, Christian smile. "Besides the fact that Sampson says that dog won't be worth a damn without you working it?"

"Besides that."

"Not much else, honestly. But I'll give you something. How about because you want to live. You've got a reason beyond survival. Am I wrong?"

The man looks away from Printz to the dog but he's thinking of his girls.

"It means you've got character," Printz says. "That you're honor-bound, and that's what it is to be American, isn't it? That's the bedrock. And for damn sure it's what the new version of America will be built on. I guarantee you that. We're taking it back, once and for all." In Printz's eyes he can see the true crazy, the fanatic, the kill-first believer.

"How'd you get so wrong?" the man asks.

Printz shakes his head but the mannequin smile stays. "America wasn't built by people like your friend Sol. People who live scared, cowards that don't know how to pull the trigger and move on. Wasting his time to save that bear when it's already dead. I keep thinking about that. It's a fatal flaw. That kind of thinking will get us all killed."

The man maintains his focus on his dog and shakes his head. "I'm going back to the trucks. I'll load my bike," the man says. He donkey whistles for the dog.

"That's the spirit," Printz calls after him.

Behind a boulder, he empties his bowels. Keeps the dog out of it. Doesn't feel better after. At the trucks he breaks down his rig and hefts it into the back of one of the troop carriers. The others are up now and, one after the next, they stow their gear and wander down to the trucks, pack the solar, and climb in.

The man and the dog are in the back of the second vehicle with Latham and the gear totes. Printz and everybody else rides in the cab because of the chill. Latham waits until they are under way before he says anything. The man has the dog pulled on top of him for warmth.

"You've got cancer," Latham says over the wind. He points to the man's sunburned ear and a scab that has been there for what seems like months.

The man touches his ear, considers if he should tell Latham how sick he's been feeling, if it may be related to the cancer, or the ticks, or the bear meat.

"It's just a guess," Latham says. "I'm not a real doctor but I play one in the Preservation." Latham smiles. He's in his twenties but already bald. He has a beard like everybody else and military/heavy metal tattoos on both arms.

"Printz is a Nazi twerp," the man says.

The smile drains from Latham's face. "Nobody's perfect." He gives his ear a tug. "I could cut it off," he says. "Might keep it from spreading, if it hasn't already." The smile returns to Latham's face. He points at the horizon, the broiling sun. "All day hot is what that is."

They leave the pavement and soon after stop at a locked gate. Printz gets out and kneels down with lock-picking tools and in under a minute he has the gate open and waves the trucks through.

The road climbs steeply and traverses the hillside in an endless series of switchbacks. Near the top they come to another gate and the trucks are shut down. The road continues beyond the gate and there're fresh tire tracks in the dust. The militiamen pile out and suit up. The man refills his water bottle and feeds and waters the dog. His empty-handedness is obvious. He might as well be naked.

"Does he go armed or no?" Sampson says to Printz.

"I'm not giving him a weapon," Printz says. "And neither is anybody else." He makes eye contact with his crew until he gets their separate acknowledgments, then points up the hill through the burn. They head out. The ash is skinned with a hard crust that crushes and breathes dust with each step. Farther up it's baby-head-sized rocks buried in the ash that roll ankles and trip up the serious men and make them look foolish. The dog cuts for scent and they follow the dog. Then it's the usual mess of deadfall and the high stepping and crawling that comes with it. The man throws up. The dog tries to eat it but gets shoved back. Printz doesn't push it. They all take a break.

"We're splitting up at the ridge," Printz says to the men. "The dog and our friend here will go first. We'll keep an eye on them and see what comes out."

"Don't send the dog," Sampson says.

"I thought you said you couldn't use it unless it was trained in Dutch."

"I could learn a few Czech commands and I know the hand signals. Just send him."

"You can't have my dog," the man says.

"He doesn't want you to have his dog," Printz says.

"Judas goat," the man says.

"You're learning," Printz says. Their faces and bare arms are coated with ash. A breeze blows and one of the standing dead nearby cracks six feet up the trunk and falls down in a cloud of ash. After that it's quiet but they move from under the trees anyway.

AT THE RIDGE THE DOG FINDS A PATCH OF SHADE AND LIES DOWN. The man drinks then waters the dog and gives him a scratch. While he's on his knees his stomach churns and cramps but he manages to keep the water down.

Far below them in the opposite valley is a copperhead of a dirt road. Through the trees the too-dark shade of a PV panel, a fence line, roof edge.

"Whenever you're ready," Printz says.

"Who's down there?"

"Doesn't make a difference to you, does it?"

There isn't any movement below but judging by the recent tire tracks on the road, someone is there.

"They'll see you first and being unarmed with the dog," Printz says, "they'll want to say hi before they fire on you."

"You don't know that," the man says.

"You're right. I don't." Printz grins at his comrades. "But if we start shooting, I'd suggest getting low."

"And if you don't?"

"Then we'll have a beer and laugh about it."

The man finishes his water and folds the bladder in half and slips it into his belt in the back of his pants. He keeps the dog in a focused heel as he moves downhill. Dust swirls and drives him to a coughing fit that hurts his ribs. Being quiet doesn't matter, moving slowly either. He wants to be seen as soon as possible. He doesn't want to surprise anyone.

The dog sees movement, and following his eyes the man finds him, just a haze from the dust, a shadow in the trees. They step slowly and come upon boot prints. The dog is looking the other way now. The man sees two of them, downhill and to the left. Thirty yards.

"I'm unarmed," he says.

No answer. The man stops the dog with a glance and they wait. He can see the house now and three vehicles, no markings or flags.

"One hand on your dog," a voice in the trees says. "The other held high."

He does as he's told.

"You take your hand off your dog, I shoot."

"OK."

"You lower your hand, I shoot."

"OK."

"Come to my voice."

The man moves to his left, scanning for the speaker, but he never sees him. A moment later two men emerge from the dead-fall, ten yards away and slightly uphill. They're militia, white and clean cut, but he can't see any insignia.

"Don't fucking move." They have their barrels up and trained on him and the dog. "Who's with you?"

"I'm alone."

"You're a fucking liar."

"STT?"

He hesitates.

The closest man yells at him: "Yes or no. Goddamn answer the question."

But he doesn't know how to answer. He says no at the same moment that the shooting starts. He pulls the dog toward him and tumbles to the ground behind a downed tree. In seconds three of the four are down. A moment later, the fourth is hit low and folds at the waist as he's hit several more times in the back and rolls down the hill. The man gets to his feet and shoves the dog toward the trees and runs after him. The kicked-up ash cloud has visibility down to twenty yards or less. They continue downhill because it's faster but the house is down there so the man works his way into a climbing traverse. He can't keep pace. He calls the dog back and they walk slow and steady. Gunfire swells and tapers off like something blowing in the wind.

The dog sees him first, a man coming from the valley, hurrying uphill. They duck into the trees. He's trying to flank the action and gain the high ground, same as them. He stops before crossing their tracks, close enough to hear his breathing, raises his weapon and scans the trees. As he turns his back, the command is given and the dog covers the ground in a blink and hits the militiaman high as he turns. They tumble into the dust and disappear in a cloud. Two shots and screaming, a steady working snarl from the dog. The man leaves the trees and enters the skirmish ground and finds the dog and the man farther downhill than he expected. He snatches a rifle from the ground. The dust has mixed with the blood on the militiaman's hands and formed a paste. His eyes are open and filled with panic as he tries to push the dog away. But the dog is locked into an almost robotic shake-and-hold pattern, shake and hold. The man calls the dog back, keeps the rifle trained on the bleeding man's center mass.

"Toss your pistol," the man says, shakes the rifle to make his point. "I mean it. Toss it now."

As blood spills down the militiaman's shirt from his neck, he searches his empty holster for his pistol, shakes his head. Then he sees the blood on his shirt and hands and claws at his throat to feel out the damage. He's in his twenties—scrawny arms, small hands, an incipient beer belly.

"Apply pressure," the man says. "You got a med kit?"

The militiaman fumbles in his cargo pants until he comes up with a stop-clot compress and tears it open with his teeth. He's crying when he slaps it onto the dark punctures pumping blood on his neck. He has defensive wounds on his arms and hands. Pale and soon to pass out, but he'll live. The man scans the ground for the pistol but it's lost in the dust. He lays the rifle down on the toe of his left shoe to check the dog for injuries, picks a bit of what appears to be skin from his teeth. The blood on his muzzle is already tacky. He gives the dog a good-boy and a one-armed hug. He's reaching for the rifle and looks up to find the militiaman has his pant leg raised, an empty ankle holster, and a .380 or whatever it is in his left hand, the right still holding the compress, and he's firing like he's joking almost, not aiming, hitting sky then dust and dust again but far uphill.

The man trips and falls over backward as he's getting out of the way and somehow finds his feet and then he's running, the dog five yards to his left. Gunshots behind them but nothing hits. He had a rifle for about a second, held it in his hands. He looks back once and can't see anything but dust and the treetops. He keeps moving and the dog is with him.

From the ridge he can clearly see the house and surrounding property. The shooting continues below him but it's intermittent and tappy as hailstones. He's maybe a quarter mile from where they first crossed the ridge, less than two miles from the second gate and his bike and the redwood box. Glancing back, one of the vehicles parked at the house is on fire and men move like fleas, building to building, working their peashooters, *tap tap*. The man spits into the dust and lopes downhill.

[34]

R < 45
CA 96118

April Simmonds arrived in an unmarked van. Aaron wasn't with her. The man that was driving was out of uniform but he had a badge around his neck and a pistol on his belt. Roy tried to make light and joke about the cops dropping April off but neither April nor her escort smiled.

"Where's Aaron?" Roy asked.

Karen walked by him with her hand over her mouth. "I just saw my phone," she said. "I'm sorry. I had it turned off." She hugged April and April leaned limply against her.

"He's gone. They shot him."

Wiley and Sarah were on the porch playing with a runty piglet they'd been keeping on a leash like a dog. Wiley tied the pig to the rail and took her little sister's hand. They timidly descended the stairs, shocked to see their mother crying. They went to her and were pulled into a hug. April picked

Sarah up and nuzzled her tear-soaked face into the child's neck.

The driver of the van approached Roy, introduced himself as Sang-Chul, *call me Sang*. Roy had never met him but he'd heard some things. Ex-Ranger, combat vet, service dog handler, currently the lead dog trainer with the Sacramento PD.

Sang opened the back of the van and unloaded two dogs from their separate crates. A German shepherd named Gem was first out. Roy knew her as Aaron's K-9, but before that she'd done three tours in Iraq with Sang. Wiley called her over and gave her a hug. The other dog, a Malinois puppy with a golden body and a black face, flung itself out of the van and charged around the yard and ended up knocking Sarah down. Roy picked her up and brushed her off while Sang corralled the puppy. Sarah's pants were ripped and her hair was ratty in the back. Since she'd learned to walk they were lucky to keep clothes on her at all.

Karen and April were climbing the porch stairs. Wiley kept an eye on her mom and April while she put Gem through the commands she'd learned on their last visit. Sarah rested her head against Roy's shoulder. It was time for her nap but Roy didn't want to bother Karen and April. Sang shut the doors on the van. He made the puppy sit and put a leash on it. He had a clicker in his hand and used it to reward the dog.

"You didn't know we were coming?" Sang said.

"With the Jeffs running things, cell service is spotty at best anymore. Did you have trouble with the roadblocks?"

"Not really. They stopped us but didn't hold us up. I don't get why they stop people at all. What are they even looking for?"

"Security," Roy said. "They want to establish the illusion of control. Like all of us." He craned his neck to see if Sarah was asleep yet, she wasn't. "We'll talk in a bit," he said to Sang. "I don't want the kids to hear."

"Got it. April wanted to come here to see them, your girls. The reporters were at her house."

"Wiley," Roy said. "I want you to put that pig away before you play with Gem anymore."

Wiley had Gem sit and stay and unhooked the pig from the baluster and walked it back to the pen.

"Let's go to the barn," Roy said to Sang. "This one will fall asleep in a minute."

"I won't," Sarah said.

"It's OK, sweetheart." Wiley came back swinging the pig's leash like a trick roper. "We'll be in the barn," Roy called to her.

"OK." Wiley approached Gem, stopped ten yards away, called her and then had her stop and lie down and crawl to her.

"She's got the gift," Sang said. He let the puppy off its leash. "Get this one to do that and you can keep him," he said to Wiley. The puppy jumped on Gem's back and ran off before the older dog could catch him.

"Seriously?" Wiley said.

"Not seriously," Roy said. "What are you doing?" he said to Sang.

"You'll have to talk to April. I probably should've kept my mouth shut."

AARON'S MOTORCYCLE BUSINESS IN LOYALTON HAD FAILED LONG before Roy had returned, but he'd still had his shop and a half-dozen bikes. Before Sarah was born Roy had spent a lot of afternoons and evenings at Aaron's tinkering with bikes and drinking beer and listening to NPR. Aaron had a job installing cabinets, but he was usually home by three. He'd taken Roy hunting and was there when he shot his first deer. He was Roy's only friend, really, outside of the random skateboarder that stopped by every now and again to skate.

A job opened up in the Sacramento PD and Aaron went for it. They were understaffed and willing to overlook his history of alcohol abuse as long as he went through an expedited version of their basic training program and submitted to random UAs. April enrolled in night classes and finally finished school and had just recently opened her own veterinary practice.

Sarah fell asleep on Roy's shoulder while he and Sang were looking at Roy's bikes, handing motorcycle parts back and forth. Wiley came in with Gem and the puppy, and soon had them up the ladder running around the skate bowl chasing a tennis ball.

"Who did it?" Roy asked Sang.

"We don't know. Aaron was in his car. The shooter approached from behind. He never saw it coming."

"What the fuck? What's going on down there?"

"It's not good, man. None of it's any good. You got militias, we got the rest. It's chaos."

"Do you have kids?"

"No."

"Hell of a world for kids right now."

"Yeah."

With Sarah still sleeping on his shoulder, Roy climbed the ladder to the ramp so he could watch Wiley and the dogs. Sang followed him up. Wiley was out of breath when she climbed out of the bowl, said, "Watch this," and grabbed her board. She dropped in and had the dogs chase her around and around until they gave up and settled in the bottom of the bowl. They kept their eyes on Wiley, tracked her as she worked a speedline high on the walls, as if they were watching a bird.

Sang-Chul went back to Sacramento that day but April stayed until the funeral and came back with Roy and Karen and the girls afterward. She didn't want to go home. Gem and the puppy stayed with her. The Malinois was a beautiful dog, and days and then weeks passed with April sitting on the porch wrapped in a blanket, Gem sleeping at her feet, instructing Wiley and Roy on how to care for him and train him to keep him in fighting trim. He was special, a one-in-a-million dog.

Near the end of the month, just as they were sitting down to dinner, Sang called April's phone and told her that the shooter had been arrested leaving a Walmart in Van Nuys with a box of ammunition. He was a kid, seventeen. He'd shot his own mother and three other cops besides Aaron. He'd worn a GoPro.

April was packed to leave the next day. Roy gassed up the truck so Karen could drive her home. She was leaving the puppy for Sarah and Wiley.

"He'll keep you safe," April told the girls, through her tears. "I want you all to keep each other safe." Gem looked at them from the open passenger window. She and the puppy had never been apart, and although Roy didn't have to restrain the younger dog, it was obvious that he wanted to follow his old pal, wherever she was going.

[35]

M<55
OR 9XXXX

THE GATE IS STILL CLOSED AND APPEARS TO BE LOCKED. PRINTZ'S vehicles haven't moved. Nothing has changed. He and the dog wait for a few minutes to make sure no one is around, watch their backtrack. The dog breathes heavily on his neck. Bloody muzzle, dry now. *Lucky you weren't shot. Both of us.*

He breaks the passenger window of one of the troop carriers with a rock, finds the tire repair kit under the rear seat. He uses the small octagonal key to unlock the hubs and with a tire iron removes the lug nuts from the tires of both vehicles and throws them by the handful in three different directions into the forest. He keeps the key. Whatever weapons are still there are locked in the gangbox in the bed. He doesn't waste time trying to get in.

He waters the dog first, then refills all of his bladders and bottles from a polytank in the lead vehicle, leaves the tap open. He watches the road behind the gate, listens to the silent woods.

He retrieves his bike and trailer and shoves the redwood box and all of his water, whatever else will fit, into his panniers. He's leaving the trailer behind. Thinks to go through the vehicles for hidden weapons but doesn't want to waste the time. One gun won't save him. Ten guns won't. Rolling away, he brakes hard and dismounts, takes time to stab some dead pine needles into the keyhole of the padlock. As an afterthought, pisses on it.

His brake pads melt on the descent and by the time he hits the lower gate he's dragging his feet to stop. The dog has the squinty look he gets when he's fatigued. The man closes the gate and locks it, the pine needle trick is repeated. Before they leave he gives the dog more water, has a few swallows himself but he throws it up, managing to land some on the padlock.

Back on the pavement, he puts his head down and pedals without stopping, breathes deep, paces himself. There's nothing left in his stomach to throw up. He pedals through his dry heaves. The dog is hanging in beside him with his tongue out.

The dog is out in front. He stops and stands broadside at the top of a low hill and tests the wind. The man dismounts and pushes his bike to join him. Below them, on the road ahead, a shredded Winnebago is blocking both lanes, broken glass like spilled water. The man slides into the ditch and with his binoculars sees the bodies on the road. The fields are empty, no other vehicles. He and the dog approach slowly and from the side.

The corpses of what looks to be two separate families are scattered on the blacktop and in the ditch. Two teenage boys with bottle flies blanketing their eyes and red-black blood, exposed flesh, are tangled together as if one had been trying to carry the other. Both sets of parents have been shot with high-caliber weapons and are missing large pieces of meat and bone.

The swarming flies are thick enough to offer shade. Empty shell casings on the road tell him that they'd fired back or fired first.

It's the dog that discovers the boy cowering speechless in a culvert under the road. He's docile and allows the man to pick him up. He's small, maybe six or seven years old. There are bicycles on a rack on the back of the RV.

"Can you ride?" the man asks.

The boy stares at him. He carries the boy to the shady side of the RV, away from the bodies, and sets him down.

The man takes the keys from the RV and unlocks the bike rack. He takes the smallest one to the boy but he shakes his head no. The next-smallest bike is pink with a flower basket. The man returns with a medium-sized bike with gears and the boy stands and takes it by the bars and climbs on.

"Is there anyone else here?" the man asks.

The boy ignores him and rides away. The man follows.

The sign has been altered: Klamath Falls to Klamath Fell. He turns from the highway as soon as he can and plots a new course on his map. The child stops beside him but won't speak. The man offers him what packaged food he has left—some saltines and peanut butter, water. He doesn't offer any of the bear jerky because he suspects that's what's been making him sick.

When they make camp the man gives the boy his sleeping bag. The dog curls onto the bottom of the bag and the boy works his feet underneath to warm up. The man pulls on his extra clothes and stays up with his cramping stomach and body aches and watches the boy and the dog and can't help but think of his own childhood. The logic of his life strikes him as impossible.

For breakfast he boils a few pieces of bear jerky thick as yellow pine bark and mixes in a pack of Lipton's onion soup mix to cut the taste. The boy eats first and finishes the last of the crackers. Shivering in the trees, trying to piss before they go, the man throws up the little bit of broth he supped. When he returns, the dog, or maybe the boy, has finished the soup and licked the pot clean. The boy is pitching pebbles into the pot and the sound vibrates in the man's head.

The man joins in the game and as they plink stones into the pot he tells the boy his name and that he has two girls of his own, and mentions as offhandedly as he can that if he decides to come along, he can meet them. He gives the dog's name again, earns a look from the boy for repeating himself, and speaks for the animal in saying he hopes the boy will join them. Unconvinced or still in shock or both, the boy blinks but doesn't speak. The man tells him his daughter's names and about the farm they used to have, all the animals they raised and the vegetables they grew in their garden. He doesn't tell him about his wife or the end. He doesn't tell him that he's worried he has trichinosis. The boy tires of the game and tips the pebbles from the GSI cookpot and rolls up the sleeping bag and puts both in the pannier where they came from, nods toward the waiting road.

[36]

R > 45
CA 96118

ROY WOKE THE GIRLS IN THE DARK AND HERDED THEM TO THE kitchen and cooked them a breakfast of fried eggs and toast, venison sausage. Sarah asked for honey but they didn't have any, hadn't for a long time. They had six Warres in the field but the bees had split for greener pastures.

"Blackberry jam," Roy said. "Take it or leave it."

Wiley slid the jam jar toward her little sister. The dot-to-dot India ink tattoo, supposed to be a rose, on the back of her hand had already begun to fade, but it still got Roy's hackles up every time he noticed it. Not as bad as Karen. She wanted amputation or a belt sander. But with the Preservation drawdown and the drought, the militia families mostly gone and the school having closed its doors for the last time, the crowd Wiley had been running with evaporated. It was as if she'd been in the current while her family was in the slack water and they'd just plucked her out before she disappeared. Wiley obviously felt differently. She'd liked the current. She wanted a life outside of survival.

Sarah pushed the jam jar back toward her sister.

"She left it," Wiley said.

"I didn't." Sarah reached for it and knocked it over but it didn't spill and when it rolled toward the edge of the table Roy caught it and set it up right.

"Want me to do it or you?" Roy said.

"You," Sarah said. Roy ladled on the jam but didn't spread it, knowing that if he did, Sarah would yell at him.

Roy fed the dog and sent it outside, then did the dishes while the girls got dressed and used the bathroom and brushed their teeth. When they came back they pulled on their Bogs and went outside in the dark to do their chores. Before he followed them, he stood at the door and listened for Karen but she was still sleeping. The girls tracked down an escape-artist goat while Roy took the eggs inside as an excuse to get more coffee.

Karen was up, reading the news on her tablet.

"Anything good?" Roy said.

"Farmer's Almanac says weather's coming," Karen said.

"I'll believe it when I see it."

"I made lunches for you, don't forget."

"OK."

"Are you staying all day?" she said.

"How hot's it gonna get?"

"A hundred and four by this afternoon."

"We're not staying all day."

At the bottom of the porch stairs, under a reddening sky, Karen handed them their lunches and gave out kisses. She patted Roy's waistband to see if he had his pistol.

"It's in the safe. I don't need it."

"OK," she said. To Sarah, "Don't eat your lunch early if you get bored or you'll go hungry."

"I know, Mama."

"That goes for you, too," Karen said to Wiley.

"I didn't ask for a sandwich, did I?"

"Nope, you didn't. Have a nice day," Karen said, and gave Roy a look.

Roy already had his sandwich out and took a big bite and grinned at Karen as he climbed into the truck. The dog was in the crew cab with Sarah. They'd loaded the vegetable crates last night. As he was headed down the driveway, he rolled down his window and yelled to Karen that they had the dog.

Dust and smoke mottled the horizon. If he hadn't seen it himself, he'd never have believed that this valley had once been sown deep with alfalfa and for much of the summer the air smelled wet and earthy with it. The sprinkler pivots were gone and dust had swallowed the abandoned pipe. The haybarns big enough to be seen from space, stacked to the rafters with four-by-three bales, had either been burned or sold off for the lumber. The hope was that it would get better but that kind of hope wasn't something Roy could maintain. He hoped for his family's safety and for water, but he didn't bother hoping for it to get better—whatever *it* was anymore—because all of that had long ago slipped out of his hands, everybody's hands.

He turned and looked at his girls. "What're we doing for your mom's birthday? I need ideas."

"We could bake her a cake and maybe watch a movie," Sarah said.

"We could set up the projector in the barn," Roy said. "That's good. What movie?"

"*Out of Africa*," Sarah said.

"Done," Roy said.

"And what else?" Wiley said.

"What else, what?" Roy said. "Movie, popcorn, a nice dinner."

"That's not much of a birthday. I mean, what about an actual present, something she wants?"

Roy suggested a new meat grinder, his one solid idea. "She was just saying how the gears in ours are shot and it's going to die," he said, the apology already in his voice.

"No and no?" Wiley said, with her near-constant teenage exasperation. "We'll get a new meat grinder no matter what, or you'll rebuild the old one. We need to get her something special, something she'll cherish."

"Maybe I'll get her a tattoo," Roy said. "A rose, maybe?"

"Don't start," Wiley said.

"OK. All right. I don't know what to get her, though," Roy said, getting a little annoyed. "That's why I asked. We only have two weeks."

"Two and a half," Wiley said. "We'll think of something by then."

"We could make her a painting," Sarah said. "We could work together and Papa could make a frame for it."

"I like that idea, sweetheart," Roy said, glancing at Sarah, giving her a smile. "I don't know where I'd be without my ladies."

Wiley shook her head and looked out the window.

Roy passed the first marker announcing the upcoming roadblock. He let off the accelerator and the truck began to slow.

The light was red on the barricade and it began to flash as they approached. "Come on, dipshits," Roy said, leaning forward on the steering wheel. "Where are you? I don't wanna talk and I don't wanna stop." The militiamen appeared with their weapons slung on their shoulders. When they saw who it was they raised the gate and waved them through. Roy gave them a middle-finger wave.

"Are they always going to be here?" Wiley said.

"No," Roy said.

"Then how long?" Sarah asked.

"I wish I knew."

A chain was strung across the gate at the farmer's market and the sign was down. The girls stayed in the truck with the dog while Roy wandered over to the horse trailer with two flat tires that was the market office and talked to Mr. Florence. After shaking hands, they moved from the cool of the trailer to the premature heat of early morning. The girls had gotten out and opened the camper shell and put down the tailgate and sat down, legs swinging. Behind them, small wooden baskets of tomatoes and peppers were lined up and stacked three high, along with their chairs and table and the hand-painted sign that Karen had helped them make. The dog was in the shade by the back tire, intently watching Roy.

"You already paid for your spot, so go on and set up," Mr. Florence said. "I can give you your money back otherwise. Everybody else took it. I was just waiting here to make sure I squared with everybody."

"They worked hard for this," Roy said, motioning to the girls. "I'm not handing them a refund check." He smiled and Mr. Florence looked at the ground.

"It wouldn't be a check, I can promise you that."

"Mr. Florence," Roy said, making a run at cheering up an old man. "You're the only person—since I dropped out of high school, when it was actually required of me to do so—that I call mister."

"You know my first name is Nathan, don't you?"

Roy grinned. "Sure, I do." Mr. Florence took his keys out of his pocket and gave them a shake.

Roy cleared his throat. "I don't even like tomatoes, so we either sell them today or I'm going to have to eat them."

"You can take them to the food bank," Mr. Florence said.

"Jefferson or state?"

The old man didn't seem to notice Roy was joking. "State. The J's'll just try to sell 'em again. It's against their religion to miss capitalizing on a financial opportunity."

"Some people say greed is good, Mr. Florence."

"Those people can kiss my ass."

"Guess it doesn't matter where we put our table, then," Roy said.

"I'd say take a piece of shade beside the trailer and chase it until you head home."

With Roy's help, Mr. Florence unlocked the chain, took the extension ladder down from the roof of the horse trailer, and flipped the gate sign to open. The girls set up their stand and Roy moved the truck to the far side of the lot under the shade of a dead locust tree.

By the time they took their seats and opened the cash box, Mr. Florence had wandered off, most likely to the porch at the boarded-up feed store where Mr. Florence and the other independents that had never joined the Jeffersonians usually held court. Roy and the girls had two gallons of water and the sandwiches that Karen had packed for them, along with all the tomatoes and peppers they could eat. No cars came. A few people wandered by. The Preservation had made it a boomtown but that was over now. The girls waved and everyone waved back, but nobody bought anything.

After the girls had lunch, Roy spread a blanket and made a kind of bed for Sarah on the ground and she and the dog took a nap. He kept busy shooing the flies and yellow jackets away.

"You said tomatoes take too much water," Wiley said. "But I thought people would buy them because they took too much water. I thought we'd get more money and that they'd sell right away."

"When you started this, you couldn't have known how it was going to turn out," Roy said. "You and your sister worked really hard. I'm impressed. So's your mom." She didn't like compliments. They made her angry. She sat there scowling and wouldn't look at him. He complimented her all the time, win-win.

Roy picked up a bell pepper and twisted off the stem and fished out the seeds and ate it like an apple, talking with his mouth full. "You don't have to listen to me. You're old enough now that you can trust yourself."

Wiley leaned against his shoulder. "I don't want to stay here forever."

He didn't know if she was talking about the farmer's market or their home. "We won't," he said. "But the day isn't over yet."

"It's those stupid food banks feeding everyone for free."

"Nothing's free, kiddo, and none of those folks would be there if they had a choice."

Sarah was awake and crawling into her dad's lap. "So let's give them away," she said. "Let's give them all away and go home." She had dents from the blanket on her cheek and a spot of dried drool on her chin. She nuzzled into Roy and he pulled her close and smelled her hair.

"We'll can them," Wiley said to her sister.

"I hate canning," Sarah said. "It's so hot. And we already have a ton in the cellar."

They looked to Roy to break the tie. "It's up to you guys. I don't have a dog in this fight." They weren't familiar with the expression so he had to explain it. They couldn't believe dog fighting was an actual event that people had watched and bet on.

A woman and her three children wandered through the corner of the park, close enough to see Roy and the girls sitting there, close enough to be embarrassed that she wasn't buying anything. Roy thought she wouldn't have come that way if she'd known she was going to have to face somebody, particularly children selling produce. The worst part of farmer's markets for Roy had always been the desperation of the vendors.

Sarah stood and ran to catch up, stopped the woman, pointed back at the fruit stand. They returned as a group and Wiley handed over a flat of tomatoes and another smaller one of peppers. Roy hadn't seen the woman before. Her kids were hungry and they'd cracked open a couple of the red bell peppers and started eating before their mother had finished thanking the girls.

When they got home, Karen came out to help them unload,

her face lighting up when she saw that their crop was gone. "All right," she said. "Way to go, girls. Another weekend like this and you'll be rich." She gave Roy a kiss.

"We gave them away," Sarah said, baseball hat pulled low over her eyes.

"One guy gave us a dollar," Wiley said. "So not all of them."

Roy held up his hands, it was their idea, I didn't tell them to do it, and Karen gathered Sarah in her arms and lifted her up.

"Farmer's market is done," Roy said. "Mr. Florence shut it down."

"That's too bad," Karen said. "Maybe next year, huh?"

Roy sent the girls inside to wash up while he unloaded the table and the chairs into the barn. The dog followed him and gave him the sad eyes so they worked through the commands April had left them with. Roy pronounced everything like he was from South Boston. Whitey Bulger, dog whisperer. *Kaynosa*—heel. *Set-knee*—sit. *Zee-radish*—attack. The dog shot from his side and launched into the air and seemed to take great joy in ripping into the goat-leather training dummy he'd hung up in the barn.

Roy let the dog rip and kill and tear while he stashed the sign under the ramp, then *poost* and *kem-yee* and he gave him a piece of goat jerky from his pocket. *Set-knee. Zoston.*

The dog sat robot still and watched Roy climb the ladder and grab his board. When he dropped in and disappeared from sight, the dog looked toward the ceiling and followed the sounds from rafter to rafter. The ramp was in bad shape, Masonite tears, popped screws, broken coping. The girls used it more now than he did. Wiley was dangerously good and Sarah mostly clowned around but she had her moments. He needed to fix it or get rid of it. This could be said of pretty much everything he owned. He only had two motorcycles left and both needed work to get them running again. The garden looked great though. So did the goat shed and the chicken coop. He was kind of half-assing the pigpen but they were hardly in there anyway. They ran them on paddocks bordered by solar-powered electric fence. If the pasture held up, they'd be able to keep it up. Otherwise, so long pigs.

At some point Karen had talked him into getting bicycles so they could get out and do things together without burning fuel. No one drove much anymore with the shortages and the high costs so traffic was minimal. It was safe enough. Cycling was tiring and slow but there was something about it that Roy responded to, and after giving it some thought he decided that it was the obvious independence. Sure, a motorcycle or car could take you farther faster with minimal effort, but that was only true to a point. When a motor stopped, everything with it stopped, but when a bicycle stopped, even someone with the most basic knowledge could usually get it going again. Unless the frame broke, it was pretty hard to get stranded. Uphills end in downhills, and tough climbs made you stronger. The dog loved it, chasing the girls all over the countryside, ranging in the barren fields.

Kay-nosa. They left the barn and crossed the yard to go inside but the lights from the drill rig were still on so he wandered down to check on Sullivan and Jerzy to see if they'd made any progress. They were at four hundred feet that morning and still no water.

"*Revere,*" Roy said to the dog, and it was gone in a puff of dust. He hoped it didn't bite anyone. He kept walking, waiting for the sound, but none came.

"You'll see the stars better if you switch off the lights," Roy said.

"Wouldn't see you though," Jerzy said. He had the dog by the scruff and was hauling him back and forth, playing rough. "I wouldn't see this monster coming at me."

"I don't know that seeing him would change anything."

"He's a killer." Jerzy had him in the air now and flung him out into the dirt but he landed like a cat and sprung and body-checked Jerzy onto his back.

"*Kay-nosa*," Roy said. The dog walked right over Jerzy to return to Roy's side.

"If he decided to," Jerzy said, as he picked himself up, "I think he could rip my throat out."

"It's not up to him," Roy said, gave Jerzy dead eyes. "It's up to me." He liked to scare the kid. "Where's Sullivan?"

"Where'd you think?"

"I think you should give me one of those smokes." Jerzy passed over a cigarette and explained to Roy that they'd only made it another twenty feet and had nothing to show for it but another broken bit, an empty water truck, another empty fuel drum. Jerzy was fifteen. Going on forty. Going on about diesel prices and rock types, aquifers and the nature of displacement, the rudiments of fluid dynamics.

"What's your guess, then?" Roy asked.

"That you're about as screwed as everyone else. Me and the old boar, we both figured you'd be in luck. With one well still producing. We weren't planning on wasting your money and our time, but what the hell. There aren't any guarantees."

"Never mind what it says on the side of your rig."

Jerzy glanced at the door decal. *Guaranteed results.* He pulled a red bell pepper from his jacket pocket and took a bite. "Results may vary," he said, smiled as he chewed.

"That one of mine?"

"One of Wiley's. She brought out a pile of them, tomatoes too."

"Are you a gentleman, Jerzy?" he asked. "Because if you're not, you're gonna have a hard time walking around taking free vegetables from my daughter after my dog eats your legs. Your balls."

Jerzy kind of froze and swallowed hard. "You don't have to worry about me, Roy. I'm on your side." He finished his pepper and dropped the stem and seeds into the dirt. "I'm on your family's side. I'll end the life of anybody that hurts them."

"Did you practice that?"

"Not bad, huh?"

"Nah, we're on the same side. Let's go skate."

"That's what I've been waiting for." Jerzy shut the doors on the cab and killed the lights and they walked leisurely with the dog running out front toward the barn and the warm lights of home. "Your buddy Barry Miller came by again," Jerzy said.

"I hate that guy," Roy said.

"I think he gets that, but he still wants us to pack up and go to his place and drill him a new well instead of you."

"It's up to you and Sullivan."

"He offered big money. Double what you're paying."

"Yeah, shit," Roy said.

"And he said all his militia bros want us to work for them too so we'd be set for years."

"What are you saying?"

"I'll never work a well for the Jeffs. Neither will Sully. Not after what happened to my folks we won't. I talked to him about it. We're staying here until we get results. If you don't mind."

"I don't care but my wife is gonna murder you in your sleep if she catches you sneaking around with her little girl." He stopped the kid with a hand on his chest. "I'm serious. Don't fuck around. This isn't an empty threat. We were kidding before but I'm sure as shit not joking now."

"I know."

"You think you do, but you don't." Roy ripped the barn door open and hit the lights and they staggered to life and lit the hard-used wooden bowl. Jerzy grabbed his board from where it was leaning against the ramp and hurried up the ladder and bomb-dropped into the deep end with no warm-up.

"Punk," Roy said.

SULLIVAN, THE WELL DRILLER, MADE SUPPLY RUNS TO RENO THAT inevitably involved a bar stool and virtual poker so Jerzy mostly ate at the Binghams'. He'd been sleeping at the rig but Roy suspected he and Wiley were meeting up in the night. Neither of them was stupid and life was short was how he looked at it. Karen thought young love, particularly concerning her eldest daughter and some middle school dropout, skate punk, drill rat, wasn't anything to encourage.

"If she gets pregnant," Karen said. "What then?"

"She won't," Roy said. "She's too smart for that, so's Jerzy. I already put the fear into him. He knows what happens if he fucks up. He's a hundred times better than those fuckheads she was running with before. Jerome. Remember Jerome?"

"Yes, I remember Jerome. But no fourteen-year-old knows what happens."

"He's fifteen now."

"Fifteen-year-olds are even worse, bigger, with more room for hormones . . ." she hesitated, "and sperm."

"Don't say that. I can't go that far. You always go too far."

"They're all little animals that grow up to be big animals."

"All right. Fine. We'll let Sullivan take one last shot. After that, I'll tell 'em they gotta go. That'll be it."

"But we can't let them leave."

"What'd you mean? We've been paying them to punch dry holes for almost a year. They've used way more water than they're likely to find. And I can't even think about the fuel. We could've run our generator for a decade with all the fuel they've burned. If he hasn't found anything yet, I don't know—"

"Don't say it."

"We've gone over this, and over this. We have enough water now for us and a few animals. Outside of that, I think we need to rethink standing our ground."

"I told you a long time ago, I'm here to stay and that means my girls are too. We'll wait this out. You always want to run."

"That's not true. I'm just stating the facts. As long as our well has water, we're good. After that, we need to be ready to go. Ninety percent of this valley is dry. To my mind that means it's only a matter of time."

"Back to the matter at hand, Jerzy and Wiley," Karen said.

"OK."

"I like him, don't get me wrong. He's a good kid, and I know he lost his parents and that's terrible, but he's just a kid."

"He can't help any of that."

"I know he can't. But, as you may or may not remember, we were just kids once and I think it's fair to say that we—you a lot more than me—were both total fucking morons."

"He skates like a man."

"He sucks compared to Wiley, you said so."

"She's been doing it her whole life. He's only been at it for a year or two."

"You said he isn't any better than Sarah and she's only a foot taller than her board right now."

"OK. I shouldn't have said it."

"'Skates like a man,'" Karen said, mocking him. "Asswipe."

"I'm just saying you can judge a lot about a person from how they skate. He's smart about it and he's not afraid."

"Anyway, my point is—"

"Your point."

"He doesn't have a place to go, right?"

"He has a room at Sullivan's, but he's been crashing on that rig so long, who knows if he's even house-trained anymore."

"I think he should move in here," Karen said. "Stay with us."

"Wait, what? He practically does live here already and that seems to be your biggest complaint. Why do you want to give him his own room?"

"Because that's the only way the little beast is going to understand what he's signing up for."

"He's not signing up for anything. He's in teenage love with Wiley. And if I had to bet, I'd say she was in love with him, too. The fucking idiots."

"That's why I want him under our roof, so I can bend the little fucker to my will."

"Is there no one you can't bend to your will?"

"You can learn a lot from goats."

"About goats."

"About getting what you want, and compromise." She smiled. "But mostly about fences. Goats teach you all about fences."

"You're saying we keep Sullivan going and give Jerzy what? Sarah's room? She moves in with Wiley?"

"Yeah, I think that's the answer."

"She's gonna be pissed."

"I know. And she's gonna watch her sister like a hawk and snitch on her whenever I ask her to."

Roy laughed. "Why don't you give Sullivan our room and we move into the Airstream? Fuck it, hook it up to the truck and we'll just leave the lot of them behind."

"I thought of that." She took Roy's hand and kissed his knuckles.

"Really?"

"No. Don't get your gypsy hopes up. We're staying."

THAT FALL, SULLIVAN WENT TO SLEEP IN HIS HUNTING TRAILER with the heater on and never woke up. He'd called Jerzy before he went to bed and Jerzy said his spirits were up and that he most likely died drunk and happy. He'd been a lifelong bachelor with no kids, not much for real property outside of his drill rig and his junk show of a house, a camp trailer, a few guns and tools, a rusted-out Dodge one-ton with a crane that he used for hauling well casing. His will named Jerzy alone and he got all the money that the Binghams had paid and Sullivan's savings besides. Then it was Jerzy and Roy, drilling dry well after dry well. What else was there to do? Throw money and material at the problem. America.

End of September and the weather was foul with hail and wind. The drill rig was hammering away in a muddy pit, a dirty island in the white, hailstoned landscape. Roy had driven the rig down the hillside into this small clearing, a quarter mile from the house, knowing they wouldn't get it back up such a steep hill, but also knowing that it was the last section of the Binghams' land to be drilled, the last of their well casing, their last chance at hitting water.

"We'll work until it gets too shitty," Roy said loudly, wincing at the hailstones pelting him in the face.

"I think it's too shitty right now," Jerzy said.

"This is the good stuff, right here. Exfoliating weather. People used to pay big money for this shit."

They returned to their stations on the rig and went about their work mechanically. Jerzy was on the controls, face turned up to the vent. Roy was swinging steel well casing from the Dodge with the crane and welding them up as they went. Then something changed, the tune of the hammer and the drill and even the motor shifted to a higher register. Jerzy killed the hydraulics and whooped at Roy, threw his hat at him to get his attention. They'd finally hit water.

Two days after they'd capped the new well, Barry Miller, the neighbor, was in the driveway with his hat in his hands. The weather had turned hot again. Dust clouds on the horizon. Roy and Jerzy did a fine job of ignoring Barry and climbed the porch stairs and sat down in the rickety ladder-backs against the wall. They'd been in the machine shop all morning trying to figure out how to power the pump in the new well. Solar needed to be pilfered from another system and a secondary pump would be required to feed a yet-to-be-built uphill cistern. They'd been about to go inside for lunch.

The boy stretched out his legs and wiggled his stockinged feet. "My boots are killing me today. My insoles are like crepe paper."

Roy peeled off his socks and stuffed them into his boots and shoved them under his seat, looked at Barry. He had the face of a younger actor that had been made up to play an older version of himself in the later scenes, but it wasn't makeup. It was just his fake-ass, older-than-you, wiser-than-you white-guy face.

"You had some luck, huh?" Barry said to Jerzy, with his phony smile. "How about you come over to my place next?"

"How 'bout you leave the kid alone, bud," Roy said. "I think he's already said everything he has to say to you."

"I'm waiting," Barry said, earnest now. "I've been waiting patiently."

"First thing that you learn," Roy said. "Is you always have to wait."

"There's human decency too," Barry said. "Not to mention the logical sense it would make for all of us to be on water. It would strengthen your position too, not just mine."

"Go home, and quit leaving all that militia shit in my mail-box."

"You're making other people—meaning me—secure your sector. It takes a lot of work."

"My sector?" Roy said. "Shit, here I was thinking we had a place or a spread or a farm, maybe even a *ranchito*, and this whole time all I've had is a lousy sector? That sucks."

"I'll tell you right now," Barry said. "The sooner you understand that you can't trust the feds or even the state government anymore, the better. Jefferson is it. This is the new state. The Preservation is real. We're the only ones you can trust. Period."

"Most of those kooks, Jeffersonians, roadblock dipshits, National Guard rejects, they aren't even from here," Roy said. "I don't know any of those guys." He looked at Jerzy. "Do you know any of them?"

Jerzy shook his head. "Not really." He pulled the insoles out of his boots and gave them a once-over before stuffing them back in upright so they would dry.

"Everybody I know," Roy said. "The people I trust, that still live here—except for you—they take care of themselves and help their neighbors when they need it. They don't have any use for sectors."

"You're wrong about that," Barry said. "Pretty soon, I'd wager, you'll be glad to know me."

Roy pointed at Jerzy. "You think he owes you something? That he should take his rig to your place and get to work? Fuck that, is what I say. You talk about preparedness and security? You're the only ones I need security against. I never saw you at the water meetings or any other community meetings, soil conservation, schools, none of it, and now it's all gone and you didn't do shit to help. Fuck you, Barry. You don't know shit about this valley. That's a fact."

"I know enough," Barry said. "I know that those meetings didn't change anything. Just a lot of talk with no action. The neoliberal *modus operandi*, gab 'em to death."

"Your neighbor Doris." Roy watched Barry's eyes, making sure he knew who he was talking about, where he was going. "Remember her?"

"Of course." Barry took off his hat again. "I went to her funeral."

"One time she showed up here on foot, exhausted. She'd walked for miles and she told me she'd asked *you* to help her get her car out of the ditch and *you* said for a hundred bucks you'd bring your big-ass Caterpillar crawler over and pull her out. You tried to make that old woman pay you."

"To cover fuel costs. It wasn't any kind of disdain for her as a person."

Jerzy stared Barry down while he spoke. "Doris took me school shopping after my folks died," he said. "I'd never spoken to her until then. She didn't know me. She just showed up at Sullivan's one day and took me shopping. She knew he wouldn't do it. Sully wouldn't think of it. He was just my dad's friend that got stuck with me. He didn't know anything about me or kids, stuff like that. Doris helped me out. Because she was a good person. That's the point."

"Go on and screw," Roy said to Barry.

"I don't quit that easy."

"I guess not, but I'd bet you're pretty quick to bleed." Roy stood up and Barry touched his sidearm and backed away.

Roy laughed. "There is nothing as cowardly as a dough-assed white man with a composite pistol," he said. "Cargo pockets. You keep your extra clips in there, tough guy? Where's your bug-out bag? Why don't you bug out?"

"Why don't you try me?" Barry said.

"Make my day," Roy said. "Feeling lucky. You're a Hollywood hero, Barry. I'm gonna call you Chuck Norris. Hey, Chuck Norris!"

"Just a tattooed piece of shit," Barry said, and turned to leave.

Karen opened the door and glared at Roy. Wiley and Sarah were behind her. They'd been listening the whole time. "Hello, Barry," she said.

"Karen," Barry said, not looking back, raised his arm to wave.

"Sorry, girls," Roy said. "I didn't mean for you to hear that."

Jerzy followed Wiley inside. Roy picked up Sarah and sat down on the steps. Karen sat down beside them. They watched Barry hustle down the road. The dog was shadowing him at the fence line but he hadn't noticed.

"He's going to come back," Karen said. "You know that, right?"

"I know."

"Why don't you and Jerzy just help him out?"

"How would *you* feel about drilling a well for the Jeffs if you were Jerzy?"

"Barry didn't have anything to do with what happened at that roadblock. He wasn't there."

"He's guilty by association."

"We're all guilty of that."

"Why don't you like anybody, Papa?" Sarah said.

"I like plenty of people, sweetheart. I like you and mama and Wiley, Jerzy, Aunt Ape. But I don't like that self-righteous old turd."

"Self-righteous old turd," Sarah said, laughing, eyes sparkling.

"That's right, sweetheart. That's what he is." Roy laughed too, but Karen didn't think it was funny, not at all.

●◆●

THEY SAT OUTSIDE AND WATCHED AS THE CLOUDS ROLLED IN. THE goats were bashing one another in their shelter and rattling the corrugated metal walls in a kind of pre-thunder. The dog was between Sarah and Wiley on the stairs, intently watching the horizon, and he looked at the girls when they startled at the first sign of lightning, and seconds later, thunder. A pig squealed out of sight behind the barn and they could hear hoofbeats on the wind. The chickens must've gone into the coop. They weren't around. As the rain started, it looked like twilight but it was barely after two. Strafing gusts worked fat steely drops up the stairs and chased them laughing indoors.

It wasn't long, three days, and their joy turned to watchfulness and worry. The drill rig sank in the mud. The root cellar flooded and they had to move everything inside the house. The electric fence shorted out and the pigs and a couple of goats disappeared in the night. Roy tried tracking them but they were gone. The radio squelched and buzzed and warned against mudslides and floods, interstate travel, intermittent streams, water over roadways, downed power lines, fires.

Then it got cold and the rain froze. Ice cocooned and eventually killed all but a few of their fruit trees and collapsed their greenhouse. The big oak in the yard dropped a massive limb that could've killed somebody. Roy and Jerzy bucked it up and stacked it on the porch with the fir and lodgepole they'd cut during the summer, some smaller stuff that'd been salvaged from the creek's floodwater.

Enough snow fell that it took Roy an hour to shovel the porch stairs, paths to the barn, goat house, and machine shed.

The wind picked up during the day and drifts unscrewed themselves from the driveway and in the fields. Roy watched out the kitchen window, a mug of rosehip tea in his hand. They were conserving coffee. He didn't mind tea but rosehip was his least favorite. He was in a mood. The girls were playing blackjack for actual dollars. Karen's sewing machine was thumping and whirring in her work room. Jerzy was rebuilding the transmission in Sully's old Dodge just for something to do. It wasn't worth saving. What was?

He finished his tea and left the mug in the sink. In the entryway he pulled on his coveralls and his rabbit fur hat and went outside to clear the snow from the solar panels. The goats heard him outside working on the roof and bleated and cracked their horns against their stall until he went in to check on them. Well fed, so far. Giving a steady gallon and a half a day. More than they could use but it helped fill out the pigs' rations, or it used to. He made some offhand feed calculations, assessed their individual life spans.

"Keep it up," he said to them. He scratched the hard ridges of their noses and tugged on their horns. "Hang in there. I'll figure something out."

The tractor didn't want to start and smoked a lot once it did. He poured in another four ounces of fuel additive and hoped for the best. While it idled and warmed he shoveled out the doorway again so a hump wouldn't form. His rabbit hat kept his ears warm. He wished his work gloves did the same for his hands.

He broke a shear pin before he'd made it out of the driveway. Cold work fixing it but he had a box full of them. The dog showed up and threw its body into his shoulder and knocked him over. Angry, with snow caked on his bare hands, he picked himself up.

"*Sedni*," he said. He wouldn't say it twice. He waited until the dog sat down and composed itself.

He was on his way back a half hour later when he saw the dog still sitting in the same spot, covered with snow, watching him. The best dog.

When the storm finally broke and the sun came out, the fields rolled endlessly open and unclaimed to the horizon. Cornices hung heavy and twisted along the ridges. The fences were buried under a foot of snow and the driveway looked as if it were cut in a mountain pass.

They needed to get moving. Get some air. Get out of the house. Roy and Jerzy spent the morning cobbling together the cross-country skis they'd discovered in the hayloft. Used short screws and cam straps to make bindings so they could fasten their snow boots to the skis since they didn't have enough ski boots. After some searching, Karen found two pairs of old leather nordic boots in the back of the hall closet in a box labeled Winter Etc. Roy wore Wiley's dad's boots. Extra socks.

The dog went through the snow as a porpoise would water. Roy had never put skis on before. It was more like walking since the snow was so deep—they weren't doing much sliding or gliding. They looped the property and had a snack at the top of the hill and surveyed their buried holdings. The winter felt eternal but from elevation less threatening. The dog's whiskers were frosted, as was Roy's beard.

Barry Miller had plowed his pasture and his cows, fifteen head, were kept in their mud-trampled corral by the massive snowbanks. As a family they watched as Barry used his tractor to plug a round bale into his big circular feeder. He had the bale on the forks and had to slip beneath the roof he'd built with steel pipe and sheet metal. It was a delicate operation and the structure showed the scars and dents of when he'd missed his target. When he saw them, he killed the motor and climbed down, muck boots, walked through the feeding bovines with his hands out, giving gentle touches to passing necks and haunches.

"Come on around and I'll open the gate," he said.

"That's OK. We're going for a ski," Roy said.

Sarah shuffled over in her skis and grabbed the fence to have a better look at the cows and Roy swatted her hand away. "Hey," she said, clutching her hand to her chest, glaring up at him.

"What're you doing?" Karen said to Roy.

He used the back of his hand to test for a shock. He could hear the charger popping. He was used to getting shocked. He was ready.

"This one isn't live," Barry said. He turned and pointed toward the house. "That one'll knock you into next week."

"I heard it popping," Roy said.

"So," Karen said to Barry. "Are you holding up all right?"

"I am. Thank you. How are you all faring?" He looked lonely and tired, a man trying to hold off despair.

Jerzy and Sarah began sword fighting with their ski poles. Wiley told them to knock it off.

"We're happy for the snow," Karen said. "It'll be great in the spring."

"I'll tell you," Barry said. "I wasn't quite ready for this."

"You're not the only one," Roy said.

"If you need anything," Karen said. "Don't hesitate. We don't want you to feel alone out here."

"I appreciate that, Karen. Thanks for coming by." He pulled his heavy jacket down to cover his pistol and gave Roy and Jerzy a nod. When the tractor fired up, Roy swung his skis around and broke trail toward the creek bottom. A pond had formed during the rains and he had thoughts of clearing the ice and letting the girls skate, but he'd have to find skates first.

Karen sailed past him on the downhill, with Sarah and Wiley and Jerzy close behind, following in her tracks. Roy trudged along with a fat layer of snow bonded to the bottom of his skis. Karen had rubbed wax on everybody else's skis but Roy had been too impatient. He'd wanted to try out his gear. He'd wanted to move. They'd been in the house too long.

When one after the other they came to a stop on the flats, the ice humphed loudly and Karen made everyone hurry back toward the safety of the hillside. Roy saw this and tried to run on his skis. He made it a couple of steps and fell on his face. He got up in a panic and went to take his skis off but by then everyone had started to move on.

Roy's face and his rabbit-fur hat were covered in snow and it was packed down his boots. He was cold. He wasn't happy with being the slowest or the idea of his girls falling through the ice. The girls started toward home. Jerzy tried to pass but fell down and they laughed at him, left him to wallow in the powder. They hadn't seen Roy fall or they would've said something. The fear on his face. Karen had, she waited. "Look at you," she said, wiped the snow from his face.

There was a cardboard box on the porch when they got back and fresh boot tracks in the drive. Wiley and her sister clattered out of their gear and ran up the stairs. Jerzy lay sprawled in the driveway. The older girl unfolded the package lid with one hand while stiff-arming her little sister with the other.

"It's a roast," Karen said when she looked in the box, smiling big. "Ten pounds of ground."

"Hamburgers!" Sarah said.

"I'm going to bake him a pie," Karen said.

"Feeding old bachelors is a bad idea," Roy said.

"Putting you and Jerzy on skis was a bad idea."

He was still struggling to free himself from his bindings. His hands were frozen. Sarah ran down the stairs and shoved him to the ground. Before he could get up, Wiley joined in and kicked snow in his face.

"I thought you were going to fall through the ice," he said, catching Sarah by the ankle and dragging her toward him. He kicked his skis off and got to his feet, hung Sarah upside down by her leg. "I think you need to cool off," Roy said. He crossed the driveway and tossed Sarah in the deep powder on the other side of the bank. He chased Wiley but she was too fast and he gave up.

They left their skis on the porch and had hamburgers on sourdough for an early dinner. Nobody asked for or even mentioned ketchup.

CHRISTMAS EVE DAY. THE STORMS CONTINUED, SNOW BLOWING sideways. Barry Miller was parked in front of his open security gate, blocking the road, waiting for Roy. Roy didn't bother to turn off his tractor. He leaned over the steering wheel and pulled down his balaclava. "Merry Christmas," Roy shouted.

Barry opened the door of his cab a bit wider and leaned out. "You, too."

"Your Jeff buddies must not like the snow, huh? Been awful quiet."

Barry shook his head and halfway smiled. "Snowbirds, I tell you. They're fleeing if they haven't already fled."

"You?"

"I live here, Bingham. Like it or not."

"You want to get this road cleared? I'll go first and you catch the other side and my berm. We can switch on the loop back. Be a lot faster that way."

Barry nodded. "You got enough fuel?"

Roy turned and gauged the distance to his house and his fuel supply, did the mental math of the highway loop. "It'll be close but I think I'll make it."

"Follow me." Roy trailed his neighbor through the massive security gate and down his driveway and parked alongside one of his two elevated fuel tanks, killed the motor. Barry climbed the ladder and unlocked the tank and passed Roy the filler hose and nozzle.

"I'm getting some coffee," Barry said. He walked alongside Roy's tractor and snagged his frosty travel mug. "Do you take sugar?"

"Black. Thanks."

Roy topped the tank and hung up the hose. Barry was still gone. His house was a single-level ranch with lap siding, solar-cell roof, same as Roy's. With the snow it was a huge pain in the ass. Hail damage didn't help either. Barry had the fuel tanks and several large propane tanks. Roy figured he must be in some militia loop for getting them filled because no one drove out this far anymore. He had several concrete outbuildings with two corrals and his Herefords. No milk cows or goats, no horses. Roy wondered where he got his hay, figured it must be another militia connection. The barn looked Soviet bloc, like a nuclear bunker that he'd forgotten to sink in the ground. Barry was walking back with the coffee.

"You alone here?" Roy asked.

"For now."

"You got a girlfriend stashed somewhere?"

Barry winced, looked away as he passed up his coffee. "Did you lock that up?"

"No, didn't know if you had to use it too."

"I'm full." Barry watched Roy fumble with gloved hands until he'd set the latch and closed the hasp and finally slapped the lock down and secured the tank.

They worked together in a staggered pattern, but even then the going was slow. When the road turned east/west, the snow had drifted four feet high. Roy was soon covered in a thick layer of snow and ice and hated Barry for having an enclosed cab.

The highway hadn't been plowed but it had been driven on with snowmobiles and what looked to be a snowcat. Barry opened the door of his tractor and got out.

"Get down from there. You're gonna freeze to death."

"I'm fine."

"Go on. Mine's got heat. I can drive your little piece a shit. I promise I won't hurt it."

"It's not a piece of shit. Just an old, underpowered, worn out—" Roy climbed down and gave Barry a swat on the shoulder with a frozen hand. He pulled himself inside and shut the door on the cab of Barry's tractor. He took off his gloves and held them over the heat vents. Barry engaged the blower in Roy's tractor and took off. Roy followed him. There was a printed photograph of a woman on the dash. She was standing before a table cluttered with antique firearms, and a banner above her announced the Reno Gun Show.

Barry stopped just beyond the gate of his property and climbed stiffly from the Kubota. He motioned Roy through the gate and once he was clear of the swing he set the brake and got down from the tractor. He left the engine running.

"If it keeps up," Barry said, in a mask of white, "and it looks like it will, I'll keep an eye out for you and we'll hit it again."

"OK."

"And I'll get on the radio about the highway too."

"See if the Jeffs will plow it?"

"Somebody has to. If no one else, Cal Trans."

"Now you want Cal Trans." Roy laughed.

"Nobody saw this snow coming."

"Karen did. She said it was going to happen just like this. She said it was cyclical, California always is."

"I bet it's worse at the low elevations with the flooding."

"It's always worse somewhere else. Thanks for the coffee."

"Yep."

Roy stopped and turned. "Hey, Barry."

"What?"

"You want to come to our place for Christmas dinner?"

"What're you having?"

"The roast you gave us, potatoes. Blackberry pie."

"No, thanks. Maybe next year."

"OK. Karen'd kill me if I didn't ask."

"You're off the hook now." Barry turned and walked away.

Roy climbed on his tractor and slipped it into gear. Barry was already on the other side of his fence, chaining his gate closed.

[37]

M < 55
OR 9XXXX

FROM A DISTANCE THE SMALL TOWNS THEY COME TO APPEAR deserted, but desertion is never complete, there's always someone. The poor kid is crying as he pedals. The man tries to talk to him but he doesn't want to talk. They pedal: chain noise, bottom bracket creak, wind. With uncomfortable regularity he checks over his shoulder but there's no one behind them. It's difficult to keep moving and they're going too slow to ever make it anywhere. It's as if they aren't moving at all. His girls appear in the road before him. *Strange children. Dead on the road.* The dog is limping and the man has *oh shit oh shit oh shit* on the brain, a dull panic. They are out of water. He turns to say something to the boy about being out of water.

He wakes up at the side of the road with blood on his face and his hands, drag marks in the dirt that lead to him. The boy and the dog are gone. His bike is in the ditch but the boy's is gone with him. He sees a patch of green high on the hillside and when he listens he can hear an irrigation pump running. He picks up his bike and wheels it onto the pavement. The dirt road is lined by dead and broken cottonwoods. The boy's bike tracks weave up the hill. The dog's tracks zigzag over them. He turns a corner and comes upon a single-level house with a sod roof, a large, high-fence garden. Mismatched chickens in the yard and in the road. The barn is small and he can smell goats. Their scent makes him happy.

An old woman in jeans and a T-shirt comes out to meet him. "We were just coming to get you." She motions to the garage. Her hair is thick and curly, red streaked with gray. A truck is backing out. The boy and the dog are in the back. "We couldn't get a word out of the kid, but we figured it out eventually."

The truck's reverse lights turn off and it returns to the garage. The dog hops out and the boy follows him. He pets the dog when it collides with his legs. The boy approaches and digs the empty water bladders from his rear pannier. The man that had been driving the truck is out now. He's old but built like a runner, wearing a red T-shirt and a dingy baseball cap, Ben Davis trousers, New Balance shoes. His name is Hugh. His wife is Patty.

The boy holds up the empty water bladders for the old couple to see.

"We can do that," Patty says.

"Better come on up here," Hugh says with a wave of his hand.

The boy follows Patty inside. Hugh motions the man through the door too but he's still bleeding a little from his bike wreck so he stays on the porch stairs with the dog. Hugh walks to the barn and when he returns he passes the man a wet rag and another dry one along with a bottle of hydrogen peroxide.

"They're clean, even if they don't look it," the old man says.

"Thanks."

"Do you want a mirror? You only have the one cut on your temple there that's still oozing a bit."

The man does his best to clean up. The peroxide foams and sludges pink bubbles down his jaw and neck.

The dog is drinking out of a water dish at the bottom of the stairs. The man searches for another dog, to prevent a fight, but doesn't see any.

"Ours is dead," Hugh offers. "If you were wondering. Remind me and I'll give you some kibble when you go."

"Thanks again."

"Is he mute?" Hugh asks of the boy.

"I don't know," the man says. "I don't know anything about him."

Patty comes out of the house, followed by the boy. They set a pitcher of water and four glasses on the table. The old woman motions the boy to a chair with a smile and he sits down and immediately drinks down all the water from the glass he's been offered.

"Take it slow now, sweetheart," Patty says. "We still have bread, don't we?" she says to her husband.

The bread is hard enough to make the man's gums bleed but the strawberry jam and butter that Hugh slathers on it makes the discomfort inconsequential.

"So he's not yours?" Patty nods to the boy.

"No," the man says, trying to keep the bread down, mouth watering.

"His people?" Hugh asks.

"They're gone," the man says, hesitating. "I found them on the road. He was hiding in a culvert. I don't know who did it, which militia."

The boy sets down his bread and looks at the old woman, butter and jam on his upper lip. "They were in a helicopter."

"Who?" the old man asks. The boy doesn't answer.

The old woman looks at her husband. "We saw helicopters, was it yesterday? Coming and going. They were militia, not federal. A man waved at me from the door."

"They took my sisters," the boy says. "They told my dad and everybody to put down their guns and then Tommy fired his but it was an accident. They started shooting out of the helicopter and it didn't stop until they landed. Until they took them." The boy swallows hard and takes a deep breath.

The adults at the table glance at one another, fidget in their chairs.

"And what about you?" Hugh asks. "You're ill? Drink some bad water maybe?"

"If I had to guess, I'd say trichinosis," the man says. "Bear meat."

"That's a tough row, that one," Hugh says.

"We can't spare any antibiotics," Patty says. "And if memory serves, I think you can ride it out just as soon as treat it."

"What I picture going on in my stomach," the man says, "is worse than the physical part."

"What's going on in your stomach?" the boy asks.

"I'll tell you," Hugh says, laughing a little. "But you have to tell me your name first." The old man glances at his wife. "And how old you are. And where you're from."

"My name is Roland. I'm eight. I lived in Sacramento before we left."

"Not at the table," Patty says to her husband.

"Roland, age eight, from Sacramento," Hugh says, smiling, making crawly fingers with his hands. "It's worms, thousands and thousands of worms squirming in his belly like a nest of snakes."

"Now you've made me sick," Patty says, standing up. "You can come with me, Roland. I don't want to leave you alone with these two. One's sick and the other's just plain gross."

The boy follows Patty inside and Hugh clears the dishes. When he comes back he motions the man around the corner to the lush grass of the backyard. "You can rest there," he says. "The hose bib is live if you're thirsty."

The man sleeps through the heat of the day in the shade of a fig tree. They have goat stew and roasted vegetables for dinner but the man can still only manage the broth.

After they eat, the man insists that he and the dog sleep outside. "I don't want to risk getting sick in the house," he says.

"You can sleep in the goat shed," Patty says.

"Can't say I'm real keen on him getting sick in there, either," Hugh says.

"It all cleans up," Patty says.

"Not if the goats eat whatever he pukes up and they get sick too."

"I'll sleep in the yard," the man says.

"Sleep in the bed of the pickup," the old man says. "It'll keep the dew off."

The next morning Roland wakes the man in the bed of the truck. He's ready to go. "Come on and get up," he says.

As he's getting himself together, digging the sleep from his eyes and tying on his shoes, Roland is going on about the soccer match that he and Hugh and Patty listened to last night on the radio, broadcast from England. The man, out of the truck now, pisses against the driveway fence. The dog moves down the line a bit and does the same. The sky is dark with smoke and the wind is blowing hot out of the south. Hugh and Patty are up and moving around in the house, the sound of cooking comes through the screen door. The man feels like he might be able to keep food down. He smells coffee and smiles. They eat at the kitchen table. A clock ticking is the only sound. Nobody says grace.

"We chose to live like this," Hugh says, passes a plate of fried potatoes and sausage to Roland, "long before it was necessary. Seemed obvious at the time."

Roland loads his plate and without pause begins eating.

"The way that people wasted their money, their lives," Patty says, passes the man a mug of coffee.

The man thanks her, sips, holds it in his mouth for a few long seconds before swallowing. "Do you have kids?" he asks.

"Our oldest was killed in Saudi Arabia in '26," Patty says, turning to Hugh. "He was a Marine."

"I did five tours in Afghanistan," Hugh said. "My father fought in Vietnam. My grandpas were in WWII and Korea. Family traditions, deadliest thing on the planet."

"We have two girls too," Patty says. "One lives in Wales and the other in Manitoba."

"They don't visit," Hugh says.

"Neither do we," Patty says.

"Jeffersons don't bother you here?" the man asks.

"Nah," Hugh says. "Never did. We're in flyover country, literally. They just fly over us. I hear the Jeffs are done anyway. It's STT now. The lady on the radio said that their general was invited to the White House."

"So they're legitimate," Patty says, nodding. "Hopefully they'll act like it."

"They're all the same," the man says.

Roland asks if he can have seconds. Of course. Much as you want. They watch him eat. The man folds his napkin and puts it on the table.

After breakfast, standing on the porch, Patty gives the boy a hug and Hugh shakes their hands, making the departure official.

"You could stay with us a few days," Patty says to Roland.

"I have to find my sisters," Roland says, as he climbs onto his bike and lifts one foot to the pedal.

"He doesn't want to stay with us, woman," Hugh says. "Good luck to you both." He turns with a quick wave and goes inside. The screen door slams.

"What d'you wanna bet that when I get in there he'll be crying?" Patty says, shaking her head. Roland gives her a scared look. "Don't worry about him," Patty says to Roland. "You can always come back. Anytime."

"Thank you," the man says.

"Thank you," Roland says.

Morning on the blacktop with full stomachs. No cars and wind at their backs. "Easy money," the man says, as much to himself as to the boy.

[38]

R > 45
CA 96118

THE HAY IN THE BARN WENT QUICKLY, ESPECIALLY AFTER THE roof leaked and they lost a ton or more to mold. They butchered four of the eight milk goats and ran trap lines to keep the chickens fed, tromped through the snow to the abandoned hay barns and nearby oak trees, chipped out watering holes from the ice and laid snares for rabbits, squirrels, feral cats. The chickens didn't like to eat animals with eyes, not at first, but they got used to it. Wasn't long before they'd peck out the eyes first.

The snow finally melted. At the edge of the western field, Wiley spotted a young ram that had escaped during a storm. With the dog's help she got a rope on it and dragged it back to the goat shed. Two weeks later Sarah crossed hog wallows while she worked her string of #2 squirrel traps along the cut banks in Correco Canyon. Roy figured they must've holed up in an old barn somewhere, or even a house. He didn't like to think what they might've dug up to eat.

Then the generator broke and no amount of cunning or ingenuity could repair it. The damage sustained to the grid over the long winter meant it was only slightly more reliable than their solar. They were lucky to have a couple of days a week at full power.

Roy left the machine partially dismantled and in a pool of its own oil. Jerzy, the actual mechanic, not the tinkerer Roy was, made short work of making the declaration of death. A slow leak had left the pistons dry and when it kicked on for the last time the damage was, as Jerzy put it, absolute. They used the tractor to load the ruined machine into the back of the pickup, then took off their hats like *so long, old friend,* and shut the tailgate.

Karen and Roy took Sarah with them when they drove the generator to the junkyard, Eli's Pick 'n' Pull, outside of town. Jerzy had come up with a list of possible replacements with part numbers they could search for. The next move was to cannibalize the generator from the drill rig. Or go to Reno, and they tried to avoid Reno. Same with Sacramento. They left with the understanding that they were leaving Jerzy and Wiley alone and doing it on purpose.

"They're going to have a kid," Karen said.

"No, they're not," Roy said. He and Sarah were playing blackjack.

Sarah showed Roy her cards and he passed her four quarters. "When do I get to have a baby?" she asked.

"Never," Karen said.

"When you're older," Roy said.

"How much?"

"A hundred years," Roy said. "Hit me." Ace of spades. "Bam, kiddo. Pay up. That's black and the jack. Blackjack." He held up his hand to make a pronouncement, as was his habit with Sarah. "The great Lemmy once said, 'You know I'm born to lose and gambling's for fools, but that's the way I like it, baby, I don't want to live forever.'" Roy was about to sing the last line, *and don't forget the joker*, when Karen told him to shut it.

"You're weird." His daughter dug into her backpack and passed her dad a butterscotch candy. "I'll get that back," she said, not joking.

The road was potholed and washed out in places. Blackened fence posts had dropped their wires but it was greener than it had been in years.

"I think Barry has the same model," Karen said.

"Same model of what?"

"Generator."

"How would you know that?" Roy said.

"Because I talk to people. I'm not a curmudgeon like you. People like me, right, sweetie?"

"That's right, Mama."

"You know as well as me that the Pick 'n' Pull is a dead end," Karen said. "Eli won't be there or have anything we can use. He sure as hell won't be sober. Might be naked."

"Probably," Roy said.

"It'll be a kind of peace offering," Karen said.

"To Eli?" Roy wasn't really listening.

"To Barry."

"Come on," Roy said. "I invited him over for Christmas. Wasn't that enough?"

Sarah held up an ace and a king. "Pay up," she said.

When Karen turned and stopped in front of Barry Miller's security gate, hung her head out the window for the camera to see, waved hello, and waited for the gate to swing open. "We still haven't met his wife," Karen said. "It's time. The opportunity has presented itself."

"I can't believe someone married him," Roy said.

"As if they don't say the same thing about you," Karen said.

"She probably came mail order from the NRA," Roy said. "Get yer new wife free with a lifetime membership and a case of 5.56 or 7.62 NATO."

"Be nice," Karen said. The gate swung open and they drove slowly down the lane.

A woman emerged from between the outbuildings and the house wearing a bloody apron and rubber gloves that went to her armpits. She had a very intense look on her face, not fear but close to it.

"Would you mind giving me a hand?" she asked, before they'd even gotten out of the truck. She was Karen's age, maybe a little older, short gray hair and bright green eyes.

"Sure," Karen said.

They followed her around the open shop door with the tractor and all its implements lined up neatly in a row to a steel outbuilding with a reinforced steel door.

Inside they found Barry stretched out on a shiny metal workbench in the center of the room. His shirt had been cut open and when his wife moved the compress they saw that he had a neatly puckered bullet hole on his left side below his ribs. He didn't look surprised to see the Binghams. He even made the effort to smile at Sarah. The room was large and well lit by overhead

LEDs. The walls were wainscoted with fiberglass-reinforced panels like you'd see in a restaurant kitchen and there was a walk-in cooler and a table with a band saw and a meat grinder. Another table on the opposite wall, beside a large double basin sink, had industrial rolls of butcher paper and plastic wrap.

"They dropped him off like this," Barry's wife said.

"Who?" Karen asked.

"Jeffersons. He won't tell me what happened. If they shot him or if someone else did. With friends like that—" She made a face at her husband then turned back to Karen and Roy. "I'm Ilah."

The Binghams did their introductions. "What can we do to help?" Karen asked.

"I flushed it and it passed all the way through so I'm ready to go in and clean it but he won't stay still. I already gave him something for the pain but he's squirming all over the place. I was about to use ratchet straps to buckle him down when the alarm beeped and I saw you on the gate camera. I'd rather we kept the human touch." She had a cool but pleasant smile and Barry obviously deferred to her. He still hadn't said a word since they'd arrived. The shame was nearly as heavy on his face as the discomfort. Roy wanted to laugh. *You're fucked, Barry*, he thought. *Your friends shot you or someone else did and you're fucked.*

"I might have to do a few internal stitches too," Ilah said. "I can't tell until I get in there."

"Are you a doctor?" Sarah asked.

"No, nurse practitioner." Barry lifted his arm and moaned a little. "Let's get it over with. Your daughter can wait in the house. There's fresh orange juice in the fridge."

"Can I stay?" Sarah asked. "I want to watch."

"No, go on inside," Roy said. "I'll come and get you when we're done."

"But I want to see."

Karen put her arm around the girl and walked her out and came back a moment later, rolling up her sleeves. "She likes blood too much. When I was her age I was a vegetarian."

"You two ready?" Ilah asked. "You ready, sweetheart?"

Barry nodded but didn't speak.

Roy took him by the shoulders and Karen held his feet. When Ilah spread the wound with her forceps, Barry fixed Roy with a hateful stare and didn't let up until she'd finished with her scalpel and took a break.

"We brought you a present," Karen said to Barry. He was pale and his skin was clammy. Roy thought he would've passed out by now, wished that he would, holding him was exhausting.

"You shouldn't have," Barry whispered.

"It's a spare generator, for parts," Roy said. "It ran dry and we killed it. Thought maybe you could use it."

"Sure. Sure, we can use it."

"Are we ready?" Ilah asked.

"OK," Barry said. He closed his eyes and Roy pressed his weight into his shoulders.

Sarah and Karen went with Ilah to feed and water the animals in Barry's weird circular barn. Once they'd finished and gotten Barry to his bed in the house, Roy busied himself moving sprinkler pipe from one side of the pasture to the other and filling the stock tank, at the same time checking out all the new structures Barry had built. He'd made a windmill from a kit and it turned a drive line that worked his main irrigation pump and there was a second PTO coming from the windmill tower that turned an ancient hammer mill for grinding silage at the pull of a lever. By the time they climbed back into the truck to leave, Roy had to admit that he kind of admired Barry.

JERZY AND WILEY WERE IN THE GARDEN WHEN THEY CAME HOME. Roy watched as Jerzy registered the blood on their clothes and his mouth fell open and Roy held up his hand and Sarah climbed out of the back where she'd been sleeping.

"We're OK," Roy said. "The blood is Barry's."

Jerzy dropped his shovel and stepped over the raised bed he'd been digging in and grabbed Wiley by the arm and they hurried together down the path out of the garden and closed the goat-fence gate behind them.

"Someone shot him," Sarah yelled to her sister. "And Ilah sewed him up like a doll."

"Who's Ilah?" Wiley asked.

"Barry's new wife," Roy said.

"Who shot him?" Wiley asked.

"I don't know," Roy said. "Guessing his militia pals, but he didn't talk about it."

"That's nuts," Jerzy said, looking at Wiley. She was acting strange. They both were.

"What're you two up to?" Roy said. Roy was caught looking at her stomach and shook his head and blew out a big breath of air.

"I'm not pregnant," Wiley said. "Quit looking at me like that." She was wearing her mom's Archers of Loaf dead hero T-shirt and a cowboy hat she'd taken from the extensive collection of Stetsons that Jerzy had inherited from Sullivan. She was already taller than Karen, stood eye to eye with Roy. She'd known hard work her whole life, even their vacations were strenuous, cycle touring, backpacking, camping. *Let's load ourselves up with a bunch of heavy shit and haul it way into the mountains and then haul it back. Maybe we'll go fishing, maybe not. Might not be any fish to catch. Same with hunting but the gear weighs ten times as much. Sound like fun? Then, when we get home, we'll haul a bunch of heavy shit around and never stop weeding and milking goats and fixing fence and working from dawn to dusk. How about that, life's a party, right?* By the time I was her age, Roy thought, I'd probably sat on my ass watching TV for a quarter of my life, maybe more. But Wiley never asked for a break, Sarah either. Jerzy got depressed if he wasn't solving a problem or sweating his ass off fixing something. *Look at them. Look at my people*, he thought proudly.

Karen glared at Wiley and shut the door of the pickup and then eased Sarah toward the house with a firm push on the small of her back. "Go on. You need to wash up. We'll be inside in a sec so we can get dinner going." Sarah didn't argue but she went by her sister giving her the big eyes, like better you than me.

"It can wait until we're at the table," Jerzy said. "We should be sitting down."

"What can wait?" Karen said.

"Spit it out, Jerzy," Roy said. "Why do you look so terrified all of a sudden?" Roy held up his fist and smiled. "I'll give you something to be afraid of."

"Roy, Mr. Bingham, Mrs. Bingham, I'd like to ask your permission to marry your daughter."

"Would you listen to this?" Karen said.

"Fine with me," Roy said. "If you want her."

"Hey," Wiley said.

"I'm kidding. You have my blessing. Babe?" he said to Karen. "Say something."

Jerzy took Wiley's hand. "You don't have to worry about me ever hurting her or leaving her."

"Words, Jerzy. Words are just words," Karen said.

"OK," Roy said. "Let's go make dinner and we'll talk about this at the table, but no fighting. There's nothing to fight about. We're happy for you and you have my blessing." Nodding at Karen, "Hers is worth more than mine so it'll be harder to come by. Probably just be patient."

Karen was headed for the house but turned around suddenly to get the paper sack of frozen steaks and green beans that Ilah had sent them home with. "We aren't having these tonight," she said to Roy.

"We could thaw them in time," Roy said. "It's a special occasion."

"No, we aren't having them tonight." As she went by she went to smack Roy with the heavy sack of meat but she missed and the handles ripped and the butcher-paper-wrapped steaks went skittering into the gravel driveway.

"See," Roy said, smiling, "they're already thawing."

Karen's mouth went from a grimace to a smile and back to a grimace so quickly that Roy was sure he was the only one that caught it. She dropped the sack of green beans where she stood and walked off empty-handed.

Jerzy and Wiley picked up the steaks, careful to wipe off the gravel, while Roy sat on the tailgate eating green beans from the bag. "Did he propose?" he asked Wiley. "Was he sweet about it?"

"Yes."

"It was romantic?" Roy fluttered his hands in front of his face and made Jerzy squirm.

"C'mon," Jerzy said.

"You can call me Dad now, or Mr. Dad." Roy pitched a bean at Jerzy and he caught it and broke it in half and split it with Wiley.

"We were in the garden," Wiley said. "It just happened."

"Crushing aphids, digging thistle, romantic," Roy said.

"It was romantic. He got down on his knees and gave me a ring." She took a ring out of her pocket and put it on and held up her finger.

"Where'd you get that?" Roy asked Jerzy.

"Sullivan left it to me. It was his mom's."

Roy smiled, the ring didn't matter—symbols and words—but Sullivan did, to Jerzy he mattered. "Let's go unthaw your mother," he said to Wiley.

But they didn't have to. When they got inside there were wineglasses on the table and a dusty cabernet they'd been saving. Karen hugged Jerzy first and then Wiley, wouldn't let her go until Roy shoved the filled glasses between them. They ate late and were a little drunk because the steaks took so long to thaw. Roy made a toast and Karen hassled him for being weepy.

[39]

M < 55
OR XXXXX

Roland pushes his bike up the hills. The man waits for him. He's feeling better and as long he keeps moving the body aches don't bother him. His nail beds are bleeding and it's weird but not painful. The dog mostly sticks with the kid. The giant power-company windmills still turn on the ridges and are sprinkled along the horizon like jacks or obviously pinwheels and the man wonders—not for the first time—what a person waking from a coma, Rip Van Winkle, would think of these alien objects. You slept too long, all the grass is dead and the rivers run dry. When they get closer they see that the transmission lines have all been taken down and many of the towers and transformers have been disassembled. The mills are turning for nothing.

They pass a U-Haul box truck with two shredded tires. The back door has been torn open and what's left of the contents, mostly children's toys and clothes, are strewn across the two lanes. The glass in the cab is shattered. They don't even touch their brakes, rubberneck and go.

A mile or two down the road, Roland leans his bicycle against an abandoned RV at the roadside and sits down in the shade. The man bangs on the door and circles the vehicle to make sure no one is around. All of the window glass is intact but judging by the large oil stain that has spread from the motor to the ditch, the sweet stink of antifreeze, the occupants have moved on.

"Your dog has the squirts," Roland says.

"Good, so do I," says the man. The pain in his hips and back swells the longer he stands. He sits down next to Roland.

"Is he sick like you?"

"I don't know if dogs get sick in the same way from what I got but he ate more of that bear than I did." He glances at the boy, his gaunt and dusty face, clumped hair. Street urchin. Road dog. From any century and anyplace except recently and here.

"I'm tired."

"So am I." The man stretches his legs out before him and rolls his left ankle until he gets it to pop.

The wind is entertaining, things blow by, trash and weeds. A farm truck drives by and the driver keeps his eyes locked to the road and never sees them, doesn't want to. The dog licks its paws and the man scoots over to have a look, searches in the webs for goat heads or other damage, finds the pads sound and well-calloused, nails dull but intact. They share the last of their water.

"Where are we going?" Roland asks.

"I told you. North. To Alaska."

"I'm not."

"You don't have to."

"My sisters."

"We'll go to Portland first. Seattle if we can catch a ride."

"You think we'll find them?"

The man glances at Roland.

"Are you going to help me look for them?"

"Yeah, I'll help you." He pulls the dog toward him and rubs his belly. "I used to skate with a guy named Roland," the man says. "Did I tell you this already?"

"No. What was he like?"

"He was from Australia. I think the name is more common there. You don't meet many Rolands in the States. But I met you." The man holds out his fist for a bump and Roland obliges him. "There was a guy named Gerald too, that's one of those names. Gerald. People called him Gerbil. He was a mess."

"What happened to him?"

"If the choice was skate or die, I'm guessing he died." The man is exhausted. He doesn't want to go on. He stands up and rips open the door on the RV but the rotten smell turns him around. Roland plugs his nose and climbs the stairs, finds a dead cat curled in the little plastic commode. The man goes in to see because the boy asks him to.

When they are back outside they pick up their bikes.

"Did you ever collect baseball cards?" Roland asks.

"No, never. Wasn't my thing."

"My dad said mine are worthless." He produces a short stack of tattered cards from his pocket.

"Do they seem worthless?"

Roland looks at the cards one at a time and then drops them on the ground and walks to his bike. The man picks them up before the wind blows them away and puts them in his pocket. They pedal on. The wind has turned and it isn't doing them any favors. Miles tick by.

[40]

R > 45
CA 96118, CA 94203

THEY'D BEEN PLANNING THE TRIP SINCE BEFORE THE GENERA-tor died, before the engagement was announced. They needed coffee, rice, flour, sugar, beer and wine, vitamins, antibiotics, and, if they were extremely fortunate, a new generator. They'd go see April first because Pecos had a bit of mange going. They always went to April's first. Most of her neighbors had left so the power company would no longer fix her lines. Last year, Roy and Jerzy had helped her rig her solar panels to her secondhand lithium-ion batteries. Roy gassed up the truck from the five-hundred-gallon tank by the barn—*thanks, Miller*—and everyone but Jerzy piled in. He'd stay to take care of the animals. Somebody had to. Wiley wanted to stay with him but Karen told her she was coming, like it or not, engaged or not. "Load up, child bride," she said, without smiling.

The roadblock was unattended and the gate was up so they

didn't stop. A makeshift plywood bulletin board at the road-side had some kind of warning or message posted on it but they didn't bother reading it.

Driving out of the mountains, Roy had to use four-wheel drive to maneuver down the embankment to skirt washouts and mudslides again and again. What the insects hadn't killed had burned in seemingly endless forest fires. Then the heavy winter and the rains brought the mountains down and had them look-ing scraped raw. Twice, he had to use his chain saw and they moved the sections of timber in pieces as a family. Sarah had never seen it green the way that Roy and Karen and Wiley had. She'd only known the Sierras as brown and charred or buried in snow and streaked with mud.

When they got to April's, Roy honked the horn and April came out and unlocked the gate and pushed it open so they could pull in. Her motorcycle was parked in front of the house, full-face helmet hanging from the right handgrip, polished chrome, wet chain, new-looking rubber, her daily driver. It was the bike that Roy had given to Aaron so many years ago, Yano's old bike. Aaron's other motorcycles had either been sold or gone to his cop buddy Sang-Chul. April had offered them to Roy but he didn't have the time or resources to keep them going.

April gave the girls hugs and took Roy and Karen by the hands and gave them each a peck on the cheek. Karen had brought her a few pounds of goat cheese and some milk and the girls gave her a flat of canned tomatoes.

"What about you, Roy? What did you bring me?" she asked as she put the tomatoes on the counter and the cheese and milk in the fridge.

"T. S. Eliot said April was the cruelest month," he said. "But I think you're a sweetheart, any day of the week."

"That's good. I like you." April laughed and then nodded to Wiley to let her know that she could take Sarah back to the kennels and see who was there. April hadn't claimed a pet since Aaron's K9, Gem, had died, but there was never a shortage of strays. Pecos lay down on the dog bed in the kitchen that was only used by him when he came to visit.

Karen told April about the engagement. She stepped back, in shock, and then opened a cupboard and took out a bottle of Glenlivet and three glasses. "Is she pregnant?" April asked, while she poured.

"She says she's not." Karen took her glass and downed it like a shot and held it out for a refill.

"If it's gonna be that kind of party, we better eat something first," April said.

"I'll cook," Roy said. "You two can get hammered."

"You'll just get hammered later," Karen said, "after you cook."

"Fair is fair," April said.

"Can we stay the night?" Karen asked.

"Can you stop asking?" April slugged down her drink and winced.

Roy opened the fridge but it was mostly pet medicine. "Is there anything open where I can get some things? Any place that's not Walmart."

"Like what?" April said.

"Food stuff, staples."

April checked her watch. "If you hurry, you can make the street fair on Auburn. There's usually a guy there selling 'beef,'" air quotes, "but he sells out early. You might be able to get some fish. Hard to say without going. There's always kelp now, always."

"Are you taking the girls?" Karen asked.

"Should I?"

"Yes, you should. Go and let us get shit-faced."

Wiley walked in, Sarah right behind her. "Who's getting shit-faced?" she asked.

"Nobody," Roy said. "You two are coming with me. Food run."

"Can we get clothes?" Wiley asked. "You said we could get some clothes."

"I heard you say it," Sarah said. "We all heard you."

Roy looked at Karen. "I thought that would be for tomorrow. With your mom."

"You can take them," Karen said. She sipped her drink and winked at April.

"OK. Fine." Roy poured a splash of scotch in his glass and downed it.

"You're not supposed to do that if you're driving," Sarah said.

"Easy, copper," Roy said.

"Go ahead and have another, Roy," Wiley said. "I'll drive."

"Wiley Jean wants to drive."

"Don't call me that."

"Mess with the bull and you get the bullshit. Cause and effect, Wiley Jean."

The gate closed behind them. He wasn't letting Wiley drive. Now she was pouting. He got lost trying to find the street fair and by the time they got there, all the beef guy had left was some greenish stew meat but Roy took it anyway and put it in the cooler with the ice packs in the back. Wiley bought carrots and golden beets and chard. Sarah found someone selling earrings and Roy ended up buying three pairs and left the fair feeling pretty good about himself.

At Walmart, Roy popped the hood on the truck and removed the fuel pump relay and put it in his pocket. The motor wouldn't start without it. He locked the doors and had to jog a little to catch up to the girls. The security line took an hour and any buzz Roy might've had was long gone. The girls were excited inside the store, as everyone was, and Roy tried not to kill it by telling them what a fucking joke the place was and that it had always been a joke. While the girls picked out new underwear and socks and shirts and jeans, Roy grabbed one of the motorized super carts, like a mini-flatbed truck, and limited-out on one hundred pounds of rice, fifty pounds of coffee, one hundred pounds of rye flour, one hundred pounds of black beans, a five-gallon jug of olive oil, and topped off the cart bed with as many cases of Wally beer and box wine as he could.

The girls found him already waiting in the checkout queue. He should've brought the dog and he should've brought Karen, or he could've waited until tomorrow. He could get rolled while he was loading all this stuff up. He'd left his pistol in his truck. He couldn't bring it through security.

The girls were trying on sunglasses and tossing candy into the cart, knowing that Roy wouldn't stop them.

"Wiley," he said, "come here. Grab your sister."

"What?" Wiley said.

"When we get by security and into the parking lot, I want you to pay attention. If you see anyone coming at us, in a car or on foot, any wrong-looking shit at all, I want you to let me know, because I'm going to be loading the truck and I won't be able to see anything when I'm in the camper, all right?"

"OK."

"You too, little one," he said to Sarah. "You're gonna be inside the truck but I want you to watch for people and if you see something, you honk the horn."

"OK."

"And what do you do with the doors?" he asked her.

"I keep them locked and don't open them for anybody," Sarah said proudly.

"That's right," Roy said. "Because I have a key and nobody is getting it from me. Ever."

The two girls hung on the side of the cart while Roy jockeyed through the potholes and vendors that were allowed to operate within the perimeter, and then it was another thirty minutes to get through security. Everything had to be weighed again and checked against the receipts, and then his "Preservation ration vouchers" had to be validated and after all that they had to re-load the cart themselves. Thanks for shopping at Walmart. The family ahead of them wasn't allowed to keep their olive oil because their vouchers had expired, never mind that they'd already paid for it. They used to ask you if you wanted an armed escort to your vehicle but not anymore.

The sun was down and bats were smudging the sky. The lights on the lampposts in the parking light were mostly broken and if they weren't they were so dim they didn't do much good. Roy grabbed Sarah from the cart and opened the truck and put her inside. He checked over his shoulder and put his pistol in his waistband. The parking lot was filled with other families loading up their cars and trucks, same as it had always been, but there were some stragglers out there too. Again, he wished he'd brought the dog. So much time in the country, when he was out in the open in the city like this his nerves went to shit and he wanted to flee or start shooting. He took a deep breath and opened the tailgate and the camper shell hatch. Then he handed Wiley the pistol, butt first. She took it and pulled the slide to make sure it was loaded. She knew how to shoot. He had to trust her.

"I got you, old man," she said. "Do your thing. I'll be right here."

One bag at a time, he loaded the truck. He was done quickly, and if he wouldn't have crawled back in to get some candy for the drive back to April's, they might've made it out no problem.

He heard Wiley say something and he asked her what and he was turning around and sliding off the tailgate when he heard her say, "Keep the fuck back!"

A man with a plastic cat mask covering his face had a sawed-off shotgun pointed at his daughter. Without thinking, Roy charged him, shoved the shotgun barrel aside as he stepped in and hit him in the jaw. The blow moved the mask over the man's eyes. He went to bring the shotgun up to shoot blind and Wiley fired three times, quick, into the crumbled asphalt at the robber's feet.

"Hey hey hey." The robber lowered his weapon and ripped off his mask, scared, blood where his teeth should've been, junky face, dead eyes. "Easy now. Take it easy. I just—"

"Shut up." Roy snatched the shotgun away with his left hand and hit him hard in the nose with a straight right. The robber took two steps back, clutching his bleeding nose with both hands, and fell down on his ass. Roy chucked the shotgun into the back of the truck. The sirens at the security gate started wailing but Roy wasn't waiting to be rescued.

"What now, Dad?" Wiley said, her voice trembling.

Roy held out the keys for Wiley and traded her the pistol for the keys. "Get in the truck and pop the hood. I'm right behind you." To the man on the ground: "Run fast."

"I'm gone, brother. I'm gone." And he gathered himself and ran. People were staring. He was a fast runner. A baby was crying. Roy shut the tailgate and the camper, shoved the pistol in his waistband, reinstalled the fuel relay, and slammed the hood.

Wiley had the truck started by the time he sat down in the driver's seat. "It's OK," he said, to Wiley, to Sarah. "We're fine. We're good. Put your seat belt on for me, honey. Hurry up now." He gave Wiley a once-over to see if she was OK. She was shaking and her face was flushed, but she wasn't crying.

"Can we get outta here?" she said.

Roy put the truck in gear and drove fast toward the exit. He glanced again at Sarah and then reached back to give her shoulder a squeeze. There was a line of cars trying to turn left and he wasn't waiting so he banked a tire-squealing turn and drove over a weedy island and smashed a rotten tree with the cowcatcher and got back on the highway.

"Next time we're bringing Pecos, right?" Sarah said. She'd started to cry and Wiley hugged her.

"It's OK, girls. I mean it. We're OK." Roy popped the magazine and handed it to Wiley. "Top that off for me." He put the pistol in the slot on the console and waited for Wiley to find the shells in the lockbox under the seat and reload the clip. He turned on the stereo and they listened to Joan Jett with Evil Stig and he couldn't remember ever being more scared, more proud.

[41]

R = M
OR XXXXX

THE DOWNHILL TO THE COLUMBIA GOES ON FOR MILES AND with the washouts and loose gravel it's slow going. In the haze there is no bottom, no river, no Hood or Adams, just rock and dirt, the ghostly wind turbines. Bones of poached cattle litter the dry irrigation canals and the roadside. After a long, clear downhill section, they have to wait for the dog and the man wishes he'd kept the trailer.

Near the burnt heap of a farmhouse—the barn still stands— they find a hand pump that delivers cold, clean water. They rest in the shade of the barn and drink. Roland wanders off and when he doesn't come back the man goes after him. The dog is sleeping and doesn't get up. The barn door is open.

Inside, a man is hanging from the main beam. He's been there for a long time, has bird shit on his skull. Roland is poking around in the clutter of the tack room, oblivious.

"Get out here," the man says. "We're leaving."

Roland pitches the crusty riding crop in his hand against the wall, glances at the dead man, and walks out the door.

The grade eases and they have to pedal instead of coast. The dog stays with them. Smoke fills the lowlands and they didn't realize how good they'd had it.

When they reach the confluence, they dismount. Roland follows the man to the edge of the blacktop to piss and they look down on the John Day. Narrow enough to step over and dirty brown with green algae at the margins. The confluence is peppered with pale and crusty boulders and a junked semitruck, no trailer. High-water marks on the Columbia's north shore seem impossible, and if the man hadn't seen it himself, he'd never believe it.

There's traffic on 84, not much, and no one is stopping for anything, but there's movement going both ways. As a group they keep inside the rumble strip, hug the shoulder, but cars give them plenty of room. The man waves the boy in behind him so he can get out of the wind.

A few miles from the park, the rubble from the ruined John Day Dam cuts the river and forms a filthy, impassable cataract. Downstream, the Dalles and Bonneville dams must be holding because the river begins to thicken.

When they get closer they see the fishing camp for what it is, a few long tables under canvas, poles and nets heaped on the shore, a dozen people of various ages sitting down to lunch at the smallest of the tables. The man and the boy stop but stay on the roadside.

An older man stands up and comes toward them. He's wearing a western-style pearl-snap shirt and camo hip waders.

He shades his eyes and studies the man on the road. "You can join us for lunch if you like."

The man asks Roland if he'd like to eat and he nods yes. The dog is looking east, back the way they came. Black trucks, troop carriers, moving fast.

"C'mon," the man says to Roland, shoves him, still on his bike, down the steep dirt road. At the bottom the man steps off his still-rolling bike and plucks Roland from his and hurries upstream, away from the fishermen, toward some boulders at the waterline. The people at the tables are standing up, watching them. The old man has seen the trucks too. He turns to the table and says something. The man calls the dog just as the troop carriers come barreling down the hill and skid to a stop. The dog turns to see what the commotion is, watches the trucks. The man calls him again but he won't budge.

Printz is first out of the lead rig. He spots the bike, then the dog. "Son of a bitch," he says to the dog. "Where's your buddy?" The dog lowers his head and growls. Printz pulls his pistol and levels it at the dog. "Come on, then." The dog barks three times, loud big barks. The rest of the militiamen are out now, weapons up.

"Always loaded for bear, you guys," the old fisherman says, staggering, wide-eyed, a pantomime of fear. Printz covers him and waves his men by, toward the people at the tables. They're all on their feet now, moving away toward the water. Nowhere to run.

The militiamen stride after them, yelling, *On the ground, on the fucking ground.* Warning shots are fired into the river. There's more militiamen than before, new faces.

The man pushes Roland down and stands and steps around the boulder, hands up. When Printz sees him he smiles and renews his aim on the dog.

"Just fishin' here," the old man says, catching Printz's attention. "You wanna buy some, come back tomorrow. We'll have more by then. Don't need to come so hard."

Printz lowers his pistol, scans the water, the people on the ground. The man calls the dog to him and Printz waves him away, doesn't care. This is about something else.

"We didn't come for fish," Printz says. "We came for our boats."

"What do I know about your boats?"

"We had a deal," Printz says.

"Not with me," the old man says. He looks away from Printz to the militiamen holding his people at gunpoint. He raises his hand, as if to block the sun, then drops it and points at the ground. Shots ring out, dozens, the air is filled with them. The man grabs the dog and rolls on top of him and covers him with his body.

When it's over he finds Roland on the ground behind the boulder. The wind is pushing the river shoreward and the ground is wet. He kneels beside the boy. The dog is there, his hot breath on the man's neck. Small-caliber fire up the hill. Pop. Pop. Mercy, execution.

"Are you OK?" the man asks, touching his back.

"Yes," Roland says.

The old man in the waders is beckoning them. "You can come up now." He has a small pistol in his hand.

The bodies are crumpled on the ground. Printz is on his

back watching the sky with dead eyes, a cigarette-sized hole in his forehead. Latham is dead. Sampson. *Sei brav.* All of them are dead.

"They knew you," the old man says, shoves the pistol into his waders, an unseen holster.

"I wasn't one of them."

"That's good." The fisherman nods to the shore, where the others, women mostly, but a few men and children too, are on their feet, hugging and moving away from the bodies, back to the tables. None of them are armed. The fisherman follows the man's gaze and points to the cliffs on the other side of the highway. Eventually he finds the dry stack-stone wall with the turrets. "We got our sharpshooters up there." The fisherman smiles. "We knew they were coming. And we already sank their boats so their buddies won't think we stole them."

The man sits down on his haunches. Roland does the same. The dog stands shivering in front of the boy and waits for a belly rub. The smell of fish guts is overpowering and the flies are thick.

"What're you gonna do with them?" the man asks.

"We'll take them to a pig farmer we know. Sell their rigs."

"Jesus."

"I don't think he cared much for bacon."

The man stands up. "I need to get to Alaska. We both do." He doesn't look at Roland because he knows he'll argue. He's not leaving without his sisters.

"You don't wanna ride your bikes."

"We wouldn't make it before winter."

"What winter?"

"Yeah, is anybody here headed north? Or to the coast? We might be able to figure something out from there."

The sharpshooters—six men, two women, a couple teenage boys—are working their way through the rocks, down the hill to the freeway.

"The feds have been sending a boat up here every month or so," the old man says. "They drop off supplies and see if anybody needs rescued. You look like you need to be rescued."

"Where does it go?"

"Points north, I hear. There's a shelter in Portland, but that's only if you got a tribal affiliation. I don't know what they'd do for you." He smiles, turns to look at Printz. "The benefits of being a white man in America seem to be dwindling."

"We had a good run."

"Compared to what? Fruit flies?" the fisherman says. "Is this your boy?"

"No," the man says.

"They killed my parents," Roland says. "And they took my sisters."

"I'm sorry to hear that, son." The fisherman holds out his hand to Roland. "My name is Mortimer."

"Roland."

"Roy," offering his hand. "And that's Pecos. The last of the good dogs."

A WEEK LATER, THE FEDS ARRIVE, TIE UP AT THE FISH DOCK. THE crew look like college kids but the skipper's older. Carries a sidearm. Two of the crew help Roland as he climbs over the rail. He's carrying a backpack he'd gotten from Mortimer's grandson,

Joshua. A change of clothes, a few pounds of smoked fish, and a bag of crab apples. The man goes empty-handed except for the redwood box and some dried fish for the dog. He slaps the rail and Pecos leaps over and lands on deck. Mortimer comes aboard and goes into the wheelhouse to talk with the skipper. When he comes out he shakes their hands and wishes them luck. The dog licks the old man's hand. "See ya, Pecos. Come back and see us."

The fed ship is an ancient steel fishing boat and once they're under way the twin diesels rarely change their tune. A deckhand has them fill out forms detailing who they are and where they'd come from, asks them to list a destination. *Alaska*. Roy writes it on Roland's too.

They stay on deck and watch from the rail as they motor downstream. Pecos sleeps. Mount Hood emerges suddenly through the smoke and just as quickly disappears. The air is hot and acrid. They tie up at the Dalles and Roland chats with the lock tender while Roy pretends to be sleeping. Takes an hour to get through, cool in the windless wet shade of the lock. Walls drip. Noisy gulls.

Structure fires dot the hillsides in Hood River. Militia graffiti on the billboards. People are fishing on the dirty shore. The vertical lift of the bridge has been destroyed and hangs twisted from its towers. At Bonneville, the lock tender is unseen, gates open and close, murky water pools and spills, flood debris, tires. They take on no passengers.

When night falls, they can see the lights of the small towns along the banks and later, near dawn, the shimmering lights and sky glow of Vancouver and later on, Portland. Bridges pass overhead and people look silently down on them. They don't stop. There is an international refugee facility near Astoria that one of the crewmen says will help them continue on their journey north.

The refugee center is at an old high school that's perched on a hill and they have to walk ten blocks through flooded streets where the water is too shallow to get the boat through, and then navigate muddy catwalks made of high-density plastic over landslides to get there. A gray-haired woman meets them outside and offers to take Pecos to the sports field where the rest of the dogs are being boarded. The man hesitates for a moment and then sends him off.

Inside, Roy and Roland are given hot noodles and bottled water and clean clothes. After they've eaten they take turns in the showers. Lukewarm water but there's soap. Roy doesn't bother shaving. When he steps out of the locker room, he finds Roland sitting on the bleachers with two little girls, his sisters. They'd been dropped off here by some militiamen three weeks ago. Roland isn't going to leave without them and the people that run the shelter aren't going to let Roy take them with him. They tell him they'll take care of the children and Roy has no choice but to believe them.

In the morning, while Roland and his sisters are still asleep, Roy slips the baseball cards, along with directions on how to find him in Alaska, inside Roland's shoes.

He finds Pecos waiting for him at the gate of the football field. They wander down the hill until the water is too deep to walk and flag down a passing skiff.

That afternoon, Roy and the dog are once again offshore. The skiff pulls alongside a massive trawler and a crane lowers a platform over the side and lifts the skiff and everything in it onto the deck. The captain comes down from the wheelhouse to meet them. She's younger than Roy, closer to Wiley's age than his.

"I need to get to Juneau," Roy says. "Farther if possible."

"If you come with us, you'll be working," the captain says. "Once we get going, we don't stop. It'll take us a week. Sixteen-hour days. Hot bunk. Food is meh." She makes a face.

"Meh is fine," Roy says. "What about the dog?"

"He has to stay up here with me."

"I can keep him out of the way if that's what you're worried about."

"No, it's because I like dogs. I like dogs more than people." She points at the first mate and then points to Roy. "Get him sorted. We'll be under way in ten."

Roy tells Pecos that he's staying and as he's heading down the stairs he looks back and the captain is clapping her hands calling him to her and the dog does his little dance and hustles over to get some attention.

The trawler has been retrofitted to harvest algae and kelp and Roy spends most of the trip in the hold filling the drying trays and when they anchor outside Juneau he stands on the deck and his arms and face are tinted strangely green from the work and the darkness. Pecos won't stop licking his hands. "Stop it, goddamnit." He won't stop. Earns himself a smack.

In town, generator fumes and wood smoke fill the streets even though the power and, more important, the phone system is still up and running. He walks into the white-marble-and-gold-handrail swankiness of a hotel lobby and without thinking of how he looks or if they allow dogs, asks to borrow a phone from the desk clerk and she cheerily obliges.

Sarah answers on the fourth ring. He tells her where he is

and she starts crying and he can't understand her. Jerzy is on the phone then. He says they'll pick him up tomorrow at noon. They'll be flying in, so he and Karen need to get to the airport, there's a new one, where the glacier used to be, not the one in the valley, that one is full of bomb holes, blasted by AK isolationists.

"It's just me," Roy says. "It's just me and the dog."

Jerzy is silent.

"Don't tell them yet."

"You can't ask me to do that," Jerzy says.

"Put Wiley on," Roy says.

Silence again and Roy is braced to hear Wiley's voice when Jerzy speaks again. "Just get to the airport."

"OK."

"Roy?"

"Yeah."

"What about Miller?"

"Dead."

"Fuck, man."

"Yeah."

"I'm sorry."

"Me, too."

"Hang in there," Jerzy says.

Roy gives the clerk her phone and she takes it and gives Roy a pat on the hand and a heartfelt nod. "You've come a long way, haven't you?" she says.

"California," he says.

"Don't tell anyone else that," she says. "I'm serious. People don't want any more Californians. They're gonna pass a law."

"I need a room for the night," he says, and before she can tell him that they are very expensive or that they don't allow dogs or Californians, he slaps down all of his pay from working the kelp boat. She thumbs through the stack of bills and reaches under the counter and comes back with a small gold nugget and a digital scale. She weighs the gold then produces a greasy set of pliers and clips the nugget in two, weighs the pieces separately, then slides the bigger half to him.

"We got mice," she says.

Roy thanks her and takes his change and his room key and mounts the stairs. The dog follows a few steps behind him. He locks the door with the dead bolt. After he's showered, he sits down on the bed in a threadbare towel with the redwood box in his lap and rests his feet on the sleeping dog. Street noise seeps through the closed window in a murmur.

"I don't want to be here without you," he says to the box, the pain showing on his face. Pecos rolls over and starts licking his toes. "Stop that, goddamnit," he says quietly. Then he lies down on the floor beside the dog with the box between them.

[42]

R > 45
CA 96118

A FILTHY GRAY PICKUP TURNED OFF THE MAIN ROAD AND CAME slowly down the driveway toward the house. It had a suspension lift and off-road tires, a camper shell and two spares like eyeballs mounted on the rear bumper, gas cans and camping gear heaped into an open roof rack and held there by a cargo net.

Roy was kneeling in a hole he'd dug beside the barn, searching for a leak in the water line. The leak had dampened the soil and made the grass grow thick and green. Before he'd stuck the shovel in and started digging, he and the dog had lain down on the cool ground for a while and watched the mudbirds build their nests in the barn eaves. Karen and the girls were with Jerzy at the Millers' canning tomatoes because they had a functioning AC window unit.

The driver of the truck got out slowly and shut the door

behind him. He was an old man and he walked with a wooden cane like the one Roy had used to herd hogs, back when they'd still had them. He told the dog to stay and climbed out of the hole and walked over, shovel in hand.

"You lost, bud?" Roy said.

The old man let go of the screen door and let it slam. "It's you."

"Who're you looking for?" But he knew the answer. He knew this man.

"Homeboy Roy," Mace said. "Look at you. Come up here so I don't have to come down."

Roy leaned the shovel against the porch and went up the stairs and shook Mace's hand. "Where is she?" Mace asked. The dog was suddenly there and Mace gave it a pat and let it run around him until Roy calmed it down.

"At the neighbors'. She'll be back later." Roy opened the door and let Mace go in but kept the dog outside. "I got tea and water. Goat milk."

"Tea is fine."

Roy stood at the counter beside the stove while Mace had his tea at the table.

"Is the old house part of this one or is this brand-new?" Mace asked, craning his neck to see into the living room.

Roy told Mace about the old house and how Karen had sold it and built a new one. Mace shook his head and rubbed his hand over his forehead. The slow-moving clouds that Roy had been tracking all morning finally arrived and blocked the sun. The kitchen darkened and Mace looked up at Roy with a confused look on his face.

"She thinks you're dead."

"Not yet." Mace turned and looked out the window. "Is it gonna rain?"

"Not likely," Roy said. "We had a hell of a winter and then it rained on the snow and caused havoc, but since then, nothing. You heard about the bombings, the flooding down south?"

Mace nodded. "Everybody heard about that."

"Clouds don't do anything but gum up our solar." Roy picked up a tomato from the glass bowl next to the cutting board, sliced it, and sprinkled salt over the slices and picked one up and ate it. He wanted to save the bread for when everybody got home but he made Mace a sandwich anyway. He waited for a compliment on his sourdough but it never came.

"I didn't think I'd be away so long," Mace said. "I got married. We had a kid. Then I got locked up. Did almost fifteen years in Spring Creek. When I got out, me and my wife renewed our vows, built a place on the Kenai together, homesteaded. I have two grandkids. Got my pilot's license but I wrecked my plane. I always meant to call."

"Here's to excuses," Roy said, held up his glass of tea.

"Yeah."

"They say it's better in Alaska."

"It won't stay that way with all of the people flooding in. Roads to nowhere now go somewhere and more roads all the time."

"We thought last winter was gonna end the drought but our groundwater is too far gone. It'd take twenty years of rain just to break even."

Mace shook his head. "I was in Seattle trying to buy a Cessna from a guy but it fell through." He looked down at his hands, back at Roy. "I left some pictures in the old house. They were stashed in the ceiling with some other stuff. I never thought I'd be gone so long."

"You should've called," Roy said.

"Yeah." His eyes roamed around the kitchen. Mace was old, slow. He pushed his plate away. "I knew that she got married, that her husband died. I looked her up. And I knew they had a kid. I didn't know about you, that you came back." The sun was low enough now to be below the clouds and the haunting light shining in was red from the smoke and the dust. "So one of them isn't yours, right?" Mace said.

"They're both mine," Roy said. "Nobody else's."

They heard the truck on the road and stood and watched it unload from the big window in the living room. The dog was sniffing everyone out and stopping for belly rubs and ear tugs. Sarah jumped out of the back with a flying karate kick but miscalculated the drop and the steepness of the slight embankment and ended up on her ass. Jerzy picked her up and dusted her off.

"Who's the boy?" Mace asked.

"That's Sarah. She decided to shave her head since I did."

"I'm talking about the other one. The young guy."

"Future son-in-law." They watched Jerzy walk around Mace's truck, checking it out. He opened the passenger door and looked inside.

Mace smiled and whacked Roy on the back with an open palm, then walked outside without his cane and held up his hands to Karen. "Hey, pipsqueak," he said.

Karen saw who it was and set down the box of jars she was carrying and walked quickly toward him. The girls watched her. When Roy came onto the porch, Jerzy gave him a look and Roy nodded that it was OK.

After the hugs and the introductions, they followed Karen inside. Later, Roy and Jerzy brought in the tomatoes and the canning stuff and put it away in the pantry. Mace took the girls out to his rig to help him unload. He'd brought presents. They had smoked salmon for dinner. Mace had mellowed with age, was tucked in and asleep by 7:30.

In the morning, after they'd had breakfast, Karen and the girls took Mace on a tour of the property. While they were gone Roy and Jerzy finished disassembling the drive motor on the drill rig and then Jerzy drove it over to Miller's to rebuild it in his shop because it was better outfitted. Jerzy and Miller often worked together now, solving the endless mechanical problems of each household.

Roy filled his coffee cup in the house and then pulled his pickup into the back of the machine shed and popped the hood. He plugged it in to charge and ran a diagnostic check on it and changed the number three coil because it came up fried on the computer.

Roy saw the shadow so he ducked down and circled around the truck and chucked a shop rag at Wiley while she crouched by the rear tire.

"You can't creep on me, kid," Roy said. Then something wet hit him in the side of the head, another shop rag but this one had been dipped in the goat trough. Sarah jumped on his back and tried to put him in a sleeper hold. Wiley was coming at him so Roy flipped Sarah over his shoulder and held her like a battering ram and chased Wiley out of the shop. Mace came toward them, limping with his cane, with Karen and the dog on either side of him.

"Are these two with you?" Roy asked.

"Never seen them before," Karen said.

Sarah was laughing, trying to get free.

"Where's Jerzy?" Karen said.

"Millers'," Roy said. He put Sarah down. To Wiley: "You can take mine if you're going to meet him. Just shut the hood. It's ready."

"She doesn't need to drive over there," Karen said.

"I'm going too," Sarah said.

"Take your sister," Roy said to Wiley.

"C'mon," Wiley said.

"Can I go?" Mace said.

"Sure," Roy said. "It's only down the road a little."

"Do you want to drive?" Wiley asked Mace.

"Nope," Mace said. "I've been driving enough, but we can take my truck. Leave your dad's in the shop."

"Did you not hear me?" Karen said. "Take the bikes, or walk. You don't need to drive."

Mace smiled. "I haven't ridden a bike in thirty years."

"It keeps you young," Karen said.

Roy helped them get the bikes situated and gave them a quick shot with the compressor for dust and lubed the chains and they were off. Mace went first, stiff and worried, bowlegged as a rodeo cowboy. The girls followed him, laughing and weaving all over. Sarah rang the bell on her handlebars. Wiley rang back.

As soon as they were out of sight Roy and Karen went inside. Without saying anything Karen headed directly for the bedroom.

"I gotta wash up first," Roy said.

"Better hurry."

Roy shut and locked the bedroom door behind him. Karen was sitting up in bed naked with the blankets off, one leg pulled up. The curtains weren't all the way closed and the morning sun edged by them and brilliant blocks of light cut the bed and struck her extended leg and lit one of her breasts. She touched her nipple, held her hand up to the sun, and smiled. Roy hadn't forgotten how beautiful she was, never would, but in the moment he was shocked anew by her attractiveness. He undressed quickly and Karen lifted the sheet over them as he got into bed. He pulled her to him and they tangled themselves together, savoring the warmth and smoothness. It was nice not to have to be quiet but they'd gotten so used to it that being free and loud seemed kind of funny and afterward they laughed for a moment at their moans and the sounds the bed had made bashing against the wall.

They fell asleep and woke to the sound of the truck starting. Roy dressed quickly and watched from the kitchen window as Mace pulled his truck into the machine shed. Roy's bike was in the yard. Karen came into the kitchen and gave him a kiss on the cheek and made a French press of coffee and Roy took a cup out to Mace.

"The girls are catching a ride back with the neighbor."

"Too lazy to pedal," Roy said.

"I doubt that," Mace said. "Can I use your welder?"

"Sure. What's broken?"

"Hole in my exhaust, thought I'd patch it."

"I can do it." Roy rolled out his welder and unspooled the lead. "I have to switch the breaker off at the house to run this," he said.

"I'll do it. Where's the panel?"

"Top of the basement stairs."

Mace's truck was high enough that he didn't need to jack it up to get underneath. He hooked the ground to the frame and put on his hood and gloves and switched on the welder. Footsteps approached and then Mace's feet were next to the welder.

"Where's the hole?" Roy asked. "I don't see it."

Mace got stiffly down onto the ground and pointed his flashlight at a broken weld in the pipe near the transfer case. Roy climbed out from under the truck and stood and took off one glove and sorted through the flatstock scrap he kept on top of the woodstove until he found a suitable piece. At the anvil he beat the scrap against a pig iron dowel of approximately the same radius with his ball peen hammer. Under the truck he scraped and tapped on the exhaust with his hammer to clean it, then used a chain clamp to hold the flatstock in place. He dropped his hood and made four quick tacks.

"Do you want something to cover my fuel tank and my batteries?" Mace asked.

"I'm not going to blow us up," Roy said, taking off the chain clamp. He dropped his hood without warning and finished his welds.

Roy switched off his welder and plugged Mace's truck into the charger. "I can't run the welder and the charging station at once either or my breaker goes. Kind of a single-stream thing we got going."

Mace pulled up a stool at Roy's worktable and sat down. "Your neighbor," he said.

"Miller."

"He acts like a cop."

"He's OK. We didn't get along at first but he's all right."

"Is he a cop?"

"No, ex-government. Ex-military. He has militia pals that he hangs out with but he's OK." Roy hung his welding hood on its hook and took a drink of his tepid coffee. "We have a don't ask, don't tell thing going."

Mace picked at the random bolts and washers on the workbench. "You know, if you could get that drill rig up north you'd be sitting pretty. With all the new folks, you'd have more work than you could handle."

"Karen isn't going anywhere. I've tried."

"This is the ragged edge, Roy. You guys can't stay here. What if that neighbor and his pals decide they want to keep your rig? What then?"

"I don't know."

"What if he wants to take your water, your whole show?"

"We're friends. We help each other out. I'm not worried about Miller. Not anymore."

"What are you worried about?"

"I got plenty to keep me up nights." Roy spat out the grounds from the bottom of his cup.

"How many people live in town?" Mace said.

"It's not much of a town anymore, not really. After the drought and then the winter of doom, everybody bailed. We got—what—drunk mechanic that keeps a junkyard of useless shit, an undertaker, a newspaperman that doesn't leave his house. Weird bachelors, militia culls, no families, really. Out here, it's us and Miller, we're on our own."

"The ragged edge," Mace said. "I'm gonna talk to Karen."

"About getting your pictures?"

"Yeah, and about leaving too. You can't stay here."

"Good luck."

KAREN AGREED TO HELP MACE IF HE WOULD SHUT UP ABOUT THEM going to Alaska. They took his truck. Roy drove. Jerzy and Wiley stayed at the house with Sarah and the dog.

The first and only roadblock they came to had been destroyed. The fifth-wheel trailer at the roadside was burned to its axles and the steel gate was wide open. Brass on the road, but that wasn't uncommon. They had to leave the pavement and drive over the exposed railroad tracks because the subway had collapsed during the winter. From there, they gained elevation and entered the blackened pines. In a few shady places, where the topsoil hadn't been washed away by the rain, the burnt ground was tinted green with new growth. Karen pointed proudly and Mace shook his head.

In the hills the land was barren, nothing worth claiming. This was militia territory. The riverbed was already dry. The snowmelt had gone fast with the rain and he could see where the water had shot through the blasted floodgate and torn a hole in the hillside below. When they topped the hill they could see the puddled pan of Frenchman Lake. Roy was ready to turn around and go home but he didn't say anything.

The fence was chain-link, eight feet high with two feet of concertina wire on top. They followed it for a quarter mile and came to a lowboy trailer attached to a dump truck parked in front of a massive steel archway. A bullet-pocked Jeffersonian Militia sign hung from the arch. The gate below the sign had been thoroughly destroyed by the track hoe parked on the other side of the fence. Beside it was a wad of twisted wrought iron that had once been the gate.

Roy parked with their tailgate facing the archway and turned off the truck. Karen got out to look around, kicked at something on the ground near the trailer's loading ramp, scooped it up and held it out for Roy to see—a handful of brass shell casings. Mace got out of the truck and walked to the shredded keypad and plucked at the wires to see if they were live and got shocked. He shook it off, spat in the dust, and shuffled to the tailgate and sat down.

"What do you think?" Roy said.

"I think, fuck this," Karen said. Karen joined Mace on the tailgate, rubbed his head, squeezed his shoulder. "Let's get out of here, huh? Down that road is death."

"You don't know that," Mace said. "I'll go by myself if I have to."

"Nothing in there is that important," Karen said.

"I drove all this way. I'm not turning back."

Karen looked at Roy and he shrugged.

"Go by yourself, then," she said.

"Goddamnit," Mace said.

"Now hold on," Roy said. "We know some of those people in there, or Miller does. Should we see if they're OK?"

"You want to go?" Karen said. "Go ahead."

"We'll just whip in and come right back out," Roy said.

"I'm not going," Karen said.

"It could be worse staying here by yourself," Mace said. "They could come back."

"This is what I get, isn't it?" Karen said. "No such thing as a harmless drive with you two. Now I have to make a life-

and-death decision, and there's no way to know which is which."

"That might be overstating it," Roy said.

"You know that, how?" she said. "From the bullet holes in that truck or from the shell casings?"

"I don't know."

"You feel like he came all this way and we should help him if we can?"

"Yeah."

"I'll help him go back to our house and have lunch and forget about this place."

"I'll go by myself," Mace said. "I'll come back later."

"Fine," Karen said.

But when they were back in the truck, instead of going home, she turned around and drove slowly through the gate.

"Don't say a word to me," she said. "Either of you. I just want to get this over with."

Roy attempted to comfort her, reached out to her. She pushed his hand away.

They followed the road through dusty fields studded with stumps and over two concrete flood-zone bridges. Karen drove faster than Roy would've liked. She was the definition of driving angry and it was almost funny, but if she went off the road the dry ditches were deep enough to swallow them up.

They'd yet to see any kind of structure or livestock, just burnt forest and scrub. They were in the mountains now but without trees it felt different, as if they were at high elevation, above the tree line.

"How big is this place?" Mace asked.

"I heard rumors," Roy said. "Other people that sold their

houses, they said it's ten thousand acres and they've got an airstrip and their own power plant."

"When they came for the house," Karen said, "they had trucks, semitrailers and a big crew. We didn't stick around to watch them break it loose. We went camping and when we came back it was just a concrete hole in the ground. I wasn't the first or the last to sell to them. This was early in the whole Jefferson thing. Nobody took them seriously."

"In town," Roy said to Mace, "you'll see all the foundations where people sold out. Lots of people did it. There's got to be half a town up here somewhere."

They came over a low hill and in the distance a roofline cut the sky, not Karen's old house; it was far too large. Beyond it there was a wooden barn with a gambrel roof and steel outbuildings of various sizes and colors, a windsock flagged a runway. They came to another gate and this one was open. As they drove through Roy saw the red dot of a surveillance camera partially hidden in the branches of a withered cottonwood.

"They've got cameras," Roy said.

"Great," Karen said.

The road forked and all the tire tracks went toward the house so Karen went the other way. The road had been washed out in places. At the bottom of a long steep hill was a valley cut by a small creek, spring fed, still flowing. There wasn't a bridge and Karen followed the old tracks along the creek and through the sandy crossing. In the distance, partially hidden in a band of scrubby trees was Karen's old house. It was lined up with dozens of others, all facing south like barracks. A black SUV with two flat tires was parked in front. The windows had been broken out of all the houses, siding shredded by gunfire, doors ripped from their hinges. When they got out of the truck they stepped onto a blanket of shell casings.

Mace didn't waste any time. He opened the tailgate and picked up a wrecking bar, using it as a cane. Roy grabbed a Maglite from the glove box. Karen tried the splintered front door and it swung open with a squeal.

Inside there were several broken deer antler lamps and two bearskin rugs strewn with shattered glass, hunks of drywall, and splinters of wood. The leather furniture was dimpled with bullet holes, but there were no bloodstains, no dead bodies.

Roy followed Mace into the back bedroom. A sleeping bag was unrolled on an army cot with an orthopedic pillow. Empty water bottles and dehydrated food wrappers were stashed in the closet and when they kicked them out of the way, they saw the hole in the floor that someone had bashed out to use as a toilet.

"Goddamn," Mace said. Then he pointed at the ceiling, the attic access in the closet. "I'll give you a boost," he said to Karen.

"Watch out," Roy said, stepping in front of them. He kicked a hole in the wall and used it to climb up through the access. He switched on his flashlight and held on to the joists and shimmied along until he saw the plastic-and-tape packages that Mace had left behind. Roy pitched them back toward the access hole and fed them down to where Karen was waiting, one after the other.

Once he had climbed down, Karen brushed the insulation from his shirt and hair. Mace went to tear one of the packages open but Karen stopped him and they picked everything up and returned to the truck. As they sat in the cab, they heard gunfire, not close, just a few shots at first but then it grew until they couldn't hear where it stopped and started.

Mace reached under the seat and brought out a pistol and handed it to Roy. "You shoot first, OK?"

"We gotta go," Roy said.

Mace tore open one of his rifle-shaped packages, brushed it clean with his hand, and racked the slide. He lowered his window and rested the stock on the door.

Karen had the truck turned around and they went fast up the hill.

At the top of the hill, Karen shifted into third and buried the gas pedal. The truck drifted sideways for a moment before she corrected. There was smoke coming from around the big house now or the airstrip, they couldn't tell which. Gunfire continued, small and far away, hesitant and random as the sound of a woodpecker. Roy spotted two trucks driving fast away from the barn. Men in both vehicles were shooting back and forth. They were fighting each other. A third vehicle joined the chase.

"What do I do?" Karen said.

"Get in front of them," Roy said.

Karen missed a corner and skidded into the deep dust and ash and circled widely back onto the road with the motor roaring and left whoever was behind them in a dust cloud. Roy turned in his seat, keeping the pistol in his right hand, and watched out the back window. Mace was in the backseat tearing open more packages and piling ammo on the seat beside him. When he finished he sat facing forward with his AR across his lap like an angry child. Karen's face was a mask of concentration.

Someone had moved the dump truck and trailer to block the exit. Karen slowed but a truck was coming up fast, trying to match them on the main road. Karen yanked the wheel and they went overland, parallel to the fence. The uneven ground was making it hard for Karen to keep control. The truck on the pavement was nearly upon them. Mace pointed his weapon out the window and fired four times and their pursuer dropped back.

"Go through it," Mace said. "Drive through the fence."

Karen yanked the wheel, and they tore through the fence and the motor wound out as they lost traction but the wheels caught again and after fifty yards of fence-tangled chaos they were up the bank on the pavement and free. The truck that was behind them had stopped and turned around and drove back toward the gate.

"That was not worth it," Karen said. Her hair was loose and blowing in her face, sticking to the sweat.

"We're OK," Mace said. "Nobody's hurt. Keep driving."

"What was that?" Roy said. "Militia versus militia? That was the Jeffs fighting someone else. They didn't know who the fuck we were."

"Good," Mace said. "They never will."

"Nothing was worth that." Karen was as mad as Roy had ever seen her. She kept glaring at Mace in the rearview mirror.

"I'm sorry."

"How could I be so stupid?" Karen said to him. "My kids could've been orphans. For some shit you stashed. Guns? Like you can't find a gun anywhere. All there is is guns. For nothing."

"We made it, OK?" Mace said. "We're safe. We're fine."

"Just some shit," Karen said. "Some useless, pointless shit. And I let myself get carried away by your stupid shit. Stupid man shit."

Roy reached for her but she shoved his hand away.

"Don't fucking touch me," she said.

Mace had a photograph of his daughter, Whip, in his lap on top of his weapon. He opened his mouth to speak but didn't say anything.

A few miles from home, the back left tire went flat. Karen pulled over and Roy followed Mace's instructions on where to find the jack and the tire iron. He had the tire off and was about to put on the spare when he saw the strange black disk stuck to the filthy, mud-covered frame. It was cleaner, newer, than the patch he'd put on the exhaust. With effort, Roy broke the magnetic pull and tore it loose. He showed it to Karen and she shook her head. He held it in the window for Mace to see and Mace took it and frowned at it, chucked it into the field like a frisbee.

"What was that?" Karen asked. "Was that part of the truck?"

"No," Roy said. "I don't know what it was." He finished with the tire and put away the jack and mounted the flat onto the bumper where the spare had been and got back in the truck. "We must've picked it up somewhere on the ranch," Roy said. "They could be tracking us. Like a transponder."

"That's ridiculous," Karen said.

"Not if we ran over it and it stuck," Roy said. "Like those guys at the gate put it on the road in case anyone got away."

"What are you talking about?" Karen said. "That isn't even a real thing, is it?"

"I don't know," Mace said. "Are you ready to rethink coming back with me now?"

"I don't want to hear another word out of either of you," Karen said. "Not another fucking word."

Jerzy was at the Millers' helping with their new well, Sarah and Wiley were with him. Roy had watched them pull out of the driveway with a truck bed full of water pipe. The dog ran after them, showing off, stretching out and kicking up dust, racehorse fast. Not for the first time, Roy thought how he'd hate to be on the toothy end of that animal.

Mace's gear was stowed, blankets on the couch neatly folded, pillow on top. A stack of photographs on the coffee table. Dead people. No sign of the weapons they'd brought from Frenchman. If you could put Karen's anger in a bottle, you'd need a big fucking bottle.

Weak sun, gray light, in the kitchen. "I'm making eggs," Roy said to Mace. Karen was still in bed. She'd come down with a fever after they got home from their ranch adventure and that morning their bedroom had smelled rank. Roy wanted her to sleep all day but knew that she wouldn't. She was calling it stress-induced illness, Mace-induced, but Roy was included with that too.

"I ate," Mace said. "Thanks." He'd been up early, might've gone for a walk. Pitter-patter footfalls outside had awoken Roy and the dog. They'd stood side by side in the hallway in the dark with the safety off, but the dog hadn't barked and the couch had been empty so Roy flicked the safety and cleared the chamber and went back to bed.

Later, maybe 10:30, Roy made Karen a cup of tea and took her a plate of eggs and fried potatoes but she was still sleeping so he left it by the bed and returned to the kitchen. He sat down at the table to go over the planting schedule that Karen had drawn up on a large piece of butcher paper with a Sharpie. Before any seeds came out, drip lines needed to go in and the tunnel-house plastic had to be patched enough to last one more season. The frames were showing damage too and he'd have to use rebar and tie wire to splint them together, again. Eventually it'd all unravel, material degrading to the point of being unusable, fabric so threadbare it wouldn't take a stitch, and once that happened, decisions would need to be made. Could be the worst thing that could've happened to them was hitting water. They'd be gone by now. But where was gone?

He thought it was the sprinklers at first, that maybe Jerzy was moving them. But Jerzy wasn't there. *Who's moving the sprinklers?* was what he thought. They could've parked Mace's truck in the barn but they didn't. They could've been careful.

Dust and small rocks peppered the living room windows and the whole house shook. Roy went to stand but Mace was yelling at him to get down. When he looked out the window he saw a helicopter hovering as if it were going to land but it didn't. A sound like a pneumatic tool, a mechanic's shop heard from a block away, and then the wall was dust and the table was coming apart. Mace was on the floor in the living room now but Roy couldn't tell if he'd been shot. Roy crawled on all fours through the thick dust and broken glass toward the bedroom. The shooting continued but it seemed that they were no longer shooting at the house. He could hear bullets tearing through the metal roof of the barn.

Karen was sitting up in bed, wide-eyed, covered in chunks of drywall and insulation. She touched her head and held up her hand to see the blood. Roy shucked the larger pieces of drywall that had fallen from the ceiling from the bed to the floor. There was blood on the bed. Roy felt as though he were moving in a dream; a whimpering, weak cry formed in the back of his throat. He touched Karen's leg and the blood was warm and wet on his hand. He pulled her to him and held her and felt her struggling in his arms. Then Mace was in the room and he had one of his rifles for himself and another for Roy.

"They're gone," Mace said. "I watched them go." His face changed when he saw the blood. He leaned the rifles against the wall but they slid down and clattered and fell heavily to the floor as he rushed to the bed. "Where's the blood coming from?"

"It's OK, baby," Roy said. He had his hand on Karen's forehead and her eyes were open and she was staring back at him with a look of utter surprise. He pulled back the blanket. The projectile had entered on her left side, just above her pelvis. He put a hand underneath her to feel if it'd gone through but he couldn't tell. Just blood. He wadded the sheet onto the wound and clamped it there with both hands.

"I don't understand," she said. Her whole body was vibrating in shock. The cut on her head was from the ceiling coming down, white dust streaked with blood, spattered on the sheets and blanket.

Through the shattered window Roy saw a fire burning but it was only Mace's truck.

"It's OK," he said. "It's OK." Daylight was shining through the holes in the walls.

Mace picked up one of the rifles and muttered something about them coming back. His footsteps on the broken glass and drywall echoed through the house. The front door squeaked open and slammed shut. Karen was taking deep measured breaths and holding her stomach.

"It's just a scratch," Roy said.

"It hurts."

"I know." He turned his head and yelled for Mace but he didn't answer so he told Karen to put pressure on the wound and ran to the bathroom for their first-aid kit himself. He clipped the lid from a large bottle of saline with the heavy-duty scissors he found in the side pouch. Karen groaned while Roy flushed the wound with saline. The bullet, or more likely a ricochet, hadn't gone through and there was already a massive purple-and-yellow bruise forming on her lower back. He didn't know what to do. They had to get her out of here, someplace clean, safe. Keep the wound clean, let it drain, and keep her warm. They had to get her to Ilah. He stood up and went to the hall closet and got clean towels and extra blankets. With a fresh towel pressed to the wound, he had Karen hold it in place and used tape to wrap all the way around her to keep it tight. Her eyes were glassy. He pushed her hair back from her face and kissed her forehead.

"Hang in there. It's not bad. Stay on your side."

She was crying now, sobbing. He didn't try to comfort her or tell her to stop. He gave her three Darvocets and one of the broad-spectrum veterinary antibiotics they'd gotten from April that had to be expired. He found her Nalgene under the bed unharmed and she swallowed the pills down and had a few extra gulps of water. Her face was wet with tears and he wiped it dry with a towel.

"How long has it been?" she asked.

"Minutes." He took note of the time and calculated when the next dose of antibiotics would be given.

"The girls."

"You first. We have to take care of you first." He forced himself to focus on human anatomy and overlay it with what he'd learned over the years of hunting and butchering animals. Foreign body, nonarterial bleeding, left side and low so the risk of intestinal or stomach rupture was low. Liver was on the right. She wasn't distended and she was responsive. She was all there.

"Just a scratch," he said again.

"Go get the girls."

"Hang on." He lifted the corner of the towel to peek at the wound again, still leaking watery blood.

"What if they go to Miller's next?"

"OK."

"Do it now. Mace can stay with me. Go."

He did as she said. The only vehicle left on the place that wasn't blasted to pieces was his bicycle. The dog met him on the road, it'd run all the way from the Millers', and Roy got off his bike and held him and they watched together as Barry's truck came into view.

Miller was driving and the girls, Ilah and Jerzy too, were with him. Everyone but Sarah had a weapon.

"We heard shooting," Miller said. "Is everyone OK?"

Roy couldn't tell him. The words wouldn't form. He shook his head no. He squeezed Wiley's shoulder and blinked back his tears. Ilah took Sarah's hand and pulled her close.

"I have my bag," Ilah said, nodding at her medical kit on the floor between her legs.

"Hurry," Roy said.

Roy pitched his bike in the back and hopped in after it and the dog followed. Miller accelerated hard. With his back to the cab, Roy's whole body was shaking and the tears came until he shook them off and straightened up. He pulled the dog to him and took a deep breath, prepared himself to face his kids and whatever happened next.

[43]

R < M

ILAH CHECKED KAREN'S VITALS AND CLEANED THE WOUND. JERZY and Mace made a makeshift gurney out of an old sheet of plywood and with Roy's help slid Karen onto it. Miller drove, Ilah sat shotgun, Roy, Jerzy, and the girls rode in the back of the truck with Karen. Mace was staying behind in case anyone came back.

When they got to Miller's, Roy held the corner of the plywood by Karen's head, Jerzy held the other. Miller and Wiley had the bottom. Sarah went with Ilah and helped hold the doors open.

The smell of bleach was overpowering. On the count of three they slid the sheet of plywood out from underneath her and oriented her on the largest of the stainless-steel tables. Ilah placed her bag on the counter nearby and spread out the various tools. The cut on Karen's scalp was black and shaped like a caterpillar.

"Hey," Roy said to Sarah. "Can you and your sister make your mom some soup so when we're done she has something to eat?"

"I want to help," Sarah said.

"You would be helping. That's why I'm asking."

"Come on," Wiley said to her sister, wrapping an arm around her shoulder. "She's going to be OK."

Once they were gone, Roy put on surgical gloves and took his place next to Ilah. The entrance wound was so small, Ilah could barely open the forceps, and when she did, Karen cried out. She was doped but not unconscious and twice Ilah had to stop what she was doing because Karen was screaming too much. The wound was bleeding again. When it came to it, Roy had to hold Karen down by the shoulders while Miller held her feet, so Ilah could fish out the bullet fragment she'd been bumping against but couldn't clamp onto. She managed to pull it free and showed the piece of metal to Karen.

"Is that it?" Karen asked. Her face was wet with tears and her lips and eyes were red and swollen-looking against her pale skin.

"It's all I could find. Do you want me to keep looking?"

"No." Roy wiped her forehead with a washcloth. He'd been crying too. Miller opened a bottle of saline and passed it to Ilah. By the time she'd emptied the second bottle over the wound Karen had passed out.

ALL TOLD THEY HAD SIX TRUCKS. FOUR WERE STANDARD QUAD CABS, one was a sixteen-foot box truck, while the last was an ancient ton-and-a-half grain truck towing a lowboy trailer and a Gradall telehandler. Twelve men, no women, all armed, exited the vehicles. They moved quickly through the house and the barn and outbuildings and set up a perimeter.

"Command structure," Miller said. "Tactical awareness." Miller and Roy were side by side in a slit trench in the field between the Millers' and the Binghams'. A spotting scope and binoculars were set up on miniature tripods sheltered behind a blind of wadded dead grass. Miller had dug trenches all over his property with his mini-ex. With the lay of the land, Roy couldn't see them from his house. Miller claimed he had weapons stashed in the trenches and claymores on pressure switches.

"Watch the road," Miller said. "We don't want these guys flanking us and going to my place."

Roy stayed low in the trench as he reoriented the tripod and focused the binoculars on Miller's front gate.

"They're taking your animals," Miller said. "Chicken chasers. Using your tractor to steal your implements. Goddamn. There goes your tumblebug plow."

"I don't care," Roy said. He didn't look away from the road and the gate beyond.

"Now it's the motorcycles."

"I said I don't give a shit." A vehicle, southbound, slowed at the Binghams' drive. Roy glassed it, side-by-side ATV, four occupants, armed. They continued on, moving toward Miller's.

"Fuck. They're headed for your place."

Miller turned his attention to the road.

"I make it four men, armed," Miller said.

Moving in the trenches wasn't easy. Miller led the way, cradling the BA50, stoop-backed and bowlegged. Roy had one of Miller's pre-ban ARs, extra clips. They'd left the scope but brought the binocs. Miller stopped Roy and pointed to the ground. This trench was an offshoot of the one they'd made their approach in.

"See that piece of yarn?" Miller said. "Don't step there."

"OK." Roy had to bend down and search to find the two-inch piece of dirty red yarn sticking out of the trench wall. It looked like a root, nothing remarkable. They bypassed the claymore and continued toward Miller's front gate.

Two hundred yards, with the binocs, Roy saw Ilah at the gate talking to the four men. She had a rifle slung on her shoulder. The gate was still closed. Jerzy and Mace were walking quickly toward her.

"Don't let them in," Miller said, under his breath. He was prone with the .50.

"If you fire that thing," Roy said, "all those fuckers at my place will swarm over here."

"I know that."

"We can't shoot them."

"I know."

Jerzy had a rifle and Mace had one of his ARs. Ilah hadn't put her hands on her weapon yet. She was smiling, pointing back at the house.

"She can do this," Miller said. "She's smarter than those fucking dimwits."

He turned to Roy. "Put down those fucking binocs and get your weapon on them. It comes to it, we'll fight our way in and make a stand."

Roy moved off a few yards to Miller's left and settled into position. He couldn't keep the rifle still. He dropped into the trench and took off his sweatshirt and wadded it up and crammed it under the stock. Jerzy was looking toward them. Mace said something to him and he looked away.

The men at the gate suddenly raised their weapons, pointing them at Ilah, Mace, and Jerzy, and spread out. Ilah raised her hands. Mace and Jerzy did the same.

"Fuck this," Miller said.

"Wait," Roy said. "They're not in yet. They still might leave."

Ilah stepped sideways to the gate keypad.

"Don't do it," Miller said.

She reached out and the gate began to swing open. Two of the militiamen went in and took Ilah's weapon and pushed her to the ground. Mace and Jerzy laid their weapons down, put their hands behind their head, and began walking toward the gate. Roy couldn't hear what anyone was saying.

"On three," Miller said. "I'm going after the two in the back, you hit the two in the front."

"Where's Wiley and Sarah? We can't just start shooting."

"We don't have a choice."

Mace, Jerzy, and Ilah were facedown on the road. Roy had a shot now. He could aim high. The militiamen in the back pulled their vehicle through the gate and got out.

"Other side of the road," Miller said. "Thirty yards, due south."

Roy was looking for whatever Miller had seen when the first shot was fired, then three more in succession. The militiaman nearest Mace and Jerzy crumpled to the road. Ilah rolled to her back with a pistol in her hand and shot the man that was standing above her. Ilah sat up to shoot again but the man nearest the ATV fired two shots into her chest and she fell back down. Miller fired and the air went out of Roy's lungs, the round struck the man that shot Ilah and he spun to the road and didn't get up. Jerzy got to his feet but Mace pulled him down and they crawled for the ditch. Wiley was in the opposite field, walking forward, weapon raised. The last man had the ATV started, looking back to reverse. The dog was closing the distance to the ATV when Wiley yelled something and fired two warning shots into the back side door of the vehicle, took aim at the driver. The dog came to heel at Wiley. The militiaman held his hands above the wheel.

When he looked over, Miller was gone. Spotted him near the road. He'd left his rifle, had a pistol in his hand. Roy got up, climbed out of the trench and ran toward Wiley. He couldn't see Mace or Jerzy. Ilah was still down. Wiley was on the road facing down the ATV. "I'm good," she yelled when she saw Miller. "Go to Ilah." Miller went to his wife.

Jerzy knelt beside her, held her hand. Miller sat down behind his wife and wrapped his arm around her chest. Mace retrieved his and Jerzy's weapons and forced the deer rifle into Jerzy's hand.

"Stand up," he said to Jerzy. "C'mon." Jerzy let Ilah's hand down gently on the road, stood up stiffly, and checked his weapon.

"She's gone," Miller said. "She's fucking gone." He slid from behind her and cradled her head as he set her down. On his feet, hands shaking. He had his pistol out and he walked by Wiley to the ATV without a word and shot the militiaman in the head. He turned and walked back toward Ilah, Wiley and the dog trailing behind.

Miller knelt over Ilah. He laid his chest on hers. Wiley put her hand on his back. He lifted Ilah's face to his.

"We have to go," Roy said. He had Jerzy by the shirt and

spun him around. The boy looked as if he might throw up. "Go to the house. Get Karen and Sarah ready to go."

"Where?" Wiley said. "What about mom?"

"You'll come with me," Mace said to Wiley. He'd already loaded the militiamen's weapons into their ATV. To Jerzy: "There's no choice now. We'll take your drill rig, whatever other vehicles we can get on the road." Mace returned to the ATV and started it and pulled it forward and waved Roy and Jerzy over. "Grab an end." They slid the nearest body into the back of the four-seat side by side.

"We have to get rid of all this," Mace said. "They'll be coming. Be hard to miss that fifty cal."

"They were running equipment," Roy said. "We might've gotten lucky."

Miller turned to look at them but didn't stand up. He had Ilah's blood on his face and his hands.

They heaped the other three bodies into the back-passenger area of the side-by-side. By the time they'd finished their hands were slick with blood and the yellow jackets were swarming.

"Help me," Miller said. Roy helped him carry Ilah to the front seat and set her down, loose-boned, gone from this life. Miller held her pistol as he pulled her onto his lap and cradled her body. Roy returned to the field and grabbed Miller's rifle. Mace drove while Jerzy and Wiley hung off the sides. Back on the road, Roy looked back and there was nobody there. Ilah's face, her lifeless hand. She couldn't be but she was.

KAREN WAS SLEEPING, DEEP IN A DARVOCET SLUMBER. SARAH WAS in bed with her, crying. She'd come out and seen Ilah. Wiley squeezed in beside Roy and he put his arm around her. He gestured to Sarah to come with them but she shook her head no. He nodded OK and guided Wiley into Miller's living room. Western ranch-themed everything, spurs and taxidermy, Remington prints. Mace came in through the mudroom covered in blood, sweating.

"Where's Miller?" Roy said.

"With his wife."

"We're ready."

Roy kissed Wiley on the top of the head. "See you in a few."

They drove the ATV with the bodies through the junkyard gate tube-steel archway studded with hubcaps. Eli's Pick 'n' Pull, the sign said. No tracks in the dust. The trailer that had served as the yard office was gone. Roy told Mace to keep going toward the back, through the heaps of fuel tanks and plastic farings, five-hundred-gallon totes brimming with shattered safety glass, to where the oil tanks were. It used to be you could bring your oil here to be recycled and Eli, the former proprietor, would resell it to be refined or most likely burned in oil furnaces. The tanks were empty now or close to it.

It took both of them to drag the bodies up the ladder to the catwalk. Roy unhitched the manhole cover and they one after the other sent the bodies slick as fish into the hold where they came to rest in the oily grime remaining in the bottom. When they'd finished, Mace kicked the hatch shut and scraped a handful of dust and ash from the catwalk handrail to wash his hands with.

Jerzy was pulling into the junkyard in Miller's pickup. Wiley was with him. They used the hand pump from Miller's truck to drain the fuel from the ATV and left it where it sat.

They were alone on the road but at every turn and hillcrest they expected to meet the militiamen. Roy sat beside Wiley. She leaned on his shoulder and he held on to her.

"Are you OK?"

"She's dead."

"It's not your fault. You did everything you could've done." He turned to her. "We're going to leave, tonight."

"Mom can't."

He didn't want to tell her he hadn't fired his weapon. He would've. He'd convinced himself he would've. *Ilah's dead but we're alive. Karen is alive. We're getting out of here. Poor Miller.* Roy didn't know what to expect when they got back. He hoped he hadn't killed himself. They needed him. All hands.

Miller was behind his house in the field digging a grave. He had equipment but he was doing it with a shovel. Ilah was wrapped in a bloodstained sheet beside him. Roy went to help but Miller waved him off. The sun was down but it was light enough to see. Roy went to the panel and killed all the breakers so none of Miller's motion sensor lights would come on. They'd be looking for their friends soon or maybe not, maybe never. Maybe they wouldn't be missed.

Roy and Jerzy worked late into the night breaking down the drill rig and getting it ready to travel. Mace helped the girls prepare a comfortable place for Karen and themselves in the back of the truck under the camper shell. At some point Miller appeared and, without saying a word to anyone, moved his truck to where he'd been digging. A few minutes later, he drove away.

Roy entered the dark house and made his way to Miller's spare bedroom.

Karen was sitting up in bed in the dark, glassy eyed and still.

Roy sat down beside her, turned off his headlamp, and dug her hand out from under the blanket and held it.

"You need to get some sleep," Karen said.

"I can't." Roy peeled back the blanket and switched on the red LED on his headlamp. Her abdomen was distended and looked black in the red light. The dressing on her wound was clean and dry, but when he touched her forehead, she had a fever.

She pulled the blanket back over herself. "I've been thinking. It's safer if they aren't seen with us. Nobody knows who they are."

"They've seen Mace."

"So Mace won't ride with them. He can take Ilah's rig. Miller won't care. I'll talk to him."

"He left," Roy said. "I don't know where."

Karen nodded. "Mace was in the back of the truck, I don't know if they could've seen him or not. They saw us. I know they did. They came for us."

"We can't let them go on their own," Roy said, not believing that she was actually thinking this, that it made sense. "We need to stay together."

"But it's not safe for us to be with them. Listen, they'll be going so slowly with the drill rig, we'll catch up in no time. We'll hide out for a day or two then go."

"If your fever doesn't go down," Roy said, "we'll have to go to Reno or go see April. We have to do something. We can't stay here."

"I'm not going to Reno. Maybe we should go back home. They'll leave soon. If they haven't left already. They won't go back there, not once they leave, right?"

"After they burn it down," Roy said. "We're not going back there. It's not our home anymore."

"OK. OK." She touched Roy's arm. "I'll tell the girls. Send them in here, will you? Wiley first."

She talked to Wiley for half an hour and then had Wiley send in Sarah. Sarah came out and ran into her older sister's arms. Roy didn't know what to do or say, but within a few hours Jerzy and Mace had finished packing and they were ready to go.

Miller returned, parked his truck out back, and went inside to talk to Karen. A few minutes later he was back outside, chucking supplies into the back of Ilah's truck. They assumed Miller was coming with them, but no one ever asked him. When the truck was full and everything was tied down, Miller gave Wiley his only functioning TNK handheld and taught her how to use it and told her to keep it charged in the drill rig with the auxiliary batteries. The main unit of the tink took up a section of wall in Miller's barn the size of a small bookshelf.

"Take all you can carry," Miller said to Jerzy, standing above the open hatch of his bomb shelter.

"You're coming with us," Jerzy said.

"No. Not yet. I'll leave when Roy and Karen leave."

"OK," Jerzy said. "Thanks, man. I'm sorry."

"I know."

Before they left, Mace shook Miller's hand and tried to give Roy a hug but Roy held him at arm's length.

"Nothing matters to me as much as those girls," Roy said. "And I'll tell you, you fucking owe this family. You fucking owe Miller and if anything happens to them or Jerzy—"

"Nobody's gonna touch them," Mace said. Mace climbed into Ilah's truck and started the motor.

Jerzy pulled Roy in for a hug and gave him a kiss on the cheek. "See you in a couple days," he said.

"We'll be right behind you," Roy said. "Let us know about the roadblocks."

"Will do."

Before she got in the truck, Roy gave Wiley his pistol and all the ammunition he had, even though Miller had them overloaded with weapons already. Sarah wouldn't look at him, even when he picked her up to put her in the cab. But once her arms were around him, she wouldn't let go. He had to peel her off him. Wiley took her and pulled her close.

"Slide over so the dog can get in," Roy said.

"He's staying," Sarah said.

"He wants to go with you," Roy said. "Look at him." The dog was sitting beside the running board of the drill rig, watching Sarah.

"Stay," Sarah said to the dog. "Keep Mama safe." Then she shut the door and Jerzy started the rig, eased it into gear, and drove off. Roy watched them drive away into the darkness and when they were gone he squatted on his haunches in the driveway. Miller came up from behind him and caught him by the arm and lifted him up.

"They're gonna be fine," he said.

"We don't know that," Roy said. He spat in the dirt and wiped his eyes, looked at Miller. "What about you?"

Miller shook his head. "I wanna kill 'em."

"They're already dead."

"There's more."

Roy left Miller in the driveway and went inside.

He slept in the chair beside the bed with the A3 on his

lap. In the morning, Karen's color was off. She had no energy. She couldn't walk and he had to help her to the bathroom. He should've never listened to her. They could have been five hundred miles away by now. Roy took his place in the chair beside the bed and watched Karen sleep. The dog was curled up at his feet.

Miller came in later and woke him up, motioned him outside.

"I set claymores on the road, so don't go anywhere without telling me first."

"OK."

"I'm taking up a position on the little knob south of the house. If you hear shooting and you decide to make a run for it, drive in the ditch to the gate, not on the road. It'll open automatically from this side."

"OK."

The day passed without incident. Roy kept the dog in the house. Karen drank water and had a bowl of canned soup. The sun set and Miller didn't return. After she fell asleep Roy used a digital thermometer to check her temperature, 102.7. He checked it again and it was even higher. The night was cold but she was sweating.

SHE WOKE HIM UP. THE MOON WAS HIGH AND HALF-FULL AND THE fields were a dull silver, the color of solder, and the light came in through the broken windows on the breeze and lit Karen's face. She looked scared. Roy knelt beside the bed.

"Get some sleep," he said. "It's always worse at night. Always. You'll be OK when the sun comes up. We'll get on the road and go. We're not staying here another day."

"I want to go home," she said.

"We can't."

"Are they still there?"

"I haven't checked. We can't go back there. It's done."

"Do you remember the frozen waterfall?"

"What?"

"The one, when you turned from the highway, you wanted to see it, and then the van broke down and we saw it when we were in the truck with Aaron, after he picked us up. Do you remember?"

"I remember."

"I used to go there after you left and watch people climb it. I'd spend all day."

"Don't."

"They just went right up it, swinging their little axes. You wouldn't believe it."

"I need to check your temperature again." He reached for the thermometer on the bedside table but she caught his hand and pulled it toward her, tucked it against her breast. "Leave it."

He squinted out the window at the full moon. "I hate the moon," he said.

Karen smiled.

"I hate the world," he said. "I hate my blood."

"I love your blood, dipshit. All of it."

"Let's get some sleep."

At dawn they shared a cup of tea, talked a little longer. Roy cried but Karen put on a good face. She was pale and weak, sweating. Her fever had gotten worse. She said she was ready to get going.

He came back from the kitchen with a bowl of oatmeal.

Her eyes were open and she wasn't there. She was gone. He didn't understand. He couldn't understand. She hadn't been dying. In a panic, he checked for a pulse on her wrist and her neck, listened for a heartbeat, breathing, anything. He performed CPR until he couldn't anymore, until he could feel that the bones in her chest were broken. He held her hand and it was still warm. He couldn't stand or scream. He tried to talk to her but ended up crying. Her skin cooled. He watched her eyes, snuck glances trying to catch her waking up. Her hand was cold and wet with his tears. After he covered her face with a sheet, he walked out Miller's front door empty-handed and climbed the fence and crossed the field hoping to step on one of Miller's bombs but had no such luck. They hadn't burned the house down. Nobody was there to kill him. He crossed the yard and went into his shop and found the chisel and, after some searching, the box of books under the workbench, and set them up and chopped off his finger.

Miller met him in the field and settled Roy down and bound his hand with his own shirt. At the house they carried her outside and put her in the back of Roy's truck, on the bed that her daughters had made for her. Miller put the truck in gear and drove slowly into the field and paralleled the driveway to the gate. It swung open and they were driving on the empty road, Miller's voice was quiet and steady.

"I already had the hole dug when I remembered," he said. "I laughed. I couldn't help it. She never wanted to be buried. And I laughed because that was like her to tell me something important in a passing kind of way. I always thought she was trying to set me up, trick me. I'm a suspicious man by nature. She wanted to be listened to. I was just getting good at it, you know?" He started to cry and Roy had to open the window of the truck to get some air. His hand was throbbing but the bleeding had more or less stopped.

"I need to end it," Roy said.

"You got kids."

"Not that. We need to find them. For Ilah. For Karen. We need to find them."

"They won't have gone anywhere," Miller said. "Not yet. They have everything they need up there. Food, water, fuel, weapons, vehicles, communications."

"Let's go, then," Roy said.

"What about what you said about your kids, about leaving?"

"I'm choosing a side."

They slid back the bunker's oak cover and Miller expertly slid the catch from the hidden tripwire and opened the steel hatch. They descended one after the other into the darkness. Miller switched on a generator and two bare bulbs came on overhead. One wall was stocked with dehydrated food, another had bunk beds and a cooktop. Off to the side was a closet-sized room with a composting toilet, a shower, and an air filtration system. In the very back there was another door, already unlocked since Jerzy had been in there. Inside were Miller's weapons.

Roy was given options but he didn't want any of Miller's tech military shit or his explosives. He'd take the deer rifle, identical to the one he owned. He wanted to line them up and knock them down. He wanted to harvest them. To live your whole life, he thought, looking at Miller's excess of firepower. To love and raise children and to end up in a place like this.

"Who shot you, Miller?" he asked. "Back when we gave you the generator. Was it the same ones? The ones at the lake?"

"The ones that lost, yeah," Miller said. "It was a mistake. As much my fault as theirs."

Roy thought back to the weight he'd put into Miller's shoulders to hold him down while Ilah was stitching him up, the same as Karen. "What're we doing here, man?"

Miller put down the crate he was carrying and stood up straight and looked Roy in the eye. "You said this is what you wanted."

"I know what I said."

"I don't know what else we could do," Miller said, and went back to loading weapons and ammunition into hard cases and duffel bags.

"We should've left with the girls."

"It's too late for that. You had to stay. You would've put a target on them. Karen was right about that."

"I'm sorry, man," he said to Miller.

"You don't have anything to be sorry for. This is best-case, right here. As bad as this is, this is the best it can be at this moment."

"I don't know if I can do it," Roy said.

"I plan on living. My life doesn't end up there. I'm not a kamikaze."

"I wouldn't blame you if you were."

"Well, I'm not." Miller passed Roy two large black duffel bags and sent him up the ladder and then climbed up after him lugging the hard cases. Miller shut the hatch behind them and showed Roy again where the release for the tripwire was, under the handle, and warned him that it was rigged with explosives and if he just lifted it, pretty much the whole place would blow up. But Roy wasn't listening. As they hefted the oaken cover and put it in place and spread the dirt and the stones and finally the harrow to hide it, he was thinking about Karen. Was she in the undertaker's oven right now? Was she watching over him? The sky was hazy with smoke.

"You hear me, Roy?"

He nodded, yes, but it didn't matter. They were going to war.

[-2]

The sound was the same as Karen dropping a book on the floor before she turned out the light and went to bed. There were no flames, not at first. The explosions were set so that the survivors would run from one building to the next just in time to be blown up there instead. Miller had a term for it but whatever. Roy held the dog. The air seemed to be drawing back on a tide and the mayhem felt far away. Neither of them moved. The sounds of falling timber, tearing plywood, and nails screeching like gulls as they were ripped from kiln dried lumber. Miller nuzzled his cheek against the .50s comb and took a deep breath.

Fires were burning in the big house, spreading to the guesthouses, barns, and outbuildings. Roy sat up with the A3 to watch. Someone stumbled from the smoke, then a few others. Miller fired and kept firing until he was empty. Nobody shot back at them.

"Don't think that was it," Miller said. "Load that mag for me."

Roy did as he was asked and was oddly grateful for the task. He hadn't touched the trigger on his weapon. He couldn't remember if he'd switched the safety off or not.

When they came, they came from the south. Not from the compound as Miller assumed they would and they must've already spotted them because the shooting started and Miller turned to return fire and Roy felt the slick of his blood and his brains and what must've been a piece of his skull or bullet fragment cut into his cheek.

Roy held on to the dog with one hand and shoved ammunition for the A3 and the 700 into his bag with the other and threw it on his shoulder. He picked up the two rifles and hauled the dog toward the spillway. Miller was draped over the Bushmaster. His hat was gone and the shattered bones in his skull looked loose and sagged where they weren't missing altogether.

Roy and the dog hunkered in the spillway. The shooting didn't stop. Concrete dust burned his eyes and the dog looked almost happy but if he let it go it'd be gone. He considered letting it go. A propane tank exploded at the compound and he thought he heard children scream. They'd move around to get to him. Circle the dam. A firing squad. It wouldn't take long. More than he didn't want to die he didn't want to die scared. No point in that. The dog pissed on his boot and began leaping and trying to break Roy's grip. The outcome would be the same. Death.

Sadni. The good dog sat and looked up at him with depthless eyes and a wild canine grimace. *Yer a good boy.*

Hugging the concrete of the dam he climbed the steel rungs with the A3. With his leg braced against the broken timber of the floodgate he unbelievably found a militiaman crouching beside a stump twenty yards in front of him, glassing Miller's body. Rifle up, targeted, trigger pulled, dropped. Not scared, killing. Easy killing. Easier than dying. Two SUVs on the road. Men shooting at the dam but they were running, not aiming. Roy waited until they were behind the vehicles and emptied his clip into the tires and under the running boards hoping to hit their feet and legs. Shot up their motors, window glass.

When he dropped back down he put in a fresh clip and picked up the 700 and his bag and ran by Miller and touched him on the back and with the dog on his heels kept running across the lake into the burned forest. This wasn't about getting away but how many would come with him. Shadows were fading and he could see well enough. The burnt trees were spikes and cracks in the blue-gray morning.

As he ran the dust and ash erupted from his footfalls and coated his clothes in powder and formed a paste on his skin. The dog made the ridge first. Roy knelt in the dust to rest. He put his face to the dog's neck and pulled him close. Miller's head. Didn't matter how smart you were. Didn't matter if you were good or kind. Had connections and powerful friends. You go looking for it and God help you.

A sound like a fast-food plastic straw twisted and flicked—snap—beside his ear and a plume of dust shot into the air beside him. Crawled to his feet, weapons, bag, dog. Find higher ground. He kept climbing. More shots, some close. At the next false summit he pushed the dog over the other side into the rocks and turned to face his attackers. The dust burned red in the rising sun and with his scope he focused beneath the cloud into the trees.

The first man edged into the clearing. Soon his comrades appeared behind him, fifty yards apart, spread along the base of the ridge. They started slowly toward him in a picket line. When the lead man was clear of cover, Roy touched the trigger and his target fell with a cry and squirmed on the ground. The others fired and got low, ran for the trees. Roy shot into their dust clouds. He yelled at them to come out but they wouldn't. He shot the trees they hid behind and the burnt alder canes snapped and danced. All at once they came out and fired and Roy and the dog turned and slid down the steep side of the ridge. Blinding cloud of dust. Rocks thudding into his boots, cutting his leg. A root snagged his bag and ripped it out of his hand. Not going back. When he finally stopped sliding he caught the dog by the scruff and they turned north and back uphill to try to flank the militiamen, to catch them as they followed. When he checked, the A3 was empty so he shoved it in the dirt and heaped ash over it.

The sun lit the forest. The shadows were long. All the way to the top and Roy was gagging, spitting mud. The dog had tear streaks on his muzzle, dull as a burnt log. In the distance an estuary of black smoke darkened the sky above the compound. They moved slowly through the forest. Roy picked up a pebble and popped it in his mouth. They waited above the spillway in a clump of trees. They hadn't found his tracks yet but they would. No hiding. They'd screw down their courage and follow him, were following him, and they'd radio ahead and that would be that. He looked through his scope for Miller's body and it was there. The SUVs on the road hadn't moved.

He spat out his pebble and fuck it, good a time as any, he and the dog ran and ducked through the spillway gate and down they went, sliding, running a few steps, falling, sliding again to the bottom, where they crunched and tumbled into the hard gravel. They couldn't track him here, not without dogs. The ground was too hard.

His truck was where he'd left it. The two of them lay down among a heap of deadfall and waited to see if anyone was waiting for them. The sun was high and red. The dog nipped at the ants that were climbing on him.

As the sun lowered, he found them by their scope flash. They were across from him on the hillside, watching the truck. He took his time with his first shot but the second was rushed and he couldn't be sure if he'd missed or not. A man stood up and threw something toward the road. Grenade. A moment later the truck rocked sideways and burst into flames. They kept shooting but they weren't aiming. They hadn't seen him. Man and dog returned to the riverbed and ran. Out of breath, he set up behind a boulder, ready, he had them in a bottleneck. He'd get at least one more. He wanted one more. They never came. He hated them most for their cowardice. When it was dark they left the river bottom and climbed higher and hid in the rocks.

During the night the militiamen passed on either side of them. They'd have night vision. If not goggles, then rifle scopes. Roy's whole body throbbed with eye-rolling, rabbit fear. Where he was blind they could see. If it wasn't for the dog, he might've surrendered. He held his breath for as long as he could but it was a trade-off because, the longer he did, the bigger the exhalation, and even if they didn't hear that he was sure they'd hear the hammering of his frantic heart. Blood pounding in his ears like footsteps. Whispers. Gear rattle. Footsteps. Any second they'd open up and rip him to pieces. High calibers at close range. Limb from limb. He wanted to keep his hands and his heart. The dog. He shouldn't have brought the dog. Either way, it was coming. Death was coming. Then, without thinking *I'm tired or I could close my eyes for a minute,* he fell asleep.

Pecos watched the slot in the rocks where the militiamen

had passed. For him it was a matter of sensation, of predation, a path clear, a path blocked. Near dawn he woke Roy with his nose and they stood in the dry riverbed and looked down on the pale, wasted valley. Smoke smudged the hills and the mountains beyond. The dog went first.

ACKNOWLEDGMENTS

The author would like to thank the Dobie Paisano Fellowship Program for their generous support. He would also like to thank Joseph Gioielli and Barry Mathias. Any inaccuracies regarding military working dogs are the author's alone and should not reflect on the expertise of Mr. Gioielli.

About the Author

Brian Hart is the author of the novels *The Bully of Order* and *Then Came the Evening*. Hart lives in central Idaho with his wife and two children.

ALSO BY BRIAN HART

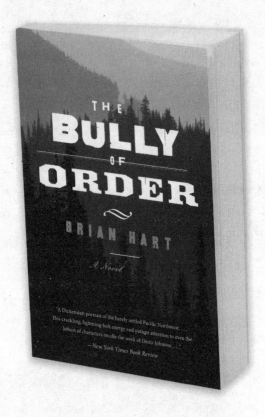

THE BULLY OF ORDER
A NOVEL
AVAILABLE IN PAPERBACK AND EBOOK

"Mesmerizing. . . . A wonderful, unique portrait of a particular landscape
I now see anew." —Amanda Coplin, author of *The Orchardist*

Set in a logging town on the lawless Pacific coast of Washington State at the turn
of the twentieth century, a spellbinding novel of fate and redemption—told with a
muscular lyricism and filled with a cast of characters Shakespearean in scope—in
which the lives of an ill-fated family are at the mercy of violent social and historical
forces that tear them apart.